ACCOLADES

"An engaging story, skillfully told."
– Pam Lecky, author of the *Sarah Gillespie Series*

"This is a tale to savor, and at its heart is the complicated, brave, and big-hearted Julia Hancock Clark. Kudos to Brook Allen for rescuing William Clark's little-known wife from the shadows of history."
– Amy Maroney, author of *The Sea & Stone Chronicles*

"*West of Santillane* transports you to a world where freedom lies beyond unlimited horizons, for those who dare to travel. An extraordinary novel of Lewis & Clark, through the eyes of the woman who loved them both."
– Elizabeth St. John, author of *The Godmother's Secret*

"*West of Santillane* is a beautifully written and fascinating novel that draws from history's shadows a woman known to many only as a name, the wife of explorer William Clark. Brook Allen brings Julia Hancock to vivid life as a cultured woman of strength and of character. The novel is also a heart-felt tribute to Julia, and the women like her, who left behind ordered, comfortable lives and, alongside their husbands and families, settled the American frontier. Meticulous and compelling."
– Catherine Meyrick, author of *Cold Blows the Wind*

"Through immense research, Allen has crafted a wonderful, vivid and heart-touching tale about Julia Hancock, the young woman who became the first wife of the famous explorer William Clark. Set in America at the turn of the 19th century, this coming of age story takes us back to the early years of America's independence — a time when women were chattels of their husbands. But Allen shows us in her engaging, empathetic novel that a woman's life can be one of adventure and discovery, too."
– Dr. Wendy J. Dunn, author of *The Light in the Labyrinth*

West of Santillane

West of Santillane

A Novel of Julia Hancock

-In Memory of Cindy Oneto-
Thanks for reading, encouraging,
and, most of all, for your friendship.
You are loved. You are missed.

Brook Allen

Dawg House Books

Copyright © 2024 by Brook Allen

ISBN 978-1-7329585-6-2 (e-book)
ISBN 978-1-7329585-7-9 (print copy)

All rights reserved, including the right to reproduce this book, or portions thereof, in any form. No part of this book may be reproduced or transmitted in any form or by any means, graphic, electronic, or mechanical, including photocopying, recording, taping or by any information storage or retrieval system, without permission in writing from the publisher.

Names, characters, places, and incidents are products of the author's imagination or are used fictitiously.

ALSO BY BROOK ALLEN...

The Antonius Trilogy

Antonius: Son of Rome
Antonius: Second in Command
Antonius: Soldier of Fate

CHAPTER I

Near Fincastle, Virginia
Late July 1801

No horse could plant his feet like King Georgie. I kicked him hard with my heels again, but he didn't budge an inch.

The old draft horse was stubborn as a mule and ornery too. Papa had named him well—after the real King George who lost thirteen colonies when we won the War for Independence. He always shook his head over that old tyrant. "Not the most intelligent man in God's creation," he'd chuckle.

Maybe Papa had named that horse such because he wasn't just a stubborn beast, he was plain stupid.

"He's scared of that water," Harri muttered from where she sat straddled behind me. I twisted about just enough to catch her batting her hand at some bothersome flies.

"I know, but it's nothing. He could hop it if he wanted."

Besides, it wasn't even a real stream; just runoff from the morning's storm in a low-lying stretch of road near Catawba Creek.

Whenever it warmed up, lots of storms brewed during high summer in Virginia's Blue Ridge. Some had wicked darts of lightning and ear-splitting thunder, making Mama's fine crystal and glassware tinkle inside their cherry cabinets, wind kicking and blowing our curtains about so much everybody scrambled to lower the glass panes.

Silly old horse.

Big as Georgie was, he didn't need to be afraid. He could plod right through if he wanted, hardly getting his feet wet. Instead, he snatched a mouthful of grass and whipped his tail around on to my legs, which were banging him in the ribs again. To him, I was nothing but an annoying bug. Sweat trickled down my back as sunlight edged out from behind the clouds. The air was stifling, pressing right up against my skin.

I was frustrated because if I slipped off to pull Georgie over the water myself, I wouldn't be able to get on again; he was so tall. And Harri would be no help. I loved her like a sister, I did, but she was no good in sticky times like we were in today. I looked all around, hoping for a small stump or something I could use as a step up.

"What should we do?" Harri fretted.

Stubborn as I was, I kicked Georgie once more, unwilling to let him win.

"Julia, *please* let's just go back. We'll be in trouble as it is."

Harri was my cousin and hadn't inherited the Hancock sense of adventure like me.

"We'll disappoint your papa," she went on, her grip around my waist tightening. "He might whip us with that switch of his—the one on the wall in the kitchen." She sounded right desperate.

"Now, Harri, I'm guessing we're maybe only two miles from Greenfield. We can make it if—"

Whistling?

I froze in mid-thought and felt Harri stiffen from where she sat behind me.

Who was whistling out here? Shrill, melodious, strong—somebody was coming up behind us on the road, headed the same way as us.

Together, we swiveled our heads toward the sound.

Up next to us rode a man in a tricorn hat on a right handsome-looking bay horse, and under that hat he had the reddest hair I'd ever seen. I declare, but I'd *never* seen hair like that.

A portly built ebony slave followed him on a mule, and he was the one whistling, the song carrying well ahead of them.

The gentleman pulled up right next to me, his horse snorting.

Above glittering blue eyes, his brows crinkled into a puzzled frown, taking in our clothes.

When we'd snuck out that morning, we'd snitched two pairs of old gray-and-white kersey breeches right off a clothesline behind one of the little cabins where some of Mama and Papa's people lived. They were child-size, so they fit us.

But poor Harri. At thirteen, dressing this way wasn't proper at all. Mama already had her wearing adult clothes, and right then, I didn't have to see red creeping up her neck and into her face. I plumb *felt* it.

"Good day, young ladies. Is something afoot here?"

Redhead had a calm, deep rumbling voice, setting me at ease right away, and those blue eyes… I swear, but no crystal glass or fancy blue jewel could ever glimmer as much.

"Sir, King Georgie here won't cross this stream."

Redhead nodded, studying the runoff. "Ah. It is quite the flow, isn't it?" he teased. "A right little Potomac. Well, you two sit right where you are, and I'll offer Georgie here some encouragement."

In one swift motion, he swung down, leaving a long Kentucky rifle hanging from his saddle. Billy Preston owned one like that. I'd seen him show it to Papa.

Before I could say anything about the gun, Redhead grabbed Georgie's bridle and we were off, splashing through the water.

"Where are you two headed, out here on your own? Mind you, there's still plenty of bear, panther, and occasional wolves passing through these parts."

"Well, sir, truth is I've never been afraid of wild beasts. Papa says they tend to be more afraid of us people than we are of them. As for where we're going? To Greenfield Plantation, home of Billy Preston. He's courting my sister."

"Now, isn't that something?" An amused smile tugged at the sides of Redhead's mouth. He laughed, a big robust laugh I rather liked, then went on. "Why, Billy must finally be thinking of settling and taking up housekeeping. Actually, I'm headed to Greenfield myself. Would the two of you mind a gentleman accompanying you?"

At that point, he stopped and released Georgie, splashing back behind us toward his horse in his high-laced leather boots.

"Oh, I shouldn't have come," Harri whined, burying her head into the back of my frock. "We're in such trouble."

I ignored her. "What's your name, sir?"

"William Clark at your service, Miss . . . ?"

"Hancock. Judith Julia Hancock. And this here is my cousin, Harriet Kennerly."

He swung back onto his bay and rode up beside us, his slave right behind on the mule. Indeed, old Georgie was a lot more willing to move forward now that William Clark's horse was at his side.

Even at nine years old, I could recognize a fine-looking gentleman when I saw one, and William Clark was well-built and muscular beneath his simple linen shirt, woolen breeches, and boots, his shoulder-length locks tied back into a queue beneath his tricorn. Oh, and he was tall like Papa—and my papa was *very* tall.

Harri spoke up, "Sir, please excuse our attire. It's hard to wear ladylike skirts riding astride."

William Clark grinned, a teasing sideways smile, where his right cheek seemed to draw up a little more than his left, making him look as though he was thinking of something mischievous. "You're fully pardoned, Miss Kennerly," he assured, tipping his tricorn at her.

Georgie up and stopped again, lowering his head to snap off stems of purple clover next to the road. I hauled back on the reins uselessly. It was so humid my hands were slipping on the leather, and every hair on my head was melting, even though it was only midmorning. "So you're a friend of the Greenfield Prestons?" I struggled to get the words out straight, as I was still straining to pull Georgie's head up.

"York, give him a smack, would you?" Clark ordered, passing ahead of us.

From just behind, the slave reached over from his mule, popping Georgie a good one on the rump, making him start. Harri squealed and squeezed my waist.

William Clark pulled up a bit to ride closer to us, answering my question. "Billy Preston and I served in the army together. It'll be a real pleasure to see him. I hope it won't be an inconvenience, especially now that he's courting a young lady."

"'Friends who surprise us with the gift of their presence are never an inconvenience,' so my Mama says."

"Wise words."

Cicadas sang a grand chorus as we skirted up a rise. Within a quarter hour, the Prestons' open fields rolled into view, and in the distance stood the stately mansion of Greenfield, built by Billy's father, the late William Preston.

We left the woods behind, the horses jogging, surrounded by thigh-high grasses, as the road cut through arable, fair land that Preston kin had cultivated since well before the War for Independence was ever won. Mud from this morning's storm sucked at our horses' hooves, and late blooming honeysuckle and purple clover sweetened the air as two turkey buzzards circled overhead.

As Georgie jogged to catch up to the men's animals, Harri fussed, "I should have worn a hat!"

※※※

Billy Preston gave us a firm scolding after arriving at Greenfield, warning us to expect punishment when we got home, but he was delighted to see his friend William Clark.

Billy Preston thought we'd get a taste of the kitchen switch.

And Billy Preston also expected me to be sorry, but I wasn't.

Not then.

Sorry came after Billy Preston and William Clark escorted us back home to Santillane, where Mama promptly hauled me to the kitchen, flipped my bare arms over to expose the tenderest skin, and doled out ten solid smacks with that dreaded switch. Jaw set, eyes squinting, I tried my best not to cry, though a few tears still squeezed their way out.

"Now, you go with Megg and wash off down at the spring. I won't have you bringing fleas inside from those awful breeches you had on. Go on now. Get!"

Megg was waiting outside the kitchen, and I followed her out to the front of the house, then into the woods along the path leading downhill toward our spring. I stared at my puffy red forearms the whole way. It was strange. Megg had always been like a nanny to us children and usually comforted me, but not today.

Instead, she was angry with me too. "You just remember something, Miss Judy. Your Mama gave you *nothing* compared to the whooping them boys is getting because of your foolishness."

I stared down as we walked, frowning. She was talking about the youngest of Papa's people—Ares and Virgil, who had just matured enough to start fieldwork this past spring.

"Well, just so you know, Ares and Virgil—they didn't have nothing to wear to hide their privates this morning, seeing you took it upon yourself to steal their breeches. They couldn't find them nowhere. Them boys was embarrassed, so they hid in the woods till Sticks done hunted them down when they didn't show up for work. And you know that ain't gonna end well."

Sticks Howard, Papa's overseer, wasn't anybody's favorite company. Mama constantly questioned Papa over why he'd hired that man. "I don't like the way he stares after our girls, George," she'd say.

After having me soak my burning forearms in the spring water and wash my legs off, Megg led me back up the trail toward the main house, but still she wouldn't leave me be. I'd never heard Megg so agitated.

"It's about time you got educated about something you ain't never had to think on none. You're a planter's daughter and privileged to live a charmed life, while us black folk is nothing but slaves and chattel to your family."

I listened in silence, my mouth dangling. Papa called the black folk "his people," and even though I saw them working, I'd never given them much thought. Most of them were grown-ups, and I lived in my child's world, playing games with Ares and Virgil—sack races, hoop and hide, and such. They were my playmates and friends. I never thought about their skin color.

"Now you're gonna head on behind the house and see what punishment Master Sticks done gave them because you're about to find out that you got the long end of the pole, hear?" Megg gave me a nudge on the back. "Go on now. I'll be there presently, but you needs to see what you done caused with your own two eyes."

I glanced back at Megg. There was an urgency to her tone I'd never heard before that made me curious, in a serious kind of way, so I did what she asked and ran on up the hill, past the carriage circle in between the kitchen and main house. Somehow I knew I was about to encounter something bad because that Sticks Howard was notorious for putting fear into everybody's hearts.

I stopped rock-still behind the house, breathing hard, and staring at an ugly truth. I'd not given a thought as to how my actions might affect anybody else.

Ares and Virgil were just getting up from where they'd been lying on their stomachs. Stripped bare of their shirts, they only wore the shabby kersey breeches Harri and I had snitched earlier. Both their faces were streaked with tears.

And their *backs*!

Broken and bloody, angry cuts oozed red and streaming. I'd never seen anybody with such wounds before, and by the looks of it, they had to have had more than my ten slaps from a kitchen switch. They must have had twenty—thirty lashes, maybe?

A movement off to my right broke my awful fascination at what the boys had endured.

Sticks Howard.

He was still holding the green switch he'd cut and used so viciously, only it wasn't green anymore. The end was darkened with blood—my *friends'* blood.

Sticks raised one hand to wipe sweat from his face. He'd always reminded me of a skeleton. Bony, long-limbed, and with a toothy smile that looked more like a sneer, I guess somebody thought he looked like a stick and called him such. That's the only thing I could figure.

"Just you two remember something," he growled, shooting a

runny load of tobacco out one side of his mouth, "ain't no excuse—*none*—for not showing up for fieldwork."

"Yessir." That was Virgil, the oldest.

"Ares, I didn't hear nothing from you," Sticks said. "You need me to clean out your ears by whipping your ass again?"

"No, sir. I heard you, sir. We's—we's sorry, sir." Ares was shy, so his voice was soft, thin, full of terror.

"Then you both best get a move on down to that east field. I saved you plenty of fresh cut down there that needs binding, and it better be done by nightfall." Sticks ended by lifting the green switch high in the air with a wicked laugh, sending them both scampering barefooted down the hill and out of sight. Then he stood a moment, still laughing and watching them flee.

"They're my friends," I whispered low and angry. "Don't you hurt them again."

Behind me, I heard Megg's heavy breathing as she arrived at the scene.

Sticks pivoted around, finally noticing me. He leaned over with both hands on his thighs to meet my gaze. "Well now, little Miss Hancock," he drawled my name out a good country mile. "They got what their kind deserves to get."

"Lord Jesus, have mercy," panted Megg, bustling up beside me. Her presence made me feel somewhat better because I didn't like the way Sticks's eyes bored into mine, like he meant to do something evil to me too. Megg scolded me again, "This here is what you caused, so just remember next time you want to go out and play with them boys. They may not want your company no more."

But they were my friends!

Weren't they?

Or did they play with me just because they were scared of what might happen if they didn't? Yes, I'd seen a few times when whippings were doled out to Papa's people—grown men. Fortunately, those occasions were few and far between. I just figured they'd done something really bad to deserve such—like me getting into trouble today—only a lot worse. Oh, my eyes were wide-open now. I saw how Mama and Papa had sheltered me; sometimes people in Fincastle whispered quiet, not-meant-to-be-heard words. *Colonel Hancock doesn't put up with anything from his people. They're overseen by that Sticks Howard, and he keeps them in line.*

No wonder Hancock's people at Santillane don't run or misbehave. Now I understood why, and it was an awful feeling, seeing my father with new eyes—a way I wish I didn't have to see him.

Papa had hired Sticks to be cruel. Seeing the boys' backs and coming to terms with it for half a minute, I'd stopped breathing.

Sticks was still there, leaning over in my face, waiting for me to do or say something. "Don't you treat them like that again," was what squeaked out as I glared at him with a loathing beyond words.

He broke out with a hiccup-like laugh, declaring, "My, but that's one stony look you're a-giving me!"

Resentful, ashamed, and oh so well-aware it was I who had deserved the beating instead of Ares and Virgil, I bolted the opposite direction the boys had run, heading down the hill toward a large meadow where a gigantic tree stood.

From behind me, Megg called, "Where you off to, missy? You come on back . . ."

Her voice faded as I closed in on that tree—my Catawba tree.

It was my special place, where I could always find peace, enjoy imaginary fancies, play with my sisters and brother, and take comfort at times when my heart was broken. Whenever something upset me, I'd lie back in the grass and stare upward among those leafy, living branches, declaring each one to represent somebody in my family, for I'd named each one accordingly. One branch was my brother, Georgie, one was Mama, and there were branches for Caroline, Mary, and Harri.

But the largest, sweeping clear down from the heights all the way to the ground, then angling back up—that branch was Papa.

Breath coming in gasps, I stood before his branch, staring at it with hot tears coursing down my face. I'd named it such because it was the strongest, the grandest, one that could take on all my climbing and childish mischief. But now, I realized that Papa wasn't always the best and kindest. He had it in his power to be a man who could be uncaring, thoughtless, or mean—just like ordinary men.

Gingerly, I crawled up his branch, balancing myself and picking my way along. I felt like I needed to tread lighter on it now. Papa had an edge he hadn't had before today. As it arced upward toward the tree's gigantic trunk, I pulled myself up higher on a secondary branch leading to Mary. Not clear to the top—for I never went all the way up there, though Georgie did sometimes, even though Mama warned him not to. As I ascended, I passed the branches I had named Caroline and Harri and another long-reaching one, stretching toward the house: Mama's branch.

But it was one that faced westward, so green and sturdy, that I sought. It was wide enough that I could stretch out on my stomach and cry, like I needed to today.

That was my branch.

That was Julia.

High up in that Catawba tree, I had a place to think, all hidden away from others' eyes. I gazed toward the horizon, the rolling Blue Ridge spanning before me in all of its gentle, purplish beauty.

But slavery? Now, I knew there was nothing lovely about that.

In my studies at home with Mama, I was always an eager learner. She explained how we depended on Papa's people to plant and harvest hemp, tobacco, and other fruits, vegetables, and grains—all grown to provide our plantation with a comfortable, self-providing living. But as I paused to consider slavery *now*, compared to the way I'd considered it before seeing Ares and Virgil in their beaten, sorry state, I realized I'd never given it any real thought, even though I'd been surrounded by it.

Megg had simply been ever-present to me and Georgie, my sisters, and Harri. She cleaned, cooked—but now I realized she had no option but to do such. Why, Megg and the others were only given time off on special days, like Christmas afternoon, after we'd all feasted. Cap, our stable boy, was always friendly toward me, helpful, eager to please; yet I'd never considered that he received no reward or pay for his trouble.

I'd never really seen white and black people as us and them. Through my eyes, I saw black folk no different than me. How blind I'd been, and now the monster was clearly in front of me. Slavery was *everywhere*. *Here*—in these United States, so recently freed from England's yoke.

High up on that branch, I knew I couldn't ignore slavery anymore. And here came an idea. I'd save up some of my own food, from my own plate, *every* day, not only on Sundays—just for Ares and Virgil. Then maybe someday they'd know how sorry I was that I'd caused their suffering.

I was little, but I could do *something*. I'd never ignore them again. I was blessed to be able to search my heart up in the Catawba tree when some people in my own household didn't even have freedom enough to let their hearts soar.

For a good while, I lay there, watching a line of ants crawl toward me, weaving their way across the bark. My eyes dried, and I guessed that thinking and coming up with a plan of kindness had steadied my heart some. I sighed, looking westward, wishing I could take flight like a bird and start over the mountains, winding up someplace new and fresh. That was my ever-adventurous spirit comforting me. It always made me want to see more—*be* more.

Then came the hollow sound of footsteps down the hill.

"What a *tree*!"

It was the William Clark gentleman. As soon as he and Billy Preston had returned Harri and me to Santillane safe and sound, Mama had invited them both to dinner.

Raising up slightly, I wiped my eyes again, trying to remove any sign of my crying.

He didn't see me, I was so far up, concealed in the leaves.

"What *are* you?" Clark smacked the trunk of the Catawba with his hand, amazed at its majesty.

I lost sight of him because he'd moved beneath me, hidden behind more foliage. By now, my orneriness had returned in full. "I'm a Catawba tree," I proclaimed.

There was that hearty laugh again. "I've never been addressed by a tree before," he declared. "Especially one with a familiar voice."

Carefully, I raised myself, creeping down the ladder-like array of branches in silence to where I could finally hop on down to the enormous Papa limb at the bottom that touched the earth. William Clark had moved around the other side of the tree's massive trunk, and he still didn't see me.

"Over here," I called, giggling.

Instantly, he appeared from behind the trunk, where he paused, leaning against it and shaking his head while chewing on a long stem of wild rye. "Why, Miss Hancock, you're as agile as a squirrel—and as impish."

He was being mighty polite—a true gentleman—addressing me as Miss Hancock, as though I was grown. I reckoned he'd be surprised to know that my own parents disagreed on what to call me. According to Megg, they'd caused quite a scene.

Christened Judith Julia Hancock, Mama and Papa were still arguing over my name at the very moment Reverend Logan sprinkled the water of baptism over my thick, dark curls.

"I'll be calling her Judith—or Judy," Papa had whispered loudly at Mama, even while my tiny forehead was still dripping.

"George, we've *discussed* this," Mama had hissed back, congregational witnesses widening their eyes during this supposedly reverent moment. "It's to be Julia, and you know it."

That's why Papa and Megg both called me Judith, or Judy, and Mama and everyone else called me Julia.

Well, I'd just let Mr. Clark keep calling me "Miss Hancock." It was polite and made me feel more adult.

"I'm sorry for your punishment today," he said, "though I'll admit to receiving my share of lashes growing up. Next time, you'd best ask permission before taking off like that."

I extended my arms before me. Raised pink welts had risen where the switch had repeatedly found its mark. "Ares and Virgil had it far worse, and I don't want anybody to suffer for something I've done ever again," I confessed.

He said nothing, just moved to the other side of the tree, facing the west and into the distance. Curious about this man, I studied him a bit. My best guess was that he was around the same age as Billy Preston—mid-twenties? Maybe older. Maybe around thirty.

I followed his gaze west.

Along the skyline, clouds were settling into the mountains, and thunder rolled within the threatening mass. We'd have another stormy night.

"There's something captivating about looking west," Clark said, almost under his breath.

"I think so too," I answered. "Someday I'd like to go west of here and see more of this United States."

I was being truthful because, as much as I loved it here at Santillane, I often daydreamed about the west. Those Blue Ridge mountains made me wonder what lay beyond. What sorts of people lived on the other side? Was it hotter there? Colder? I wanted to see more than just Virginia.

"It's an uncharted land way out there," he mused through his teeth, the wild rye quivering between his lips.

A lightning bolt flickered from within the storm clouds, followed by a low, distant grumble.

"We'll be getting weather," I said. "I'd best head back home."

"I'll walk with you," he said, following me with long, sure strides as I made for the hill leading back to Santillane. "Not many girls your age are interested in the west. You're mighty full of adventure, Miss Hancock, and that's a rare treasure in a young lady."

In just a few steps, he'd caught up with me. I doubted my parents thought me a rare treasure, for my daring spirit was so often my downfall—like it had been today.

All the same, I found it curious that somehow, in all of the topsy-turvy, tear-filled mess I'd caused, I'd earned William Clark's approval.

Chapter II

Fincastle
Five years later, March 1806

I brushed down my turquoise day-dress, hesitantly following the others into the drawing room of stately Grove Hill, home to Papa's dear friend and colleague James Breckinridge.

Mrs. Breckinridge stood to greet us. "Please, ladies, sit and make yourselves welcome. We've delightful sweets to share, and I know our visit will be lovely."

I looked over the women in the room besides our party, consisting of Mama, Harri, and Mary. Mrs. Logan would make things tolerable, at least. But Letitia?

I swallowed hard. It was another ladies' tea, and of course I was fated to sit right in front of Letitia Breckinridge, her incessant chatter beginning before I scarcely took a seat.

"Julia! What a perfect color to match your eyes."

I glanced down at my dress again, relieved to have chosen this one.

"You weren't at the public dance last week," she rambled, tilting her head coquettishly as she poured my tea.

"No. Harri and I couldn't go. Papa had some evening business, and Mama was busy with other things, so we didn't have a chaperone."

"Chaperones," Letitia sniffed in disdain, shaking her head. "Well, *all* of Botetourt's finest beaus were there, including Phillip Carrington."

I blinked. She had my attention now, for she likely knew how I felt about him. Phillip had written me several admiring notes that had been formally delivered, and Mama and Papa had grudgingly given approval for me to be courted by him if he asked.

"He's *so* handsome," Letitia drawled on. "Since you weren't there, he asked me to dance. I didn't think you'd mind. I knew you wouldn't want him bored just standing about."

I nearly choked, swallowing my tea. "You danced with Phillip? How many times?"

Letitia sighed, flipping lush dark curls over her shoulder before gazing at the ceiling as if doing the arithmetic. "Oh, I don't know—maybe nine, ten?"

Sweet Lord, that nearly filled up an entire night of dancing.

But why worry? Hadn't Phillip assured me that I was the finest dancer in Botetourt County? Besides, in my absence he had no choice but to dance with Letitia or somebody else.

Didn't he?

The real problem here was that I had a jealous streak when it came to Letitia.

She had the deepest, darkest eyes I'd ever seen, and if I'd been born a man, I would've been lost to her, for she was much more… well, *curvy*…than I. Her entire person dripped femininity. From her choice of clothes, tailored so luxuriously, to her body's womanly shape and creamy skin without blemish. Altogether, she was the type of parcel for which any gentleman would have willingly tripped and fallen down a steep staircase.

"Phillip told me a secret," she whispered, leaning in. "Said he wants to pursue a military career."

Instantly, my interest in a tray of brown sugar cakes fizzled, despite my eyeing them since coming in. Phillip had never told *me* anything about joining the military. Why had he told her? Was Letitia trying to win him over, or was I just being overly sensitive since I considered him my beau?

I always tried my best to accept my parents' prompts when it came to friendships, but my relationship with Letitia remained stiff and uncomfortable. Exactly my age and daughter to their closest friends, Mama and Papa more or less assumed we'd be bosom companions too.

What they hadn't ever considered was how different Letitia and I were. I was all about reading, educating myself, and adventure. She was dramatic and flirtatious, well aware of her effect on young gentlemen. In our earlier years, we'd had a difficult history—like the day she said I wasn't pretty, so I shoved her into the Mill Pond. Then to repay me in kind, she and two of her Papa's people confronted me out in the woods at a May horse race, throwing pails of sour, curdled milk all over my new frock.

Since then, our folks had brokered a tenuous peace between us, but whenever we were in the same room, things remained tense. An almost palpable barrier of distrust, dislike, or envy between us prevented the forgiveness and forgetting of our childish antics. Yet, despite all that, Mama, Papa, and the Breckinridges *still* urged us to bury the hatchet. Here we were, young ladies now, and they expected us to have everything in common, maturing together as friends.

When I didn't reply, Letitia reached over and took my hand in hers, soothingly. "Please don't worry, Julia." Her tone sounded sincere. "I told Phillip that he needed to share his aspirations and hopes with *you* since he was bound to court you, not me."

"You told him that? What did he say?"

"That he'd share his true feelings with you very soon. After all, you've waited long enough. You deserve to know exactly how he feels." She smiled sweetly.

My cheeks felt hot at such words, but I hoped she was right. I had waited for Phillip to visit and declare his intentions for weeks now.

"Thank you, Letitia. I appreciate you encouraging him to be open with me."

She squeezed my hand again. "I'm so happy to intervene, and it's so wonderful you're here. Mama has an idea for us to get together again soon."

Just about to inquire what that entailed, I heard Mrs. Breckinridge address me. "Julia?"

Letitia leaned in, whispering to me. "Listen—Mama's about to extend the invitation."

"Yes, ma'am?" I politely turned toward Ann Breckinridge, Letitia's graceful and courteous mother.

"Mr. Breckinridge is running for Congress next year, and we're traveling to Little Amsterdam in a few weeks to campaign. There's going to be a big camp meeting there, preached by a group of Methodist circuit riders. We thought it would be a perfect opportunity to canvass votes since hundreds of people are bound to attend from all over the county. Would you care to join us as our guest?" She turned toward Mama, including her in the idea. "We'd only be gone for one night, Peggy. Unless of course, your Presbyterian leanings—"

"Oh, never mind that, Ann," Mama laughed lightly, waving her hand in nonchalance. "You know George and I have no problem with our girls hearing about others' faiths. As long as the good Lord is glorified, she's welcome to attend, and I'm sure she'd benefit. Julia loves learning, don't you, my darling?"

Ordinarily, I would have had *no* interest whatsoever in joining Letitia in anything, but Phillip's family was Methodist, so he'd likely attend. And just now, for the first time ever, Letitia had extended an olive branch. "Of course I'll go, Mama. Thank you for thinking of me, Mrs. Breckinridge."

Letitia squealed delightfully, clapping her hands.

Mrs. Breckinridge nodded an acknowledgment in my direction but spoke on to Mama. "And we'll certainly appreciate any Hancock votes, Peggy."

"Oh, you know George will support James."

"We can always depend on the Hancocks," Mrs. Breckinridge declared, offering Mama a brown sugar cake. "Might we depend on the Logans too?" she queried.

Mrs. Logan, our pastor's wife, answered more ambiguously. "I'll certainly ask the reverend to pray over the matter. Now, *Mary*," she changed subjects, addressed my sister with a grandiose smile, "I've heard such thrilling news concerning *you*."

My sister blushed and glanced down at her hands. She was the shyest Hancock ever born.

Our family was expanding. Barely a year after Harri and I had made such fools of ourselves riding stubborn King Georgie, Caroline had married Billy Preston, just like we'd all known she would. They'd recently moved to Wythe County with their sweet little girl, Henrietta. Now, Mary, my oldest sister, who some ladies in town feared would turn into a spinster, had finally found a match that pleased her with a Mr. John Caswell Griffin, and I'd started the whole family calling him "Griff" for short.

Mrs. Breckinridge trilled, "When's the wedding?"

"Exactly what I was going to ask." Mrs. Logan nodded. "My husband will want to place you on his schedule, of course."

"We've not set a date quite yet," Mary said softly, her eyes darting toward Mama, who immediately spoke up.

"Rest assured we'll contact the reverend as soon as it's decided. Much of the scheduling rests with Mr. Griffin's plans, as he's purchasing a mercantile here in town and is due to arrive in Fincastle with his belongings any day now. George and I feel it's best if he has some time to begin his business before marrying."

"Well, of course Colonel Hancock would know best," Mrs. Logan murmured.

I knew the *real* truth of the matter.

Papa wasn't altogether pleased with the match and wanted to be certain Griff could provide for Mary. Griff wasn't landed, and both Mama and Papa preferred their daughters marrying into landed planter families, as they had done. However, Mama had been quick to remind Papa of Mary's twenty-three years and how her time was fleeting. Papa had finally acquiesced but refused to set a date until Griff moved to Fincastle, opened his business, and accrued some money first.

Poor Mary . . . faced with yet more waiting.

Mrs. Breckinridge poured herself some more tea and reached

over to Mama's cup to refill it as the subject changed again. "Ladies, did you hear? James came home from town the other day with news that those poor men who were sent up the Missouri may have perished. Some folks are calling the whole expedition 'Jefferson's Folly' and are saying that they may have been cut off."

My thoughts about Phillip Carrington faded at her words. Everybody in our United States was breathlessly awaiting word about the Corps of Discovery, which had departed St. Louis in spring of '04. By summer of '05, fascinating goods had arrived in Washington City, sent to Jefferson by Meriwether Lewis and William Clark—the *very same* William Clark I'd met with Harri on the road that hot summer day while out riding. Supposedly, they had continued west last spring, but nothing had been heard from them since.

Mrs. Breckinridge's last remark puzzled me. "Cut off?" I asked, concerned. "What was meant by that?"

Everyone's eyes turned toward me, Letitia cocking an immaculate brow and shrugging. "Does it really matter?"

Yes, it *did*. Letitia might have attended fancy private school, but I knew she didn't crave knowledge like me. Especially when it concerned someone I had met and considered both respectable and gentlemanly.

"They're presumed lost—killed, most likely," Mrs. Breckinridge clarified. "One rumor has it that the Spanish intercepted and executed the captains, enslaving the rest for their mines. But really, who knows? We'll probably never learn the truth. Poor, poor souls..."

"Last December, they were safe in Indian villages on the northern Missouri," I said, everyone's eyes sweeping toward me. I'd read about it in one of Papa's Richmond papers. "What I find puzzling is why the Spanish would have a military force that far northwest—unless it was to intentionally intercept them?"

Letitia gawked at me. "And just *how* do you know all that, Julia?"

Mama reached over and squeezed my knee—rather hard—a warning to redirect the conversation to something more womanly. "My girl loves her reading, history, and geography," she stated, to my utter delight. "But how sad if this is true." She shook her head. "Both

Lewis and Clark were Virginians, you know, and we dined with Captain Clark years ago at Santillane before he became well-known."

"I remember him," I agreed, nodding enthusiastically. "I was so young then, but I liked him. He was kind."

Harriet giggled, nodding with the memory, all smiles. "I met him too," she said. "Julia's right. Even then, I could sense he had greatness about him. And he was handsome."

"And, ladies," I added, "he and Lewis sent President Jefferson *marvelous* things last year from the northern Missouri. Furs, a huge bison robe, samples of new plants that had never been seen before, skeletons of amazing beasts, and even live animals."

The entire group of women all stared at me in speechless silence.

Before arriving at Grove Hill today, Mama had reminded us, "Be discreet with what you say and limit your conversation. Allow the other ladies to talk." Now she was giving me a stern look and had set down her tea; brow cocked, her posture was rigid.

I'd hear from her later.

Letitia broke the silence. "My, Julia, but you must think you know *everything* about what the president got from Lewis and Clark."

"I think Julia is quite intelligent to know all that she does," praised Mrs. Logan, and I mouthed appreciative thanks to her as I stood, suddenly feeling rather self-conscious and gloomy. I hadn't meant to steal everyone's attention or show off by dominating the conversation.

It wasn't ladylike.

I was merely in a tizzy—first about Phillip, *then* at the prospect of William Clark losing his life. To imagine that the impressive red-haired man I'd met could have died along with his soldiers, striving to serve his country…

I set my cup down, excusing myself, leaving the drawing room for the front of the Breckinridge house. The slave serving as Grove Hill's butler met me at the door, bowing respectfully. I nodded at him, breezing past, jerking my long gray wool cape off of a wall peg on my way out.

Outside, a March shower added to my melancholy, dampening

the red earthen clay, so there was nothing to do but remain on the spacious front porch, closing my eyes and inhaling moist, cool spring air. Then behind me came footsteps, the door reopening and closing softly. I looked back over one shoulder.

It was Harri.

"Remember, it's all just talk, Julia. Nobody knows anything for sure. There's no proof at all. *Hope*, sweet cousin. We have to hope that they're all still safe—it's not like they can just write home from where they are."

I turned toward her, grinning at her quip. Harri could always cheer me, and there was truth to her words. Indeed, hope was a marvelous thing. Yet even with the limited maps Papa had in his library, I knew how vast this North American continent really was. It was *thousands* of miles to the Pacific Ocean, miles of uninterrupted wilderness and unknown danger full of wild beasts and savages. I hoped for William Clark's sake that he was alive and had reached his destination.

And if he was dead, I silently prayed that it had been a swift, painless passing.

※

I straightened my back, considering my image in the old antique mirror that had once belonged to a Polish count—Count Pulaski.

Papa had fought at his side during the War for Independence, and when the count had been shot, Papa had dismounted in the middle of the battlefield in time to ease him from his horse as he died. His family had honored Papa for that act, bestowing him the mirror that had once hung in the count's palace as a gift. Now, the old antique hung in my room, where I stood, looking at myself with regret.

My features were nothing like Letitia's. Even now that puberty was behind me, along with that dreadful gangly stage. True, my cheeks were rosy—but the rest of my face?

Attractive. Not much more than that.

Plain.

Middling.

I turned my head sideways, straining my eyes peripherally to see my profile, which was identical to Mama's. There was her nose in all its Grecian alignment, right above a small, delicately formed mouth. Granted, Fincastle ladies all said how blessed I was to have such lush, wavy, dark hair. But unfortunately, I wasn't skilled in the art of coiffure, so most of the time it was nothing short of an unruly, tangled mess—unless Mama intervened. It was my eyes that were probably my finest feature: azure blue and lively looking when I smiled.

That being said, it frustrated me that I wasn't the lovely, feminine beauty as was Letitia or my sister Caroline, who were both perfection in manner and style. Nor did I have the womanly propensity for sewing and embroidery like my sisters and Harri.

My samplers never even made it up on the walls of our grand staircase. Mama silently stashed them at the bottom of her sewing box, hiding my halfhearted attempts. Whenever Caroline and Billy visited at Christmas with my sweet niece, Henrietta, Caroline always helped me cut chemise and nightgown patterns to stitch up for gifts, coaching me every step of the way. They were the easiest garments to make, and I never took contentment in stitching clothes the way she, Mary, or Harri did.

My passion was reading.

Oh, Mama had me tutored in music too, which I confess I enjoyed. And I possessed talent, playing the family spinet. Harri thought I was brilliant at it. But reading was my recreation of choice. Recently, I'd completed studies on the one book Papa had containing Shakespeare's sonnets. I had already devoured most of our library's geography books and was just starting to read in Latin, soldiering my way through a history of Rome by Tacitus.

However, Papa's collection of Shakespeare's sonnets was my favorite, and I wished with all my heart that I had more of his works. His poetry evoked such mysteries about love and the depth of feeling between men and women, something yet unknown for me. Whenever I read his sensual words of experience and longing, I'd think of Phillip and what we might have in store, should our courtship eventually lead to marriage. The thought absorbed me, curious as I was about such. It made me tingle in an almost shameful way. Though Shakespeare had lived hundreds of years before my birth, he had plenty to teach me. Someday I hoped I'd have all of his works at my fingertips, for Papa said that he was a famous playwright as well as a poet, but regrettably none of those works were in our collection here at Santillane.

"Miss Judy!"

It was Megg.

"Your ride is here," she called from down the staircase.

Hastily, I tucked in a few stray hairs under my bonnet and turned to snatch the overnight bag Mama was allowing me to borrow. I was off for my carriage ride to Little Amsterdam, accompanied by the Breckinridges.

"What a splendid dress," Letitia exclaimed as I climbed up. "Just perfect for this weather."

I'd worn a comfortable tweed, something warm for Virginia's changeable weather this time of year.

"I'm so glad you've come," she gushed. "You're so intelligent that should I have any questions about what all we hear, I'll be able to ask."

"Really, I imagine any answers could be found in the Bible."

"Well, I'm afraid I'm not the reader you are."

That I didn't know. But it was promising that her friendliness appeared intact since the tea. Prior to that, we'd always remained so standoffish. For the first time, I was really looking forward to getting to know her. I suspected that down deep, Letitia had an elegance and sensitivity that I'd never be able to match.

Little Amsterdam had a different feel to it than Fincastle, where the landscape was all sudden, steep hills, abrupt curves, and deep vales with cabins and cottages tucked here and there along its several thoroughfares. Terrain here was rolling and gentle, the perfect sort of wide-open landscape for horse races, picnics, and large gatherings like camp meetings. It was mostly inhabited by a number of German families who had come to these new United States to seek their fortunes in farming and dairy-tending.

The camp meeting was held in a huge field next to the village, and it was a busy place, despite a misting rain that had settled in; low-hanging gray clouds enveloped the surrounding hills, compelling everybody to wear hats and woolens. It wasn't a heavy downpour, but enough to make roads muddier than desired and persuade families to arrive early for choice seating under the tents.

These circuit riders—Methodist preachers sharing the Gospel and whatever message was on their hearts—drew hundreds of people. Therefore, the huge oiled canvas tents they used were set up and lashed together to accommodate as many folks as possible.

Mr. and Mrs. Breckinridge dropped Letitia and me over near the tents, us girls sharing a parasol and scurrying on ahead through the drizzle so we could get good seats. We were expected to attend the services while her parents campaigned, so we located spots in the middle section, close to the front.

I was all eyes, my glances darting everywhere, looking for a tawny-headed young man who stood just a bit taller than me, with a hale complexion and keen hazel eyes. Wagonloads of people from the surrounding area were pouring in now, and surely Phillip would be among them. Hymns were beginning, and just when I had lost hope—there he stood, in the very back of the tent, craning his neck.

Phillip Carrington.

"Oh, there he is!" Letitia whispered into my ear.

Yes, and he was looking for *me*!

Oh goodness, he was fine. Dressed in the newest fashion of long, straight trousers and wearing a burgundy jacket with long tails, broad lapels, and a black-and-white-striped cravat, he had cut his hair since we'd last been together, at a community outing all the way back in February.

He nodded in my direction with a slight smile, and before long we were seated side by side, with Letitia to the right of me. During the first speaker, our hands touched, our fingers entwining so that my breath caught in my throat and I felt heat on my face. Nobody was watching, of course. All eyes were on the preacher—everyone except Letitia, who stared at our hands for a few moments, then looked away, smirking. My cheeks flashed hot again, and I felt a little scandalous, even though it was only our hands touching. Phillip was rubbing my palm with one of his fingers, and the entire sermon was lost to me.

All I could think of was this lithe, youthful body beside me, the feel of our hands blending together as though in a duet. I decided then and there that if he suggested we court, I'd say yes. And then if he got bold enough to kiss me, I'd let him.

That's all I was thinking about until the key speaker for the evening, a certain Reverend Mitchell, apparently with deep Botetourt County roots, strode down the aisle and up to the podium. He was a stately man, not overly tall, but there was a way he comported himself, evincing dignity. Dressed in the older style like Papa still wore, he even wore a powdered wig and stood completely still in front of the enormous horde of people, waiting for everyone to settle.

"Beloved," he eventually began—his voice unlike the other preachers, whose words were easily lost in such crowds. Not Reverend Mitchell's. His instrument was trained and authoritative over all of us seated under the tents, even thundering outside, among overflowing crowds of people enduring the wet weather.

He commanded attention.

"I am no different than any of you here, for as a younger man, I was besmirched by a sin that has saturated this country, degrading America far below the freedom for which she was purposed. These United States are infested with a disease—" He paused for effect. "A disease called *slavery!*"

Suddenly absorbed, my fingers slipped out of Phillip's as I scooted forward on the hard bench. A fleeting recollection of bloody tracks on Ares's and Virgil's backs flitted through my mind—a traumatic memory unforgotten, even with time.

The reverend waited again, gazing down at an open Bible on his pulpit. "Now, be mindful of my own sin, good people, for I once owned men and women myself—here, in this very county. I was as susceptible to that abominable sickness as anybody seated beneath this tent. I was guilty as any man here. So allow me to ask: What good is freedom when not *all* men are free?"

I glanced over at Phillip. He had slouched back against the bench, staring outside, where someone was selling hot cider. On my other side, Letitia licked her lips. "I'm chilly," she whispered to me. "I'm going to get some of that cider. We'll meet up later."

Something else was happening around us, for the mood in the tent had suddenly changed. A few men were already standing and leaving, faces dark with disgust. One gentleman shook his head as he left, discontentment all over his face.

Turning to the front again, I wanted to hear more from Reverend Mitchell.

"Fortunately, the Almighty has placed a sense of conscience within our hearts, and when sinful man listens to that checking of the Holy Spirit, change occurs, followed by a divine reckoning of the heart. That's when God's holiness can at last take hold."

Slavery was sin? Of course it was. It had to be.

After what I remembered about Sticks beating poor Ares and Virgil until bloody, it was also an understatement of truth. Now, my parents wouldn't accept that, and from what was happening around me, it didn't seem like many other people here believed it either. Reverend Mitchell was addressing farmers, planters, and Virginia folk whose pockets were bound to slavery for their earnings. Such a message here wasn't welcome.

Not at all.

Another man just in front of me arose, snatching his wife's hand roughly, and they left, the woman glancing back guiltily. Nobody else moved; faces all around me were stony.

Then I noticed something else.

Phillip was gone. Where had he... ?

He could have at least told me he was leaving.

At first, I was torn between leaving and trying to find him or staying for the rest of the sermon.

Mind made up, I decided I'd search for Phillip later. For me,

Reverend Mitchell's words held more importance than Phillip's current whereabouts.

Reverend Mitchell opened his Bible, saying, "The Gospel of Luke tells us how Jesus Himself came to free all men from slavery, whether it be of a spiritual or legal nature and regardless of skin color. Listen to the Word of God in Luke 4:18:

> *The Spirit of the Lord is on me,*
> *Because He has anointed me*
> *To preach good news to the poor.*
> *He has sent me to proclaim* freedom *for the prisoners*
> *And* recovery *of sight for the blind,*
> *To release the oppressed,*
> *To proclaim the year of the Lord's favor.*

The manner in which he emphasized certain words made my heart dance, a tingle of faith creeping up my spine.

"When that reckoning—that tallying-up of my spiritual condition—took place years ago, God moved powerfully in my soul. That was when I felt the Spirit stirring my heart and I became a man of *action*—a patriot for the helpless and enslaved, desperate for freedom. I took up pen and manuscript, rushing to the courthouse in Fincastle to manumit my thirteen people. And do you know how it affected me, beloved? *Do you know?*"

Tell me... I was waiting, my heart ready—though someone else's wasn't.

"We don't care!" some man outside the tent shouted. "You're preaching to the wrong crowd, Reverend!"

I thought of the daily plates of food I still saved for Ares and Virgil, who were young men in Papa's fields now. How glad I was that I'd kept my promise, making it a daily habit to give them extra from my own portions or whatever was left in the serving dishes. Still, I was troubled. I didn't have the means to free them or any other slave belonging to Papa, and that was a frustrating thought.

Reverend Mitchell raised his arms heavenward, his voice trembling in joy. "I became free *myself* that day!" he cried. "That year, I experienced the Lord's *favor*, and now I'm more liberated myself for freeing those thirteen souls than they were on that day when they took leave of my bondage over them. Therefore, I plead with you, brethren. *Search your hearts*. If you own either man, woman, or child, consider *their* suffering. Consider *their* displacement upon being sold to faraway owners or controlled by threat of the whip. Are not their lives—these lives of fellow brothers and sisters in this human race—more valuable than the cost of replacing them with paid labor? If 'no' be your answer, then your heart yet needs the touch of God's Spirit."

"Get the hell out of our county!" another male voice ripped through the worshipful silence.

Mitchell merely shook his head in reply, his face glowing with fervor. With hands outstretched toward the congregation, and undeterred by the unsympathetic people finding fault in his words, his voice fell dramatically to a whisper, gradually rising in crescendo along with his emotion. "No. I'll not leave. Instead, I invite you to come. Come and repent of any sin, but tonight of all nights, consider the sin of *slavery* and how this oppression must be cauterized from the heart of America. There is a way to experience the Lord's favor in a powerful, personal way, and that is by setting your people *free*."

I looked around, curious to see if anyone was responding. The entire congregation sat stoically, impassive faces frozen. How could they all be so callous, especially after such an impassioned message?

One of the other circuit riders, Bishop Asbury, came out next, leading everyone in prayer. While heads were bowed and eyes closed, I quietly slipped to the end of the bench, hurrying out into the mist, my heart scuttering and my hands clammy.

Outside, I crossed my arms against a breeze kicking up and edged around the length of the tent to the strains of a hymn. Behind the canvas stood an awning where several of the preachers were waiting for their turns to speak, shielded from the rain. My eyes scanned their faces, looking for Reverend Mitchell.

Then I turned about, hearing a slap of canvas behind me as someone exited the camp meeting tent.

It was him.

He spared no time, immediately turning his back to his colleagues, his head bowing in prayer.

I crept nearer, so desperately did I wish to speak to this man, yet I was careful not to disturb him. The mist was turning into heavier raindrops, so I readjusted my bonnet, tying it tighter, trying in vain to stay dry. It was some time before I heard him whisper an "amen," then he turned about, giving a start at beholding a young lady standing before him.

"Forgive me, Reverend. I won't keep you long. You may not have thought anyone responded to your message, but I have."

His look of surprise softened into the warmest of smiles, and he reached out, clasping my hands into his enormous ones, so calloused from riding and work. "Praise be to the Lord that you've come forward, dear girl. Praise be."

"My problem is that my papa owns our people, and as his daughter I can do nothing to free them. Does that make me sinful by association?"

Reverend Mitchell stared at me open-mouthed. "What conscience!" he gasped. "My, but you're mature for your age. Take comfort, for God will not hold you responsible for that which still hardens your father's heart. Await His Spirit to move you and learn to respond to His still, small voice. Then *take action*. Every day of your life, you must ponder what He would have you do, for much can be done for people in servitude. Work at their sides, help bear their burdens, see to their needs. And since you're a young, unmarried girl, consider the opportunity you'll have someday to make a difference in your own household."

He squeezed my hands in a kindly fashion, his twinkling green eyes still fastened to mine. "Do you read?"

I laughed. "Voraciously!"

"Good." He released my hands, reaching into his deep pockets. "I've some pamphlets for you, explaining more about abolishing slavery, for it is my foremost prayer that the end of it will give rise to equality in this nation. Did you know that the flame of abolition has already ignited across the Atlantic?"

"No, sir."

"Right after our victory over the British, one man in England—still bound by a tyrant king himself—managed to speak to Parliament. This William Wilberforce continues to fight for the end of slavery there." He reached in his deep pocket, pulling out several printed leaflets, and handed the top one to me. "This tells us how Wilberforce is taking abolition into British Parliament. Now, this one," he handed me a second, "details writings by two black American ministers of the Gospel. They cite examples of how enslaved people they know have been caring for the sick, bound only by kindness in their hearts. Their words challenge why blacks should not be free in society to do even *more* good."

"Thank you for these. I'll look forward to reading them and learning more."

"Now, may your heart be at peace. Never fear concerning what you are unable to do, unless you spurn opportunities to do good that the Lord places before you."

I nodded, trembling with both excitement and the chill rain, tucking the pamphlets into my petticoat pouch-pocket best I could.

I needed to find Phillip. He hadn't returned to the service. Nor had Letitia, for that matter. I broke into a trot, hurrying back toward the entrance of the long-sided tent and glancing about.

"Oh, Julia!"

It was Mrs. Breckinridge.

"It's raining harder, so we'll be leaving soon. Why don't you head on to our carriage and look for Letitia? Tell her to join you and wait on us."

I nodded, disappointed. I wanted to find Phillip again. But both my feet were beginning to get soaked and cold. Mrs. Breckinridge was right. The skies really were opening up. Breathless, I began running in earnest through the crowds toward the long rows of carriages, trying my best not to soil my feet too much in the churned mud.

Still no sign of Letitia.

I managed to find the Breckinridges' carriage, but without the driver. Reaching up, I grasped a handhold, hopping up to make it to the high step. Once there, balanced upon one foot, I pulled the door lever and gasped—for I was far from alone.

Nor was I the only one breathless.

Letitia and Phillip were locked in a heated embrace, their passion only broken by my arrival. They both looked as stunned as I imagined I myself looked. Only the element of surprise wore off far more quickly for me, morphing into hurt and resentment.

"What are you *doing*?" I wailed at her. "I thought you were my friend!"

Phillip scooted toward me, away from her. "Julia—I—"

He held out his hand imploringly, but, angry and betrayed as I was, I smacked it out of the way—that hand that had so recently caressed mine and held it in such hypocritical warmth. That hand that I would have agreed to hold in courtship had he but asked, and that I would have reached for had he tried to kiss me.

"Please, Julia, I know this was wrong of me. I just—"

"*Wrong* of you?" I was appalled. "Yes, indeed. And it'll be *more* wrong for you to stay any longer inside this carriage. Get *out*, Phillip. Go, and take this last memory of me because you'll never have another!"

Phillip glanced back at Letitia, then edged forward and jumped out, darting away.

"Oh, Julia, it's not what you think," Letitia began, calmly reaching up to tidy some strands of hair that had come loose in her exertions. "We were only—"

"Only *what*?" I demanded. "Only betraying a friendship that I thought we'd finally started in sincerity?"

It was a silent, sullen carriage ride to the German-owned cabin we stayed in that night. Letitia and I were to sleep together in one of the two beds, but there was no way under heaven I'd be near her. Instead, I stayed up long into the night by the fire, reading the one pamphlet I still had; the other having gone missing, probably lost and trampled somewhere on the camp meeting's wet grounds by hundreds of carts, wagons, and carriages.

Still, the one that remained—about William Wilberforce's influence in Parliament—was a good distraction and pretense to Mr. and Mrs. Breckinridge that I was just a bookish, spiritually hungry girl, reading materials from the camp meeting.

Letitia and I didn't say another word to one another, and whenever she glanced my way, my response was a stare more lethal than Medusa's, and I swear, I *should* have been able to turn her to stone.

After reading the pamphlet several times over that night, I stayed by the hearth, warming my freezing feet and trying to winnow through the fury, jealousy, and wounded pride I'd experienced that day.

Phillip was the only young man for whom I'd ever held any romantic hopes. Obviously, his aspirations were far different, without genuine commitment or interest in me or my feelings. He was just the sort of boy Mama sometimes warned us about: the opportunist who might take advantage of a young lady if her guard was down.

Well, he'd *never* have any advantage over me.

Not ever.

In fact, why would I even be interested in courting a planter or planter's son now that I had silent abolitionist leanings? The commitment I made all to myself in front of that hearth was that if I ever did court anyone again, it would be because the man in question wanted *me*—not anybody else—*just me alone.*

Sleep finally found me, lying by a dying fire under a quilt and atop a stale-smelling fur rug. It's true I awakened the next morning without Phillip Carrington or a friendship with Letitia, but that no longer mattered since it was a message of freedom for all people that burned inside my heart.

Chapter III

Santillane
April 1806

If someone meandered up the hill leading to Santillane, they'd immediately see our main house rising in all its red-brick glory above a peaceful stand of trees. Papa had it styled on a simple Federalist design with chimneys on either end. The kitchen wing sat separate off to the right side, with the heftiest chimney of all. Beside it stood the smokehouse, where Mama hung hams and Papa cured game.

Upon entering, visitors could either turn left into the library or right into the drawing room. If they walked straight, they would wind up passing the stairs and the dining room to the back door. The house plan was ingenious, built to invite air flow straight through the broad main hall whenever the front and back doors remained open. It was a natural ventilation system for which we were most thankful during the hotter months.

Our family's private rooms were upstairs, where I shared space with Harri. Since I'd gotten no sleep in Amsterdam the night before, I was still slumbering deeply when Mama's irate voice jolted me awake.

"Judith Julia Hancock! What foolishness is this?"

I sat up erect, brushing sleep from my eyes and blinking. Mama was in the room, waving something around in her hand—a paper.

Oh no.

I recognized it immediately as the missing pamphlet Reverend

Mitchell had given me. I'd been careful to conceal the other one beneath a loose floorboard under my bed.

Mama didn't allow me time to answer. "Ann Breckinridge said Letitia saw this fall from your petticoat. Mother to mother, she thought I'd want to know what you were reading, and she was correct. What on earth were you thinking, collecting such writings?"

Letitia.

Not surprising, but it still angered me nonetheless. What else could she do to hurt me in such a short span of time? "It's just a pamphlet, Mama—distributed by one of the preachers. That's all."

"Well, it will be *ash* before your father sees it. It's a pity the good Lord didn't give you an equal helping of common sense alongside all that bookish nonsense He poured into your head."

I hadn't a clue what to say to that, and she must have seen how taken aback I was because she finally settled onto my bed, her face stern and drawn. "Whatever feelings you have about this, you keep them hidden unto yourself. Remember that we're a landed family, Julia. Your papa's people are part of our livelihood. And someday in the not-too-distant future, when Providence grants you a husband, he'll have his own people and—"

"Mama, I have decided that I don't want to be a planter's wife."

"*What?*"

How could I explain myself without stepping any deeper into the abolition issue? My words with Reverend Mitchell had affirmed that I'd have a new responsibility as a helper and guardian of the enslaved. I intended that responsibility to begin immediately, then someday follow me into the home I'd make with my husband, whomever that might be.

"It's just that I'd like to consider other men," I attempted. "Perhaps a learned man or a military man? Papa served in the War for Independence. Why shouldn't I be interested in a man willing to do such? Besides, I've always wanted to travel and see more of our country."

"What silly notions you've got in your head, girl. You'll marry a planter here in Virginia—*whomever* your papa wants you to marry—where you *belong*," she duly informed me.

Then she arose, crinkling the pamphlet into a tight wad and tossing it onto last night's coals in the fireplace. Barely a moment passed before it caught and erupted into flames, only to spark, fizzle, and crumple to ash.

Mama marched to the door, opening it and disappearing into the hall, leaving me wondering how many such pamphlets would be destroyed before the evil of slavery ever ended.

Later that day, Mama met me in the hallway, stating, "If you're to become a planter's wife, you'll need to learn the ins and outs of running a plantation, so I've made a schedule for you, Julia. I'll be expecting you to comply with it."

Indeed, her agenda ordered my days into a strict and organized regimen: an hour of embroidery after breakfast, cutting and sewing patterns in the next, and then the rest of the day's hours spent at Megg's side, learning to select meals for the ensuing week, overseeing Megg cooking, taking inventory of pantry goods, and organizing housework duties among Papa's people—a full-time task in itself, cleaning rugs, draperies, silverware, dusting, mopping… There was no end to it, for whenever I thought I'd finished, it was time to begin the whole process again into the next week.

Over the years, I'd observed Mama in action as she guided the cleaning and upkeep of Santillane. Firm, curt orders were given, and her people complied.

Well, I'd be different. Efficient, but different.

Indeed, there were benefits of my involvement that Mama hadn't considered—that *I* hadn't considered. Firstly, I was learning how to manage a household, regardless of whether I'd be a planter's wife or not. It was worthwhile being instructed on what all was involved.

Second, and most importantly, I was able to get to know more of Papa's people, discovering what their needs were and contributing to them, all under Mama's own design. Sometimes that irony made me laugh!

When it came to updating the pantry and listing sundry supplies we'd need for meal preparation, I learned that this didn't just involve food, but pots, crockery, and utensils. Megg supervised, for this task was vital to the household. Now I was the one ordering flour, cornmeal, peas, or molasses, always setting aside portions for the slaves along with their usual allotments of grain.

Megg was stunned. "Miss Judy, you ain't supposed to be getting us extra food like that. Your papa would never allow for this to be happening."

"Well, Mama and Papa want me to learn to run a household, and this is the way I'd run it."

"And all the work you been doing with me and others—cleaning and all that. I don't think that's what your mama expects you to be about."

I laughed. "Well, Megg, you all are getting more than you bargained for, then, aren't you?"

Her great eyes rolled in her dark face, and she shook her head in wonder. "Lord knows we could use the help, so I sure ain't gonna say nothing."

Family household inventories were a seasonal task and one of my favorites since they were practical and useful for clearing space. I sorted through everyone's wardrobes and chests, judging which garments might be turned into rags and patches. And again I had opportunity to give hand-me-downs that were in good shape to some of Papa's people—from Mama's wardrobe, Mary's, Harri's, and mine. Georgie had a few sets of breeches and shirts that I knew were too small for him, as he was a growing boy. It pleased me greatly to carry out a basket to the slave quarters, greeted by their excited smiles and elation in getting something new to wear.

Mama kept an ordered catalogue of inventories, and I was a quick study to adapt her style and make my own improvements to it.

Down deep, I knew that all of this supervision of housework and skills in organization would someday be a lesson well learned and used, and it kept my mind from too much anger and bitterness about Phillip Carrington, who, incidentally, had *lost* his brief infatuation for Letitia and begun courting another young lady.

No, Mama would never have reason to say I was idle or wasn't thorough in whatever I did. Especially when it came to the enslaved.

❦

When a severe bout of influenza unexpectedly swept through Fincastle, it was a blessing someone else swept in with it.

His name was Dr. John Radford, and everyone in town was delighted, for he was impressed with our community and decided to begin a physician's practice here.

One person in particular was thrilled at this prospect: Harriet.

On this bright April day, she and I climbed the steep Courthouse Hill into Fincastle.

"Today, John is going to ask Uncle Hancock if he might court me."

"Well, why wouldn't he, Harri? You've flowered. Any man would want to court you, with your dark brown eyes and warm soul." I couldn't help but be a little envious of Harri finding Dr. John. Here was a man who wasn't a planter, and to my knowledge had no slaves serving him here in Fincastle. With a trade in medicine, he could be hopeful of making a fine marriage. Even one within the landed gentry like us Hancocks. And physicians weren't known for their poverty. He'd make an excellent living.

Flushed as she was with our quick, uphill steps, I noted additional color creep up Harri's neck at my compliment. She really had blossomed, with beautiful thick, dark hair swept up away from her ivory face, free of blemish and ruddy with vigorous health.

"I can't believe it's happening. Julia, I really think he's the man for me. It's wondrous strange how this has happened so suddenly. Why, a month ago, I didn't even know he existed."

"Both you and Mary have amazing things in store."

What a fine thing this was for Harri, who was really more like a sister. I was only six when her father had come to speak privately with mine. I was never told much about the circumstances, but her mother had died, and since her Papa had to work away from home so much, he thought it would be more fitting for her to live with us, surrounded by other girls, where Mama could teach her womanly ways, educate her, and see to her daily needs. Her papa visited whenever possible, and those were special times.

"I just feel bad," Harri said, "because no young man has spoken for you yet."

"Don't you dare say such," I laughed, "there's still plenty of time for that." That was the truth, and if Harri could find a man who wasn't a planter, then why couldn't I? I might still have my own way.

"Well, I'm certain of one thing," she said. "Whoever does speak up for you will be much finer a man than Phillip Carrington."

I nodded with assurance at that. "I'm waiting for somebody who wants *me* more than anyone else. I won't accept just anybody." And that was only half the truth, wasn't it? I required someone who would have to be as against slavery as I.

We stopped atop the hill in front of Fincastle's old log-cabin courthouse, its heavy bell hanging atop rough-hewn timbers. Supposedly, there were plans to build a new courthouse, and Papa was mighty proud, for during his time in Congress, Thomas Jefferson himself had displayed interest in designing the future one, sketching a plan for what it might look like. "It's most Jeffersonian," Papa had declared proudly. Like drawings I'd seen of Monticello, the plans included a dome and classical columns out front.

Fincastle's founders had planted our village's seeds amid rolling hills, making certain that our courthouse crowned the steepest one; a beacon of justice was their intent, like some Greek acropolis of old.

"John is meeting me right here," Harri said, stopping suddenly and plopping down on a tree stump. "We're going to speak with your papa together, so I'm a bit nervous."

"All will go well because I think you and Dr. John are meant for one another," I reassured. "I'll leave you here, and you can tell me all about it later. I'm going to find Mama and catch a ride home with her. Megg said she's in the cemetery visiting Johnny."

Harri shook her head. "Your poor mama."

That was a fact. Mama often went into Fincastle by herself, straight to where Johnny had been laid to rest. Megg said that a grieving mother never got over how a child she birthed was beyond her reach, deep underground in a dense, dark grave. Sometimes Mama would have a sorrowful, wistful look in her eyes, and I'd always know she was thinking about him—the little boy she'd lost.

I hoped I'd never lose a little one that way.

After leaving Harri at the courthouse, I walked down the hill to the cemetery surrounding our little Presbyterian Church. Papa's phaeton was waiting out front, and Cap, Papa's stableman and driver, sat atop his seat. Not far away, in her usual place behind several enormous oaks, stood Mama.

I made my way over, joining her before Johnny's tiny gravesite and slipping my hand into hers.

"Julia?" she gasped. "Did you walk all this way?"

"I decided you needed company," I said, kissing her cheek.

She shook her head. "Sweet, sweet girl…"

I wrapped my arm around her waist, my gaze drifting down to the greening grass, where Johnny's gravestone read:

John Hancock, August 2, 1795
Died at 8 years, 4 months

"You know, I remember parts of his funeral," I said to her. "We girls were all expected to follow you and Papa, and we all walked here from our old house."

"Goodness. What were you—only three?"

"Fourish, maybe."

"Gracious, that was before we moved to Santillane," Mama reminisced, head shaking. "Poor Johnny. He never got to live in our beautiful new home."

Nor did his brief life allow he and I to become well-acquainted as siblings. For me, my deceased brother was only a fuzzy memory—one barely recollected. I'd awakened to Mama's sobbing one night, and naturally I'd gotten up, finding Mary and Caroline already standing in front of his door. Waning candles had flickered on either side of where he lay, Mama sitting vigil at his bedside.

By the next day, black swags had hung somber and stark over all our windows, along with a dark wreath on the front door. Mama had taken to wearing all black, and so had the rest of us—even Megg.

Johnny's passing had been my first exposure to death, and all those shadowy colors had confused me because I thought heaven was supposed to be all light and no darkness. If we were sending Johnny there, why was everything black?

A chilly breeze stirred the smaller branches on the tall oak behind us, and, shivering, my thoughts returned to the present. "Do you think he knows we're here?" I asked Mama.

"I do. I feel him near me every single day."

"You think he misses us?"

She shook her head. "I believe in my heart that he sees through a glass that only allows him to view good things—happy things." She tilted her head back, gazing up at the cottony clouds sailing high above. "All he sees of us here is our outpouring of love for him."

She paused a moment, adding, "Someday you'll understand that there's nothing more powerful or unshakeable than a mother's love. It's stronger than any steel chain or stone fence-line. Nothing can sever it—not war, not even death."

On that fresh April afternoon, I stood with Mama while she hummed a lullaby she had sung for me when I was small. Undoubtedly, she had sung the same one for Johnny too.

I held her fast so she'd feel me near her while tears soaked her cheeks.

"You're such a different sort than my others," Mama remarked after a time. "You're stubborn in your own way, but you also have a grace and charm about you that is unique, along with a kind and giving heart. I'll continue to pray for the good Lord to keep His hand upon you, for this life we live may be full of unexpected joy, but it's just as full of unexpected grief."

Unexpected grief...

Something I'd yet to encounter.

Chapter IV

Fincastle, Virginia
October-December 1806

I forced a smile through my clenched jaw. "Welcome to Santillane, Letitia."

Enter the dramatics.

"You're welcoming me? Really? Is it heartfelt?"

"Of course." I was an awful liar, and knowing her, she saw right through me. However, I wouldn't shame Mama and Papa today when so many people were gathered.

Each harvest, we Hancocks hosted an afternoon pig roast, inviting craftsmen and prominent citizens of Fincastle to close shop on a crisp autumn Saturday to revel. Weather for this year's roast was glorious—every leaf burnished and shimmering like polished copper in the dappled sunlight.

The sound of laughter caused Letitia to peer over her shoulder. Her glorious hair was swept into curls rolling down one shoulder as she watched a young Bowyer cousin, laughing at his younger brother's attempts to participate in an egg-and-spoon race. I breathed easier when she strolled away from me without further comment. Bitter memories of her in the carriage with Phillip and then spitefully making sure Mama got the abolition pamphlet were still mighty raw.

Letitia sauntered straight over to the gazebo, where the handsome young Bowyer was wiping broken egg yolk from his brother's breeches, both of them guffawing. God bless, but I'd gladly lay money down that she'd have him under her spell by the time we all sat down to eat.

Reverend Logan blessed the food, and I congratulated myself. Seated near me was Letitia, right across the table from young Bowyer, whose handsome face was fully focused on her and grinning like a fool. She twirled a curl through her fingers while telling him something she was *making* sound important, even though it probably wasn't. Then at one point, she had the audacity to look my way with a self-satisfied smile.

I'd had enough.

Abruptly, I got up, walking away from the crowd to the edge of the hill where the road curved up toward Santillane. This was my favorite time of year: dense clouds hanging over Fincastle first thing every morning and smoke from so many households preparing hams for winter. It was a time of year bursting with expectation—a sense of something coming.

I paused atop the rise, spying two horses galloping hard up the wagon road toward the house. Harri's sorrel mare was racing beside Dr. John's horse, so I made my way down to the road to meet them, waving to welcome them back from their ride through town.

Harri saw me and smacked the mare with her crop, leaving Dr. John behind to speed straight toward me, her face radiant. "Julia, I have news!"

Oh, it was coming. I felt it inside. After all, this was Harri's time, and with all my heart I wished her the *greatest* happiness, even though it would leave me as the last of the Hancock girls.

She pulled up next to where I stood and lifted her right leg slightly, tugging at her riding gown to clear it from the saddle's fixed head. She gave the horse a final slap on the rump, and it trotted on up the hill where Cap was waiting to stable it. Dr. John had come up even with us, grinning knowingly at Harri as he followed her mare, giving us a moment together.

I glanced at him, my eyes widening. "Are you and Dr. Radford—"

"*Yes!* He just proposed." She embraced me, her face glowing.

"But please don't tell your parents yet. Let me. I want Uncle Hancock to allow John time enough to write to my father before it's all made public. We want it all proper, formally asking Papa's permission."

"Oh, Harri—I'm *delighted* for you."

But Harri knew me only too well and sensed I was holding back. Was it in my tone? How did she know this was so bittersweet for me? In her eyes, I saw the care she held for me at conflict with her own excitement.

I tried explaining, "It—it just won't be the same here at Santillane without you and Mary. I can't imagine being here without you two, but *especially* you."

She kept hold of my hands, leaning in to kiss my cheek. "You've nothing to fear. Know why? Even if we're not together, our hearts are always close. That's just the way it is with us."

She was right, and I needed to put myself aside and focus on what a tremendously important time this would be in her life—as well as Mary's.

"And my engagement is only *part* of the good news."

I cocked a brow at her, waiting.

"Remember that day back in March at Grove Hill? We were both so sad at the prospect of William Clark being killed out in the wilderness?"

I nodded.

"Well, up in Fincastle just a while ago, some riders came through announcing that Captain Clark, Captain Lewis, and the men from the Corps of Discovery returned safely to St. Louis at the end of September. And they *did* it! They made it clear to the Pacific. Our William Clark is a *hero*!"

I was speechless and frozen, but my heart took flight. This was an unsurpassed moment for our new and burgeoning nation. Somehow these men had forged a way through the high and unknown mountains leading to the Pacific and survived, returning to tell about it.

"They're *safe*, Julia! *Safe!*" she cried in delight, laughing. "Imagine what their welcome home will be like when they return to Washington City."

"You're right. Oh, don't you wish we could be there to see it?"

Harri linked her arm through mine as we proceeded up the hill. My earlier melancholy concerning Letitia lifted, and as we returned to the pig roast arm in arm, my spirits were afire, assured that Jefferson's Corps of Discovery had been successful after all.

❦

It was to be a double wedding, both Mary and Harriet marrying at once.

When the sun first poked its head above the horizon, I was already lying awake. It was the final day Harri would share my bed, as she had since she had first come to live with us when we were both children. Tonight, she'd be abed with Dr. John, and my thoughts wandered as to what that would be like, as I'd only heard Caroline mention once that it hurt the first time.

"Harri?" I whispered. "You awake?"

"Mmm... I am now."

"Are you afraid it will hurt?"

She laughed sleepily as she rolled over to face me, her drowsy eyes opening. "Being with a man, you mean? John said it might at first, but only a bit. He says the marriage act is quite pleasurable if we communicate because men and women are scientifically designed to join together in that way. So once our chamber doors shut tonight, privacy will be all ours, and I can't *wait*."

I stifled a laugh with a little choking sound. What an earful—I was taken aback, for, as a rule, young ladies weren't meant to speak so openly about such. "Well then, I guess it's time for you to rise up and embrace it all." Harri squealed playfully when I nudged her with my cold feet.

"I'm too frozen to move," she complained.

"Just think," I teased, "tomorrow morning, Dr. John will be warming you better than any fire I build."

"Oh, *hush*, you!" Harri blurted, disappearing back under the quilt.

With a deep breath, I slid from the bed, my chilled feet hitting the hardwoods. Lord, my toes felt like an icehouse in January. I snatched up my woolen stockings and tugged them on, shuffling to the fireplace and snatching up a spill. My hands worked deftly, for I'd told Megg not to bother starting fires for me in the mornings. It was something less she had to do, and I could do it myself. Steadily, I held the spill to the coals from last night, and a hot one caught as I reached into the woodpile for kindling. Smoke rose from the dry wood, and I was satisfied. The least I could do on this special day was treat my cousin like a princess.

"Thanks, Julia." Harri's acknowledgment was muffled from under the quilt.

"It's your day, Princess Harri. All must be perfect for you."

"You'll be next. Wait and see." She finished that brief statement by reappearing from under the bedding. "No Hancock girl will ever be forsaken."

I watched the kindling flame up, then added a small log, silently wishing she hadn't brought that subject up. Mama and Papa were apt to focus on me now—pushing me toward their friends' sons and acquaintances. Honestly, it was a little odd that they hadn't already started doing so. It might be fun. Balls, a season or two in Richmond or Washington City, where Papa had connections...

If I ever left Santillane, I'd always fancied it would be to the west. That's the direction I'd always gazed whenever I'd climbed up to my Julia branch on the Catawba tree. Such a change would probably make me homesick. I'd miss everyone. Squeezing my eyes shut, I tried to envision what it was that I really wanted, and the bright image of the flames in the fireplace seemed to illuminate it in my head. I wanted to make a *difference*—to help people and see their lives made better, especially those who could do nothing to improve their own lot in life.

Reverend Mitchell's words flooded back, along with the memory of his gentle but commanding voice: *"Consider the opportunity you'll have someday to make a difference in your own household."*

That was what I wanted from life—though a handsome husband wouldn't be wasted either.

※

It being Christmastide, a huge garland of evergreen hung above Santillane's front door—both inside and out. Lanterns twinkled, and red bows decorated the staircase. Papa had hired a German violinist from Little Amsterdam, and he struck up a haunting folk song, signaling the beginning of the ceremony.

First down the staircase came Mary with Papa, her hand upon his arm. Next came Harri, arm in arm with her father, who had arrived only days ago. Both brides beamed brighter than any candlelight to the violin's melodious strains as they descended toward their waiting grooms.

Vows were repeated, everyone cheered, then older men and women retreated into the drawing room, library, and dining room, making space for dancing in the hallway. First was a reel, which I danced with my brother, Georgie, someone joining the German violinist with a fife. We'd be merry tonight, and the dancing was so lively that I felt my hairpins loosen. Before another gentleman begged a dance, I scurried back upstairs, impatiently standing before the count's big mirror in my room, twisting tendrils of hair into place as best I could and plugging pins back in.

Sensing another's presence, I turned toward the door, a little unnerved to see Papa's tall, imposing form in the doorway.

"Judith, might we have a word?"

"Of course." I blinked nervously. He seldom sought me out alone, and I hoped he wasn't displeased with me in some way. I found it easier to love him from a distance.

He strode into the room. "My girl, there's no better time than this wedding of your sister and cousin to share something important concerning *you*," he began. Reaching into his breast pocket, he retrieved a neatly folded letter. "Take a look." He extended his hand, offering me the letter.

I accepted, inching closer to the fireplace for light and unfolding it. It read:

> My dear Colonel Hancock,
>
> Some years ago, I wrote you rigarding the possibility of joining our famlies through marriage. My former collegue Billy Preston has always Spoken so highly of you and yours. You wisely responded, encouraging me to wait until I had a trade or Some further experience which would help Support a famly.
>
> By now you probably know that I joined Captain Meriwether Lewis and the Corps of Discovery on behalf of Congress, to jerney and mark a waterway to the Pacifick. This undertaking was long and treacherous. However, I Survived and returned.
>
> Now I hope that you will Still consider my offer. Since Some time has passed, I am certain that your daughter Mary has already been Spoken for Since your good name and famly reputashun is Such that many men would vie for her favor. However, I remember best your youngest daughter——who I met along the road. Then, She was but a child, but by now I believe She would be of marigeble age. I remember how adventurous and mischievous was her Spirit and love for the outdoors. Thus it is my belief that Judith the young lady would be even more captivating and I'd be most honored to make her acquaintance.
>
> Sir——it is with the greatest respect that I make this request: Should she respond with favor toward my interest, might you allow me to court her?
>
> I am proceeding eastward and should be in Fincastle sometime in late December.
>
> I am your humble Servent,
> Captain William Clark

My sudden inhale was more a gasp. Time had frozen, and I'd left my last breath somewhere in the middle of the letter. Captain Clark had certainly been cordial the short time we had spent together on that fateful day so long past, during my misadventure with Harri. But I'd been nothing but a child, and it was hard to imagine any impression I'd made then was enough for him to pursue me now.

Papa noted my incredulity and explained, "Years ago, before President Jefferson ever sent the Corps of Discovery into the west, I received Clark's first letter, expressing interest in joining our two families through marriage. Granted, his family is well-known throughout the country, due to his brothers' parts in the war with the British. However, at the time William hadn't made much of himself, aside from guiding you and Harriet over a runoff." Papa paused, chuckling at the memory. "Therefore, I suggested he wait until he had more of a career before we spoke again."

Still disbelieving it all, I flitted my eyes back over the letter, rereading portions, and I forgot Papa was still in the room, so when he spoke again, I jumped, gaping at him, overwhelmed.

"My hope is that Jefferson will grant him a government post as a reward for his services these past years. However, let's not rush into anything, for I want what's best for you. Let's give this time and much thought, shall we?"

Lightly, he kissed my head, turned, and walked out of the room.

Rooted to the floorboards, I stared down at the letter in my hands from an American hero.

My heart didn't need the dancing music from downstairs. It was beating a rhythm of its own accord—a heated, frenzied pulse that bespoke possible happiness and caution of the unknown.

❦

I was frustrated.

Since Harri was one of the brides, people swarmed her all evening, making it impossible for me to approach her and share my news privately. For the rest of the night, I danced in a whirlwind of possibility and nervous hope. When would Captain Clark arrive?

Would he be disappointed in this girl for whom he held such high hopes? And would he want me above all others?

None of my dance partners tonight had red hair or wore it in a queue as had the captain so long ago, but that's all my imagination saw—a tall, stately, red-haired gentleman. Twirling, skipping through steps of jigs, reels, and minuets, my heart was bolstered and excited that such a man was considering *me*.

Later that night, after the wedding guests had all gone, I tiptoed downstairs in my night shift to find my parents collapsed in the library, sipping glasses of port. Papa had his pipe lit and, between sips, was actively puffing through half-closed eyes.

"Oh, Julia, darling," Mama started, "please come join us."

I chose a wooden chair opposite them. "It was so beautiful tonight," I said. "Mary and Harri were most pleased, I'm sure."

Mama agreed, nodding. Yet I could see there was something more she longed to say. Finally, she said, "Julia, your father has told me that he spoke to you about William Clark."

"Yes," I replied, both smiling and blushing.

"Your papa and I have had some disagreement on the timing of all of this. I'm fearful you're far too young for such a union. You've only fifteen years."

Shaking my head, I countered her. "Mama, he's not even here yet. Courting or not, I rather doubt we'd marry before a year or so has passed."

"See?" Papa grumbled through his teeth, his pipe stem firmly in place. "Our girl is wiser than some women twice her age."

"But surely, we're rushing her into adulthood. And she's our youngest girl."

"Mama, I'm actually very eager to meet Captain Clark again."

"He's *much* older than you, love," she warned.

"Ho!" Papa exclaimed, removing his pipe. "Don't be ridiculous, Peggy!" He shot back, then lowered his tone. "Age means *nothing* when it comes to marriage, and you know it. Caroline was seventeen, and your third cousin, or whoever she was from Culpeper, wed when she was but *fourteen*. We were both there to see it! Besides, Judith here possesses an older soul."

I widened my eyes at his remark. My views of him had changed those years ago and created a barrier between us, though I doubt he realized it. It wasn't a chasm too wide or unbreachable. To hear him speak of me like this proved that he was much more aware of who I was than I'd thought.

"She's also our smartest child," he added. "And she's got a clear shot at marrying into one of America's most illustrious families. So let's allow the two of them a chance to know one another." He popped the pipe back into his mouth.

Mama stood and crossed over to where I sat, kneeling before me. "Haven't I always said you were different from the others?" she whispered. "But I urge you to take your time. Move things along slowly. If Captain Clark is truly the man for you, your heart alone will give answer to that fact."

With that advice, Mama leaned in, kissing me lightly on the cheek. After she arose, she said, "It pains me, seeing all of my dear ducks marrying and leaving us. Now, up to bed, all three of us. One would think we'd given a double wedding tonight or something!"

※※※

We were all upstairs in the sitting room, Mama and Mary behind me, fussing over my disobedient tresses. It was the third day in a row they'd dressed me, for we all knew he'd be here anytime. However, it was only yesterday when a visitor to Fincastle told Dr. John that William Clark had stayed the night before in Blacksburg, so we anticipated him to arrive today at the latest.

"We're dressing her for a hero," Harri reminded Mama, "so let me run and find those green ribbons in your old sewing box that match the green velvet on the top of her gown."

Once my hair was done, they all stood back, looking me over. I looked ready for a ball in the middle of the day.

Once Megg had dinner on the table, I could do little but twirl my fork through the potatoes, and I nearly jumped from my seat when the clock chimed noon.

Harri reached over, squeezing my left hand. "You mustn't be nervous. He's coming just for you."

"Indeed, Judith." Papa cleared his throat. "He is, in fact, coming just for you. All those years ago, you somehow impressed him that day you set off on my workhorse, though I don't know how. You and Harriet were wild as wolves."

Everyone laughed, for since we'd had word of Captain Clark's imminent arrival, Harri had circulated that old tale all over Fincastle. When we were just settling down again, Cap opened the front door, calling, "Your visitor's riding up the hill, Colonel Hancock!"

Everyone dropped napkins and silverware, hurrying into the hall to greet Captain Clark, but I hung back in the dining room, swallowing hard, my heart racing. Both my hands were going clammy and cold, and I needed a moment to gather my composure.

When I entered the main hall, everyone was crowding the entry, eager to welcome him. I remained in the background, watchful, cautious—*breathless*.

Papa swung open the door.

There he was, still the tall figure I remembered—though there was more of a commanding air about him now. Despite his long ride, he was well attired, wearing a long gray woolen cloak atop a charcoal-colored greatcoat.

"Captain Clark!" Papa exclaimed, clasping his hand. "It's mighty fine to see you again. Welcome to Santillane."

"Indeed, Colonel. It's been far too long since I've enjoyed Virginia hospitality."

"We're pleased to offer it up, sir," Mama voiced. "Cap, do take the captain's apparel."

Cap stepped up immediately to assist.

Georgie pressed in right next to Papa, grinning and vying for an introduction. "I'm not sure if you remember my son, George Hancock, Junior."

Clark smiled warmly, shaking Georgie's hand too. Then, looking past him, he nodded with a warm smile of recognition. "Ah! Miss Harriet Kennerly, I presume?" he greeted, moving to Harri and taking her hand with a gallant bow.

"Harriet Radford now, actually," she corrected politely, linking Mary's arm in hers. "Both Mary and I were married to these two goodly gentlemen only days ago."

Dr. John and Griff stepped up in turn, the three men exchanging handshakes and pleasantries.

Then Clark craned his neck, looking back in my direction. I took a deep breath and stepped forward as I saw his smile broaden, his eyes gleaming just the way I remembered. Blue as the border of Mama's fine China, they were.

"Miss Hancock." His address was followed with another sweeping bow, sending a shiver down my spine.

Never had my heart beat so erratically and with such restive energy. "Captain," it wound up coming forth as a whisper, and I curtsied low, biting my lip, well aware that everyone was watching.

"Oh my, you've grown up far lovelier than I could ever have imagined. You know, while journeying to the Pacific, I never quite forgot the brave girl I guided across a terrifying river not far from here."

Everyone started laughing, myself included, his humor lightening this moment for us both. I had to be blushing clear up from my toes.

"So I thought you deserved a river of your own, and I named one for you."

Everyone fell silent at that.

What? Had I heard him correctly? "You named a river after *me*?" I exclaimed. Another tingle, for how could it be that William Clark had been thinking of me while he was on the other side of the continent?

"Yes. I wish you could see it. This will sound somewhat embarrassing, but I wasn't sure what I should call it—the Judith, the Julia…"

More light titters, so I inquired, "Which name did you hazard, sir?"

Captain Clark just shook his head. "I took a chance on Judith. It's the *Judith* River—and what a gorgeous flow it is, sequestered in lush green trees with water as clear as crystal. Beyond it are the widest open spaces one could possibly imagine. I felt as though I'd discovered Eden."

I smiled, thinking how easily this man could win me over. "You chose my papa's preferred name for me, Captain. I'm Julia to most everyone else."

"That river fishable?" Georgie interrupted, eyes wide.

"It has abundant trout," Clark answered. "I saw them and walked into its depths, reached down and nearly grabbed several. None of them are used to the presence of men, you see."

Papa announced, "Captain, why don't you two enjoy a few more moments together here, then join us in the drawing room for tea?"

Everyone retreated, leaving just the two of us alone in the entry.

"If you prefer the name Julia, might I have permission to call you that?"

"Yes, please. What should I call you?"

He thought a moment. "My sisters call me Billy, but Billy Preston is your brother-in-law, and we mustn't be confusing."

"What about 'Will'? Would that please you?"

"Will. Hmm… I like the sound of that. And I like the thought of you calling me something unique and different."

In his mid-thirties now, there were a few gray streaks in his crimson hair that I didn't remember from the first time we'd met, but one had to be mindful of all this man had endured for the past several years. And indeed, either I had matured or "Will" had put me at such ease that our age difference didn't alarm me at all.

Therefore, I accepted Will Clark's arm to join everyone for tea, where we all sat around the fireplace in the drawing room, spellbound at the prospect of hearing more about the Corps of Discovery's journey.

"Captain, what is one thing about your trek that stood out most?" Papa asked.

"It had to be the Indians' hospitality, especially the Mandan and Nez Perce."

"Nez Perce?" I asked, translating the French in my head. "Did they pierce their noses?"

"Not that particular tribe. But they were most kind, supplying us with salmon to eat and even guiding us over the mountains on the way back. I assure you all—we would have perished without their mercy."

"Then they're not savages?" That was from Mama.

Will smiled at her. "Mrs. Hancock, some of the natives have finer manners and personal dignity than people here in Virginia or Kentucky. However, the Mandan, Shoshone, and Nez Perce were the most genteel of any Indians we encountered. They showed greater kindnesses than many white men I've known."

Papa clapped his hands together, enjoying the day with relish. "Oh-ho, Captain, I look forward to more in-depth conversations about your venture."

"I'll be most happy to share the details, sir. I'm pleased to have returned safely so that I'm able to be in your company. Thank you for opening your home to me."

Megg poured everyone's tea, and generous slices of apple cake were passed around. From where I sat next to the hearth, I could see into the hallway. Cap and another slave I faintly remembered from the first time Will and I had met were hauling heavy chests to the guestroom on the first floor.

Everyone was asking Will questions, but all I heard was the grunting of two slaves heaving a weighty burden.

My heart sank as reality struck me square. William Clark was a slave owner.

Chapter V

Fincastle, Virginia
Late December–January 1807

Now that Will was visiting, Mama, Papa, my brother, and I joined him daily after breakfast to hear more about the Corps of Discovery journey. It was an invaluable time for me, learning more about the explorer inside the man who wanted to know me.

"How many men were lost along the way?" That was Mama.

"Thank God only one," Will replied, head shaking. "His name was Charles Floyd, and he succumbed to a ravaging illness. We buried him high atop a bluff overlooking the plains. That was a dark day for us, it happening so early in the mission, with everyone expecting he was but the first and not the last to die. As he was lowered into the earth, I swore to myself that I'd do everything I could to ensure he *would* be the only soul to give his life for our undertaking."

After a brief silence, Papa was next. "Tell of the places you spent the most time?"

"We camped seasonally in a few places and used a few stops for days of rest. In the winter of '04–'05, we were at Fort Mandan, named for the natives who hosted us. Same for Fort Clatsop last winter, whose natives were less savory, in my humble opinion. They'd been corrupted by sailors trading along the Pacific coast."

Georgie piped up, "Captain, how were they corrupted?"

"*That's* not your concern, my boy," Mama informed him, making Will and Papa both laugh knowingly. "Thank you, Captain Clark, but we needn't put those sorts of things in his head just yet."

"Understood." Will complied with a grin. "Let's see… at a place we named Traveler's Rest, we allowed respite for a good number of days, both coming and going. That was a magnificent place—right at the foot of the mountains."

"What of the dangers?" I asked.

"Constant—*unending*!" Will exclaimed, frank and wide-eyed. He had such an easy manner, but I still blushed, so he immediately put me at ease with his answer. "There were too many perils, really. It took all of my skill to see us safely through waterways that were unknown and risky. And often we used native-styled canoes too. By God, was that ever a ride when we hit rapids or the Missouri's falls! Another time—early on—the Sioux tried to commandeer our keelboat, and we barely escaped an outright attack with the whole warband surrounding us. Then once, the weather turned on us when several Corps members, including the native woman Sakakawea and myself, were in a dry riverbed. A sudden, violent storm flooded the area and nearly claimed us all. I found myself shoving her up the embankment before I was hauled up too, soaked and battered as I was by the muddy water."

These conversations allowed me to vicariously meet those with whom Will had traveled. First and foremost was his dearest friend Meriwether Lewis, whom he considered a brother. Added to that was the indomitable sharpshooter George Drouillard—half-Indian and all courage, then the fascinating Sakakawea, who introduced the Corps to her people, the Shoshone. And even the youngest of the expedition, George Shannon—not much older than me.

It was captivating, hearing how the Corps had become as close as blood kin, seeing to one another's needs, illnesses, and travails. Like any excellent soldier, each had contributed to Will's safety, as he had theirs. He was gregarious and outgoing while sharing his memories; the sort of personality that drew one into immediate friendship.

Naturally, he wanted to know more about me, but I became cautious. I wanted to open up, for here was a man truly interested in me and me alone, who had come specifically to see me—exactly what I'd desired.

Regardless, I trod carefully, deciding at this point to share only the obvious—not the strife pulling at me, that *hidden* Julia, who was at an utter loss of what to do with the responsibility to the enslaved I'd promised to take on in the sight of the Almighty within my heart.

If only Reverend Mitchell was here for advice.

Thus, I showed Will the many books in Papa's library that I enjoyed—especially the volume containing Shakespeare's sonnets. "I only wish I had his plays," I said regretfully. "I hear he wrote thrilling ones, but I've not had opportunity to read them."

Those first several days were full of relaxed conversations at mealtimes and family games in the drawing room in front of the fire. Not only was Will a jovial sort with a hearty laugh, but he had a dignity and comportment in a group setting that impressed me—a self-assurance putting him fully at ease. That trait must have served him well on the trek to the Pacific. It was a character of greatness.

Another thing of which I was certain was that he was a staunch family man. On the last day of December, on the afternoon before our annual New Year's festivities, we found ourselves alone in the library. There, he told me about his oldest brother, Jonathan, and of their closeness. Then there was his other brother, the war hero George Rogers, with whom he lived in Kentucky.

"George is prone to solitude and depression," Will confessed, his brow wrinkling in concern. "He had an illustrious career during campaigns against the British and their Indian allies. However, he was never reimbursed for supplies purchased on his own credit. Neither the state of Virginia nor Congress has repaid him, despite everything he did on behalf of soldiers while defeating enemies in the northwestern Ohio wilderness. Now I'm trying to help him out of financial and emotional ruin, and sometimes it seems futile."

My heart tugged inside me, tempting me reach out and take his hand in comfort, but still I held back, despite the emotional attachment I was beginning to feel.

That night, we prepared for New Year's Eve. Fincastle had a yearly tradition of ringing the city's church bells—and of course the old courthouse bell too. Everybody close enough to town attended the event, and many folks who lived a good way off stayed overnight with friends or family so they'd be able to join in the fun.

Naturally, James Breckinridge was first to greet us when we arrived. "Hancock, I *must* meet your guest." He hurried to Papa's side, extending his hand to Will. Everyone in town had heard about our famed visitor and the principal reason he was purported to be here, which only heightened my anxiety.

I glanced about.

If Mr. Breckinridge was here, it meant Letitia probably was as well. Fincastle was too small for us to avoid one another completely, and I knew she wouldn't miss an opportunity to meet and flirt with Captain William Clark.

James Early, the local tailor who made Papa's suits, was hauling a small wooden box over in front of the log courthouse. Someone would be speaking. Mama drifted away with ladies from church and was completely engaged, probably answering their questions about Will and me. I found myself suddenly alone and couldn't decide where to go, wishing to avoid any confrontation with questions.

Then someone grasped my arm.

Harri! I hadn't seen her since Will had arrived a few days before.

"Julia, how are things with Captain Clark?"

"I—I don't—" Why I became emotional right then, I had no idea, but my eyes turned wet and teary, stinging in the freezing air.

Harri glanced about, looking for privacy and pulling me over to one of the courthouse's walls. Shadowed and dark, now we could be alone.

"Sweet cousin, what's happened?"

"If I share it, you mustn't tell, for my feelings wouldn't be popular here."

"We've always kept each other's secrets, haven't we? I'd never betray that."

Sniffling, I nodded. "Last year, when I went with the Breckinridges to that camp meeting, one of the preachers spoke against slavery. He didn't have to persuade me much, for I already hated it."

"Ah. And Captain Clark owns slaves."

"At least one—that man York we met along the road years ago—and probably others, though I've not discussed it with him."

For a moment, she was tongue-tied, shaking her head. "Julia, your own family has slaves. I can't understand why this is such an issue, even with your convictions."

"Because if my husband owned slaves, in theory, I'd own them too. I'd be married *into* it, regardless if they were legally mine, and I never want to own another person, Harri."

"It's a way of life here. If you don't court and marry Captain Clark, then your parents will just introduce you to someone else—*another* slave owner! And should you refuse that, then where would you be? A spinster?"

True enough. "I know you think I'm being foolish, but I'm struggling with this."

Harri paused again and sighed. "Tell me something. Do you feel so strongly about it that you'd sacrifice your own happiness?"

I brushed away tears, shaking my head. "And that's just it, Harri. I already feel something inside my heart for him—even though it's just been a couple of days. He's good to me, always the perfect gentleman and so handsome, but I'm afraid to tell him about my convictions because he'd think I was some sort of radical and look elsewhere for a woman with her head on straight."

Harri grabbed both of my hands. "He may not free his people, but think of the difference you could make in their lives if you were their mistress. You could help them—just like you help Megg, Cap, and the others at Santillane."

I nodded. Indeed, her words were so similar to those of Reverend Mitchell. I wondered—how *would* Will respond if I told him? Honestly, I wasn't sure, and that concerned me.

"Do you *desire* him?" Harri asked in a low voice.

There was nothing for it but to nod admission, for it was true. Will cut a dashing figure, and I thrilled whenever we were in the same room and his eyes followed my every move. And what would it be like to have that face hovering closer to mine—about to kiss me?

When a shiver crept up my spine, I realized my body had answered the question for me.

By the time Harri and I reappeared in front of the courthouse, Henry Bowyer, one of our town's beloved veterans of the War for Independence, climbed up on the speaker's box.

"Citizens of Fincastle," he cried, "friends and families all! Hear, hear! Tonight, we celebrate the incoming year of our Lord, 1807. We'll welcome it with the sound of bells in just fifteen minutes' time. Meanwhile, I invite you all to join me here on January 8th to welcome home the illustrious explorer Captain William Clark!"

Crowds in the square exploded into enthusiastic cheering at that announcement.

I craned my neck, seeking Will out. He was just beyond the podium with Papa, Mr. Breckinridge, and Patrick Lockhart, another well-respected veteran.

"As many of you know," Bowyer continued, "he's a fellow Virginian, the nation's finest outdoorsman, an army friend of Billy Preston, and most recently, a close friend to the *Hancocks*!"

More cheering and laughter followed at his emphasis on our name, and I was thankful for the darkness, as I still felt more than a hundred sets of eyes, all seeking me.

"In a week's time, we'll celebrate the captain's return and his triumphant journey to the western ocean. *And* he has promised us a few remarks of his own!" Bowyer ended with an elegant bow as another hearty round of cheering commenced.

I couldn't help but feel pride, which only added to my conviction that, yes, I was developing deeper feelings for Will.

After that, New Year's Eve festivities were in full swing. Cider was passed around; men fired rounds into the air, spooking every carriage horse in sight. Groups of gentlemen gathered together to open a keg of whiskey in celebration—Papa and Will among them.

Mama called Harri and me over to join up with Mary, Mrs. Logan, and other ladies from church, holding hands and singing hymns around the bonfire in the town square. When midnight tolled, the night filled with ringing bells and cheering. I glanced over at the men, where Patrick Lockhart was leading some old War of Independence songs, full of bawdy lyrics about scandalous British ladies. Will moved over to join them, laughing merrily, pausing to reload his firearm and shoot it high into the night.

Mrs. Early's brood of children ran up to me for hugs. Then Agatha Bowyer caught my arm, taking my hand in hers. She was a fascinating woman—Patrick Henry's niece and Mama's dear friend.

"Sweet, sweet Julia, how you've grown up. Captain Clark's interest in you is such fine news, my girl. He'd be a fool not to pursue a Hancock."

"Thank you," I replied, accepting her kiss on my cheek.

As she walked away, I looked back over at Will. He hadn't yet asked to court me, probably since we'd been alone so little. But at least now I'd decided upon an answer for him if he did.

※※※

On the day before Will was to speak to the people of Fincastle, he pointedly asked Papa at breakfast, "Colonel Hancock, might I have the honor of strolling with your daughter this morning?"

I stared into my tea, feeling every eye at the table on me.

"Certainly, Captain."

Thus, we were truly alone for the first time, Will politely offering me his arm.

"Where shall we walk?" he asked.

"Is there a particular place you'd like to go?" Honest to goodness, if one blinked while riding a coach through Fincastle, they'd miss the entire community.

"Might there be a walking path nearby?"

Shivering, I bit my lip and pulled my coat collar closer against the January air. "There's a short trail down by the Mill Pond, and it'll be a brisk walk even before getting there."

"Perfect."

It wasn't too long a distance, and once there we stood for a spell along the shore, taking in the sight of crisp brown reeds and grasses, whose days were done. The water was like glass, and Will pointed at a big blue heron standing as though it were a statue. "Those birds even inhabit the Pacific coast."

"You've quite the eye for animals," I marveled.

He laughed, eyes twinkling. "When the possibility of dinner depends solely on hunting it down, then yes, one learns quickly how to locate game."

I felt so relaxed with him, and my, but he was distinguished-looking. Dressed in his thick, dark gray overcoat, I couldn't help but imagine a muscled form underneath. For a heartbeat, we gazed at one another, and I took in his face, ruddy as it was now in the cold air. Fine lines formed slight parentheses around the sides of his mouth, but in my estimation they added character.

"Julia, I hope you haven't minded my visit."

"Minded? Why, it's been an honor, and we've all enjoyed hosting you, especially hearing about your travels."

He guided me toward the footpath around the pond. "I've shared a great deal of my life with you and your family, but I've yet to learn much about Julia Hancock herself. I sense you're aware of my real reasons for coming. Have I been talking too much, or are you holding back?"

I was quick to answer. "There's not much to know about me. I'm just a girl from Fincastle—one who longs to help people."

"There's nothing greater than someone who wishes to care for one's fellow man." He studied me as though longing to read my mind.

A real warmth ignited within me, and, not watching where I was going, I stumbled on a tree root, Will catching me.

We both laughed.

While standing still again, holding hands, he said, "Julia, I must declare my intentions before any more time passes. In just a few days, I must leave for Washington City. That's why I was anxious for some time alone with you, for I need to hear your feelings on this matter." He paused, thinking hard and choosing words carefully. "When I was growing up, my sister Lucy had a friend of whom you remind me. Hannah always made us Clarks laugh and kept us guessing. From the very start, you reminded me of her, with your captivating personality. I told myself that if I returned from the Pacific whole and in one piece, there would be no other girl I'd want to know better than that Fincastle girl at Santillane whose horse was afraid of rainwater. Therefore, I would like permission to court you. My intentions are honorable, and should either of us decide this relationship is not worthy of further effort, then we must be open and voice it, painful or not."

"Papa showed me your letter," I said, nodding. "So, yes, I was aware of your interest. I've just needed time—time to consider everything."

"Dare I hope for your favor?"

Could it have been Providence that had brought him alongside us on that road years ago? Little matter, since my mind was made up. I would be courted by William Clark. A thrill of excitement flooded me, for as much as I did love my home and family, I craved the adventure of seeing more—being more.

"Yes, Will Clark. I will court you—on the terms you've just offered."

"They're fair terms, don't you think?"

"More than fair."

He grinned boyishly, lifting my hand to his lips. I trembled through my leather glove, wishing I could have felt that first brush of his lips on my flesh instead, for though I was young, I was also a woman and fashioned for such. I was even ready to boldly declare my opinions on slavery when he gave me a mischievous grin, and I paused, long enough not to speak further.

"I've a gift for you." He reached into a deep pocket within the warmth of his overcoat, drawing out a small, soft-looking oblong package wrapped in brown paper. Whatever it was wasn't boxed and looked lumpy. "I hope they fit," he added with a touch of worry, handing the bundle over to me.

Curious, I tugged on the string. What was inside was all supple leather and delicately beaded doeskin.

Moccasins!

The smell of woodsmoke from a thousand fires clung to them, and I pressed my cheek against their softness, imagining winds of open prairies and bellows of buffalo. Even the rawhide lacings were light to the touch—almost silky. Sewn into the hide were birdlike creatures—sparrows, maybe—brightly crafted with red, white, and sky-blue beadwork. Inside, the leather was lined with rabbit fur and topped at the ankles with a light fringe.

"They're extraordinary," I gasped, for I'd never received such a gift.

"Sakakawea made them. She was married to one of our interpreters. She herself turned out to be a fabulous help on our journey."

"How old was she?"

"Around your age, I imagine."

"And what was her husband like?"

"Truthfully? A scoundrel."

"Were they not in love, then?"

"Absolutely not. But Toussaint was a far better cook than she was! That's something."

We both laughed. *Sak-ak-a-wea*. What an intriguing name.

"I hope you like them," he said.

"I *love* them, and they look to be a perfect fit."

"Good. I'm most pleased, and she would be too. Sizing them was a gamble, so I had her tailor them to her own feet. She was happy to make them when I told her who might wear them."

I shook my head, humbled. He had told others about me—about his hopes?

For a time, we walked along in silence, arm in arm, listening to chickadees call out in the brush. When at last he broke the quiet, his words were full of the same awe in which I was basking.

"What a fine day it was when I accidentally came upon two girls on a stubborn horse, and one of them amazed me with a bright smile like the sun, an innate sense of frolic, and a mischievousness that made me laugh."

Grinning, I tugged at his arm. "Come, let's hurry and get home to Santillane to share our news!"

BOOM!

Horses tethered around the courthouse square jumped involuntarily. Old Patrick Lockhart was busy firing his cannon. Fincastle folk said he'd brought it home with him from the war, when it was used against the British, and now he kept it in his barn under old quilts except for special occasions, such as today.

Wiggling my nose at the sulfurous odor of gunpowder, I stuffed my hands deeper into my fur mitt where I sat with Mama, Mary, and Griff.

Today, Captain William Clark was to be officially welcomed home by the people of Fincastle.

BOOM!

My ears rang.

Mary began waving wildly from her seat next to me, and I saw Harri and Dr. John weaving their way through the crowd to join us in the seats we'd saved for them. Undoubtedly, Dr. John was running late from a call to a patient.

I couldn't help but shake my head, amazed at the throng that had literally tripled since we'd taken our seats. Word had spread about Will's visit, and folks were flocking in from as far away as Bedford, Blacksburg, and Richmond. At breakfast, Papa had even mentioned several gentlemen having traveled all the way from Harper's Ferry.

Mr. Bowyer was pulling out the same wooden box upon which he'd spoken last week on New Year's Eve, and to let the waiting crowd know that the festivities were about to begin, someone started ringing the courthouse bell.

BOOM!

Harri crept over, kneeling down, eye to eye with me, placing a comforting hand on my shoulder.

"How are things?" she whispered.

My ears were ringing from Lockhart's cannon, and it was hard to hear with the crowd and the bells, so I simply nodded, giving her a hopeful smile. "Much better," I assured. "Let's talk soon."

She kissed my cheek, stood, and followed Dr. John to their seats.

Mr. Lockhart moved away from the cannon, using an old handkerchief to wipe gunpowder from his hands. Officially, he was Botetourt County's sheriff, though only in name now since he was a ripe seventy years old. Still, he comported himself like a soldier. Grizzled and gray-haired, his steady gait never faltered, and he stood tall—living proof that many veterans enjoyed as healthy a life as they'd had a quarter of a century before, at war with England's crown.

Marching up to the speaker's box, Lockhart stepped up, raising both hands for everyone's attention. Behind him, the courthouse door opened; Mr. Breckinridge, Papa, and Will strode forth to their appointed places.

Once everyone settled, Mr. Lockhart raised his voice, "Welcome, friends, neighbors, travelers, and strangers! Fincastle ain't a town for outsiders, so you'd best get acquainted with people next to you." He laughed at his own words good-naturedly, and a few people tittered, some introducing themselves to those nearby.

"Today, I'd like to welcome back to the bosom of our nation the daring explorer Captain William Clark, offering sincerest congratulations for his perilous and laborious service."

He turned to Will, who stepped forward for Lockhart to address him personally. Lockhart clapped his hand on Will's shoulder. "Sir, your prudence, courage, and good conduct have afforded us joy without restraint. In whatever situation God might place you, it will ever be a source of gratification to remember your appointment, leading you to navigate bold and unknown rivers and mountains never before impressed by civilized man. You've extended the knowledge of the geography of our country, enriched science, and opened this United States to inexhaustible wealth. And in the midst of it all, you respected the rights of humanity. Your fame will be pure and unsullied, for you've taught us all how discoveries—even the most difficult—may be affected without the effusion of human blood. Therefore, indulge us in declaring that your grateful country thinks it proper to bestow greatest reward upon you for these past perils, difficulties, and privations."

I pulled my hands out of my mitt to applaud with everyone

else, and in a show of utmost appreciation and honor, everyone rose, granting Will a standing ovation.

As he stepped up onto the podium to speak, Fincastle cheered, many even waving flags. One hand tapping his heart lightly, he evidenced his deep appreciation at the welcome while humbly nodding his head, mouthing silent thank-yous. An inner warmth spread through my entire being as I considered how this man might well be my future husband.

Once the crowd quieted, he addressed them:

"Ladies and gentlemen, such sentiments of esteem and care over our personal safety are much appreciated. Indeed, it will be a pleasing reflection in my future life to find the expedition has been productive for our country, geography, and science. To respect the rights of humanity had and ever will be the leading principle of my life, and no reflection is more pleasing to me than knowing we spilled so little human blood. Your friendliness and attention are highly flattering, and I'll make your appreciation known to both Captain Lewis and the faithful party that accompanied us."

Short and sweet it was when he finished. My heart fluttered and my mouth was dry as cotton, for I was the one privileged person here with a hold on his heart. It really was no small thing, the fact that he was pursuing me and wanting me above all others—this newly returned American hero.

Then I saw her—Letitia Breckinridge—meandering her way forward from her seat toward the front of the crowd. I knew she intended to speak to Will. Yet just as she was within an arm's length, so close she could have reached out and touched his sleeve, he turned away, shaking hands with Lockhart and thumping Papa on the back.

For a few more heart-pounding moments, I thought she was going to keep going and interrupt their conversation. Then she stopped, cocking one of her immaculate eyebrows as Will turned around, beckoning and calling to me. "Julia, come join us!"

I went forward to meet him, leisurely pacing past where Letitia stood, her face flustered, unable as she was to breach the crowd that parted for me.

"Excuse me, please," I said tersely as I passed her by. Once I reached Will, I placed my hand lightly on his arm, glancing back at her and smiling broadly.

It was enough, knowing that this time she couldn't ruin a thing.

⁂

Two days after his triumph in Fincastle, Will left for Washington City.

A separation would be a good thing, giving me time to assess my feelings, for once he left, stirrings of uncertainty had gripped me once again.

Full of pride and bursting with burgeoning emotion that I felt was love, I'd asked Will if I might reread his response to the people of Fincastle. As I did so, one phrase—something I'd not caught while he'd spoken the words—gave me pause, causing me to doubt the feelings stirring within me.

Ever discerning, Harri saw me at church and pledged to come by for a chat.

Her bright blue taffeta day dress rustled as she removed her gloves to settle onto the leather chair across from me in front of the fire in the library. "At the courthouse, you said all was well," she commented. "Has something happened since? By the look on your face, your doubts are back."

Oh, how she could read me!

I smiled. "We did speak—alone. I agreed to court him, and he has made it clear that should either of us wish to end the relationship, then we are free to do so."

"He won't end it, Julia. He wants you and you alone. It's obvious. He *adores* you. However discreet you may be to others, I can always tell when something is bothering you, so what is it?"

"Look at this." I picked up the copy of Will's speech, handing it over to her. "Once more, my conscience is pricking me."

"Over slavery?"

I nodded. "Will's speech was magnificent, Harri. At the time, he left me breathless and the crowd went wild in their accolades. Then later, I reread it. Look at what he says here." I leaned over, pointing at the exact phrase in the speech. "I'll never forget these words: *'To respect the rights of humanity had and ever will be the leading principle of my life...'*"

My cousin stared at the words, then at me, silent. Did she not understand? "They're hypocritical!" I exclaimed. "My convictions run deep, and I don't know if I can marry a man declaring such noble sentiments while living his life in such *dis*respect for other human beings."

Harri glanced down at the speech again, perusing the words. "You've not yet told him about your concerns, have you?"

I shook my head.

"I know this is tormenting you, but—"

"But *what?*"

"If you haven't broached the subject, then you don't know what lies in his heart. Even if he owns more slaves than that man York, he may be as kind as a shepherd is to sheep. You mustn't judge him for a societal malady—if that's the way you see it."

She got up from the chair and sank down before me, grasping both my hands. "Know what I think? I think you're falling in love with him *despite* your beliefs. Is that true?"

Becoming emotional again, I could hardly form words, so I simply nodded.

"I've known you most of my life, Julia Hancock. You've always been stubborn and prone to thinking things through too much. Stop *thinking* with that brain of yours, stop *arguing* with yourself, and just let love happen."

I set aside Will's speech and determined to move forward, letting my emotions finally have full rein to lead me where they would. My beliefs would never change, but instead I'd lean on the faith that should Will and I marry, the good Lord would allow me to work in the lives of any of Will's enslaved.

That became my fervent prayer.

Chapter VI

Fincastle, Virginia
February 1807

Will didn't tarry in Washington City, returning to Santillane by mid-February. On the very day he returned, we donned warm woolens and coats to take a long walk together, reveling in the frigid air and watching a pair of hawks flap circuitous paths through the sky while hunting. We took a shortcut down into one of Papa's fields—the one with the Catawba tree, then trudged on down the road to the Mill Pond. We'd had a heavy snow three days past, and since then everything was frozen.

The Mill Pond was a sheet of ice.

"I was the brunt of many a joke in Washington City," Will confessed, the edges of his eyes crinkling with mirth. Even as cold as it was, freezing temperatures didn't faze him.

"Tell all, Captain Clark."

"Apparently, President Jefferson was planning quite a welcome-home party for Lewis and me at the presidential house."

"I'm most curious about Lewis."

"He's a man with an arduous task ahead of him, for his next step is publishing our expedition journals."

"Really?" That sounded fascinating, me being so fond of books. "Tell me about that."

"Certainly, but let me finish first. Jefferson waited and waited after Lewis had already arrived in Washington, but I tarried here so long they wound up having the token celebration in my absence." He laughed aloud, shaking his head.

I stopped in my tracks. "*What?* You missed your own party, given by the *president?*" And he'd missed it to be with me? My mind and heart had been playing tug-of-war so much this past month, but now I felt completely humbled.

Will stopped walking, turning toward me and taking my hands in his. "I was with *you*, Julia." He grinned in earnest, his hands squeezing mine. "So it really doesn't matter to me that I missed it."

Heart hammering, I was speechless, gazing into his eyes.

"Now, you said you were curious about our journals and their publication?"

"Yes," I affirmed, eager to set aside my awkwardness.

"Well, it's mostly tedium, preparing a manuscript. First, Lewis will solicit help from men in the scientific community and get their penny's worth of advice. He'll need help editing passages on flora and fauna that he recorded, so there will be specialists to consult and hire for the job. Then there's finding a company to publish the work. And, of course, our field journals from those two years require attention. They must be completely rewritten, something Lewis and I began—copying them to neater renderings. But we're not close to finishing, and I confess that my own spelling and writing skills are far from superior."

From his letters, I had noticed his colorful spellings and capitalizations, though none of that mattered to me. However, it did appear that Lewis would have a taxing job, for compiling a book sounded far more complicated than I'd ever imagined.

Abruptly, Will released me, walking over beside the pond and leaning against a tree. "I have some news—news that may or may not suit you. For now, it needs to remain between just us until I have confirmation. Lewis consulted with Jefferson and Secretary of War Dearborn. They intend to offer me a position in St. Louis."

St. Louis?

"Such a far-off place—and west of here too. How certain are you of this appointment?"

"Quite certain, but I'm awaiting official word in writing." He waved his hand nonchalantly. "A typical formality." Then he chuckled.

"What's so funny?"

"It's not actually, but if I share something in confidence, will you promise never to tell anyone?"

"It'll be hidden all the way to my grave."

"Well then... right before we set out on our expedition to the Pacific, I was to have received the rank of captain, just like Lewis. Even Jefferson was party to this agreement. However, what nobody knows is that I never officially received that honor. Dearborn wrote to inform both Lewis and me that I'd be nothing but a second lieutenant."

"How horribly unfair!" I cried out, stunned. "You're not a captain at all, then? Even after risking your life in such a grand way for your country?"

"Ha!" he expelled mirthlessly. "My poor brother George has been treated far worse. It's truly a wonder the man hasn't committed treason by the manner in which our government has spurned his many favors toward liberty."

"So you kept this slight to yourself but continued with the expedition despite not receiving what was promised?"

Will nodded. "Lewis and I thought it best to keep it to ourselves while we proceeded on, for all our men already assumed we were equal in rank. Since it was news that arrived at the eleventh hour, very near the time of our departure, there was nothing to be done except to move forward."

I was dumbfounded.

He could have quit, relinquished the opportunity Lewis had extended, but he didn't. Instead, he remained steadfast to his country, the Corps, and every man involved despite the disappointment of a lower rank and not receiving the expected courteous nod from his betters in Washington.

And how had I treated this man who had risked so much for his country under less than satisfactory conditions? My fickle thoughts and emotions had swung like a pendulum due to my stubborn conscience, but at least I'd decided to commit myself to loving him now—to follow my heart's desire.

"You're a remarkable man, William Clark," I breathed. Ever so gently, I placed my gloved hands upon both sides of his face, and just as tentatively, he leaned in so that our lips brushed. Then we embraced, staying there for several moments, holding one another.

Oh, but my feelings were complete.

"Ah, well," he murmured softly in my ear. "I confess that whenever I think back on that message from Dearborn, I was thunderstruck—no, *furious*. I felt slighted in the worst possible way, and yes—*cheated*. But if I had known it would have this effect on my ladylove?"

We both laughed, pulling apart, though I already treasured the feel of being pressed against him and kissing for the first time.

"Did Dearborn's message make you want to quit the Corps?" I asked.

Will shook his head. "No. I simply realized there was nothing to do except swallow my pride, so I forced myself to do so. How thankful I am that I did. Sometimes we must make sacrifices to achieve our life goals. *But*," he added, "it gave me the *deepest* satisfaction to send my resignation of that 'official commission' right back to Dearborn once we returned."

My head was nodding in full, wondrous agreement when we heard playful shrieks pierce the still of the pond's surroundings, making Will turn around. Still holding his hand, I took a step forward too.

On the other side of the pond were three small enslaved children, bundled up in tattered coats and old clothes, all giggling and sliding about on the ice. The two girls remained close to shore, but the third—a boy who looked to be about eight—slid toward the middle of the pond's frozen surface. For half a minute, he was giggling and spinning about until I saw him freeze and look down.

I dropped Will's hand, shuffling forward in the snow to the edge of the pond. "Go back!" I screamed. "It's not safe, it could crack—"

The boy glanced up at me, panic registering on his cherubic round face, then looked back down at his feet. "It be cracking right now!" he squealed. "And I can't swim none!"

Now we heard it too—a snapping like the sharp breaking of fine porcelain, only loud enough to make me jump.

"Can you go *back*?" My desperate question echoed over the frozen landscape.

"Miss, that crack is *behind* me!" He starting crying in panic. "My feet's done soaked!"

Then Will was by my side, bearing a long-reaching branch of sizeable deadfall, probably knocked from some tree this past autumn. It was a good twenty feet long. I realized his intent, and I was thankful that the Mill Pond wasn't overly wide in circumference.

"There's nothing to be done but to pull him toward us." He eased the branch onto the ice but shook his head after pushing it out halfway. "Damned thing's not long enough, and as large as I am, my weight would shatter this ice, especially out toward the middle."

"He's sure to fall in." My decision was made without hesitation. I took a step out onto the pond's surface.

"No, Julia!" Will exclaimed. "That water could kill you."

"I'm lighter than you, and we can't just leave him—especially if he doesn't know how to swim. Give it to me." I went over and took hold of the limb. What mattered at that second was getting it to the child for comfort and stability, if nothing more.

We were face to face, holding the branch now. "Don't do this," he begged, "*please* don't."

On the other side of the pond, the girls were crying out to the boy, fearful, imploring him to come back to where they were.

"Girls," I shouted, ignoring Will's plea. "Come around here to this side of the pond. We're going to try to pull him out over here, and if he falls in, you'll need to hurry him home."

They didn't hesitate, immediately running around the bank toward us. By then, I was taking more tentative steps forward, pulling the limb away from Will.

"Julia, if you won't listen to reason, at least lie down. Spread your weight over the ice." Then he raised his voice, gesturing and shouting to the boy to do the same, "You too, boy! Get down like her. Spread out your weight."

I did as Will said, taking my time and trying to be careful with every movement. Wouldn't the ice be stronger closer to the edge of the pond near the frozen earth? And hadn't Will mentioned something about the middle being more prone to breaking—exactly where the boy was? I certainly wasn't sure, but we'd had a hard freeze for three days straight with no thawing.

I'd be testing it now.

Never had I realized how heavy wood was; maneuvering that limb out in front of me was more difficult and awkward than I'd first imagined. I forced it forward slowly, breathing deep and shoving with every inch of progress I made. Like a slow-moving fish, I was swimming—but over a thin veil of snowfall atop the ice. Indeed, the thought of falling through gave me pause, but the child needed help.

Somewhere ahead, near the boy, another sharp crack resonated in the still air.

"Oh, Julia, don't do this…" Will groaned fearfully behind me. "Come back!"

I kept going.

Snow feathered around me, and the vacuous silence augmented everything—the cold, the sound of my own breathing, my heart's rush. One scoot, then another, and another. How odd I must have looked from a bird's view, reclining facedown on the ice and repeatedly pushing off with help from my arms to slither forward. It was slow going, and my winter clothes and long skirts didn't exactly help.

"What's your name?" I called, hoping to divert danger from the child's thoughts and mine.

"Nace, miss," his voice tremulous.

"Well, Nace, don't you move. With the good Lord's help, we'll have you high and dry in no time. And should the ice break and you fall in, you just kick with your legs, you hear? That's how you'll stay afloat."

I reckoned I was near enough to the center of the pond, so I slid the branch toward Nace as far as it would reach. Lord be praised, he snatched it perfectly, hanging on for all he was worth.

"Don't let go," I instructed. "Hang on." Taking care, I began moving in reverse, tugging on the limb as best I could.

"Julia, I'm coming out just a ways. Once you've pulled him in far enough, I want you to slide the limb toward me as hard as you can and then get off this ice."

I looked back over my shoulder. Will was on his knees, gradually easing himself out a short distance from the bank. Everything was moving at so slow a crawl.

When I sensed I was back far enough, I turned slightly and, with all my strength, shoved the branch at Will.

He lunged out as far as he could, and—*success!* He caught it squarely. Far stronger than me, he backed up on his haunches, pulling Nace toward him easily in comparison to my efforts. Close, *closer*, my heart thrilled when Will exclaimed, "I've got you, boy!"

Relieved, I closed my eyes and started to resume my own backing up.

That's when I heard it.

Beneath me began a high-pitched keening, a straining of the ice, complaining of my weight. Glancing over my shoulder again, I realized I was only halfway back to the shore, not having come as far as I'd thought. Maybe if I hurried…

CRACK!

Everything gave way to a million needles piercing my flesh. Even worse was my reflex, to gasp at the shock of the cold, inhaling water instead of air. Choking, I squeezed my eyes shut, my lungs screaming as I plunged downward, and I could hear my throat retch as my entire body rebelled against drowning. In panic, my arms flailed and my legs kicked to propel myself up, and when I opened my eyes, all was dark and cloudy amid mind-numbing, frigid water that even made my eyeballs ache.

When my fingers resurfaced at the break where I'd fallen through, I was so insensate I could hardly feel the sharp edges of ice as my fingers clawed to find purchase.

Then something poked my shoulder.

"Julia, take the limb!"

I saw the branch Will offered. Yet now it was difficult to force my body to respond, trembling as I was. Oddly, I saw myself take hold of the rough wood, but I couldn't *feel* anything.

Dimly, as if in the distance, Will was calling, "Hold on! Hold on!"

It's a surreal feeling when you can't control your limbs from juddering. Mine were more than shaking—they literally smacked the water with little splashes. Coughing, sputtering, my immediate goal was air, yet every breath was an effort, even though I was now above water.

"Julia! *Julia!* I've got you, my love. You're safe now."

"Nace?" my own voice wheezed "Is he—"

"Yes. He's with his sisters," Will assured. "They're taking him home."

My teeth were clicking so hard I could hear them resonate inside my skull. Then his hands found me.

"I'm wrapping you in my greatcoat."

He still sounded so distant. I wanted him to hold me—get me warm—but my shaking was so uncontrollable I couldn't form any words.

Then somehow I rolled, despite my quaking limbs. I coughed up water in a warm, involuntary gush. Exhausted after spilling what seemed like half the pond onto the bank, I focused on trying to breathe, coughing so frequently I still couldn't talk.

Will was talking in gasps, for he was carrying me now. "I'm taking you home. Stay awake with me, and we'll be at Santillane soon."

His footsteps were uneven, and he stumbled once or twice, but not once did he stop, and I felt safe in his arms.

Georgie saw us first as Will heaved me up Santillane's brick stairs. Then voices rambled, Georgie and Mama sounding fearful, Papa's first remarks reproachful toward Will, as though this was his fault, which it wasn't. I'd remedy that once I was warm again and able to speak.

Mama was all organization, ordering Megg to get me clean clothes and bring in a stack of quilts from the cedar chest. I wanted to reach out to her, but I was still wrapped up in Will's heavy greatcoat, and my energy was spent.

We were in the drawing room, and Papa was coaxing the fire into a roaring blaze. Will disappeared as Mama's gentle hands removed my heavy, soaked clothing from my shaking body, toweling me dry and guiding my limp arms into the sleeves of warm flannel. Megg toweled off my wet hair, temporarily lifting it from my back and neck.

As the fire warmed the room, I gave in to sleep when it found me, overcoming me above everything else. Never had I fallen into such a deep slumber, dreaming of a stalwart, redheaded man rushing me home, holding me close in his arms.

❧❦❧

I spent the night on the settee in front of the fire. Will kept it well stoked, returning to a wooden chair next to where I lay.

By morning, I felt well enough to eat one of Megg's biscuits smeared with cinnamon butter. Mama and Papa retired upstairs to catch some sleep since everyone except Georgie had stayed up late to look after me the night before.

As the day crept on, my coughing seemed to be increasing instead of decreasing, and by afternoon my whole body felt cold and clammy. I joined everyone for dinner in the dining room, still in my flannel gown and wrapped in a quilt. Megg was serving up pork chops—one of my favorite meals, but I had no hunger, and in only a few hours my cough had worsened even more—noisy and deep in my chest. Sleep was beckoning, and occasionally I'd feel a stab of pain inside my ribs.

Mama urged me to bed, and Megg and Will helped me upstairs until I had to stop, dizzy and weak.

Megg studied me. "You feeling poorly, ain't you, Miss Judy? You's white as clean linen."

I blinked, thinking that surely whatever it was would pass and I could continue upstairs. My heart was pounding as though I'd bolted from the dining room all the way down to the Catawba tree.

"I'll be fine," I asserted, though I wasn't certain of that at all. Something clearly wasn't right. My head swam for a moment, and before I could do anything more, Will had swept me into his arms and carried me up the rest of the way.

Mama hurried into my room, and as my head made contact with the pillow, her soft hand covered my forehead for an instant. "Have *mercy!*" she cried. "She's hot as Hades!"

Following that, my thoughts became jumbled, and I alternated between wakefulness and a fitful sleep, losing track of time. Megg and Mama tended me, but sometimes I heard Will's voice in the room too.

I floated on a silent haze of delirium, saving my breath by not talking, for it hurt to breathe, and my inhalation consisted of rapid, tiny gasps. Somebody—Mama, Will, or Megg—kept wiping my face with a cool, moist cloth.

Eventually, I heard Papa's voice from the doorway. "Peggy," he said to Mama, "I've sent for John. He's coming over to tend her."

"Thank God, George," she replied. "She's mighty ill and isn't any better."

It pained me, hearing such despair in Mama's voice and being unable to communicate with her. Later that same day, John hovered over me.

"Do you know whether she inhaled any water?"

Will's voice: "She coughed up a lot after I pulled her out."

"Hmm..." John was thinking. "It's not unusual for someone to inhale water when falling through ice because they gasp at the cold. Let me listen to her lungs, if I may."

Mama: "Please."

Fitful and writhing in fever, I struggled to lie quiet as John pressed his head to my chest, listening.

His fingers found both sides of my neck, took my limp wrist in his hand and held it still for a time, as though waiting for something. Next, he felt my forehead like Mama and Megg kept doing, pressed on my abdomen in places, then spoke softly to whoever was still present.

"Her lungs are crackling and rattling a bit, so I'm fairly certain she's got a light case of pneumonia."

"How can you treat her?" Papa said.

John sighed. "Julia's a healthy girl, so let's stuff pillows beneath her head to raise her higher. That should help her breathe easier. I've been told that sometimes this sort of thing happens after near drownings. Right now, I'm more concerned about that high fever. Get her into a cold bath and try to bring her temperature down. Fluids like hot tea will be good for her too."

"Will she recover?" Poor Mama sounded terrified, not wanting to lose yet another child.

"Like I said, she's young. Let's focus on bringing the fever down and see what tomorrow brings. After her cold bath, pack ice from your springhouse around her to keep her cool."

So began more misery.

I cried and moaned in protest when Papa lowered me into the cold bath. Afterward, ice even surrounded me in bed—another rude disruption to my sore, miserable state, but it helped. And John's suggestion to position me upright with pillows made it easier to breathe without as much sharp, stabbing pain.

After what I reckoned was days of lying abed, I squirmed to sit up, finding Harri sitting next to me, embroidering.

"Harri?" My voice was so hoarse from coughing.

"Julia!" she exclaimed. "My word—this is the first talking you've done in almost five days."

She was all lively, perched on the edge of my bed in a warm, high-waisted green woolen gown: a picture of fashion. I smiled to myself. Dr. John was doing fine business, keeping my cousin thus attired.

"Captain Clark will be so relieved to know you're awake again—everyone will, for that matter! He's been by your side for days. Your papa finally implored him to go to bed last evening, so I came over to give your parents some relief. You've been terribly ill."

"Please. Go get Will?"

Not three minutes later, he was by my side. "Thank God you're awake and well," he whispered, plopping into the chair next to my bed. He looked worn out, and he'd obviously not shaved for several days.

Harri grinned from the doorway, jesting, "You two behave yourselves, and I'll shut this door for some privacy. You more than deserve it."

Without words or thought, I reached over, grasping Will's hand, bringing it to my lips. My breath was still ragged, and illness certainly didn't tempt romance, but I wanted him to know of my love—that his was reciprocated. "I heard you on the ice, Will. You called me your 'love.'" I stopped there to swallow. My voice sounded as rough as whittled wood shavings.

"You are, Julia. You are my love—truly the only young lady I desire to come to know deeper and marry."

Such simple words, but now I knew for certain. I wanted William Clark. I wanted this steadfast man who was calm and willing to stay up when I was ailing, holding my hand. To have his unconditional presence at my bedside—*oh*! If we were wed, then I'd have this love for the rest of my life.

This is the man I want to marry!

Will pulled strands of hair from my cheek with his spare hand, then his rough thumb caressed my face. "We should marry when we're able, Julia."

I felt tears of happiness sting my eyes, biting my lip in excitement. "I love you, Will," I whimpered. "Please, *please* do marry me."

Eyes closed, I let his hand trace patterns on my face for a long while, reveling in the peaceful silence, assured by his caring, gentle touch. Sap from a log in the fireplace sizzled and whined, and for a moment time stood still as William Clark kissed each of my fingers slowly before speaking again.

"There's something of which we must be conscious. Despite the fact that my successful return from the Corps of Discovery may have made me a hero in people's minds, it does not secure me with the means to support a family."

"What about St. Louis?"

"That would provide a *suitable* income, not a lavish one. You would have to accept that." He snorted. "My, but your father was mighty sharp with me when I brought you home, half-drowned and nearly frozen to death. Both your parents were quite taken aback. Fortunately, they also know their daughter's nature, so they can't blame *too* much on me. I think I'm finally back in their good graces. But had you—" He stopped, his eyes becoming wet with emotion. "God, I don't know what I would've done. I would never have weathered that."

A cough racked me for over a minute before I could speak again. "Surely, you told Mama and Papa that we had saved a life. Please tell me I heard you correctly—Nace is safe, is he not?"

"I imagine so. His sisters rushed him home."

I smiled in relief.

"As for the possibility of living in St. Louis," I said, returning to the original subject, "I'm sure we could manage on whatever President Jefferson affords you, and I've always wanted to see the west. Mama has always fancied me a planter's wife, but I want to experience this country, for I'm envious of what you've seen."

Will leaned in enough to kiss the top of my head. "Ah, here is the adventuresome girl I remember sitting atop that horse with her cousin. How relieved I am that she's returned to me."

Chapter VII

Fincastle, Virginia
March 1807

Santillane's doors were thrust wide-open, driving winter out of the household with spring's first rejuvenating breezes.

When a messenger climbed the steps to the doorway, he called out to the first person he saw—Mama—sitting in the drawing room, sewing.

"Messages from President Thomas Jefferson and Governor Meriwether Lewis for Brigadier General William Clark, ma'am. I was told I'd find him here."

Brigadier General?

I froze where I was, sitting in the library next to the fire, reading across from Will, who was busy jotting a letter to his brother Jonathan. He smoothly set his pen aside and rose, walking into the entry with me close on his heels. Mama was at the door with the messenger, letters in hand.

"*Frazer?* What a surprise!" Will exclaimed.

The messenger recognized him at once, stamping to immediate attention and saluting with a friendly smile. "Yes, sir—good to see you, sir. I's here from Jefferson and Dearborn to present your orders in writing."

"Excellent. Everything is official, then."

I stepped up next to Will, and he glanced at me, smiling proudly. Oh my, it was happening—so, so quickly.

"I also has leave to accompany you on to St. Louis, sir. Orders of Governor Lewis."

Will grinned his playful sideways smile that was so disarming. "*Governor*, is he? Ah, this is all well done. And as for your company, it will be most welcome. It's a long journey. I'll probably be stopping in at my brother's on the way, so from there, I may send you on ahead."

I coughed briefly to one side—vestiges of my illness that lingered. Mama offered Will the letters, and he accepted them, breaking one seal and unfolding it. "Well then… Jefferson wants me to do some excavating for ancient bones in the Big Bone Lick, a salt lick up near the Ohio."

Rackety thumps and some tromping announced Papa's entry from the back door. "I saw a rider—what news?" he demanded, running each boot over the scraper before entering.

"Colonel, President Jefferson has appointed me Superintendent of Indian Affairs in Louisiana Territory and given me command over militia there, which I'm to further develop. I'll be stationed in St. Louis."

Papa had been removing his boots, still at the back entrance, but he stopped. An uncomfortable, prolonged silence descended that made me bite my lower lip. I still couldn't see him well from where he was, but his pause was palpable. After a few heart-stopping seconds, I heard his footsteps along with a lengthy sigh, and he joined the rest of us at the doorway. "Back to the military in St. Louis, eh?"

"Yes, Colonel," Will veritably crowed. "It's a great honor, for now that the west is opening, St. Louis will soon be bursting at the seams. It won't be long before it rivals New York or Philadelphia in size and culture."

How unsettling. Will was having to remind my father that St. Louis was destined to be more than just a frontier backwater, and I sensed Papa wasn't pleased with the assignment. Too far away? Was it unsafe in his opinion?

"Mmm," was the only affirmation Papa offered. Not even a congratulatory slap on Will's back!

I started coughing again while Mama said, "You've much for which to thank the good Lord, William."

Once my fit ceased, I enthusiastically entwined my arm through Will's. "I'm so excited for you!" I exclaimed, hoping to break through the discomfiture that had descended. Papa's response was far too shallow.

Next to me, Will relieved the situation even more by clapping the young messenger on the back and introducing him. "Forgive me. I must introduce someone of merit. Be pleased to meet Robert Frazer, a fellow member of the Corps of Discovery, who is now entrusted with responsibilities straight from the president, such as messages of import and seeing me safely to my point of command."

"When must you leave?" I ventured, glancing about and forcing myself to smile, for shreds of the uneasy heaviness in the room still remained, and I wondered if Will felt it and was simply masking it.

"In a few weeks, now that all is official."

Of course, my parents welcomed Robert Frazer in as another houseguest, and time at the dinner table was full of reminiscing between him and Will as more stories of their way west were shared. But both my parents were subdued, and I caught them exchanging glances that looked to be full of concern or regret. Somehow Will's appointment must have fallen short of their expectations.

"I was the one who actually signed Frazer into the Corps," Will recollected, slicing off another piece of smoked venison from the sizeable roast Megg had prepared that night.

"That's right," Frazer said. "I were one of the company from Captain Stoddard and hadn't expected to be permanent in the Corps. But John Newman—he were insubordinate and had to be let go, and Pat Gass was appointed as sergeant in his place after that. It opened a position for someone to travel the entire way, and I was mighty pleased to be given the chance."

"And, Colonel," Will pointed out, "here's a man with a steady hand. We were in a tight spot with the Lakota, and he manned the swivel gun I'd fixed onto the bow of our keelboat—"

"Oh, aye!" Frazer broke in, relishing the moment and giving

a broad smile that exhibited several broken teeth. "Lewis ordered me to fire on them, but General Clark here—he was on the bow with me, trying to keep them Lakota calm. He drew his sword when the chiefs kept bullying us, telling me to hold fire. Them chiefs was greedy," he laughed, shaking his head at the memory. "They wanted more gifts than we'd already handed over, but one thing about General Clark here—he wanted no blood spilled on our journey."

"Ah, the stories we have," Will murmured to himself, spearing some venison into his mouth.

Frazer said, "My own journal's out for publication soon. There's already a prospectus for it. I've a copy I've brought I can show you."

"So soon?" Will looked unprepared for this news, explaining to the rest of us, "Lewis gave Frazer here express permission to submit his journal to publishers."

"And a few others is planning to publish too," Frazer added, excitement for the venture evident on his countenance. "Pat Gass and even Private Whitehouse. Maybe more."

"I should think the two captains' accounts should be the first to greet readers," Mama voiced, one eyebrow skeptically cocked.

"Mmm… that shouldn't matter, Peggy," Papa answered her after a taste of small ale. "None of the others have the scientific knowledge of flora and fauna as did William and Captain Lewis."

"My word!" Will exclaimed, laughing in good humor. "I've been remiss. Colonel, you weren't present at the time, but Frazer here also reported that Lewis is no longer captain, but *governor* of Louisiana Territory." He reached for his pewter tankard of ale and lifted it. "To Meriwether Lewis, governor of the richest territory in our United States, and for myself. I drink to ventures westward with hopes of peace with the Indians and prosperity for the territory, not to mention growth in St. Louis."

"Huzzah!" That from my little brother, Georgie, who had been courteously silent for most of dinner.

We all responded with laughter and lifted tankards, "Huzzah!"

Following the toast, Papa remarked, "My, but I look forward

to when these journals of you gentlemen become available. They'll make for excellent winter night reading."

"Hopefully, Lewis will revive his editing soon and solicit help in Philadelphia to move things along," Will said. "Though I'm sure Mr. Frazer here has plenty to add to the story, it's integral that readers receive the official account as soon as possible."

"I'll read them too," Georgie declared.

Will set down his glass and leaned in toward Papa. "Colonel, later this evening, might we speak privately?"

Privately.

I was sitting right across from Will, and my eyes sought Mama's, but she was looking steadily at Papa, her lips tense.

I could scarcely breathe. Surely, Will intended to ask for my hand.

※※※

There was a place in Santillane's dining room where Mama's tall China cabinet allowed just a slip of space alongside two glass-paned French doors leading straight into the drawing room. As slender as I was, I fit into that space perfectly. Past experience had proven that even with those doors shut, that tiny niche was where every single breath from the drawing room could be heard.

Once dinner ended, Mama sent Georgie into the library to study arithmetic, then she and Megg led a weary Robert Frazer upstairs to one of our extra rooms. As I suspected, Papa had invited Will into the drawing room, so I assumed my position, sliding into the slot, jittery with anticipation.

I heard Papa close the other door nearest the front of the house. Then Megg entered from seeing Frazer to his room, and she wiped down the dining room table, completely unaware of my presence. Barely chancing to breathe until she finished, I pressed my ear to the drawing room wall.

"It is a fine position, Clark. I won't argue that," Papa was saying. "You're suited for it perfectly. However, Judith is not."

"Please, Colonel, let's not rush to conclusions, I beg you. Perhaps we could give her another year or two. I'm willing to wait."

"She's far too inexperienced for such a place as St. Louis. Besides, you'll have your hands too full with a new position to have to deal with Judith's stubborn nature, such as she displayed at the Mill Pond."

"I'm aware St. Louis isn't altogether suitable for a lady, but—"

"She cannot be expected to make such an enormous decision about her own welfare." Papa's voice escalated. "God, man! She's never been away from Fincastle, much less to the frontier, filled with criminals, savages, and filthy boatmen."

"It is rugged—"

"*Rugged?*" Papa thundered.

I squeezed my eyes shut at his tone, picturing his reddening face. Pulse racing, my breath hitched in my chest, and I suppressed a cough. Megg blew out the dining room candles, heading outside to the kitchen.

"It's nothing but a filthy *village*—that's all St. Louis is," Papa insisted. "A place full of drunken scallywags. You cannot *imagine* I'd allow a daughter of mine to live there!"

For a moment, silence—such quiet that I could hear the fire crackle from my hiding place.

"Colonel," Will spoke at last, his voice even and patient, although I knew he was frantic, "I'm not here to argue and cause any unpleasantness. However, I now have a position, one worthy of your daughter's hand and bestowed upon me by the president himself. Perhaps I can persuade Jefferson to transfer me elsewhere once a year or so has passed. Louisville, perhaps . . ."

"Hmph. Mere speculation. In the meantime, my daughter would be homesick and miserable in a reckless, wild place. And what if she conceives?"

"Sir, please. I understand you desire her happiness and well-being, as do *I*."

"Judith is mature for her age, but I cannot—I *won't* allow my slip of a girl to be subject to a life of which she knows nothing, one rife with hardship. It's true I once assured you that I'd consider joining our families once you had a permanent career. But *this*? I am sorry, but I cannot accede. I realize you're both very fond of one another—"

I determined that I'd had enough, and before even realizing what I was doing, I'd quit my hiding place and hauled open the French doors, breathlessly standing before both men, who were already standing—the meeting obviously over, as far as Papa was concerned.

"Papa—"

"*Judith?* Have you lost your senses?" he roared, his face a crimson scowl.

"No. I've gained them. And I'm no longer a child for you to order about as you please."

He thrust up his hand, pointing in the direction of the dining room. "You walk back out that door, girl, and I'll forget that you've been spying on everything we gentlemen have said in here."

"Papa, hear me out since this whole business revolves around me." I cleared my throat, forcing down another persistent cough.

Papa hesitated, and I saw real sorrow in his eyes. Oh yes, he cared for me and had hoped that Will and I might be joined—but only under *his* conditions.

Well, I saw my chance and snatched it, aiming to prove that I wasn't as easily put off as Griff and Mary had been. I'd inherited all of the stubbornness he claimed I had straight from him. Now he'd confront it.

"Yes, it would be a huge leap of faith for me to leave Santillane, the hardest thing I've ever done," I declared. "You, Mama—*everything* I've ever known would be removed from me. But, Papa, William Clark has chosen *me*—wants *me*! It would be impossible for me *not* to marry Will, knowing that we'd never have a life together. That's how much he means to my heart, Papa. I *love* him!" Trembling but dry-eyed, I took a deep breath, stepping over to Will and joining him. Boldly, I linked my arm through his. "William Clark has not just chosen me; I've chosen *him*."

Papa, for all his lofty, authoritative stature, looked somehow smaller to me at that moment. His jaw was sagging. Did I detect resignation?

He stepped closer to me. "You could *die* out there, Judith." His voice dropped to a hoarse whisper. "You could fall ill and never recover."

"That nearly happened a few weeks ago, but here I am. If it happened in St. Louis, I'd have to submit to the good Lord's will, as we all do. I'd just be doing so there instead of here."

I felt Will's fingers interlacing with mine, responding to my reckless entrance with a slight squeeze. "Colonel Hancock," he said softly, "as you can see, our hearts are already joined, but we will wait until next year to wed. It will give us all time to think things through and prepare. And as God is my witness, I will strive to make your daughter a fine husband. We both request your permission *and* your blessing."

Wearily, Papa turned away from us, and I glanced at Will, who was still following him with his eyes. Papa picked up his pipe from where he always set it on the side table at the end of the settee. Into the bowl he stared, coughing lightly and lifting his finger to tamp down the tobacco where Megg had filled it. Without a word, he moved to the fireplace, reaching for a spill, sticking it into the flames, tucking the pipe between his lips and lighting it.

Only after several puffs did he turn to face us. "Then I suppose you've checkmated me, leaving me no choice," he muttered over the ivory between his teeth. Then to me, he added, "My, what a tenacious girl you are."

Was I dreaming?

Shocked and hardly believing my own ears, tears of relief clouded my vision. My risky move to enter the room had just led to Papa's consent!

Next to me, Will threw his head back, laughing. "Now *this* is the fearless and honorable Colonel Hancock I look forward to coming to know as a father. Bless you, sir. You will never live to regret this decision."

Papa harrumphed. "Indeed, I'll always have to be at your disposal, *General*—for now you outrank me."

Will laughed again and the two men embraced, Papa adding, "Do teach that girl to fire a damned rifle, will you?"

※※※

The day came for Will to leave, and we took a portion of the early morning to spend a little time together before our parting. We'd not seen much of one another for the past several days. Will had been out combing the county for pack mules and acquiring necessary staples he'd need for his travels ahead.

Already, I missed him.

In the past, Mama had told me plenty of stories about people during the War for Independence; patriots marching to fight the British had no guarantee they'd ever see their loved ones again. Though Will wasn't going to war, St. Louis was still fraught with dangers of its own kind, and there were risks along the road he traveled.

There was no possible way to set a firm wedding date, but we'd marry sometime early in 1808. Sometime after that, I'd leave gentle Virginia behind. It was true that I'd inherited Papa's adventuresome spirit, but I also had a fair ladling of Mama's commonsensical reality, and that piece of me was alert to what was ahead.

At least we'd marry with a promise of future success, which was far more than many couples began with at the altar. Will and Meriwether Lewis had both received sixteen hundred acres of land west of the Mississippi. Congress, on behest of President Jefferson, had also awarded them extra compensation for facing privations and perils during the trek west, amounting to over four thousand dollars each, and Will's annual salary was to be fifteen hundred a year. Papa was more than pleased about all that, though he repeatedly told Will and me both how he wished we'd be closer to home.

Will and I walked arm in arm, breathing in the cool air of dawn. Early spring crowned Santillane's surrounding hills with low, puffy clouds, giving the heavens above an illusion of mystery. As we descended the hill, before us stood the majestic Catawba tree, still void of its late spring foliage.

"Are you well, my angel?"

Will's thumb rubbed gently against my palm as we reached the tree's bare limbs, yet to acquire their lush heart-shaped leaves.

For fear of losing my composure, I found it hard to meet his eyes, so I looked westward. "I feel as though a costly gift is about to be stolen from me. But costly doesn't really express my sentiments, for you're such a vital part of my life now; you're the very air I breathe. Yes, that fits better, even though there aren't words within the English vocabulary poignant enough for a real description." Summoning courage, I finally turned to face him.

At that, he drew me in, kissing me and making me weak-kneed with an intense hunger that had become more consuming and unquenchable each time he touched me, kissed me, or held me. And those moments had become more frequent since we'd become betrothed. I craved his arms about me now.

After the kiss, he whispered against my ear, "I rather like being your 'costly gift.'" His deep voice was husky.

He felt what I did—a longing to touch more, kiss longer, to remain *together*.

"Just remember what will be when I return," he said. "Our *wedding*. Granted, now that I'm a government man, I'll need to travel occasionally, but by then we'll belong to one another, and homecomings will be all the sweeter. Let's both look ahead to next year in anticipation."

He leaned back against the tree, still holding my hands. "I forgot to tell you. I met a friend of yours in Fincastle while picking up supplies yesterday."

"Oh?"

"Yes. She was accompanied by her father, James Breckinridge."

"Ah." I sighed heavily, looking down toward the ground and coughing; that stubborn, diminishing remnant of the pneumonia. "You met Letitia?"

"I did."

"I must confess that she and I are not the best of friends. We've both been terribly hurtful to one another at times." My mind went back to that awful day in the rain at Little Amsterdam, discovering Letitia with Phillip Carrington inside the Breckinridge carriage. Now, that hurtful humiliation seemed like another lifetime ago.

"Has she been spoken for?" Will asked, coaxing me from my sour memory.

"Not to my knowledge. She needs a special man, I think," I ventured.

"I've decided to mention her to Lewis," Will said. "In his last letter, he said he wants to visit your family when he travels to St. Louis. He too is looking to marry in the foreseeable future. I only wish I could be here when the two of you meet."

"I'm looking forward to meeting him," I said, then shook my head in earnest. "But I'm not sure about introducing him to Letitia. She might not be a satisfactory match."

Will looked down at me with eyes that often penetrated my very soul. "Bear in mind she's as youthful as you, and in our younger years we are all often foolish. I daresay that with the right man, she'll transform into a lovely personality, and she deserves that opportunity."

Such wise words, though until I saw a major change in her, I couldn't be certain. Humbled, I spoke in a soft voice, "I pray you never come to think your choice was an error in judgment."

"Never. And I know my family will be so thrilled to embrace you as their own. I have a wonderful brood. They'll be anxious to see us happily married and settled. Prepare to be doted upon, for you'll love my brother Jonathan and his wife, Sarah, who are closest to me. They are the best of hearts and will love you dearly."

He took my hand, lifting it to his lips and kissing it. His lips rested there a long time before he spoke again. "Julia, I confess that occasionally I worry that I'm asking more of you than I should. Your father was right, you know. As of now, St. Louis is nothing but a frontier back of beyond. Not an ideal place for a lady."

"That doesn't matter to me."

"Doesn't it? There aren't many American women there. It's a

place that was occupied by both the Spanish and French, and French is still widely spoken. It will seem rather foreign to you with so much Creole culture there."

"What is 'Creole culture'?"

"French people from down New Orleans way."

"Well, Fincastle is a frontier town too. It might not be so different for me after all."

"*Was* a frontier, more like," Will corrected. "I assure you—it is no longer. However, St. Louis is. It's a diamond very much in the rough. Indians are everywhere on the streets, and so are fur trappers; ofttimes not the best of men. It's a wild and unseemly place, really. Be mindful of that. Nor are comforts of home as easy to come by as they are here. Goods must travel farther to arrive in St. Louis, and so does the post. You won't hear from your family as often, for the service is rather scattered and undependable, even for officials—especially in winter. Now, everything I've mentioned should improve with time as the city develops, but I must be honest. It's likely you'll feel isolated in comparison to the life you've always had here."

In his cautious concern, he had forgotten something—my adventurous self, something compelling me to be impetuous and accept risks. "Will, I really have thought about all of this a great deal. I'm sure St. Louis will have its problems, but there are worries anywhere with anything, are there not? Besides, if I commit myself to you, I will learn to adapt because I must."

He scrutinized me. "Very well. I just want you to be completely certain." In one smooth motion, he knelt down before me on one knee, my hand still captive in his. "Judith Julia Hancock, I've not yet had opportunity to officially ask you as a gentleman should, so now I shall. Will you do me the honor of becoming my wife and come to live with me in St. Louis?"

Little did I care if the ground was damp with morning dew. I knelt down too, where we were eye to eye and on equal terms, our hands woven together and eyes locked, speaking to him with clarity, "Yes, I'll be your wife. I'll support you and live wherever you live, even if it means traveling all the way to the Pacific again."

He grinned like a schoolboy and raised me up, fumbling about in his trouser pocket for something.

"I've a gift for you. I'm thirty-seven now; no longer a young man, but not old either. Nowadays, I hear how younger gentlemen are giving poesy rings to their beloveds." He held forth a glistening gold ring. "I'm hoping it fits as well as the moccasins."

I gasped. Delicate and carved with the tiniest curling branches, it was of exquisite workmanship with a tiny blue sapphire twinkling in its pronged setting.

"Nor am I a poetic man," Will said regretfully, "though I do my fair share of writing. As you know, my spelling is deplorable and my words direct and to the point. So consider this ring as I am: not overly fancy or filigreed, but *secure*—the way I want us to be as a couple. Despite my lack of being the Shakespeare you so deserve, my heart will remain here with you at Santillane. In fact, right now it's overflowing. I love you with my whole heart, dear angel."

Gently, he nudged the ring onto my left finger, the same one upon which Mama always wore Papa's wedding band.

We kissed under the Catawba tree, and I didn't want these heartbeats of time to pass. Harri had told me tidbits of what she'd anticipated prior to her own wedding, and now I wanted the same. My hands moved up to Will's face, feeling his wind-whipped skin, touching him lightly as he drew me close and kissed me harder. I responded hungrily, feeling his hands travel down my back and over my warm, wool gown.

Whatever these moments of hunger were, they were a treasure—a warm, physical one that I couldn't wait to experience in full.

Chapter VIII

Fincastle, Virginia
November 1807

October 1, 1807

Beloved Angel,
    I have been at the place called Big Bone Licke now for a month. My men and I have laboured hard, hawling dirt and rocks from a quarrye in which we dig for skeletens of ancient cretures. I have found many virtabrae and a few larger bones to send to the President.
    During the expedition, Lewis and I invited Sheheke — chief of the Mandans — to visit President Jefferson. We provided him with a suitable escort, the visit was sucesful, and when he was to be returnd to his people, I assigned another Corps of Discovery man, Ensign Nathaniel Pryor, to lead the party. However, the Arikaras attacked, forcing the escort back. In the fighting, one of our finest Corps of Discovery men was shot in the legg. George Shannon, youngest member of the Corps, endured amputashun as a result, causing my heart to grieve. Just as troubling, as of now there is no safe means of returning Sheheke, with the Arikaras blockading the river. It concerns me greatly, as I see it as unfinished expedition busness.
    Now my thoughts tern to you and the months ahed. I will leve for Virginia some tyme in December. Soon you

and I will be housekeeping together, and it is with much longing that I think of starting a family with you at my side. When we last embraced, I could tell you felt the same way.

You shall soon meet Governer Lewis. Know that you have my love. Take care of yourself and the rest of my new family in Fincastle.

With all of my heart,
William Clark

With great pleasure, we welcomed Governor Meriwether Lewis to Santillane late in the year, on his meandering way to St. Louis. In his company were two men and a large dog.

First was Reuben Lewis, the governor's brother, a robust, social sort, desiring to seek his own way in Louisiana Territory. The second was Lewis's free mulatto servant, John Pernier, a quiet, reflective man who cared for Lewis's personal needs.

Pernier gave me reason to wonder about the governor and his opinions on slavery. Had he freed Pernier himself, keeping him as a hired servant? Of course, I didn't pry, but it piqued my interest.

Lewis's dog, however, captured my heart.

Wooly and beautiful, with inky black fur and a white star on its chest, his name was Seaman, and he had accompanied the Corps of Discovery clear to the Pacific.

There was really no way to sum up Governor Lewis in a simple sentence. A perfect gentleman—ever polite and deferential to me, warm and gracious to my parents as their guest.

However, his peculiarities commenced just past that.

Though handsome, he was nothing like Will, who was rugged and built for frontier life. Lewis was slighter, with delicately chiseled features and a noble profile. He was most attentive to his dress, cutting a dashing figure, and at first meeting appeared to be all confidence and self-assurance.

Yet, past all of the salutations, usual comments of new acquaintance and welcome, I found the senior Corps of Discovery officer less approachable than Will. Lewis maintained a stiff and formal posture, and I longed to chisel my way through that exterior to reveal the *real* Meriwether Lewis—the man Will knew and with whom I longed to form a lasting friendship.

He wasn't the type to make airs, though honored by President Jefferson with his title of governor and being the toast of Washington City. Nor did he solicit congratulatory comments.

On our first evening together, Mama had Megg lay out a magnificent Virginia smoked-ham feast, complete with yams, carrots, and apples from the cellar. Dessert was Megg's magical sweet vinegar pudding—a favorite Hancock family recipe.

Following dinner, Papa suggested taking brandy in the drawing room, where the roaring fire would warm our guests on such a cold night. Lewis and his brother followed Papa in, both settling on the settee.

"My, but that was an abundant feast, madam," Lewis praised, nodding to Mama. "Do give your lady cook my praise."

"We're most honored to have you in our presence, sir," Mama replied.

"Governor Lewis," I said. "I'm an avid reader and love all things literary. Could you tell us more about the plan to publish the Corps of Discovery journals?"

"Julia," Papa cautioned, "that may be business the governor isn't yet ready to disclose."

Lewis smiled. "On the contrary, Colonel, I'm happy to indulge her. Clark has told me much about Miss Hancock's fervor for books. A love for reading and writing is a worthy pursuit for either gender, I believe. I spent far too much time in Philadelphia planning the publication, but it needed doing since other members of our Corps have already secured publishing contracts."

"During his stay here, Robert Frazer announced his publishing intent," I said.

Mama reiterated her previous words to Will and Frazer, "I believe the *captains'* journals should be the single most important document on the whole experience. 'Tis a shame they won't be published first."

"Agreed, but what choice had I in the matter?" Lewis chuckled briefly, waving his hand to dismiss concern. "Men like Robert Frazer and Patrick Gass labored hard on the expedition and deserve recognition for what they wrote. It's even been brought to my attention that I had no right to 'lend permission' for either of them to publish, being tersely reminded that our experiences to the Pacific were shared ones, and they own freedom of speech as much as I. Some men have even suggested I desire complete ownership over all the journals that were compiled. And *that*, dear lady, is untrue."

I was curious as to the road to publication. "Sounds like you'd need some sound, gentlemanly advice prior to publishing, then. Who did you consult?"

Reuben, obviously proud of his brother, spoke before Lewis had opportunity, "He visited the most famous men of science and learning in all of America."

Lewis thanked Megg courteously as she served him and his brother snifters of brandy. "I needed to find men specific in their fields to edit, sketch, and correct mistakes in my notes," he explained. "I've hired a German botanist to do detailed sketches of the flora I managed to bring back and artists to portray the fauna—including Charles Wilson Peale."

"Goodness! Who else?" I asked, eager to hear more.

"Well, I needed a mathematician to correct our mileage to and from the Pacific," he explained. "In science, one must comb over facts to ensure as few errors as possible. The chronometer I had on the journey was less than accurate, and for that I suppose I must assume fault. Thus, it became necessary to hire Ferdinand Hassler."

"Another German…" Papa mused, tamping his pipe.

"Swiss, actually," Lewis amended, standing and coming forward with his own pipe to share Papa's burning spill and setting it alight.

"Hassler teaches mathematics at West Point Military Academy," boasted Reuben, finishing with a lengthy draw on his brandy.

"My, what a project," I laughed aloud. "It sounds like half of Philadelphia is involved."

Papa took some more of his own brandy, smacking his lips. "Have you a publisher for the work?"

"I do, sir," Lewis replied. "I've secured a contract with C & A Conrad and Company. I've much editing to do on our original field notes. William and I began the laborious task of copying them from our rough originals into a more legible format, but that was over a year ago, while we were still heading eastward. I'll say this about your future son-in-law. He's meticulous when copying his account, preferring red Moroccan leather notebooks for the task," he concluded, shaking his head and snickering to himself.

"Whatever he does, he does with meaningful diligence," I stated. "I suspect his work looks more professional that way."

Lewis gazed my way, nodding and inhaling smoke from his pipe.

"I've a copy here of the prospectus." Reuben fished in his pocket and withdrew a folded paper. Handing it over to Papa, he confided, "My brother doesn't much like crowing his successes, so I do it for him."

"Three volumes!" Papa exclaimed. "Good God, man—I recently told Clark that I'd have plenty of reading to do about your journey, but this—"

"Let me see, *please!*" I begged, and he acquiesced, handing me the prospectus.

I gasped in excitement. There would be maps, in which I was certain Will would have a hand in creating, as well as illustrations. The first of the books was to be a narrative, featuring the journey itself and adventures along the way. The second would focus on Louisiana Territory's geography and its Indians, the third delving into scientific research.

Once I'd finished devouring the prospectus, Lewis's eyes affixed on mine. "Now, Miss Hancock, William mentioned you had a friend I should meet. After all," he indicated helplessly with the hand not holding brandy, "I am but a lonely bachelor, and I'll make no secret of the fact that I'd find the discovery of a wife to be nothing less than Providence."

Reuben nearly choked on his brandy. "I declare, but the new governor of Louisiana Territory aspires to enter St. Louis with a bride in tow."

Papa's brows lifted, "Who did Clark mean, Julia?"

"Letitia," I sighed. Then to Lewis, I added, "I'm afraid that she and I are more acquaintances than close friends."

"No matter, I mean to meet her and pursue her, should I find her charming."

This overly direct manner was one of those traits that was off-putting with Meriwether Lewis. His next words had Mama and I staring at one another open-mouthed and at an utter loss.

"I've only two days' time here in Fincastle before continuing my progress westward. Might it be possible to arrange a meeting with this Letitia Breckinridge before I depart?"

※

The "meeting" was a hastily assembled tea with only Mrs. Breckinridge, Letitia, Agatha Bowyer, and Margaret Logan in attendance. Oh, and of course Harri and Mary too.

Everyone wanted to know when Will would return, though he'd been occupied with his fieldwork at Big Bone Lick, and I explained as much.

"Field work for the *president*?" Margaret Logan was astonished. "Oh my. Peggy, your family is mighty honored to have your sweet Julia marrying such a well-respected and famous gentleman."

I had personally helped Megg with the tea's details, so quickly was it thrown together. She and I had made gingerbread cakes and chilled some fresh cream. I determined to take full joy in the gathering, the ladies present, and even Letitia.

It had been a year and a half since the incident at the Little Amsterdam camp meeting, although now it felt like another lifetime ago. Here I was an engaged woman, so wasn't it time to embrace our ripening maturity? Yet while most of the guests were enjoying the event, one guest clearly was *not*.

From where I sat, keeping Reuben Lewis company, I couldn't help but notice Letitia's discomposure.

She sat stiffly in a fashionable golden-yellow gown, complete with long sleeves trimmed with white silk-embroidered cuffs. She looked positively flawless, as always, her dark, lustrous hair stylishly piled with several curling tendrils cascading down on either side of her face. But today, her usually graceful, relaxed countenance was as stiff as the starched collar Reuben was sporting. Every single time she smiled, it was forced. I knew it, though others in the room—*especially* Meriwether Lewis—didn't.

All my life, I'd seen Letitia Breckinridge flirt and linger with youths in Fincastle who would never have the hope of marrying an affluent man's daughter like her. Now, however, she appeared downright frigid, her usual outgoing personality snuffed out like a cold candle. With her showing such palpable reticence and discomfort, I knew she had no interest whatsoever in poor Lewis. Truthfully, I thought she looked ready to bolt and make a run for it, never to return.

Still, Lewis lounged at her elbow, solicitous and intrigued, enthralled by every move she made. He was completely oblivious to moving in too close to her, and he interjected comments to attract her attention that instead defeated his best intentions. He said far too much; his excessive doting not to his credit—

"*Miss Breckinridge, allow me to serve your tea. Would you care for sugar or honey?*"

"*Please accept this bouquet as proof of my utter joy in making your acquaintance.*" Alas it was November, and the bouquet consisted of dried flowers he'd asked me to pander from Megg's stores. I'd urged him to offer her silk ribbon instead. It wouldn't have changed Letitia's sentiments, but it would have been more appropriate.

"*I hope you're enjoying this day. How kind of Mrs. Hancock and Julia to put themselves out for us, don't you think?*"

"Do have another gingerbread cake. They're incredible concoctions, aren't they?"

"I daresay no other lady in Fincastle is bedecked as beautifully as you."

My eyes were sore from rolling. At one point, Letitia rose when she saw another seat open up. Understandably, she fled there, assuming she'd be safe, surrounded by Mama on one side and Mrs. Bowyer on the other. But up leaped Lewis in heated pursuit, and I couldn't help but gawk at how gracelessly desperate he was acting. Especially when he planted himself between Agatha Bowyer and Letitia's seat, leaning over so close to his prey that she shifted, nearly winding up on Mama's lap!

Once I'd decided to allow Will to court me, it had been easy and natural. This farce of Lewis's was disconcerting.

That night, after the tea, he joined me at the fireside in the library. I was braiding strands of golden silk into what would be a tassel for my wedding cape.

"Am I intruding?"

"Not at all. Please sit down." I gestured to a chair across from me.

Lewis got straight to the point. "Miss Hancock, as of tomorrow, I intend to court Miss Breckinridge."

My fingers froze on my project. "You've already spoken to her of your intentions?" I doubted it.

"No, but certainly she's aware of them from today's efforts."

Sighing, I set aside my tassel-in-progress on the side table next to me. "Governor, you've only seen her once—and not alone, but with other ladies and your brother present. You've had no time to get to know her on a personal level, and you're only staying one more day."

"True, but—"

"As a lady myself, who is already engaged, I strongly advise you to slow down." I couldn't believe I was giving advice to a man of his status, older than I and more experienced at life.

Once I'd said my piece, he frowned, falling silent at my words, so I continued. "As it stands now, you have no idea of her feelings or thoughts, do you? She only spent two hours in your company. Do you really think that's time enough upon which to base a serious courtship?"

Lewis gave a cumbrous smile. "I suppose I must hope so since I haven't much time. St. Louis awaits, so I'll speak to both her and her father first thing tomorrow."

"At peril of sounding too direct, I need you to see that you're moving *far too fast*—rushing into this headlong and forcing her first impressions. You mustn't do that. Let things be as they are for now and write to her when you get to St. Louis. That way, she'll have a chance to sort out her feelings."

He stared down at the rug in our drawing room, then jerked his head up. "Miss Hancock, my mind is made up. I only ask you to wish me the same good fortune that you and William have had."

"Of course, but…"

Lewis refused to accept no for an answer. He was a man of definitive absolutes. There was no putting him off, though I knew through female intuition that he was going about it the wrong way.

I may not have been good friends with Letitia Breckinridge, but I had seen every obvious sign that she was *not* interested in Meriwether Lewis.

❧

As usual, I made it my business to assist Megg in the kitchen as much as possible. I was with her at dawn, kneading dough for the day's loaves. Early mornings were peaceful, and though Megg rarely ventured much deep conversation, I knew by her occasional smiles that she enjoyed and valued my help. Despite me being her master's daughter, I felt a certain fondness from her and hoped she felt my love. My heartfelt desire was that she understood how differently I viewed her compared to the rest of my family.

Flour dusted my hands when I first heard a soft tapping at the kitchen window behind me. Megg and I both glanced over our shoulders, exchanging wide-eyed surprise.

Letitia Breckinridge?

Grove Hill was well outside Fincastle, so she must have risen hours before dawn to be driven here.

Wordlessly, I snatched a dish towel off a peg on the wall, rubbing dried, flaking dough off of my hands before opening the door. "Letitia? Whatever are you—"

"*Shush!*" She burst inside the kitchen, her face pink-flushed from the cold. "Is the governor awake?" she whispered low, glancing out the window toward Santillane's high windows. "I don't want him to hear us or know that I'm here."

Lewis's window was still dark.

"It's not even dawn yet. He's likely still asleep." Near us, Megg tossed another log onto the fire, wiped her hands down, and brushed past, out the kitchen door toward the house. "What's wrong?" I asked Letitia, though I already knew.

"It seems Governor Lewis wants to court me with the intent of marriage." She looked down, shaking her head emphatically, her hands fidgeting.

I nodded. "He's *completely* taken with you, but everything he knows about you is superficial." Actually, my *own* knowledge of Letitia was superficial.

Her next words addressed that very dilemma. "I know we've never been close, Julia, and that's mostly my fault. In the past, my behavior hasn't always been easy to excuse. I never should have dallied with Phillip Carrington like I did. And the time you pushed me into the Mill Pond, I said something so cruel. You wouldn't have done it otherwise."

"Well, we're young ladies now, aren't we? We needn't be at odds anymore."

She nodded, smiling tensely. "Should he ask, could you please tell Governor Lewis that I am most flattered by his admiration and honorable intent, but that I'm not at liberty to court him?"

"Shouldn't you tell him yourself?"

Head shaking, Letitia went on, "You see, there's someone else for me in Richmond. Papa and Mama have cultivated many friends and connections there. Last spring, he introduced me to a man he favors. His name is Robert Gamble, and both my parents think he'd be a proper match for me. Governor Lewis may be courageous and honorable, but Papa fears what might happen to me if I moved to St. Louis."

"And you?" I asked. "What do *you* think?"

Letitia sighed in frustration, glancing outside toward Lewis's upstairs window again, obviously concerned he might suddenly appear. "I think it's a difficult thing we women do, marrying so young, when we've barely tasted of life. However, in this case I believe Papa has my best interests in mind. Mr. Gamble is a man of means, and I'll never want for anything. And he'll never go to some uncivilized place like St. Louis." She hesitated, then finally added, "Think on it—when you marry General Clark, you'll be moving there. Doesn't such a place scare you witless?"

"It's always the unknown that frightens us, isn't it?" I mused. "But strangely, I'm at peace because the general and I share a great love. Truth is, Letitia, I *want* this for myself. Of course, the thought of leaving Fincastle, my family, and all I've ever known makes me tremble. But I want to see more of our country, and most of all, I believe I'm *meant* to marry William Clark."

"My, you really do have a love match," she acknowledged, taking my hands in hers and smiling sweetly. "You're the lucky one."

"Shh, you. If Governor Lewis really cares for you as he says, he'd want what is best for you too, and I can tell how ill at ease you are in his presence."

Shuddering, Letitia whimpered, "Was I *that* obvious yesterday?"

I giggled, and she lifted a finger to my lips to hush me. "He's a good man—no a *great* one," she stressed. "Just not the one for me."

"You owe me no more words, but I'm glad you came. Whatever ill regard there was between us before—I think it's finally patched up."

She nodded, and I was amazed to see her eyes watering with tears. "We made a big mistake when we were girls, not being good friends when our parents encouraged it of us."

Then we embraced, holding one another for a brief time as if to seal our peace. "Fully reconciled," I whispered in her ear. "Now you'd best hurry back to your coach before the governor awakens."

She nodded, sniffed, and gave my cheek a swift kiss, exiting out the kitchen door and scampering toward the front of the house to the waiting carriage.

No, Letitia Breckinridge and I weren't destined to own a great friendship, but it warmed me that she had trusted me at last, coming to me so that things were now settled.

Things between the two of us—and Lewis.

❧

That night at dinner, Reuben Lewis expressed his brother's regrets.

"I'm afraid my brother is feeling rather ill."

Mama insisted Megg take up a tray for him, but I intervened. "I'll take it to him myself." After all, I suspected I knew why he was indisposed.

I ducked out to the kitchen, selecting tidbits from our meal for which Lewis might be tempted. Then I re-entered the house, treading carefully upstairs to the second floor.

Outside the guest room, I called, "Governor Lewis? It's Miss Hancock. I've brought up dinner for you—something light since you're not feeling your best."

No answer.

Perhaps he was asleep? I raised my voice slightly. "Governor? I'll leave the tray here on the service table next to your room."

At that, I heard shuffling; glass clunked onto wood, and a creak of floorboards betrayed approaching footsteps. I heard him catch himself and swear under his breath. He was staggering.

Abruptly, the door swung open, and there stood Meriwether Lewis in a flowing black silk banyan embroidered with Chinese flowers and vases. His mien was entirely different from the distinguished governor who had visited with us these past two days—the man vying for Letitia's attention.

His squinting eyes were bloodshot, his hair matted and flattened on one side, and I couldn't help but step backward at the odor of his sour breath. My eyes flitted beyond him of their own accord, catching the glint of a Pitkin flask atop his bedside table.

What would be inside but gin or whiskey?

Heart sinking, my mind whirred. Yesterday, he'd shared his plan to visit Letitia. I hadn't seen him all day. I thought back on Letitia's early morning visit. Undoubtedly, Lewis's attempts to meet with her had been futile, and now I was staring at the result.

"My apologies," he managed, his speech slurred. "I'm afraid I'm not at my best tonight. You've a most unappealing guest—an ill and boorish man." He barely finished his phrase before suppressing a belch.

"No—no—not at all," I stuttered. "I'll just leave the tray here in case you change your mind."

As I set it down on the service table, he caught my elbow. My whole body tensed at the unexpected contact, for not only was it improper, but Lewis was hot to the touch; I felt it clear through the thick wool of my sleeve. I whirled about, and my movement forced him to release his grasp. "My brother-in-law is a local doctor. Since you're feeling poorly, we could send for him."

"No," he sighed, his head wagging from side to side. "But perhaps just speaking with you will help. By gaining any insights you have to offer, I might staunch my wounds and be healed. Especially since you and Letitia are friends."

Admittedly curious, I gestured to the intimate sitting room just outside his doorway, where my family and any overnight guests could visit at leisure. "Please sit down," I invited, nodding to the settee. Once he accepted and leaned back on the cushions, I shared the other end, distancing us and waiting for him to speak.

"I rode to Grove Hill earlier today," he began, leaning back against the cushions and closing his eyes as he rubbed his temples. He looked terribly pale.

"Grove Hill is magnificent, isn't it? Such a fine house."

"More like a palace. Twenty-six rooms?" He blew his cheeks out and shook his head in awe, letting it drop back so that he stared blankly at the ceiling. "Truly, I was anticipating a welcome."

"You weren't invited in?" That was a surprise.

His head rolled from side to side. "I was informed at the door that Breckinridge and Letitia had departed for Richmond before dawn."

Letitia hadn't revealed she was leaving Fincastle. Apparently, it had been her own father bringing her here to see me. "With all of your kind intentions, it's a shame they left."

Lewis's eyes snapped open, locking into mine, as though penetrating my soul. "I was hoping you'd enlighten me on the situation."

My, but this was unnerving, the way he was staring me down so intensely. I could only pray my face didn't betray any guilt that Letitia and I had spoken that morning. "I'm afraid Letitia and I aren't as close as you might think."

"That may be true, but I believe you're withholding something I should know. Has she another suitor?"

My tongue was cotton-dry, so I swallowed, trying to wet my mouth sufficiently. It didn't work and I simply nodded, glancing back at the tray of wasted food.

"Let me guess," he sat up, hands on his knees, "you're beholden to Letitia not to tell me anything more."

Finally, I found my voice. "Would it change anything if I told you?"

I didn't want to see him hurt. Will considered him like another brother, and I wanted to invest in a friendship with him myself. At least I thought I did. Right now, his peculiar behavior and overall condition had shaken me, and I felt ill at ease with him, overcome with drink and in his nightclothes… It seemed there was a reckless nature to Meriwether Lewis that Will had not mentioned.

He rubbed his grizzled chin with one hand. "Truly, I have no hunger this evening, Miss Hancock," he said, waving at the tray in dismissal. "Do tell your kind parents that Reuben and I shall not trouble them further. We'll leave at first light."

Dismayed, I stood up, glancing at the tray of soup, bread, and sliced apples. "Then I'll go down and wrap up this food and a few more victuals for your travels. We are your family while you're our guest, so please don't hesitate to let me know should you need something more."

The next morning, Reuben was able to persuade his brother to take a light breakfast with us. The younger Lewis was his usual chatty, outgoing self, definitely the sunnier side of the family. The governor, however, barely ate, only drinking several cups of steaming tea while absently stirring his fork through his eggs.

Papa peered at him over his spectacles. "Surely, you're looking forward to your arrival in St. Louis as governor." It came out like a statement, not a question.

"Oh—yes," Lewis assured him. "I'm sure it will be a . . . a challenge."

"Ha!" this from Papa too. "I'd say so. What sorts of things require attention once you arrive?"

"I've a list of tasks," Lewis replied. "We've many Indian issues. Tribes war against one another, and there's the situation north of us along the Missouri where the Arikara are blockading river travel. It impedes the fur trade."

"I heard about that," I exclaimed. "Will wrote about a delegation carrying the Mandan chief home and how they were attacked—forced to turn back."

Lewis shook his head. "Not a good situation at all, and it reflects poorly on us, in keeping our word to the Mandans and to their chief, Sheheke. I shall have to look into another means of returning him, requiring more manpower to assure safety of everyone involved."

"I'd be most interested in going on such a venture," Reuben pledged.

"We shall see," Lewis told him. "When it comes to dealing with natives, you're bound to get your feet wet, one way or another. Colonel Hancock, there are many other things demanding attention. Squatters, amending territorial laws, development of militia . . . I could go on and on."

Mama piped up, "How will you ever find time for work on the journals?"

"*That* will be a challenge indeed," Lewis admitted.

Reuben nodded toward his brother. "I'm proud of Meriwether receiving a governorship. What greater honor could he have from the president?"

"We wish you the best with it," Papa said. "And hopefully, some young lady in St. Louis will catch your eye."

Lewis bristled a bit. "Perhaps," was his terse reply, along with a forced smile.

I sighed. Papa was seldom subtle. Was Lewis hurt from unrequited feelings or simply the sting of wounded pride? My wager was on the latter.

The front door opened, shut, and Cap appeared at the entrance to the dining room. "Your horses is ready, Governor," he announced. "And your bags is strapped on the pack-ponies. John be waiting for you outside, along with your dog."

Lewis nodded tersely, then abruptly set his teacup down and rose. "I've something for Miss Hancock before I leave, if you'll all excuse me a moment."

As soon as he was out of earshot, Mama said under her breath, "Poor man. He's so melancholy."

"Madam, I've never seen Meriwether as taken with a young lady as he was with Miss Breckinridge," Reuben replied in the same hushed tone.

We all arose from our seats as we heard Lewis re-enter the hall. When we met him there, he was holding a book—a large, thick tome bound in supple, tooled calfskin.

"Miss Hancock, before taking my leave, I wanted to extend my warmest congratulations once more and offer you this humble gift. William has told me how much you love literature."

"Oh, she sure does," affirmed Georgie with relish, breaking the silence he'd politely kept during breakfast. "She reads all the time!"

"Indeed, I do love reading, writing, and—" I stopped mid-sentence, blinking in astonishment as Lewis presented the gift. I was overjoyed at seeing what it was. "*Shakespeare?* His *complete* works? Including the plays?"

"Every single one. You'll need some distraction during St. Louis winters."

I gasped in utter delight. "Oh, what *joy*! But you shouldn't have."

"Aren't you pleased he *did*?" Reuben snorted, heading toward the door.

Lewis ignored him.

"I cannot thank you enough. Shakespeare is my *favorite*. Did Will tell you?"

"That he did," he disclosed with a warm smile that completely overshadowed his previous melancholia. "I found this at a bookshop in Philadelphia."

I lifted the book to my nose, inhaling the smell of its elegant leather binding.

"Now, now, you're marrying my dearest friend," he reminded me. "William and I are more like brothers, so we must dispense with formalities, don't you think? I insist you call me Meriwether."

"Well, if you're permitting me to call you by your Christian name, then you must respond in kind by calling me Julia."

Meriwether bowed to me with flourish. "I will do so with honor—Julia." Then he bowed low to Mama too. "And what happiness it's been to be the guest of such a genial, welcoming host and hostess. Now, we must depart. According to William's most recent letter, I've tarried far too long in the east and my presence is much required."

Mama, Papa, Georgie, and I stood on the porch, watching the men ride off, followed by Seaman's loyal company. The gift of Shakespeare had touched me—a tangible reminder that Governor Meriwether Lewis was my friend. However, my memory of the previous night and his bizarre behavior made that November day feel far chillier than it was.

Chapter IX

Fincastle, Virginia
Late November-January 1807-08

My Angel,
 It has been too long Since I've been in your presens, cheered by your sweet face. I take comfort knowing that Soon we Shall be together once more and be wed. Please give my kindest regards to your famly.
 Since I was absent for Some time at the Big Bone Licke, my work in St. Louis has only just begun. I Sint Sevral large bones to Washington City for the President. Now I am back to my true perpose, resuming my office in Indian Afairs, but as in all important tasks, it comes with frustrations.
 There is a gentleman here by the name of Frederick Bates who bears watching, as I fear he may not be trustworthy. Recently, I delt with a Settler who planted corn on land allocated to the Indians. Bates disagreed with the maner in which I handled it, criticizing me harshly and making the matter public. There will be many challenges in my new position, and this is proof of that fact. Now Bates is fussing about Lewis not yet arriving when his governorship was asigned over a year ago. I often remind him that Lewis has had plenty of business afoot, and here in the west we must be pashient regarding long distances.

I hold you close in my heart and look forward to seeing you in the next month.
           I am faithfully yours,
           W. Clark

Christmas passed with no sign of Will, and for me there was a saturating profusion of *whens*.

When would he arrive? When would the wedding be? When would we depart for St. Louis?

For nearly all of December, I listened for riders approaching the house. Whenever I heard hoofbeats, I ran to the window. When that happened on a blustery, chilly late afternoon, I set Master Shakespeare aside, scrambling to the window and wiping frost from the pane.

Not him. Not yet.

Instead, it was an armed soldier with a padlocked saddlebag, making me wonder what sort of official business he had at Santillane. By the time I reached the front door, he had dismounted and was busy unlocking the bag, drawing out a small parcel, neatly wrapped.

While I swung open the front door, Mama was calling for Megg to warm some tea on the stove for the traveler.

"Greetings, miss," the young man said. "I'm looking for Miss Julia Hancock."

My heart thudded. "I'm Miss Hancock."

"Miss Hancock, I've ridden from Washington City to convey warmest regards from President Jefferson," he announced, climbing the stairs. "This here is a wedding gift from the president himself."

He presented the parcel, and I accepted. Utterly astonished, I wandered into the library's privacy with it.

"Please," Mama invited, bustling to the entrance toward the soldier. "It's freezing outside. Do go around the side of the house to the kitchen. We've warmed some tea for you, and my woman Megg will see you're given a hot meal before you continue on."

"Many thanks, ma'am. That's greatly appreciated."

Once she'd shut the door, Mama came up behind me, where I was admiring the packaged gift. "What is it?" she asked, insistently peering over my shoulder.

"I don't know—"

"Well, *open* it, child!"

I peeled away the outer layer of wrapping carefully to find a smoothly sanded and polished flat-latched box of walnut with a crisp note of official presidential stationery attached.

"Oh, Julia, he's written you a *private* note."

Blinking at my own disbelief, I lifted the folded stationery, feeling the raised print under my fingertips. It was engraved with the presidential seal and Jefferson's name. Beneath was his message—the author of our Declaration of Independence had written me in his own bold script:

> *My dearest Miss Hancock,*
>
> *I'm sure there are hardly words to express the delight and happiness you must feel as you celebrate the advent of your marriage. If William Clark has chosen you as his bride, then I can only assume what an upright and purposeful woman you must be. Therefore, I beg you to accept this small gift, representing the sentiments I hold, not only of your worthy person, but of Clark's esteemed service and character——all of which I hold dear. May your days together be many and full of joy.*
>
> *I am indeed in your service and in the service of our beloved country,*
>
> *Th. Jefferson, President of the United States*

"Oh, Julia—*open* it!" Mama fussed again.

In disbelief, I set the note aside upon one of our library tables. Using my finger, I slid the box's delicate brass latch up to the right. The lid released, and I opened it the rest of the way, gasping. Beneath a protective flap of emerald satin was a magnificent brooch of carnelian and gold, and on either side were displayed matching earrings. They were exquisite, and not even my parents had ever gifted me with such extravagance.

I stared at Mama, shaking my head, stunned. "How can I accept this? It's far too rich for me."

Ever so gently, she placed her hands upon my face and whispered, "Daughter, you are marrying into greatness, and even our president recognizes that fact. You will accept it with humility, with dignity, and wear these baubles in St. Louis with pride, where people will be *amazed* that the president sends you such."

I was humbled.

What an incredible time this was—a year full of newness, a year of firsts.

Like receiving gifts from the president.

⁂

I waited.

Some days, I'd sit on the edge of my bed, gazing westward out the window, listening for approaching hoofbeats. I'd close my eyes, concentrating, willing him to come.

On the day after hearing Fincastle's New Year's bells, I sat in that very spot, alone in my bedchamber, staring down at the ring Will had given me. Slipping it off, I admired it. Really, I'd hardly removed it since he'd slipped it onto my finger, but on occasion I reread the words he'd chosen to have the engraver carve inside the band: *In thy sight is my delight.*

While inspecting it, a tendril of my hair fell out of place and the hairpin dropped onto the bed in front of me. I lifted the little pin, toying with it in one hand while my other still held the ring. I slipped it back on, leaned toward the window, and, using the hairpin's point, carved something of my own—straight into the windowsill.

J.H & W.C.

Perhaps I'd leave Santillane and never come back. It was possible. But at least I'd leave written proof of my love for William Clark. The inscription on the sill was evidence that our romance commenced here and only here. As long as Santillane stood, my inscription would be here.

Later that very day, I sat reading one of Shakespeare's plays called

Othello. The story captivated me; a Moorish black man married Desdemona, a white woman. How contrary to our own society, and yet Shakespeare had written that story three hundred years ago. The mere fact that Desdemona loved and married Othello would be nothing less than scandalous now. I adored this play, though it was still full of prejudice, depicting a black man who had risen to great success and a woman who loved him, seeing more in him than just black skin.

"*Julia!* Come outside! I've a gift for my bride!"

In a sudden inhale, my breath caught in my throat. It was *him*!

I'd been so absorbed in the play I'd not noticed the clatter of hoofbeats. Master Shakespeare would wait as I bolted into the hallway, grabbing my warmest coat. Then I was leaping down Santillane's steps, two at a time.

Will had already dismounted, Cap taking the reins of his horse while York was busily jerking something free from behind the cart he'd been driving.

Then I was in his arms. He lifted me, twirling, laughing—there was *nothing* like William Clark's glorious laughter.

Finally setting me down, he looked back for York. "York, bring her up. Look, Julia. I bought you a mare. We'll be buying a wagon of some sort before leaving for St. Louis, but I wanted you to be able to ride if you wanted."

I had never had my own horse, though everyone knew I loved riding. She was a beautiful chestnut, and Will led me over to the water trough, where York let her drink deeply.

"I'm guessing she's about twelve years old," Will said, "middle-aged, but in excellent shape. A perfect lady's horse."

"I *love* her!" I cried, clapping my hands together and unable to prevent a girlish squeal from stealing its way into my voice. The mare flinched and I reached out, stroking her face to calm her. Really, she needed a good brushing, and I'd see to that, but she was lovely all the same. "What's her name?"

"The Spaniard in Louisville who sold her to me said he called her 'Castanea.' If you don't like it, feel free to name her something else."

"Oh, I do like it, but I'll call her Cassie for short."

Now that Will had arrived, there would be no more waiting. Our special day was set for that very next week—on Tuesday, January 5th.

Billy Preston, my sister Caroline, and their precious daughter, Henrietta, were still visiting, having stayed on after Christmas in anticipation of our wedding. Early on the mornings leading up to that Tuesday, Will, Billy, Georgie, and Papa took off hunting before we women arose, so dinners were hearty for all and full of fresh game. The entire family was together: Mary, Griff, Harri, and Dr. John coming every night to enjoy wild turkey, venison, or rabbit—anything the menfolk brought in. Seldom were there any leftovers, but I was ever careful to save something for Ares and Virgil, just the same.

Georgie took it upon himself to ride all over Fincastle and its nearby hollows, inviting folk to our celebration. Papa took care of the business end of things, including the task of writing and delivering an announcement of our nuptials for Mr. Ammen, owner and editor of the *Herald of Virginia*, Fincastle's small newspaper.

Mama allowed me several days prior to our wedding to do whatever I wanted, so Will and I took long rides through Papa's fields and the roads surrounding Fincastle so I could get used to Cassie. On our way back from one of those jaunts, we cantered back onto Papa's land, and I galloped hard, even gaining ground ahead of Will, not pulling up until we reached the old Catawba tree.

Will swung off first, laughing. "You got ahead and enjoyed that, didn't you?"

I let him snatch me by the waist as I slid from my sidesaddle, feeling his lean body against mine the entire time, culminating in a wildly pleasurable and abandoned kiss. Our intimacies had become more frequent, longer, and more urgent. The night before, his hand had traveled down my backside and against my thigh. No man had ever touched me like that, but I didn't stop him because I didn't *want* him to stop. I sensed that Will had previous experience with women, and Harri tittered about that, saying, "Be glad of it. He'll show you delicious things you'll enjoy."

As he held me, I tightened my grasp on his manly form. Oh, how well-built he was with powerful, sinewy shoulders and a well-muscled neck.

"By God, but I think you want me, don't you, Julia?" he breathed in my ear, playfully nipping it afterward with his teeth.

"I do—in a way I don't fully understand."

"You'll learn soon enough." Then he pulled back, hesitating a moment before stepping toward the Catawba tree, where he leaned back against its trunk.

I walked over and sat down on Papa's branch—the thick one bowing toward the ground before sweeping skyward. I bounced on it just a bit, and like a rope swing, it swayed.

Enjoying the movement, I deliberated, "To think that we'll never be parted. Granted, I know you'll travel, but it's so satisfying knowing that within days we'll *belong* to one another."

"I only regret that you must leave all of this," he said, sweeping one arm toward Santillane. "Your family has been your world, and there are moments when I'm full of guilt for tearing you away from them."

"*You* will be my world, Will."

He lowered his eyes, looking at his feet. "Julia," he began in a tentative manner, "though Virginia may still have some of its wilderness, Virginia is *civilized*," he emphasized. "St. Louis, despite what some of its families and leaders are striving for, is not. There are still threats of Indian raids and even of foreign invaders, like the British."

We'd trodden this path numerous times, so I arose from Papa's branch, striding back over to where he was and wound my arms about his neck. After kissing him, I whispered, "Don't you go sounding like Papa—trying to convince me not to marry you."

Again, we kissed, this time deeply, and I slid my tongue into his mouth to dance with his. When I pulled away, I shook my head and teased him, "I'm sorry, General, but not even an order from you will keep us from wedding now. I am fully committed to this adventure of ours, regardless of where it leads."

On the morning of January 5th, Will, Papa, and Billy went to the old log courthouse, where Will paid for and signed our marriage bond, Billy Preston standing as witness. For us women, the whole afternoon was spent getting me ready up in Mama and Papa's room. Harriet and Mary were there, as were Caroline and Mama. We all stood in front of her dressing mirror, staring at the finished product—me.

"You're beautiful, Julia," Harri whispered in my ear. She held my hand on one side, Mama clasping my other.

As a gawky adolescent, I'd spent so many days standing before mirrors, thinking myself plain and not overly beautiful. Now, I realized that I'd probably been comparing myself to too many others—women like Caroline, graced with such poise and loveliness, and Letitia, who possessed such feminine allure.

To me, my face had never been overly lovely.

Just attractive.

But now, gazing at myself all done up for my own wedding, I had to admit that I looked stunning.

Mama and Mary swept my hair up on both sides, with only the very back loosely falling into curls between my shoulder blades. My one dimple appeared as I smiled, and a sparkle lit my eyes.

Despite my leaning toward blue, Mama's favorite color was red, so I'd let her select a deep crimson satin and matching velvet, and it turned out to be a flattering color.

"You needed a bold color to make a statement," Mama said, as though reading my mind. She turned her face to peck my cheek. "You're marrying a hero and gentleman of great reputation, so Papa and I wanted to see you arrayed like a princess. And you are, my girl—even adorned with Jefferson's jewels."

I smiled at that, my hand flitting upward to fondle one of the earrings as I eyed the glittering gold broach between my breasts.

The gown's design was based upon a single picture—just a sketch, actually—of Empress Josephine in one of her gowns. Her styles were in demand all over Europe. Oh, and Mrs. Early, wife to Fincastle's finest tailor, had donated ivory lace for the trim of my sleeves and around the neckline, the last of which had been used for an elegant cream-colored sash.

A chill crept up my spine. Today, I would become Julia Hancock *Clark*.

From the top of the stairwell, I looked down at warm, gleaming candlelight illuminating Santillane's hallway.

"Little Judith—last of my girls," Papa murmured, more to himself than to me. Gently, he took my arm to escort me down, and I squeezed his hand in response.

Despite the thrill of dazzling our guests with my finery, the greenery giving our house a cozy pine scent for the ceremony, and the warm melody from Harri's violin as she played, my eyes sought only Will's. We gazed at one another as I descended toward him until we were joined before Reverend Logan. Will's red hair flamed against the dark, formal military uniform he wore, epaulets on his shoulders catching the warm candlelight, sword at his side. I saw nothing more—only our gazes fastened together, the words of our vows lost in my overwhelming happiness. And when it was done, I felt his warm lips as everyone applauded and Georgie and Billy started whooping.

Next was the barn dance.

As stately as Santillane was, it wasn't overly spacious for such, so town folk who had come to honor us were waiting outside in the barn for the dancing afterward, many spilling outside in the winter cold to enjoy a bonfire that Papa's people had started behind the gardens.

Friends and neighbors had brought outdoor braziers to keep coals warming the air inside the barn, and Megg had organized all of Papa's people to decorate it as best they could with berry-dyed straw swags and greenery from our property. Music for the evening was courtesy of Billy and Caroline, who had hired a skilled handful of Germans from Little Amsterdam to play dancing tunes. Our celebration went on for a good three or four hours until it began snowing hard and people had to leave so their carriages could make it home. Papa made an announcement, welcoming those who had traveled far to take refuge in the barn for the night. "And we'll provide a warm porridge breakfast in the morning," he added, cheering and applauding following his kind promise of hospitality.

Will and I stood by the barn door next to one of the braziers for warmth, wishing our parting guests farewell. "My hands are freezing," I whispered as the last ones departed.

Will grinned, breathing a titillating promise into my ear, "Soon we'll be alone, and you won't be cold at all. I'll see to that."

When it came time for him to lead me back into the house, we paused at the foot of the stairwell to wish my siblings and parents good night. They all clapped and cheered as Will led me up to my chamber door.

Now it was *our* chamber.

Once inside, he bolted the latch, turning back to me. "You needn't be afraid or nervous," he assured, lips grazing my ear.

Heat rose to my face, and my entire person went all a-tingle. Megg had started us a roaring fire, and extra firewood was stacked neatly to one side. My bedsheets had been changed, and there were new lacy pillowcases and dried lavender strewn all over the bed.

Will led me in front of the fire, where it was warmer, then circled back behind me, placing his arms about my waist and nuzzling my hair. Then I experienced the unique feel of his fingers slowly and methodically unlacing the back of my gown. The occasional feel of his lips on my neck made me inhale in delight and helped me relax in a cascade of shivers.

When my gown dropped about my feet in a soft swath of gossamer fabric, I turned around, standing before him in nothing but my silk shift and stays, which I untied myself. Then I lifted my arms to the back of my head, pulling out hairpins one at a time as he watched, blue eyes glittering. Ever so slowly, my hair spilled onto my shoulders.

"May I ask you a personal question?" I asked as I lifted my shift above my thigh, detaching a garter from my silk stocking. Harri had told me how fun this could be, and what had I to lose? At the moment, I felt rather empowered, holding this man enraptured as his gift unwrapped itself before him.

Will had taken to lounging against the hearth, his eyes never leaving me, nodding permission, his gaze locked to my every movement.

"Earlier, I told you to teach me. Thus, I assume you've been with other women?"

"Yes, I confess I have, Julia. However, I've pledged myself to you now, and I'll keep that vow sacred, as I promised before the reverend. Never have I known a young lady more loving, considerate, or comely than you. Seeing you now . . ." he paused, swallowing, his eyes intense with want. "By God, you have never looked more desirable or beautiful."

"So teach me," I heard myself say.

With that, he returned to me, taking my wrist before I could remove my other stocking. His hand moved slowly up my leg, making me gasp, as he eased my calf out of the rest of the silk. It was my turn to take the initiative, placing his hands on my other thigh. Hungrily, I reached up to take his collar, drawing his mouth back to mine. Even through closed eyes, I felt his broad smile against my mouth, and then—unexpectedly—he swept me up into his arms, carrying me to bed while I dropped my head back, giggling.

There, on clean white linen and quilts, I let William Clark have me—body and soul. His hands visited places about which I would ordinarily have felt shameful, but we were married now, and I was at peace. We became one, and when he took me for the first time, I forced myself to relax so that pleasure would come. Hadn't Harriet promised that it would?

And oh, she was right.

Chapter X

**Virginia, the Midland Trail, and Louisville
March–May 1808**

Winter ended with an exhale of warm air, melting snow clear up in the mountains. The break in the weather allowed us to travel with Mama, Papa, Georgie, Billy, Caroline, and her little Henrietta up to Bath County, where the healing waters of Warm Springs awaited us. We traveled in a cavalcade of carriages, carts, and horses, visiting friends and extended family along the way. It was a joyful time.

Warm Springs was a special place, and men and women in our party took turns luxuriating in the pools within the spa. Bubbling medicinal springs, mornings spent riding Cassie through the woods, exuberant laughter, and dreamy lovemaking at night—the arousing sensation of my bare skin against Will's…

While we were there, he surprised both me and my family by delaying our St. Louis departure until May. "I want our life together to begin surrounded by your loved ones," he told me.

And then came May.

I missed my courses.

It sometimes happened, so I thought nothing of it. But then one morning, I rushed from breakfast, scrambling upstairs and snatching the chamber pot from beneath the bed. There, I heaved up the little I'd eaten. For several days, I'd been feeling queasy after waking, but this…

Settling back on my haunches, I sensed the presence of another in the room, and I turned. Mama had followed me upstairs, and she knelt down at my side. Still nauseous, trembling, and taking great breaths to steady myself, I shook my head, trying to summon words. She beat me to the task, "Well, the good Lord be praised. Seems I'll be a grandmother *three* times over."

Only weeks ago, Mary and Griff had announced that she was with child. But the thought of a pregnancy so early in my own marriage was completely unexpected. Far too soon. I knew it could happen, but I wasn't prepared for this timing, and my reaction was to break down crying, my tears spilling in a volatile expiation of turmoil.

"Dear child, why the tears? This is a blessing."

All I could do was bury my face against her breast. "I'm not ready—everything's happening too quickly—*if* this is what it is."

"I've seen these signs many times, and nonsense. You're a married woman now, so dry those eyes. It was bound to happen sooner or later, and for you, it's to be *sooner*."

I said nothing, my stubborn nature still grasping for my other life that had suddenly vanished.

"Mmm..." Mama crooned. "Married only five months and with a hero-husband's babe in your belly. Get up now. You're a Hancock and made of stern, steely stuff." She nodded once at the pot. "I'll have Megg toss this, and you go back down to breakfast."

"Shouldn't I tell Will?"

"I'd wait a bit. That way we'll be certain."

"That's how I should handle it?"

"It's how I always handled it, and what's done by one Hancock should be good enough for the next, I'll wager. Now scoot on down, and remember that you're bearing *two* worthy names now."

I picked up the chamber pot.

Mama shook her head. "I said I'd have Megg fetch it."

"No. I don't want her—"

"Julia." Suddenly her voice had changed into chilling sternness. "I'm well aware of your opinions on this matter as well as your affection for Megg, Cap, and the rest of our people. I also know how you continue to feed Ares and Virgil extras because of their whipping so long past."

I blinked at her in surprise. She'd said nothing more about abolition since the day the pamphlet had fallen into her hands, thanks to Letitia.

"Silly girl!" she laughed. "You'd be surprised at what all I know that goes on in this house, but I'm mistress of Santillane, so I make it my business to know what happens here. Only too soon, you'll be mistress of your own home, and you'll be doing the same. But let me tell you something. Whatever people belong to William, you'd best learn to keep them in their places, managing them fair and firm."

"But—"

She flipped her hand up, demanding silence on the matter. "Does William know your thoughts on slavery?"

I swallowed hard, my mouth forming a hushed, "No."

"You never *told* him?" She sighed, shaking her head. "Do you not realize that this is something that could affect your marriage in the future? You've always had too soft a heart when it comes to our people, but if your papa ever learned about what's behind it, he'd be outraged. What might William think? You'd best work to keep it from him and step up to be an iron fist in velvet when it comes to managing whatever property he owns."

Of all the truths Will and I had shared between us, this was the one thing I'd kept to myself—a priority my heart held in the greatest magnitude.

Or did it?

I'd held back this secret—so afraid it would destroy the relationship I so cherished. Sheer cowardice had thwarted my honesty. And yet there had been a time, not long ago, where I'd valued my abolitionist leanings even more than any prospects of marriage. I'd let that precedence slide through my fingers as though it were sands in an hourglass, and now I faced my guilt. Guilt that I'd lost sight of what was a personal mission along with guilt over not being completely honest with the man I loved. Mama had shot to the very heart of the matter, and now I had to admit how afraid I was that this secret might ruin the happiness I'd found with Will. There was no way I could argue it; this vital detail's concealment had been fully intentional on my part.

Granted, he'd never really spoken about his people, other than York, who traveled with him, and always assisted him with shaving, dressing, caring for his horse, and any other day-to-day details. I'd probably meet any other of his slaves that he'd inherited once we moved west.

Now, my stomach was all knotted up again, and I scrambled back over to the chamber pot. But this time, it had nothing to do with pregnancy.

※

Powder.
Wadding, then set the ball.
Ramrod and compress the powder.
Reattach ramrod.
Cock the hammer.
Powder in the pan.

"Slowly now, take your time when aiming. You needn't hurry. We're not at war."

Cold, unforgiving steel pressed against my cheek. I steadied myself, squinting, looking down the long barrel at a scarecrow Will had fashioned out of an old coat and handfuls of straw from the barn.

"Just remember… miss and you'll have to reload."

"I don't intend to miss this time."

"Good. Sometimes it helps if I pretend I'm shooting someone I don't like."

"Who?" That upended my concentration, but I breathed deep, trying to settle back into focus.

Will shrugged and snorted. "Right after returning from the expedition, it was Aaron Burr. I detest the man. We hadn't heard he'd killed Hamilton until we got back to St. Louis."

Pulling a trigger was the most delicate part of learning to shoot. It was so subtle, and though I hated the loud explosion setting my ears to ringing, it was the peripheral sight of fire in the pan that nearly made me drop the gun on my first try.

But not this time.

I didn't hate anyone enough to pretend shooting them, but I hated slavery. This time, I'd try to kill it.

No, it didn't take much at all to pull that trigger.

Fuh-BOOM!

The scarecrow jerked where it was staked.

"You did it!" Will shouted.

"I hit it!"

He swept me up in his arms, rifle and all, spinning me about, both of us laughing. For me, it was a victory, for my lessons in shooting had only begun with the warmer weather, and I found that learning to load and fire *plus* hit a target took skill I'd never thought to admire.

Will took me hunting twice with Papa and Georgie, and when I continually missed, my younger brother laughed at me. I ignored it at the time, but now I respected the Corps of Discovery soldiers and veteran patriots more than ever. And Georgie would discover that his sister learned quickly and wasn't a bad shot for a girl.

Together, Will and I hurried down to the end of the field to examine the scarecrow.

"He's dead!" Will proclaimed loudly. "You killed him."

I grinned, cocking my brow at him. "Finally! It's about time." I wiggled one finger into the torn hole the ball had shot straight through the coat's wool and straw. "It's even on the left side," I noted.

"Indeed. Straight through the heart. You're a quick learner, compared to some."

"Then let's go home. Now that I've proven I can kill something, I want Georgie to know."

"Fair enough. And I have news."

I looked up at him, curious.

"A letter from Lewis. He's found us a house—to rent monthly, but only until I save up enough to buy us a place."

"Really? What's it like?"

"Not large, I'm sorry to say. There's a dining room, several bedchambers, and a tiny room in the back for guests or office space. In addition, it has a garden area and a covered porch."

"A cellar?"

"A small one. And Lewis will be living with us."

"*What?* He'll be *living* with us?" That was news. "It will be rather tight. You hadn't told me that. What about guests? Will there be adequate space for such? A small room in the back sounds like very little, especially doubling as an office."

Will grasped my hand as we walked. "Let's trust him enough to give it a try. We owe him that since he's found us a place. And don't worry about him sharing our living space. He's like family."

"But if it's too small—"

"Then it'll be too small." He laughed lightheartedly, drawing me closer to drape his long arm over my shoulders and relieving me of his gun. "No sense being anxious. If it's not satisfactory, we'll move once something better presents itself."

The thought of us living under the same roof with Lewis sounded awkward, being newly married. However, I had been told repeatedly that living in St. Louis would be different, so I decided to force myself to wait, test the waters, and then express any dislike of the accommodations if things weren't satisfactory.

We'd be leaving in a matter of days. With spring heading into summer, the Ohio River would be ideal for flatboat travel. According to Will, it was a literal roadway for anybody heading west. Our time at Santillane was slipping by.

If there was one thing I was learning, it was that life's moments often felt much shorter than a clock hand registered. Sometimes I wished time would remain stagnant, like a frozen pond after new snow. But it never paused. Everything edged forward, ever transient. Not all was travail and darkness, of course, for melting snows brought spring and vivid gardens of iridescent color. But life always pressed on in an ever-forward momentum through both the good and bad.

As did new life.

In the weeks since Mama had first helped me realize my condition, my body itself was directing me into treasuring this new journey. That, and she kept sneaking me old baby gowns for me to pack in my trousseau and take with us. Gentle changes occurred within me: a weariness at times making me feel lethargic and lazy and my breasts becoming tender. I stopped wearing my stays—even to go to church. I calculated that I'd give birth sometime next winter.

Adventure was what I'd wanted and was *exactly* what I was getting.

I paused a moment, dizzy from the brisk walking and not eating much since it had been difficult to keep food down early in the day. Will stopped too.

"Something wrong? You're not ill, are you?"

I shook my head. He still didn't know, and memories of my pneumonia still haunted him. On impulse, I decided it was time. "No. I'm fine. Just dizzy."

His forehead crinkled in concern. "That doesn't sound fine to me."

I grinned, biting my lower lip to keep from laughing aloud. "Maybe not, but it'll be mighty fine when you're a papa early next year."

His eyes nearly popped from their sockets, and this time I did laugh.

"You mean—you're saying—"

"Yes, William Clark! You're going to be a *father*!"

"*Really?*"

I nodded. "It's not exactly what I'd planned, so soon—"

"It's *wonderful*! When and how should we tell everyone?"

"Mama already knows."

"We're leaving next week, and everyone *must* know before we go."

"Why not tell them at dinner on our last night here?"

"Perfect. It'll make for a festive occasion. Get Megg to bake us a cake, would you?"

I nodded, warm and well inside because of his ardor.

"And no more riding Cassie. You'll be traveling by carriage the entire way to St. Louis. I'll be taking care to keep you safe."

That disappointed me, but I conceded without argument. "If you insist."

"I do. We mustn't take any risks." He stopped from climbing the hill to take me into his arms again. "I'll do anything I must to care for you and my son or daughter."

On the eve of our departure, dessert came out with a flourish. Megg's cake was tall and covered with fresh crème Chantilly, brown sugar, and cinnamon—a confection fit for a prince or princess, whichever I carried.

Nearly everyone was there: Mama, Papa, Georgie, Mary, Griff, Harri, and her Dr. John—just not Caroline and Billy. They'd already left for Wythe County after their extended stay. As Will accompanied Megg out with the cake, I met Mama's eyes and saw her smiling with pride.

"Julia and I have a special announcement," Will veritably crowed. "Come next winter, we'll be parents!"

Papa led the family in rising for a toast, lifting his glass of port. "Hear, hear! And may many more little blessings follow this one."

Everyone drank to that.

❧❦❧

A rickety old T-post was the only signage for the Midland Trail, with spelling as dubious as Will's.

Midlin Trayl, it read.

We halted, and I climbed off of the wagon. Papa had accompanied us thus far, and this was where he'd be turning back. He trotted over to where Will and I stood together, holding hands.

"Sweet Judith," Papa murmured, dismounting. "You're making me mighty proud. Married and with a grandson on the way."

"How do you know it's a grandson?" I teased. "You may wind up with a grand*daughter*, and I hope that wouldn't disappoint."

He shook his head. "You're having a strapping boy this time. Will thinks so too."

I shielded my eyes from the sun, peering up at Will, who grinned broadly, his hair slick from sweat beneath his tricorn. "Well," I teased, "now I feel pressured into giving you a son. Myself, I'd be just as fine with a girl."

Will's only answer was to pull me closer, chuckling and kissing the top of my head.

Papa's laughter echoed through the hills—he and Will shared such a similar timbre in their deep voices. "Come here, daughter!" he bellowed.

We held each other. I'd so miss my family. Yet hadn't I heard Reverend Logan share scripture before, saying: *A man must leave father and mother and shall cleave to his wife: and they twain shall be one flesh*? Surely, Will and I clung together in such a fashion.

"I'll miss you and Mama so much," I managed, swallowing a tightening in my throat and steeling myself not to cry.

"You'll have a household to run, then a child to rear. By God, you'll be so busy you'll forget about us," he chuckled, pressing me against his rough cheek once more, grizzled as it was with stubble.

"Please be well, and take care of Mama and Georgie. Remind them I'll write from St. Louis."

"And you take care, for you're carrying a precious load." His eyes narrowed as he turned serious. "I tell you, find a midwife as soon as you arrive in St. Louis." He nodded at Will while still holding my hand. "Clark, you see to her health, you understand? My greatest trepidation is her welfare, along with the baby's."

"Colonel Hancock, while there's breath in my body, I promise to see to her every need, sir."

"Then with that, I'll take my leave."

With a final peck on my cheek, Papa turned and remounted, removing his tricorn and placing it against his breast. "Safe travels to you both. Write soon. Your mother and I will expect it."

"I'll miss you all!" I called, waving and taking a few steps toward his horse.

He said nothing more, turning the animal and clicking to it, cantering off. My eyes followed him. Would I see my parents again?

Leaving home brought so many unknowns that I'd not considered when daydreaming about seeing the west. There were so many faces I didn't want fading from my memory with time.

I shut my eyes a moment, then reopened them.

Good. I still saw Papa as clearly as the minute before, when he was holding me so tight. Perhaps he and I thought differently when it came to his people, but he was still my papa. I'd always love him in my own way.

And what a relief! Mama, Georgie, Megg—yes, I still saw all of them in my mind's eye too. And I hadn't cried a single tear, though emotion churned inside. "It's best we keep moving," I said to Will, sniffing away the tears building up. Briskly, I walked back to the wagon, climbing up on my own.

Our journey proceeded well, though inns along the way were often nothing more than log cabins with straw mattresses. It struck me how gentle a life I'd led. Fleas and bedbugs became daily inconveniences, and the itching was pure torment. At least my morning bouts with nausea subsided, and I found myself capable of stomaching unsavory fare offered at some of the places at which we overnighted.

For now, our wagon traveled light. Will had hired a wainwright in Fincastle to adapt a wagonette to be sturdy enough to handle rough roads. The craftsman had even built a custom roof over the driver and passenger bench, which would help in wet weather. York rode Will's horse, and we ponied Cassie behind the wagon next to an extra mule.

We planned on purchasing furniture and goods in Louisville, so the wagonette would be full to bursting by the time we arrived in St. Louis. "You'll get a finer assortment of furnishings and such in Louisville. I'll let you shop there until your heart's content."

We'd need furnishings for the house, so getting to pick out those items was something I anticipated with pleasure. Never before had I been able to select my own bed or armoire.

Along the trail, wildlife was everywhere. Several times along the way, York or Will shot quail, supplementing the fare we had at inns.

We often saw deer, especially in the mornings, and once, York shouted that he'd seen a panther slinking away.

"You should have seen the game on our trek west," Will said, slapping the reins onto the mules' backsides. "There were places where we could literally walk amid deer or elk. They hadn't yet learned to fear men."

There were high places along the Midland Trail, and before long I heard rushing water as we descended into a lush river valley.

"Is this the Ohio already?"

"No, the Kanawha," he replied. "But it feeds the Ohio, and we'll be following it until we get there."

While in these wild regions, I adored the sound of the water's flow when passing near the banks, coupled with an aromatic smell of pine needles permeating the air. Woodland birdsong was an unending symphony, and Will taught me the names of many of them along with birds of prey that majestically glided high above us in the blue.

One afternoon, in a higher region of the Kanawha wilderness, Will had to reshoe one of the mules, so I volunteered to help York gather firewood. Frankly, I was hoping to get to know the man a bit. York had never even spoken to me, though we'd been traveling together now for several weeks. I was hoping he'd tell me more about Will's people, but he walked briskly ahead, sure-footed as a packhorse—and about as talkative.

"Plenty of deadfall over there," he indicated gruffly, pointing around some large boulders near cliffs that dropped down toward the Kanawha.

Sensing that he desired as little contact with me as possible, I followed his lead and silently picked up the driest pieces I could find, wrapping them in an old shawl I'd brought for that purpose. In only a few minutes, we met up and—again, with few words—I watched York load it all in a large leather pack and hoist it up on his shoulders.

"Missus, you'll need to carry the rifle."

I nodded as he handed it over, shouldering it the way Will had taught me, and together we began the trek back, mostly uphill.

Brawny and fit, it occurred to me that York had drastically changed since our first meeting in 1801. Back then, he'd been rather rotund, but his years with the Corps of Discovery had hardened him, turning him muscular and agile. Just like Will, he could move as dexterously through the woods as a deer, while I panted, breathlessly trying to keep up.

Just as we approached several more of the standing boulders, a large black form shot out from behind one of the rocks in front of York. It happened so quickly that I froze in my tracks, stunned.

York shouted something I couldn't decipher as the bear knocked his feet out from under him with one swipe of a burly paw. The poor man seemed to topple slowly like a felled tree to the earth, and the bear was so fast—one moment confronting, the next atop him, its teeth gripping his shoulder.

Strange how it made no sound, no snarl or roar, but kept at the attack, and it was York who did the howling. With surprising calm, I lifted the rifle, knowing I'd have to make one shot count. The bear was turning, pulling York around—struggling and shouting where he was amid the spilled firewood.

Careful. Don't shoot York.

But the bear started dragging him, and now it was positioned perfectly for me. York was splayed out on his stomach, and I had the advantage of aiming straight at the beast's backside. The gun was already cocked and ready to fire.

Fuh-BOOM!

The report echoed down the canyon and across the river. Sweet heaven, but people probably heard it all the way back in Fincastle, the way my ears were ringing. Whirling, the bear bolted, my eyes following its jerky movement as it bounded at an odd gait, sprinting down the hill and disappearing into underbrush.

I was still amazed that it hadn't made a sound, for there was no doubt in my mind I'd shot the creature in its buttocks.

"*Julia!* Julia, where are you?"

Coming to my senses, I scrambled up to York to assess his condition, shouting back to Will as I moved, "Just down the hill. We're both here."

Soon I heard his shuffling footsteps approaching, and as I knelt next to York, the slave was already sitting up, grumbling about spilling the firewood.

"I'll help you with the firewood, but let's see where it bit you." There was blood on the front of his torn work-shirt, so I tore into the fabric to where his wound was, and that's when Will half slid down the hill to us.

"What happened?"

"A bear attacked him," I said. "A right large one. I shot it."

Will glanced about, obviously half expecting to see it.

"Oh, it ain't dead, Master. It done run down toward the river."

Will smiled proudly. "Well done, Julia! Well done!"

"Well done?" York scoffed with an abrupt snort from someplace down inside his throat. "She ain't shot nothing. She done scared that bear. That's all she done did."

I stared at York, speechless and insulted. I'd just saved his life!

"You best be glad she scared it off, then," Will fired back, examining York's shoulder. "You head on back to the wagon and wash off this blood."

Craning my neck, I thought he'd been mighty fortunate. Only one bloody bite was on his arm.

Will went on. "I'll take another look at this back at camp and make you a poultice. Squeeze out some more blood. It'll help to clean it. But don't you go speaking rudely to Mrs. Clark again, you hear? You be respectful."

"Yessir."

York abruptly arose, gathering the firewood back into the leather satchel, heaving it up on his back, and striding in the direction of the wagon while Will made his way on down to me. Seeing the look on my face, he laughed. "Let him go, angel. I'm mighty proud of how you kept your head. You've proven you can protect yourself and others as well."

Frowning slightly, he stopped again, staring at some disturbed ground where the bear had run away. Leaning over, he swiped at a leaf. When he held out his hand, I saw the blood. He looked up at me, one brow cocked and pride glistening in his eyes as I stood there, still holding the rifle.

"You hit it! You really *did!*"

※※※

Anybody from Fincastle knew about Point Pleasant.

It was memorialized by veterans back home in Botetourt County because of the bloody battle that had taken place here before I'd been born, back in '74—before we had become the United States. Virginia militia, including men from Fincastle, had fought and defeated a native alliance under Chief Cornstalk.

Will halted the wagon in some trees and offered me a hand down. "Let's walk a piece. I want you to see the view."

Hand in hand, we hiked a quarter of a mile through the woods until everything opened up. Here, the Kanawha joined the broadest body of water I'd ever seen. Just like the bear, it wasn't noisy, but moved in powerful surety: steady and strong.

"Behold the Ohio," Will said, nodding toward the powerful flow.

"It's huge."

"Wait until you see the Mississippi. It's at least twice as wide in most places."

My head shook in awe, and I heard a soft sucking sound as the water lapped against the bank, as though clinging to the silt in vain.

We rested at Point Pleasant for two days while Will hired a flatboat man to take us first to Louisville, then on to St. Louis. Once that was settled, our wagon was eased onto the boat along with our stock and tack, everything tied down and secured with wooden chocks wedged beneath the wagon's wheels. While Will and York were immersed with that task, I busied myself preparing a list of items we'd need to purchase for housekeeping in St. Louis.

Upon docking in Louisville, we spent most of the afternoon shopping for furniture. I'd never seen such a large city, with impressive shops, churches, and even a hotel. Among the sundry things we bought were two lovely cherry bedsteads—one for us and one for houseguests—a medium-sized mahogany secretary, a dozen chairs, a settee, numerous cooking utensils, and fine china. Will arranged for the items to be delivered to the dock prior to our departure for loading, after which they'd need to be transferred to our wagon.

While we shopped, York rode to Jonathan Clark's home at Trough Spring, alerting the family of our arrival. Upon returning to the dock from our purchases, Will and I gathered a few loose possessions from the wagon, which would remain on the boat. Hoofbeats and the grind of wagon wheels announced the arrival of his brother's brood, coming to drive us to their homestead.

I stepped off the flatboat to a shrill female voice heralding me from the arriving Conestoga wagon. "Julia Clark? I've been longing to meet you!"

A compact, stout woman leaped down, embracing me with arms like a vise. Both of my hands were full, porting baskets of personal articles as I was, including my heavy Shakespeare book and a week's worth of clothing, all of which prevented me from returning her affections. All I could do was smile foolishly.

"You must be exhausted, and in your condition too," she rambled on. "We'll get you home, get you fed, and I'm having a warm bath drawn for you as I speak."

I squeaked in ecstasy. "A *bath*?"

She laughed at my glee, warbling on like a bird as she snatched one of the baskets from me. "Yes, a *bath*, sweet girl. And I'll add peppermint oil to it too. If that doesn't spoil you, nothing will. Now hand over that second basket. We're here to help you load anything into our wagon you don't want drunken sailors a-pilfering."

I managed to squeeze in one phrase, "You must be—"

"I'm *dreadful* sorry! I'm Sarah Hite Clark, Jonathan's wife. We're sisters by marriage now, you and me, but just consider me your Kentucky mother. Why, I've been a-praying for this to happen now for years and years. William was one tough mule to hitch, but you took care of it easy enough. Come along now," she beckoned with her head, and I followed.

Sarah made me smile. Crinkles surrounded her merry eyes, suggesting a challenging life of years on the Kentucky frontier. Her hands were calloused as tanned leather, but her hair was still thick and brown as molasses, neatly tied beneath a bonnet.

"Is this my Aunt Julia?" a similarly high but youthful voice demanded.

"Yes, Nanny, but don't you trouble her today. She's too tired to talk, I'll warrant." She glanced back at me. "Oh my—just *look* at her—a genuine Virginia *lady*, all elegant and proper. Look at that lovely dress."

I laughed. My lovely dress was actually a hand-me-down Harri had given me for travel, covered with an old apron of Megg's because I wanted something to remember her by. I focused on this girl who was my new niece—Nanny—one Will had said was only a year or two younger than I. "I'm so delighted to meet you, Nanny."

Sarah popped the whip at the mules, and the wagon tossed me forward just enough to lean in and kiss the girl's cheek.

I hadn't realized how starved I was for female company. As Sarah Hite Clark drove us on to Trough Spring with Nanny by my side, I didn't even bother to look back for Will, who, along with Jonathan, was leading our stock off the flatboat.

Having lived at Santillane as I had, Trough Spring seemed more like a glorified two-story cabin with long logs, chinking, and a few windows covered in oiled paper. *This* was a true frontier homestead, and it caused me to wonder about the dwelling Meriwether had found us in St. Louis. That being said, I loved Jonathan and Sarah's place, for it was cozy—a clean and pleasurable haven, full of delightful cooking smells and laughter. Perfect hospitality.

Several of their children still lived with them. Mary was a year or two older than me, and Bill was their youngest son, named after my husband. While Sarah continued preparations for our meal alongside Mary and an enslaved woman, Nanny ushered me upstairs to a loft of sorts, where a steaming bath awaited in a large tub, similar to one we used at Santillane. My new niece even helped me undress, and soon I was sinking into warm water up to my chin, holding my breath, and allowing myself complete submersion. I hadn't been able to wash up much at all since before leaving home, so never in my lifetime had a bath felt as good.

After scrubbing until my flesh tingled, I dressed and went back down where Will and my brother-in-law Jonathan now sat at the dinner table next to Bill, each man sipping ale, their stockinged feet propped up on a couple of chairs. Nanny stood at the fireplace, spooning steaming food into bowls, and Sarah brought warm bread to the table.

When the men spied me, they scrambled to their feet.

Jonathan, the oldest son in the Clark clan, whom Will considered his closest sibling, was a distinguished sort with graying hair tied back into a queue with a scrap of leather. Though he was powerfully built, like his youngest brother, I still saw age weighing upon him. His eyes were as dark as chips of cobalt glass, but wrinkles lined the edges. Still, the brothers' resemblance was uncanny in the shape of their faces, from forehead to jawline.

"Julia Clark," Jonathan said, embracing me with his great arms, fatherly-like. "Welcome to our family. I can already see the sweet soul my brother has so admired in you."

"You should see her writing," Will quipped, settling back down onto the bench again. He sipped some ale before adding, "And she loves to read too. I married for intelligence, brother. And right before arriving at Point Pleasant, she rescued York from a bear! Shot it right in the ass."

Jonathan laughed loudly, a big, booming laugh like his brother had—like Papa's. "If this young lady can fire a gun into a bear's ass, then I reckon she'll make one *hell* of a Clark!"

"And don't forget her genteel loveliness," Sarah added, toting a large pottery pitcher of small ale our way and smacking Will in the head with a wooden spoon. "Bear's ass…"

Jonathan directed me to the bench across from him and I sat

down, the men reseating themselves as Mary placed a bowl of steaming venison stew before me. I ate my full share, including homemade white bread and butter and the heaping slice of dried-apple pie that Mary and Nanny had concocted from last autumn's harvest, served with chilled cream.

"George visited a month back," Sarah said after we'd all eaten and Nanny poked the fire back to warmth. The evening had turned cool.

"How's he faring?" Will asked.

Jonathan wagged his head, sighing. "Those Washington City bastards have no idea what they've done to such a good man—one who sacrificed so much for them—to just sit by, smoke their fancy pipes, and eat their custards. They've still not acknowledged or supported George with any payment whatsoever. So he's been back to drinking of late, and what a damned unpleasant drunk is our brother." With a quick nod to Sarah and me, he added hastily, "Excuse my temper, ladies."

"You're more than entitled to it," Sarah said. "'Tis a good thing your late parents aren't here to see him, William. Lately, he's been in a sad state, he has."

Jonathan shook his head, his face sorrowful.

Will reached over, clapping him on the back. "I wish I had time to cross the river and see him this trip, but we have to leave in a few days. Much work lies ahead of me in St. Louis, plus setting up housekeeping. I'll try to send him more financial assistance if I'm able."

Sarah changed the subject, asking Will, "Which of your people will be going with you?"

"I've made a list. Lewis has arranged for most to be hired out once we arrive since we won't have room for them all. It'll help put a little savings into my pocket for a house."

"I know you'll insist on keeping York with you, but that Scott is a good sort," Jonathan commented. "Of all of them here on the property, he's the hardest working man—does chores inside the house and out. Great at fixing things. You might want to pack him along with his woman, Chloe, and their little daughter. They'd be fine house-slaves for you, just starting out."

Sitting there listening, I took note of those names: Scott and Chloe. I'd have to remember them.

Chapter XI

Louisville on to St. Louis
June & July 1808

Will's people were mostly inherited from his parents, and until he had a place of his own, Jonathan kept them. The list of those traveling with us to St. Louis was longer than I expected: *Juba, Sillow, Scott, Chloe, Rachel, Aleck, Tenor, Venus, Ben, Frankie, Lew, Kitt, James, Easter, Nancy.*

Desiring to begin my acquaintance with them, I requested an introduction. The meeting took place in Jonathan's barn during a June rain. It was humid, and every ebony-skinned face before us shone with sweat. A few sat on hay bales, attentive and listening, while others stood against the wall or slouched in corners, arms crossed and sullen.

Will took my hand and spoke with that deep, rich voice of his, "I've gathered you all together today so you're aware of our plans, and I wanted you to meet your new mistress, Mrs. Clark."

I smiled as warmly as I could, nodding to them politely.

"We'll be leaving here tomorrow," Will continued. "I'm aware that many of you traveling with us are apprehensive about St. Louis, as we'll temporarily be living in a smaller house for a year or so. Once we arrive, most of you will be hired out and placed in houses or businesses according to your skills and abilities. However, should you be placed somewhere and expected to work at different tasks, you must be willing to adapt. Remember, this will be a temporary inconvenience for all of us—not just you."

I swallowed, for as Will spoke, I saw faces already expressing disgruntlement. York in particular stood in the back and spat on the floor, looking away in malcontent. For a man who had traveled all the way to the Pacific with the Corps of Discovery and was considered Will's trusted slave, his behavior perplexed me.

He was a bitter man.

When the meeting broke up, he strode forward, straight to Will. "You already know what I's gonna ask, Master."

"I do, and you already know my answer. You'll also have a special task once we arrive at the Cumberland."

York glared at Will, his dark brown eyes deep, unyielding, hard.

"We'll be stopping at Fort Massac for some militia to board and to load government goods. After that, we'll be short on space, so you'll lead the others off the boat and proceed overland to the Mississippi, then boat over to St. Louis. I'll provide you with a wallet of money to see all of you to us safely."

"That's a long way for some of them folk to walk," York stated.

"Clearly not as long as it was to the Pacific, so no dawdling. Upon your arrival, we'll manage the hiring out."

York slowly shook his head, his jaw working about in dissatisfaction. Will grabbed his arm, speaking low. "I'll expect you ready to leave tomorrow morning at dawn with everyone else. Don't you *dare* be late, or we'll have things to settle between us."

Will's imperious tone sent shivers up my spine; York's stifled ire was bottled up—explosive. The slave pivoted about and stalked away, saying nothing more, his jaw still
grinding rhythmically in a stiff, repetitive motion.

Every set of enslaved eyes were upon him, following him as he returned to slouch against the back wall.

I knew too little about this man who Indians from St. Louis all the way to the Pacific coast had marveled at, his obsidian skin and intimidating size dwarfing most folk. I'd need to learn more about him, for he had been with Will through thick and thin, yet he was a very angry man.

Before we left Louisville, Sarah took it upon herself to school me in a new skill: the art of Dresden lace. Embroidery on its own had never fascinated me, but working Dresden lace was more interesting, and since I always enjoyed a challenge, Sarah took the time to teach me.

"Your little one will need a sweet cap to sleep in and for christening, so I've made up this pattern for you," she explained, presenting me with a stiff paper form upon which muslin was secured. Next, she guided me in aligning some wooden bobbins around the dainty fabric, where it was fixed.

"Mama had us girls embroider and cross-stitch samplers, but I never practiced like they did. I've always preferred reading," I said, taking care in each step of the work.

Sarah was all encouragement. "Well, with us practicing together, you'll be able to finish this cap on your own in St. Louis. It's something I thought I could share with you for the baby."

Indeed, my waist was just starting to expand, a constant reminder of the tiny life developing inside me. Peaceful patters of gentle rain blended with the crackling fire, and all morning, working on this little cap kept my mind on the tiny child I'd be greeting come winter.

Sarah prompted me whenever the bobbins needed readjusting. Will and Jonathan had gone to see to the loading of the flatboat, so it would be a while before they returned—a perfect opportunity to inquire about York.

"Sarah, when Will introduced me to his people, York spoke to him and seemed awfully angry. Did something happen between them that I should know about?"

Sarah nodded. "Ah, yes. I know all about that. It started shortly after they returned from the Pacific. See, York has a woman here, owned by another family not far from our place. That's why he desperately wants to stay in Louisville. Jonathan's tried to get William to trade him for one of our folks or simply free him, but he won't."

I paused my work, looking at her in puzzlement. "Why not?" It didn't make sense. The solution was so simple and obvious. Allow York to stay, or set him free to enjoy his life.

Sarah shook her head and blew out her cheeks, revealing her own consternation. "Only the Almighty knows what causes men to act the way they do, but I think William resents the fact that York wants a life separate from his. York and William grew up together as children and once had a powerful bond, straight through to adulthood. Never was it stronger than when they went west together. Out there, Indians thought York was powerful medicine, and he was a hard worker, treated fairly and kindly by the men in the Corps. But once they were back..." Her eyes locked on to mine as she shook her head again. "Now, we both know that William's a good, good man. But after returning, York was nothing but his property again. Sure, he was a slave when he went west, but he felt freer out there than he does now here. 'Tis a sad state of affairs, slavery. Were it up to me, every one of mine and Jonathan's would be set free as birds."

I set aside the Dresden work, grasping Sarah's hands and looking at her in utter joy. "Oh, Sarah! That's *just* how I feel!" What joy to have discovered another soul with abolitionist leanings—one within the Clark family. And it was so helpful having her insight on this matter.

She squeezed my fingers in hers, smiling. "You'll need to learn to care for your husband's people by working at their sides, looking after their health and grooming, and keeping them well-fed. Those three things will make their desolate lives an easier burden. That's all we women can do for now."

I'd take that to heart and remember her words well. Then, thinking back to what she'd said about York, I asked, "Does York have children with this woman in Louisville?"

"Oh yes. He spends every moment he can with them whenever he and William visit."

Such a heartbreaking state of affairs. To do any good by York or any of the other enslaved, I'd be walking a delicate line, especially since Will's emotions and opinions were likely at play in this matter. But help them as Sarah said?

Oh, I would. I'd find ways.

The flatboat trip from Louisville to Louisiana Territory was more crowded than the first segment. Lots of folk were aboard, all of them eager to head west.

My first glimpse of St. Louis was its river moorings, behind which rose solid, whitewashed walls of stone delineating the waterfront. From my initial perspective, all appeared neat and orderly.

Sailors were still securing lines when Will offered me his hand to disembark. I stepped carefully over a rough, narrow wooden plank through mudflats at the edge of the quay. All around us were smaller bobbing boats tethered to broad stakes. Upon smelling rot and hearing loud squeals and snorts, my first impressions of the city faded. Just paces away, a boy in mud up to his knees chased a muck-covered sow through the flats.

I waited while Will hired a wagon to take me to our house. He'd be staying at the docks to help unload the furniture to be transported there. Twenty or so soldiers from Fort Massac had joined us, led by Nathaniel Pryor, another of Will's Corps of Discovery comrades. They disembarked the flatboat behind us, awaiting Will's leisure.

From the shore, I scanned the area. St. Louis had fooled me on our approach. It was as muddy as a pigsty, without a single cobbled road in sight. The town had undoubtedly experienced heavy rains in the last day or so. Regardless, life and work continued, even in quagmire-like conditions.

Men astride hardy little ponies ploughed through the mess, headed to their destinations, while those on foot sloughed along, wearing high boots or laced-up moccasins. Light two-wheeled willow carts embellished with caning, similar to chairs back home, rattled effortlessly through the muddied paths. I noted several driven by women wearing odd-looking turbans on their heads and shapeless skirts that looked more like sacks.

I'd stepped into a world devoid of refinement.

Close to the dock where we stood, the raised stone walls I'd seen from the flatboat had hidden groups of fur trappers and rugged workmen, arguing in animated French. Low clapboard buildings were interspersed with double-storied brick structures of both American and French architecture. I couldn't help but favor the two-storied French styles, complete with galleries where people could peacefully sit above the street activity.

Then I beheld my first Indians. Some were women, their infants in stiff, beaded cradleboards strapped to their backs. Their men stood nearby, talking among themselves with rapid hand signals as well as verbal conversation. Many wore copious feathers in their hair, and their attire was an eyeful, with skin leggings up past their thighs and another flap—or loincloth—of hide, concealing their privates.

Just when my fascination with dyed leather and quilled native costume had consumed me, a huge mud-spattered buckboard pulled up and Will said gently, "Welcome to St. Louis, angel—exactly what I meant when I described it as a frontier town. And this," he gestured at the driver, "is Monsieur LeBeau. I've sent a private on ahead to let Lewis know we've arrived. He'll be awaiting you."

LeBeau grinned down at us, displaying a worrisome array of rotting teeth. He didn't strike me as particularly dependable, but Will apparently trusted him enough to deposit me wherever we'd be living.

"Our place isn't far," Will assured. "I need to see to the unloading of the boat. My men will help me haul everything over later today. I promise we'll sleep in our new soft bed tonight."

He assisted me up onto the tall buckboard—the highest, most unstable monstrosity of a conveyance I'd ever seen. The seats were nothing more than rough, unevenly planed planks of wood, and I steadied myself, trying to sit as far from LeBeau as possible without risk of toppling off the other side. Behind me, soldiers loaded my personal belongings onto the back of the wagon. Then LeBeau cracked his whip and the mules jerked forward. Sludge splattered everywhere, and I felt wet goo land on my right cheek. I risked a quick swipe to clean it off as we pitched forward.

While passing through the village—for now I saw that St. Louis could hardly be considered a town like Louisville—I heard some French women calling from one of the elegant-looking galleries above us. There, painted and scantily dressed prostitutes whistled and laughed. One of the girls, dressed in an ill-fitting corset and tattered yellow petticoat, hailed LeBeau. "Ay, LeBeau! Come tonight and I'll wash the mud from your cock!"

"*Bien sûr*, mademoiselle!" LeBeau shouted back, honking a lust-filled laugh.

I found myself blinking in shock, for I'd not heard any man except for Sticks Howard use such language in my presence before. And that had only happened once.

Another of the loose women bared her breasts, flopping them around for all to see, giggling shamelessly and hooting to workmen below, who paused from unloading barrels to look up, whooping and pointing. I tightened my grip on the rickety bench, fixing my eyes on the furrowed road ahead, dismayed to see two skeletal dogs foraging on the carcass of a donkey right in the middle of the street.

And yet many of the buildings along the way were fashionable, neatly constructed clapboard structures that appeared reputable. Even a few stone houses were mixed in, most being simple one-story affairs that were neat as pins. One log-cabin house was especially striking. Made partly of stone, its log beams ran vertical instead of horizontal, as I was used to seeing back east.

"Monsieur, what sort of building style is that?" I ventured, pointing at the place.

"*C'est Français,*" he replied, gruffly.

Fortunately, the house in which we'd live was not along the rowdy street. With the busiest part of town behind us, we entered a quieter area with several other homes nearby—all of which were unpainted clapboard with wide-open views of the Mississippi.

LeBeau reined in, and I saw a respectable little house built in the French style except that the covered veranda was on the first story. It looked pleasant enough—quaint, like a cottage.

A dog was barking, and Seaman bounded out to greet me. Just behind him, bursting out in welcome, came Meriwether Lewis. "Julia! You must be exhausted. Welcome home!"

He hurried to the wagon, and I allowed him to lift me down safely, relieved to be done with Monsieur LeBeau's company.

Lewis nodded curtly to Monsieur, who lifted my things from the back, depositing them in front of the house.

"And how fares the bride?" Meriwether cheerfully inquired.

"She fares very well," I forced, smiling to mask the uncertainty of my new surroundings, not to mention the memory of Lewis's feverish and unkempt state one night at Santillane last November.

"Of course," he said. *"Love sought is good; but given unsought—"*

"—is better," I completed for him, charmed that he'd brought up Shakespeare. Then I added quickly, *"Twelfth Night—*Act III, I think? Didn't Viola say that?"

"Ah, you've been reading. But I'm afraid it was Olivia," he corrected, bowing politely and offering me his arm.

We entered the house as John Pernier materialized to port in my bags. Meriwether was obviously eager to give me a tour. "There's a cellar accessible on the side of the house, though I won't bother taking you down there now. Let's start with the interior, shall we?"

Immediately, I noticed a sparsity of space in the entry, where a narrow hall led to the back of the house. Pausing in front of a room, Meriwether gestured. "This front room is where I imagined you and William sleeping. It's right across from what I've started using as a drawing room."

Oh, but every room was tiny. How spoiled I was by Santillane. As for the room designated for Will and me? I glanced inside, biting my lip. Most of the space would be gone once our bed was set up.

Meriwether beckoned me to look back into the hallway again. "Here, across from my room, is an additional chamber where guests might be comfortable. And to the rear is a small cubby in which William and I might share office space. Should he require more room, I'll move into a separate office in town."

"Is there any other living space besides the drawing room?" I asked.

"There's one more room behind the back guest chamber that should suit for dining. Here it is," he said, showing me in. It was surprisingly well-lit, with a large glass window displaying the backyard and outbuildings, one of which was especially large, with two chimneys."

"Is that—"

"The kitchen? Yes. And it's huge, with two fireplaces and a bake oven. And right above us there's attic space enough for a couple of servants, accessed by a fold-down ladder here in this wall." He patted it, a hollow thud of empty space sounding. "If you and William keep a couple of his people here, they're welcome to live up there. My man Pernier sleeps on a separate pallet in my room."

It would do for now. It had to.

"I hope you realize how welcome you are," he said. "Let me see: *Good company, good wine, good welcome can make good people.*"

I jumped at his challenge, for I'd just read this. "*Henry VIII*— Guildford?"

"Correct! Come out to the kitchen and I'll offer you some tea."

Thank goodness for Shakespeare. It was the only civilized thing I'd experienced in this wild country so far.

❦

Scott, Chloe, and Rachel.

Jonathan had recommended Scott as a good, hard, and honest worker, and I intended to see that he'd never be separated from his woman and child. Today, they stood behind me while I completed the hiring out of the last two slaves, destined to leave with their temporary masters.

It was horrible, making such decisions over people's lives. Every shred of my being rebelled at what I was charged with doing. Though the alternative—selling them—was less favorable. If only Will had left more of them with Jonathan. However, they'd been there for an extended period, and he'd wanted to move them nearer to his own residence. And, of course, the bottom line was that money would be made from hiring them out.

These last two turned out to be York's siblings. Nancy and Juba were his half brother and sister.

"I's just as good a cook as Chloe," Nancy challenged, her face stony and hard. "Ain't no reason why I shouldn't stay put here instead of her." She had an odd habit of sucking on her teeth, and she commenced with such after stating her qualifications.

"I'm afraid the decision has already been made," I said as gently as possible, though I was nearly crawling out of my skin, saddled with this dreadful task. Conscience in knots, I'd be losing sleep over this for months. However, to do them any good in the long-run, I had to play my game wisely. "I'm merely carrying out the general's wishes on the matter. Remember, your hiring out shouldn't be for more than a year, and should we move elsewhere with more space, you'd be returned to us. Governor Lewis made provision for such in the contracts."

Indeed, I prayed they could all return sooner than later, but now that the deed was done, I acquainted myself with the three who were staying.

Scott had a gentle, well-meaning countenance; his dark, round face was honest and forthright. He wasn't overly tall like York, but he was built stocky and erect. Chloe liked to hum or sing while she worked, something I found pleasing. With full lips that easily curled into gentle smiles, she had a motherly disposition, naturally acquired from tending her little girl, Rachel, a charming child, petite and well-mannered.

Jonathan had been right to have spoken so highly of this little family, and I tried to put the past few days of the hiring out behind me, focusing instead on getting settled. All three of them worked with me to set up housekeeping. Chloe crafted white linen curtains, Rachel swept the house daily, and the three of us cooked meals together, Chloe teaching me how to make yeast rolls.

She wasn't dear Megg, but I could see how we could become close, Chloe and I.

Meanwhile, Will settled into his many responsibilities along with Meriwether, both men deciding on office space elsewhere in town so that the tiny room in the back could be used for storage.

Each evening, I'd see to the last of the dirty dishes at Chloe's side, then go back inside to the drawing room or our chamber, where Will would be waiting. We were still celebrating a honeymoon of sorts, for I was still early enough along in my pregnancy to crave lovemaking.

Tonight, I found Will stretched out on our bed, propping his head up with crossed arms. Noticing a slight frown of concern, I asked what was wrong.

"It's Lewis," he explained. "He's just not been himself—not since we've started our official positions here."

"How so?"

"Well, first off, politics here are damned mercurial. Jefferson appointed a Secretary of the Territory—Frederick Bates. Now that Lewis is governor, Bates has turned into a sort of 'second,' and he much prefers the captain's chair, which was what he more or less had until Lewis arrived. Granted, I've locked horns with Bates myself on more than one occasion. However, he and Lewis are like fire and gunpowder, setting each other off into angry bouts of arguments. I tell you, when that happens, being around either is never pleasant. At times, I find myself caught in the middle, and as much as I hold Lewis in esteem, his behavior around Bates concerns me, for whenever they argue, things get tense and he turns to drink. He's complained more about his health lately, and at times his overall state of mind seems to be . . . I don't know how else to say this—*compromised*."

Bates... I recalled that name from one of Will's previous letters. I sat down, brushing my hair and plaiting it. "Hearing you say such does sound worrisome."

He sighed, shaking his head. "There's an instability about him I've never felt before. Certainly not on the expedition. Lewis had perfect clarity of thought and clear-minded leadership then."

"How has he been different?"

"Sometimes in meetings he's snappy and curt—especially with Bates's colleagues that he should be trying to win over. And here's something else—after all of that time spent in Philadelphia garnering a publisher and hiring specialists to add art and edits to all of the scientific observations, would you believe he's done absolutely *nothing* on our journals? Frankly, I'm beginning to wish Jefferson had had him focus on that task alone and granted the governorship to someone else. It's as though Lewis is struggling to manage his own business."

"Are you sure he's done nothing on the journals? The publisher printed a prospectus. I even saw a copy of it when he visited Santillane last November. Won't they be depending on him to deliver a complete manuscript to them soon?"

"Yes, but I'm certain. He's done *nothing* on them. Nothing at all."

I secured my second thick plait with some yarn, tucking my hair up under a linen nightcap. "What a shame. That prospectus made the end product sound incredible. Maybe you should gently press him to get busy on it?"

"Believe me, I have, even offering evenings of my time if he'd just sit down with me and show me what needs doing. By God, Patrick Gass and Robert Frazer are bound to steal all of our readers from under us."

"My hope is that their books merely whet the appetites of readers for yours."

"Doubtful. When folks dine at a banquet, first helpings are always the most satisfying. Fewer people return for extras."

Unfortunately, that was true.

"When did Meriwether's problems with Bates begin?"

Will scratched his head. "I'm really not sure. Lewis was a good friend with his brother Tarleton, who was also vying to acquire the position of Jefferson's secretary. As you know, the president awarded it to Lewis instead. Bates is petty enough to hold something like that against Lewis, even now." He snorted before adding, "Frankly, I think Bates is jealous at the strong partnership Lewis and I have."

I smiled. "The Corps of Discovery defined you both. It made you two what you are today. You can't argue that."

"No. I can't. I just hope he'll exercise more wisdom and discernment now that he holds the highest office in Louisiana Territory."

"I imagine he's lonely at the top, and we both know he wants to marry. You have my company—something he isn't even close to acquiring."

He nodded. "Indeed. We've nothing to be concerned about, the two of us, except for the house."

Ha! *He'd* brought it up, and I whirled about on my dressing chair. "It's *so* small, Will. If I stand and take two steps, I'm at our bed. With your long legs, you're only a step or so from the door, and should I swing my own out of bed in a hurry, I smack them right into our wardrobe. You and Lewis both have to take your meetings with other men elsewhere, and there's just no privacy here for us as a newly married couple."

"Problem is there aren't many houses to let in St. Louis, and we need to save up before finding our own place, for I want a special home for us."

"Might I help by looking for a new temporary place?"

He smiled, patting the empty side of the bed where I slept. "That's more than reasonable. But not a word to Lewis about it. He did his best finding this current abode. Now take your two steps over here and come to bed."

I smiled, rising and stepping twice, slipping beneath the linens.

Chapter XII

July-Late August 1808
St. Louis

St. Louis's most prominent family was a French-Creole brood by the name of Chouteau. Their massive mansion couldn't be missed, standing tall and capacious along the main street of the town. Between furs and wise investments, they'd made their fortune even prior to the territory passing from France to the United States.

With a new governor and staff in place, the Chouteaus invited Meriwether, Will, and me as honored guests to a reception to be held at Christy's Tavern, the very place where the two explorers had been feted upon their return from the west. The prospect of attending this social gathering filled me with excitement, for I believed that the more people I met and the more I learned about the lay of this land, the better I could support Will in his career.

Christy's Tavern, owned by the entrepreneur Major William Christy and family, was surprisingly fashionable. In no way was it the typical rustic Virginia or Kentucky tavern. Hors d'oeuvres in the serving line were arranged on fine china with silver service as sparkling as Mama's back home, accompanied with fine crystal wineglasses. Draperies of rich burgundy velvet separated individual sitting areas so that guests had privacy in a stylish way, and candles on each table flickered inside cut-glass globes, casting magical lighting throughout the gathering space. How surprising that such tasteful sophistication existed in a community so remote and often inelegant.

Once we arrived, it was naturally the Chouteaus I met first, just inside the entrance. Will introduced me. "Julia, I present to you Monsieur Auguste Chouteau and his wife, Marie-Thérèse."

"*Bienvenue,* Madame Clark," Auguste bowed deeply over my hand. He seemed a serious man, middle-aged, with a receding hairline. Marie-Thérèse possessed a motherly face and round, matronly figure. She gently took my hands, welcoming me to the west.

Next was a dashing gentleman, dark-haired and handsome, greeting us with a trumpet-like flourish. "Général! Let me meet your lovely bride!"

I couldn't help but smile at his flamboyance.

"Julia," Will said, "this is Jean-Pierre Chouteau, the younger of the Chouteau brothers."

"*Oui,* and the most gallant," Jean-Pierre said, laughing and snatching up my hand for a light kiss.

Lewis ambled up to our little group, escorting the most austere woman I'd ever seen.

Since my first day in St. Louis, I'd noticed hardworking Creole women on the streets dressing in simple wool or cotton skirts and blouses, but I hadn't expected any woman at such an elegant event to be as humbly attired. Who only knew what color or length was this lady's hair, for it was completely concealed beneath a plain turban-like headdress, knotted neatly in the center. Her chemise was dull gray, and the skirt she wore clear to the floor was a darker shade of blue. Despite straight and sure posture, she used a magnificently carved wood-and-ivory walking cane, the only ornamented part of her ensemble.

Having heard Will and Meriwether speak of this family, I knew she could be only one person—the eccentric matriarch of the Chouteaus, known around town as the "Mother of St. Louis." Of her two sons I'd just met, she more resembled Auguste than Jean-Pierre.

Meriwether introduced her. "Madame Chouteau, I present to you Mrs. Julia Clark, the general's wife, newly arrived from Virginia."

I curtsied slightly before her, grateful that Will and Meriwether had prepared me for such introductions.

Madame's proud blue-gray eyes swept over me; her head tilted sideways as I was awarded the phantom of a smile. "Général Clark has brought loveliness to *ma ville*," she assessed in excellent English, touched only by the expected French words and accent. "Le Général is an adventurous and noble man, deserving of such a well-born wife."

"*Merci*, madame. I'm honored by your hospitality this evening."

Only days ago, Will and Meriwether had given me an earful about her. Decades earlier, well before the turn of a new century, she and her lover, the daring fur trapper Pierre Laclède, left New Orleans, where her husband had deserted her. Together, they settled this village on the frontier, where scandal could be avoided and their sin overlooked. Now, her generosity and humble nature were celebrated by the people of St. Louis, and she remained the heart of the Chouteau family.

Meriwether smiled, interjecting, "Now that you ladies are so well met, I'll excuse myself and join the general so you two may chat."

I was eager for new friends in this foreign place, so I inquired, "Do you enjoy reading, perhaps?"

"Oh, not me, no. But my sons devour books. In fact, they have spent a great deal of time and money on a library at our home. For myself, I have my bees."

"Bees?"

"*Oui*. They are my pets—*ma joie de vivre*. All of St. Louis values my prized honey, and I will send some to you as a gift, *ma cherie*."

"My, that would be lovely, thank you. General Clark and I are expecting this winter, and I'm craving sweets." I touched my lower abdomen lightly, for current high-waisted fashions still kept my secret.

"*C'est pas vrai!*" she exclaimed, glancing down at my stomach. "You are slender and tall, concealing it well. Indeed, you and the little one shall have honey soon."

"You're most kind, and this reception is wonderful—the first I've had since getting married and leaving Virginia."

"You are most welcome, but understand that St. Louis is full of a different sort of people—some of whom will not be to your refined tastes, I know. But you must never look askance at those who are different. Many times, they are the ones who will be true." She nodded across the room at a woman who was well-attired yet unescorted, speaking in a low voice to several fur-trapper types. They were also fashionably attired, aside from unkempt hair and beards giving them away. "That lady is Mademoiselle Escoffier. She runs a local brothel, but do not judge her too harshly, for if there is a child or widow in need, she is always the first to offer them provision."

After seeing half-naked prostitutes on my way into town that first day, I was stunned at Escoffier's modest and excellent taste. Her simple but fashionable silk gown was rose-colored and altogether tasteful, not at all suggestive of her trade.

Madame nodded again, this time to the left, where a middle-aged couple sipped champagne, conversing with Jean-Pierre in animated French. "That is Dr. Saugrain and his wife, Genevieve. He was the very first physician to settle here and underwent a frightening initiation to the frontier, being wounded and chased by Indians. He left France when la Revolution was becoming dangerous, and you must know this"—she pressed her lips close to my ear—"his sister married Monsieur Guillotin, who invented *Madame Guillotine*!" She drew away, sweeping her hand beneath her neck in a cutting motion.

My jaw went slack. "Really?"

"*Oui*. He met Genevieve here, after his trouble with the Indians. They fell in love, settled in St. Louis, and he is an excellent physician."

As unusual as she was, Madame Chouteau entranced me. She took my hand, walking me about the spacious tavern room, nodding to someone, telling me about them, their background, and even whether it would be best to be alone in their company.

After a time, I noticed Will speaking with a gentleman in the back of the room. "Who is my husband speaking with?" I asked.

Madame cocked a brow, pursing her lips in disgust. "A man whose worth to the *territoire* I still question," she sniffed. "Go and meet him. Decide for yourself."

What did she mean? I looked back again to where Will stood

among a small group of men, noting that most of his conversation was directed to a young, stately gentleman.

"Ah, hello, my angel," Will exclaimed as I joined him. "Here's someone you must meet." With a knowing wink, he said, "I present you to Secretary Frederick Bates, who originally hails from Ohio."

Ah! Meriwether's cantankerous Bates.

"What a pleasure, sir." There was an awkward moment when I extended my hand, as I'd done to everyone else that evening. However, Bates ignored it, nodding in my direction instead.

"Mrs. Clark," he said simply, his gaze appearing to pass me by and rest elsewhere.

Haughty man.

"You've not had champagne, have you?" Will asked me. "I'll remedy that. Bates, if you might entertain my wife, I'll fetch her something to drink."

Bates had one thing in his favor, for like Jean-Pierre Chouteau, he was yet another strikingly fine-looking man, with a face more youthful than his purported rank and experience. Deep-set brown eyes glistened below dark hair, stylishly tousled per the fashion trend, and the back collar of his black suitcoat rode high on his neck. At his throat, he sported an impeccably tied white cravat pierced with a sparkling silver pin.

He didn't seem inclined to chat, so I pried him for conversation myself. "You, my husband, and Governor Lewis must have few spare minutes with such an enormous territory."

"Indeed, and I'm most grateful that your husband has been more helpful than the governor," was Bates's trenchant reply. "Lewis's delay in arriving was unprecedented. Most men given his position would have hastened to their post, but by God, he didn't bother arriving until an entire year had passed from the date of his appointment. I can't imagine that's what the president intended." He capped his spicy vent with a swift swig of gin.

"There was much for him to do," I said in Meriwether's defense. "Jefferson himself is anxious for the Corps of Discovery journals to be published. They're integral for a national comprehension of our western lands."

One of Bates's friends behind him interrupted abruptly. "Freddie, look there what's a-coming through the door."

My eyes followed Bates's just in time to see a native man in white-man's attire enter, surrounded by a small entourage of militia.

"Oh, damn it *all!*" Bates hissed under his breath. "Why is *he* here?"

"Probably for the free drink, like most Injuns," another of his friends crowed indiscreetly enough for everyone in the entire tavern to have heard.

Altogether, Bates had four fellows at his side, a hodgepodge who obviously worked closely with him and followed his lead on most everything. They reminded me of bullies, ready to taunt whomever their ringleader targeted. And in this case, the sport was a hapless native, just arriving.

Bates growled to his retinue, "First, he complains of his board, then he demands to live closer St. Louis. Now, I've heard he calls himself Jefferson's *brother!*" He shook his head in disgust, and a chorus of derisive male laughter ensued.

"Filthy native," muttered another of them.

"Who is he?" I ventured.

"Chief Sheheke of the Mandan. He was supposed to go home, but your husband's efforts to send him upriver were disastrous."

I blinked, shocked at how rudely Bates stated Will's failure, which wasn't actually failure, but bad luck and timing. Even after such brief interaction, I could well understand why Will and Meriwether disliked him. His mouth was a loaded cannon.

Intrigued by Sheheke, I used my sweetest, ladylike voice and placed one hand lightly on his arm, imploring, "Please, Secretary Bates, would you introduce me?"

It was a moment to relish, for Bates stiffened and stared at me in arrogant annoyance. Forced into courtesy, he took another swallow of gin before setting the glass down with a clunk and escorting me to where the chief stood.

Indeed, Chief Sheheke's entrance had captured the attention of everyone in the tavern. The Chouteau men were gathering around him, already exchanging pleasantries, and now Will and Meriwether were sauntering over too—Will's intent to bring me champagne interrupted by the Indian's arrival.

Thinking back on stories Will had shared about the exploration, I remembered how much he and Meriwether owed this man. He had seen to their overall care during the harsh winter of '05 along the northern Missouri. Most probably, he was instrumental in the very preservation of the Corps of Discovery's success.

Will saw Bates and me threading our way through the curious crowd and immediately gestured for me to join him. Before leaving his side, I heard Bates gripe to his friends, "Just *look* at them all. You'd think it was the second coming of Christ!"

The crowd parted for Will, and he led me forward.

"General Red Hair," Sheheke acknowledged, bowing stiffly toward us. His western etiquette was impressive, but then again he'd been entertained by Thomas Jefferson and a multitude of other dignitaries and men of note.

"Chief Sheheke, I'm most pleased to introduce my newly wedded wife, Julia."

I dropped into a curtsy, Sheheke reaching out and taking my hand as though we were in Virginia and not on the riotous frontier. He bowed over it politely, and instead of kissing it, he simply gave it a gentle squeeze. In short, he was the perfect gentleman and had already shown me more regard than Bates, who had finally come up even with the rest of us, his loudmouthed friends at his back.

Sheheke spoke slowly, clearly, his voice a masterful baritone. "Mrs. Clark, I am pleased to meet you." As expected, his English was slightly staggered, with an unusual accent, yet clear and precise.

My hand remained in his, and I returned the slight squeeze. "Meeting you is *my* pleasure, sir," I insisted. "I know of the kindnesses and hospitality you and your people extended to my husband and the Corps of Discovery. It was both life-preserving and of generous character."

Little had I realized how many people were listening, but to my utter surprise, everyone in the tight circle, excluding Bates, applauded my statement, Will and Meriwether both nodding and joining the ovation.

Sheheke possessed a captivating demeanor. His complexion lighter than that of other natives I'd seen since arriving, with his high cheekbones, ruddy with vigor, it was impossible to gauge how old he was, for his face's only evidence of age were crow's feet on the sides of his eyes, which twinkled with a serene demeanor.

Dressed as he was in western attire, he only resembled a chief from the neck up. Above his cravat were two narrow horizontal tattoos the color of charcoal, and his ears bore discs patterned like a five-spoked wheel; his dark hair loose over his shoulders.

Beside me, Bates just couldn't seem to grasp how to be pleasant, inquiring of my husband, "Have you and Lewis connived a way to pay off the Arikara and get him home any time soon so he's not eating out of our pockets all winter?"

I shot him a look of disdain as one of his cronies raised his voice loudly, "He'll never get home 'cause it'll take a damned army to make sure he gets there. We ain't got no army in these here parts. Them politicians back east is keeping soldiers close, in case the British try anything."

Chief Sheheke turned his head toward the man who had made the remark. I felt a stirring in my heart, seeing anxiety in his eyes.

Will clapped him on the shoulder, answering Bates, "The *chief* here will be the first to know of any plans made on his behalf," he pledged, then added to Sheheke, "and be assured, sir, we are *honor*-bound and have not forgotten you."

At my elbow, Bates snorted. "Washington City will want to know about any plans you devise, and I'll be keeping them apprised, don't you know."

Unable to control myself, I rounded on him, repulsed by his words. "Are you threatening to *inform* Washington about official business before any of it is confirmed or made public? Chief Sheheke's visit to the president was a *state* visit, thus his return is state business too. Be mindful of that, Secretary Bates. What sort of assistant to the governor are you by saying such?"

"Julia . . ." Will whispered, leaning into my ear.

With a sneer of obstinate pleasure, Bates waved him off and retorted evenly, "I'm the sort of assistant that uses something called *freedom of speech*, Mrs. Clark. I've heard tell it's an American ideal."

It gave me joy to turn my back on Bates, feeling the heat of a flush at his affront. I nearly ran straight into Meriwether, who had obviously overheard our last words to one another.

He stood puffing his pipe, piercing Bates with his gaze—one of pure hatred.

❧❦❧

Before Will could help me up into the hired carriage that night, I was begging for more information about the chief whose full name was Sheheke-Shote, the Great White Coyote.

"Tell me more about Sheheke. Why does Bates dislike him?"

"Because of his bigotry and low opinion of any culture other than his own," Meriwether answered contemptuously from his corner of the carriage, pipe between his teeth.

Will rapped on the carriage's outer shell, signaling the driver to depart. "I'm sure you sense how my friend here feels about Bates, and I agree with his assessment. However, Bates has other reasons to despise Sheheke. He's punitive when it comes to the territory providing funds for anything, and until Sheheke and his family are able to receive a safe escort, we must provide for him since he's still considered a guest of the United States. Then," Will laughed at this part, "there's the simple fact that Sheheke received invitation into Jefferson's inner circle during his visit east—something the whole Bates family has desired for years yet never attained."

"Well, I must apologize to you both for losing my temper with Bates tonight," I said, "but then again, I don't regret it either."

Will grinned, chuckling. "Next time, you needn't come to our defense. We're both more than aware of Frederick Bates's manner and bravado."

"Don't you *dare* reprove her, Clark!" Meriwether exclaimed in all seriousness, tapping his pipe's tobacco ash out the open window. "Bates more or less threatened to spy and inform Washington on whatever I do here. Julia, I owe you my heartfelt thanks. He needs reprimanding from someone and certainly doesn't heed me when I try to muzzle him."

For a few minutes, we were quiet, the carriage nearing our house. Will's and Meriwether's comments formed a clearer picture in my mind of why Bates might dislike natives—but especially this Mandan chief.

I spoke up again, "Sheheke looked mortified when someone said he'd never make it home. Please tell me that's not true. Surely, another attempt will be made to return him to his people?"

Will and Meriwether exchanged smiles, Meriwether swiftly saying, "It's a quandary coming up with the number of men necessary to send him upriver a second time, thereby guaranteeing his safe return. Before jumping into a keelboat and pointing the prow north, a lot needs to be thought out. Mandans and Arikara have been enemies since before white men ever entered their lands. We simply can't afford another disaster as happened last time."

"So true." Will shook his head in remorse. "It was a stain on my honor here, during the first months at my post, and upon the honor of our United States."

Meriwether shook a finger at Will's words. "True, returning him is a matter of honor, but what happened the last time wasn't your fault, Clark. It was completely unexpected and caused in part by Manuel Lisa." Glancing at me, he explained, "Lisa is a Spanish fur baron who was traveling just ahead of Sheheke's party on the river and informed the Arikara that another flotilla of boats was coming up just behind him—and how that party was loaded with valuables along with Sheheke himself and two of our Corps of Discovery comrades, Nathaniel Pryor and George Shannon. Lisa *sold* them to save himself. As a result, Shannon even lost his leg."

"A painful fact I'll never forget," Will sighed, shaking his head.

How horrible. "Can't Manuel Lisa be tried and punished for such?"

Will shook his head. "It occurred outside the territory, and even had it happened here, without tangible evidence of what Lisa said to the Arikara to save himself, there's no way to take him to task. It likely happened exactly how Lewis just described it. Lisa is a slippery fish, but he's also a valuable one, with many contacts among influential men in the fur trade. When needed, he's a powerful ally."

What a hypocritical world was politics. "So there's no plan in place and not enough protection to return a man who risked a great deal to leave his homeland and meet with the president as a native diplomat?"

Will took my hand. "Lewis and I have discussed a skeleton plan, but mind you, it's not yet ready to present as a proposal to anyone who would be involved. Any militia here, guarding our surrounding interests in St. Louis, doesn't amount to numbers we'd need to venture into Arikara or Sioux territories."

"Please tell me it wouldn't be you going," I whispered to him, though truly I hated the thought of Meriwether's involvement too. It would be a dangerous mission.

Will smiled, reaching for my hand, lifting and kissing it. "No. Right now, we are tied down to other affairs and can't venture that far afield. Whoever leads the next expedition to return Sheheke will be someone else."

I didn't think twice, leaping at the magnificent opportunity. "Might we—might *I* help Sheheke and his family, Will? *Please?* We could begin by having them to dinner. It's something I could do that might help you and Meriwether. Besides, I'd love to meet his wife. What's her name?"

"Yellow Corn," he answered. After a pause, he smiled at me warmly. "You do have a heart for helping those in need, don't you?"

I nodded, eagerly anticipating his answer.

"Then, yes. Why not have them to dinner? You can send Scott out tomorrow with the wagon, and the three of us can learn exactly what they lack and provide whatever it is they need—within reason, of course."

Come morning, Scott took our wagon to bring Sheheke and his family to our home for a meal. Finally, we'd entertain someone, but more importantly there was a possibility of helping these people and making a real difference for them.

※※※

Chief Sheheke's son giggled, bouncing upon my knee. He had an unusual name, White Painted Lodge, and among whites on their journey east everyone called him "Lodge" for short. Only a toddler upon leaving his lands, his parents had taken him into a completely different world. Now, he was dressed in play-clothes like my brother's and his English was impressively fluent.

It made me wonder how he'd adapt upon the eventual return to his people.

"We hear you've moved to a new place," I said to Sheheke. "May I ask why you left Cantonment Belle Fontaine? I know it was a place meant to keep you safe."

Sheheke sat back in his chair, brow furrowing. He wore the same suit he'd worn the night before at the reception. "Fort flooded, river rose, and Lodge-boy got sick."

Meriwether nodded. "I spoke with Jean-Pierre Chouteau this morning. The river's eroding that old stronghold bit by bit, and there's so much moisture that when he visited them to address their complaints, he found the walls in their quarters cracked and covered in mold. Looks like we'll need a replacement fort. Just another item to add to our list." Overwhelmed, he shook his head and lifted his mug of ale to his lips.

Even in their temporary circumstances, those were terrible conditions to endure. No wonder Lodge had been sick. I looked down at him, lightly touching his head, adorned with a colorful quill band. His hair was shiny with animal grease, used as a pomade, Indians finding sleek hair beautiful.

Sheheke spoke again, "I tell Chouteau we leave fort. Now we live in lodge outside St. Louis. Air clean, better to breathe."

"So you're happier now?" I asked.

"Sííka'—Yellow Corn—not happy. She misses home."

I was beginning to feel pangs of homesickness myself, so I could relate. Yet they'd been absent from their homeland for nearly three years. Yellow Corn had every reason to grieve.

I was fascinated with this Sííka'—Yellow Corn—a woman who looked to be in her late twenties. Long, wavy black tresses adorned her shoulders, and though she was wife to such a well-known chief, her attire was simple: a long doeskin tunic painted with a dark red-and-black collar-like design below the neckline, belted snug at her waist. In her ears, she wore simple drop earrings of silver. Her simplicity was her loveliness, and I sensed a gentle spirit.

Chloe brought out steaming bowls of chicken soup, home-baked bread, and butter. As soon as she set the bowl before Yellow Corn, Lodge hopped off of my lap to scurry around the table, joining his mother. She spooned some of the hot soup into his mouth.

"Careful…" I murmured, worried he'd burn himself. But that didn't stop him; his mouth popped open again, wanting more.

Yellow Corn spoke to her husband in their language, and he translated. "She thanks you for this. We eat dry beans and corn. Settlers want no hunting on land where we camp."

There it was—their *need*. I glanced at Will, and he nodded. "Sheheke, do you remember your words to me and Lewis when we first came upriver with the Corps? You said, 'If we eat, you shall eat. If we starve, then you shall starve.' Well, as you can see, we're not starving, and Julia has suggested we bring you food to supplement your stores."

"*Supp*-el-ment?"

"Extra food," I explained. "Something other than dry goods. We want to bring you meat, chickens—whatever you need. Clothes? We'll provide them for you."

Sheheke stared at me for a moment, then softly spoke to Yellow Corn again in Mandan. Her gaze swiveled around to me, tears brimming in her eyes. She touched my hand, and I took hers, holding it fast.

"Thank you," she whispered, slowly, deliberately.

She didn't speak much English. I could tell that much. Not like her husband. Perhaps I could engage her in conversation, teach her more. I felt her loneliness—a sadness, in longing for a home she missed. I looked back at the chief. "May we visit you at your camp?"

"Yes. You visit. We share what we have." He nodded for several seconds, looking at me with what appeared to be newfound respect. For my part, I was simply relieved that now we knew where they stood.

"I'll speak with my staff tomorrow and see if there are additional rations we can send as well," Meriwether said under his breath.

Will nodded, looking my way. "We'll have Scott take one of those big hams we brought with us from Jonathan's when he drives them back tonight. Perhaps you can pack extra blankets to send along too. And whenever I'm able to hunt on our property outside the city, you and I can make occasional visits to take them fresh game."

"And chickens," I added. "Let's send a couple of laying hens with them today too."

It was a start, and when our guests left that evening, Yellow Corn took my hand again, squeezing it and nodding with a shy smile.

I likened that tiny spark of trust to a priceless jewel.

*

Dearest Angel,

We are making headway on the fort's construction atop a bluff I spied when Lewis and I were headed north on the Missouri in '04. Indeed, this defense should be a fair detterent to Indian skirmishes. Curius Indian visitors have come to watch us build and are encouraged by what they see, for they are anxius for a place to trade. Once the fort is complete, the intention is to build a factry and trading post, fulfilling a promise Jefferson made to the Osage people.

Unfortunitly, I have joined my men in sickness.

Many of us are down with the dysentery. Hoping for the next week to be better. I look forward to returning home to good meals and your healing touch. That above all things will make me well again. And as for you, eat well, rest, and care for yourself and our child. Look for me toward the end of August.

I am ever your loving husband,
W. Clark

I had known from the start that Will would be absent at times, and by summer's end plans were made to build a fort west of us. He would be gone for weeks. Though he urged me to remain at home, caring for myself in pregnancy, I wasn't one to be lazy and useless.

I took it upon myself to transport weekly baskets of vegetables and fresh fruit to Sheheke and Yellow Corn. Chloe and Rachel always accompanied Scott and me, riding the brief four miles or so to their camp for visits. Lodge and Rachel scampered around the earthen lodge, squealing and laughing, playing together with the utter abandon of children. And Yellow Corn always chose a time during each visit to place one hand upon my burgeoning abdomen, resting it there until she felt my child move.

Being with child was a wonder.

Now that my belly was distended, I often sang lullabies to my baby when I was alone. My singing wasn't as lyrical or pleasing as Chloe's, but at least my son or daughter would know my voice. My appetite increased threefold; this new life inside was making me hungry like never before. A favorite treat was Madame Chouteau's honey, which she sent monthly. I indulged every morning, spreading it liberally on bread or Chloe's biscuits. It was the finest honey I'd ever sampled. Will and Meriwether called it liquid gold.

Despite forcing myself to stay busy, Will's absence during Fort Osage's construction was difficult, especially after learning of his illness. I found myself fighting off dense, dark clouds of worry and despair. Part of it was homesickness. I kept imagining what was happening at Santillane, wishing I could be both Will's wife *and* a Hancock daughter. Though I sent and received occasional letters from home, sometimes at night my whirring mind was relentless. I'd clench my jaw until it ached, apprehension transforming into real, physical pain.

After all, dysentery was a dreadful illness, stealing the life of many a soldier.

Thankfully, Meriwether was calming company.

We'd sit on the porch together in the evenings, where he'd smoke his pipe, enjoying lively conversation about St. Louis and life in general. On a night when the air was too still and my worry over Will had sapped my spirit, we took our places in silence, listening to a distant meadowlark.

Once he was puffing contentedly, I finally spoke. "Yesterday, a letter from home came. Letitia married Robert Gamble on June 2nd. I thought you'd want to know."

Removing the pipe from his mouth, he replied, "Ah, well. Another one lost. I shall remain the fusty, dusty bachelor that I am, then."

I stared down at my hands, regretting I'd brought it up. "May I ask you something, Meriwether?"

The pipe was back in his mouth, so he simply nodded, a faraway look in his eyes.

"While visiting Santillane last year, you grasped my arm when you were indisposed and you were hot as Hades. Granted, you'd had a dreadful day without getting to speak to Letitia, but I've noticed Dr. Saugrain's visits here. Are you well? I mean, we all live in the same house, and if it's something serious, don't you think Will and I should know about it?"

He removed the pipe, his eyebrows arching. "My, but you're perceptive."

I allowed a smile to cap my reply. "And stubborn too."

He smiled. "Well, both Will and I have the ague, though his doesn't trouble him the way mine does. Fevers, shakes, horrible feelings inside—sometimes they make me want to rip my own skin off." He snorted a mirthless laugh. "Other times, well, it interferes with my very nature and how I act, which concerns me. You know, Jefferson recently wrote me a reprimand, demanding that I write more and come up with a plan to return Sheheke to his people." He paused, taking another toke on his pipe before continuing. "William and I had spoken of it briefly, but I put it off due to my condition, which makes it more difficult to communicate and stay on task. My temper can take flight, and I'm uncontrollable. I'm afraid things are especially tenuous if I'm around Bates."

While I was still considering his answer, he added, "It's getting worse—my ailment."

"We're here for you. Know that much," I assured him.

"You mustn't worry," he said. "Not in your delicate state. And I know you're concerned about William, but he'll be back soon. He'll be fine."

"I'm praying he's better," I said, my concern seeping out.

"He'd send for help if he wasn't."

"You're sure?"

He nodded in certainty. "He's always been one to take care of himself and other people. You should have seen him among the Walla Walla on our return trip, Julia. He tended to their illnesses better than I, even with my training from Dr. Barton in Philadelphia. Eye ailments, broken limbs, fevers—and the only thing he asked for was safe passage for us, food, and horses."

I smiled. Meriwether really was a comfort. Here Will and I had been married for over half a year, but Meriwether Lewis still knew him better in some ways than I.

Chapter XIII

October & November 1808
St. Louis

I barely recognized Will when he returned.

The dysentery had left him quite emaciated, and when we made love, I felt his ribs beneath my fingers. With ample portions on his plate, I saw to his recovery. Fortunately, he was a physically powerful man and quite able to mend, but what a terrible scourge was dysentery.

By the first of October, I'd located a larger house, right across from the river and just outside of the town center. Will was delighted with it, for curious to the design, there was an extra room on the first floor with a separate entrance around the side. He claimed it as his personal office space, and now associates and native clientele met him there. Meriwether remained in the old house, joining us at our place for breakfasts and dinners.

At times, I'd look out a back window on the second floor and barely recognize our yard, for whenever tribal elders traveled to St. Louis to meet with Will concerning land squabbles, trade, or simply to learn more about what white men wanted from them, we allowed them to camp behind the house. Teepees would rise, and Scott and York dug latrines in the forested back end of the property for their use.

Late October sunshine streaked longer shadows across our new home's spacious drawing room, where I sat contentedly with little Rachel, trying to finish the baby cap Sarah and I had started. Rachel sat very still, focused on keeping the bobbins tight and motionless while I did the work. "Tired yet, Rachel?" I asked, smiling to myself, for she always had the same answer.

"No, ma'am. I's just fine." Then she'd bless me with her cherubic smile.

This family had become invaluable, for Scott was gifted at carpentry and a willing worker, repairing rotting fence boards and designing a chicken coop out back. He and Chloe were also knowledgeable gardeners, promising to help me seed come spring.

Just as I was thinking of Scott, in he walked through the front door.

"I has something for you, Missus Julia." That's what they all called me now. He held forth a torn, folded piece of paper, scribbled with a terse note inside:

STAY AWAY FROM THEM INJUNS.

I frowned, staring at the script. Anyone could have written it, intentionally using sloppy handwriting. "Where did you find this?" I asked Scott.

"In the crack outside the front door."

He and Rachel were watching me, inquisitive. "Have you seen anyone loitering here on the property—anybody different who you might think suspicious?

Scott shook his head. "No, ma'am."

"Well then. Thank you for sharing it with me." I folded the paper and tucked it within my bodice.

Who on God's green earth would consider us a threat for *helping* Sheheke and his family? For the present, I'd keep this to myself. Now, there were two secrets I was keeping from my husband. My silent abolition and this odd note which wasn't *exactly* a threat. But still…

Later that morning, while Rachel and I still labored on the baby cap, Chloe came in. "You know how we done lost that crock of honey that Madame sent over?"

The missing honey had caused quite a stir two mornings ago at breakfast, and I had to admit it was frustrating not knowing where it had disappeared to. We were all spoiled, enjoying it as we did.

"Well, I done found it," Chloe reported in a low voice.

"Where?"

"In the cabin with Juba's things. He done stole it, Missus Julia, but I left it be. I's just telling you so you knows."

"Oh my," I sighed.

With the boon of increased domestic space, I had pleaded with Will to contact each party who had hired his people to return them. One by one, the Clark slaves came back, accommodated by two small outbuildings behind the house, both with small fireplaces.

If what Chloe had said was true, I feared what Will would do to Juba. He was York's little brother, and York wasn't in Will's good graces right now. Lately, he'd earned Will's ire, doing what Will described as "half-assin'" his job. Recently, I'd heard him yell at York after the slave grumbled about an assigned chore. When I had hurried into our room where the two men had been, York had skulked away.

I'd never heard Will use such a threatening tone with anybody, and it chilled me.

When it came to his people, I'd found an unsettling hardness existed in his heart, and with all of them returning, it was only a matter of time before Will discovered the truth about my beliefs.

With Will presently out in his office, I thought it would be best to deal with this elsewhere—someplace he never ventured. "I'll meet Juba out in the kitchen," I suggested. "Bring him to me out there."

"Yes, ma'am."

Rachel and I cleaned up from our crafting, and I made my way out to the kitchen while Chloe fetched Juba. I was racked with nerves. Juba was only fourteen or fifteen, I guessed, and I wasn't entirely sure of what to do. Pacing from one end of the kitchen to the other, I was certain about one thing: the outcome would be more reasonably settled by me. No doubt, Will would be heavy-handed, punishing the boy harshly—a thing I wished to avoid.

Finally, the door swung open, and I looked up from where I'd stopped my marching. Juba came in, Chloe right behind, shutting the door and waiting just inside.

Juba had sprouted since returning from his hiring out. His impressive height was perhaps the only attribute he shared with his older half brother, aside from their ebony-black skin, for Juba was wiry—not muscular, like York.

"Thank you for coming to see me, Juba," I began. "Tell me, where were you hired out?"

"At the docks, Missus."

"Hard labor, then?"

He said nothing, just nodded while staring at his feet.

"You've not been back long, but do you find that living here is better than sleeping in a rundown shanty along the riverside?"

"Yes, ma'am."

"That's good to hear, for I wish to make it my business to see that you're well-fed and treated fairly. How does that sound?"

I received another unenthusiastic nod.

"Then I'll need something from you in return."

Head still down, Juba raised his eyes, staring at me, rocking slightly on his heels. Nervous, perhaps? "Don't you want to know what I want?"

A long, silent pause.

"I require *honesty*, Juba. I require the return of what belongs to this household."

He was still silent, though his fingers were fiddling with the fabric of his breeches.

"Juba, return my honey and apologize for breaking trust with me. Do so, and I shall strive to forget you stole it. Give it back, and the general will never know."

His eyes grew wide, and then he dropped to his knees. "Don't be telling him, Missus! I *begs* you—I'll give it back, but I *begs* you, please, don't tell him *nothing*."

"You have my word, provided you return the honey crock to the kitchen by breakfast tomorrow. Place it on the kitchen shelf where Chloe and I keep it. If not, I'll speak with my husband. Also, always remember that whatever is in this kitchen or in our house belongs to the general and me. Not to anyone else."

That night, when Chloe came in to help me into my night-shift, she brought me a biscuit atop a porcelain plate. Will was at his small desk, writing a letter to Jonathan. Though not overly hungry, I bit into the biscuit, instantly tasting the sweet, sticky goodness of Madame Chouteau's honey. I looked at Chloe, my eyes wide, and I smiled, licking my sticky lips.

"That was some nice work today, Missus," Chloe murmured under her breath. "Nice work indeed."

I kept chewing, unable to reply, for I was taking mental note. Yet another secret—purposefully kept from my husband.

※≫≀≪≫

Will always packed one of his rifles, loaded and stashed beneath our buckboard's bench, where it lay inside a specially carved insert. At first, I thought him over-cautious since Sheheke's encampment was but a few miles from St. Louis. Until I received the mysterious note Scott found stuck in our front door. From then on, I knew it was for the best, praying that gun would continue to lie where it was, inert and unused.

When not buried in work, Will accompanied me to Sheheke's, and as we left the house on a crisp, late fall morning—just the two of us this time—he spoke to me seriously. "You're getting great with child now, my love. I don't want to risk your health or the baby's, so today must be your final visit until the babe is born and you're feeling yourself again."

Just as when he'd banned my riding before leaving Virginia, I swallowed any argument. His care was an expression of love, protecting me and the child. Determined as I could be, I would not counter that.

We always passed a clutch of farmhouses shortly before arriving at the encampment. They were humble abodes, most of them of scrappy clapboard or log cabin affairs, unpainted and bespeaking rugged lives for the farmers who lived there. A half mile past that stood a recently built militia cabin beside an American flag raised on a pole near the chief's earthen lodge, reminders that Sheheke was still considered an official guest of the United States, formally protected by American soldiers.

Will set the wagon brakes and leaped down, coming around to lift me off. Admittedly, my stomach was ungainly, and I no longer felt quite as balanced. After calling out our arrival to Sheheke, Will opened the flap to the lodge, a round dwelling made of dirt and sod, and I awkwardly ducked—best I could with my bulging belly—to enter.

Sheheke was standing, conversing with another white man dressed simply in worn breeches, a shirt, vest, and coat. Unpolished and grimy, the stranger's face was covered in unkempt stubble.

"This is Ramses Phipps," the chief introduced as we came in. "He is farmer and visits sometimes."

"Well, hello, Farmer Phipps," Will greeted cordially, extending his hand. "General William Clark at your service. And this is my wife, Julia."

Phipps's eyes widened for a split second. As tall as Will, and brawny, he said, "General Clark himself, eh? I live in the settlement over yonder." He nodded his bushy head toward the farmhouses. "Visiting the chief here to see if he's staying the winter. Snows are hard round these here parts."

Will laughed. "Believe me, they're *much* harder around Sheheke's own country. He's used to such. But yes, he'll be wintering here."

"Says his woman here is homesick and all, being so far from their own lands. When are they heading north?"

"It's late autumn now," Will replied dismissively as I made my way around to join Yellow Corn, who was smiling a greeting and patting a buffalo-skin cushion, inviting me to join her. "As you've clearly pointed out, winter is on its way."

"A shame," Phipps said. "He's so far from his people, and I didn't know this here was Injun land. None of us settlers knew we'd be sharing land with them."

"Phipps…" Will looked lost in thought. "Have I heard that name before?"

"Yes, sir," Phipps answered evenly. "You met my brother, Odysseus Phipps, and forced him off his land."

Will cocked an eyebrow. "Ah, that. But it's not the whole story. Your brother *encroached* onto Indian lands set aside for their use."

Phipps set his jaw, giving Will a hard stare. "Secretary Bates let him settle there, then you came along changing things."

Will was used to such, giving Phipps a shrug. "I'm afraid Secretary Bates was *wrong*," he promptly corrected. "He should have carried out the designated land allotments, for those natives had every right to be there."

Phipps shrugged, letting the conversation die and aiming toward the entrance. Before leaving, he donned a worn felt tricorn. "Chief, remember I'm happy to sell you another chicken, but you'll have to pay, fair and square." Curtly, he nodded to Will and then to me, his voice dismissive and surly. "Afternoon, General, Mrs. Clark."

Once he'd ducked outside, beyond hearing of our conversation, Will asked, "What's that about a chicken?"

Sheheke shook his head and spoke, engaging in Plains sign-talk, the language of gestures that the natives used broadly. Both Will and Meriwether understood it well, though it was lost on me.

"I no understand some white men," Sheheke said, signing and speaking. "Land is sacred and meant to be shared by all, but Phipps says one of my chickens went on his land and was killed by his dog. I tell him that since his dog killed it, he should give me another chicken. He says no. He says he only give me chicken if I pay."

Will couldn't help but laugh, signing back and assuring Sheheke, "Please don't worry. We'll give you another chicken. Julia, have Scott come out tomorrow with another. We have a whole coop full of chickens. But I do remember Odysseus Phipps. He was trouble. Refused leaving Kickapoo land until I had to send armed militia to escort him off it."

I smiled. "I'll bet Scott would help Sheheke build a small coop so his chickens won't wander again."

Sheheke nodded at me with a rare smile, for he tended to be a serious sort. "Good idea," he said, tapping his head in approval. Then he regarded Will again with seriousness. "Phipps asked important question. When do we go upriver? Yellow Corn misses home, and farmers here do not welcome us or want us near them."

Will nodded. "I plan on meeting about this with a group of men who are coming together to form a new trading company. The St. Louis Missouri Fur Company is what we intend to call it, and I think it would be excellent to ascribe your safe return to posterity as its first success. Therefore, I'm going to try to convince them to take on the responsibility of getting you and your family back home safely. However, we will also have to work with Great Father Jefferson, for he will be the one paying for it."

Sheheke still pressed. "If he agrees, then when?"

Will used signage again as he spoke. "It's really too early for me to say. Perhaps when the flowers return and the buffalo calve? But that's only a guess. However, I promise it will happen, for our Great Father Jefferson desires it to happen, as do I and Governor Lewis."

Per their tradition, Yellow Corn pulled out fresh corn cakes and dried berries for us, and while the men continued conversing, she reached over, gesturing to my stomach. With a smile, I nodded, and she gently placed her hands on me. Lately, Baby Clark had become much more active, and it wasn't long before I felt a stirring and saw Yellow Corn smile broadly.

"The baby is happy to see you," I told her, laughing.

"Hap-py?" she queried, cocking her head.

I tapped my heart, then outlined my own smile with one finger. "Happy to see *you*," I repeated, pointing back at her.

"Ahhh..." Yellow Corn nodded with a grin, then offered me more berries. She knew I loved them. They were sweet like candy, and these days I was always hungry.

Will sat back, watching us two women getting on so well, then he spoke again to Sheheke. "Our women are friends. That is good."

Sheheke looked our way, nodding his approval.

"This will be Julia's last visit until the baby comes. But we'll still send Scott out to bring food and gifts through the winter."

Sheheke translated Will's words into Mandan for Yellow Corn, who looked over at me with wide eyes, nodding. Still gazing at me, she spoke something back to her husband, then got up and went to the other side of the teepee.

Sheheke addressed me, "Yellow Corn has gift for you."

There was a rustling, and Yellow Corn returned to my side with a beaded leather bag, which she presented. Pointing to herself, she said simply, "I make," then she reached over and touched my stomach again. "For baby."

I reached into the bag, pulling out a bundle wrapped in the softest rabbit fur and tied together with rawhide. I pulled apart the leather binds, the furs flopped open, and the tiniest moccasin I'd ever seen tumbled out. "Oh! How precious!"

Yellow Corn gently took my hand, placing it on her heart, then reached over and placed her own upon the left side of my chest so that we felt our female hearts beating together. Incredibly, my baby chose that very moment to squirm again, and a unified feeling of oneness swept over me that overcame language, tradition, or race.

※※※

Month seven of my pregnancy made me feel ponderous as a cow and lazy too. I felt sapped of the usual energy I possessed, constantly craving rest.

"That's the Lord telling you to sleep more and get ready for the birthing," Chloe said.

There was nothing for it but to pay attention to what my body was demanding. My activities became more homebound: organizing, sewing simple nightshirts and clouts for the baby that I'd learned to make, and at last, finishing the Dresden lace christening cap. It took a long time, for I simply wasn't as adept at such as my sisters, but I put my full effort into it, adding grapevines and cornucopias. It was certainly the most ambitious handicraft I'd ever attempted, and though I lacked the passion for it that other women seemed to have, I was proud of my work.

My book of Shakespeare from Meriwether became my daily indulgence, next to the drawing room fire. And that's exactly what

I was doing on a cold, late-autumn night, keeping silent company with Will as he sat at the large secretary against the wall, writing his usual letters to family. A peaceful time that dissipated as soon as York entered the room.

Just one glance at the burly slave made me tense. He stopped right next to Will, hovering, his straw hat tight in his fists as they ground at it, fingers flexing and straining.

"Master Clark, I's got something to ask."

"I'm listening," Will said, still writing.

"You knows I got a wife and children back home in Louisville."

Will responded sourly, "Yes, you never let me forget it, York."

"Well, I hear tell that Master Jacobson in Louisville's wanting to buy some people, sir. I was a-hoping you might be willing to sell me to him so I could be near my family."

"You see Mrs. Clark here, York?"

York glanced back at me over his shoulder. "I sees her, sir."

Yes, he did, and he was just as uncaring of my presence as ever. It puzzled me why he disliked me so. The only time he'd ever spoken to me at all were the brief words we'd shared on the day I'd shot the bear, scaring it off of him. The only thing I could think of was that perhaps I'd become just another obstacle between him and the William Clark he used to know as a boy, who had been as much of a friend to York in those early days as he was a master now.

Will went on to make his point. "Well, she has family clear back in Virginia, and she's homesick too, but not once has she demanded to go back to visit."

It was less than pleasing being made an example of in this conversation. Not pleasing at all. So I helped myself right into the dialogue, keeping my voice pleasant. "Will, I really can't compare my homesickness to York's *inability* to be with his family. Marrying you and coming here was my choice. Wouldn't it be possible for him to visit his family several times a year? We have plenty of help, and Scott has proven to be more than capable. I could arrange to have him or even Juba assist you during working hours if York is away."

York froze, staring down at his feet, his face clouded in frustration. My idea wasn't what he'd requested or expected, but at least it was a way to get him to Louisville for a visit.

Hushed and lacking impetus, he breathed, "I was just hoping—"

"Surely, it would be no problem for York to return there for a short time," I interrupted so Will wouldn't get riled. My husband had already glanced my way once, his brows sunken in a frown, obviously not pleased with my idea. "Even a short visit of a couple of weeks would be better than nothing," I added.

"I suppose that might be managed," Will acquiesced. "However," and this was directed sternly to York, "I'll expect you back with the New Year, and don't you dilly-dally about it."

What a chasm distanced York and Will.

If they had played together as children so long ago, hadn't they been free of prejudice and blind to skin color? Mercy! They'd traveled clear to the Pacific, both of them working toward one common goal instead of against one another.

With all my heart, I wished I could see the day when enslaved people would be free. But at present, that wasn't reality, and to help them at all in their suffering, I had to tread carefully.

❦

"Sit down, my love," Will invited, guiding me to the drawing room settee before the fireplace.

I'd just helped Chloe remove dinner's remnants to the kitchen, and my feet hurt—a telling sign of my pregnancy's final months.

"We need your opinion," Meriwether announced. He followed behind Will, making himself useful by dropping another log onto the fire. "You've become close to Sheheke and Yellow Corn and know the history behind the first attempt to return them, so you're to be the first to see our plan for the second attempt."

Will promptly pulled a folded sheet of paper from his suitcoat and sat down next to me. "This is just the first draft, mind you." Then he snickered, stilling my eager fingers from taking it. "Uh-uh. Not yet. As you know, of late I've concocted the St. Louis Missouri Fur Company to attempt a peaceful union between fractious traders—"

"Namely Manuel Lisa versus the Chouteaus," Meriwether interjected with a nod.

Will nodded. "Yes. And as you also know, we've sold shares in the venture to various men in the city. Now, Lewis and I have included the company in the mission to return Sheheke."

This new "company" of Will's was meant to alleviate tension between the contentious factions of traders. "How would they be involved?" I asked.

"The St. Louis Missouri Fur Company would be the very entity that the United States would hire to return Chief Sheheke to Mandan Territory," Will explained.

Though questions were already forming in my mind, I started by asking the obvious. "Who would lead this . . . mission? Certainly not you or Meriwether."

"Oh no," Meriwether confirmed. "We're needed here to address territorial concerns."

"Lewis and I are going to press for Jean-Pierre Chouteau to lead and for René Jessaume to interpret. Chouteau is fully invested in the company, and Lewis and I trust him. And Jessaume is trusted by Sheheke, having traveled with him as interpreter to Washington. It makes sense for him to go."

"Makes sense. *Now*, may I read it?"

"Just remember, it's only a draft," Will reminded me, conscious that his writing skills weren't as honed as mine.

I giggled. "Don't fret, I'll remember."

"But we want your honest input, Julia." That from Meriwether. Will finally let me open the paper. It read:

> *Said party would leave in Spring of 1809, the St. Louis Missouri Fur Company providing krafts to head upriver. Said transports would support fit acommodations for Sheheke and family as well as an interpreter. Said party will be prepared to defend themselves with rifles and munishuns purchased by the Company. Mishun is to Safely convey Chief Sheheke and family to their homeland, Safe from any attacks, if necessary, by force of arms, even at*

> *physikal risk to lives of Said party. Said party will carry goods, munishuns, uttensils, Supplies, and gifts for natives along the route as deemed nesessery, which will be approved by Governor Lewis. Upon the Sucess of Said mishun, those employed are free to engage in trade.*

After the initial read, I went back and reread it again, then paused, gathering my thoughts before saying anything. When I looked up, both men were staring at me intently, awaiting my reaction.

"You've not stated how many men you intend to take," I began.

Will swiftly responded, "After returning from the failed attempt, Pryor insisted we needed at least four hundred men to succeed this time."

"But even with improvements made to our militia, we haven't those numbers," Meriwether added. "We need trader types and marksmen."

"And that's why you're opening up the possibility of trade once the mission is completed and Sheheke is home."

"Yes." Both men nodded in unison.

"If I was Secretary So-and-So in Washington City, I'd be worried about this venture not being *entirely* under United States military auspices. If they're paying for it, then wouldn't they want the military to have exclusive rights to it? Including any money from trading?"

Will sighed. "An excellent point, Julia, but we don't have the military manpower to send on such an endeavor. That's why we had to create this secondary venture into the plan."

Meriwether returned to the first concern: numbers of men. "Actually, I can't see us sending more than two hundred men, militia included. St. Louis is still volatile amid native tensions and current sentiments with the British. In short, as governor I must protect our interests here too."

"Understood, but how would these lower numbers of men be supplemented?"

"Even one hundred more men than last time would be more effective," Meriwether stated. "Especially given enough rifles and ammunition, and provided that most are marksmen."

Will pursed his lips. "I have an idea," he broached. "If we assemble the *minimum* of two hundred men on our end, why not get creative in enlisting the rest? Not *all* Missouri tribes are friendly to the Arikara or Sioux. Couldn't some of those rival natives be persuaded to bolster our strength and join our men? If approached in the right manner, it could even be done in the name of peace."

Meriwether smiled. "I like that. A mere show of numbers would discourage an attack."

"When would the mission depart?" I asked.

"We'd like to see things moving by the end of April," Will replied.

"Will Washington fund it?"

Both men paused before Meriwether affirmed, "I would certainly hope so. This was Jefferson's idea, to arrange for an Indian delegation to visit Washington in the first place."

I nodded. "Then I think there's only one deterrent that would give me pause if I were on Jefferson's staff. As stated earlier, the venture combines *both* state and commercial affairs. That's just the thing to spur the likes of Frederick Bates into complaining about it to Washington."

"Frederick Bates is not a member of the company," Will told me flatly.

I shrugged. "Eventually, he'll hear about it, and that won't stop him from informing whoever he communicates with. You *both* know that."

There was a period of silence before Meriwether agreed, pointing out, "Men like Manuel Lisa will *strive* to involve Bates into reproachful discourse with his contacts. I'm afraid we'll just have to move forward, hoping we're able to succeed despite his interference."

I looked at him frankly. "Meriwether, you'll have to show real grace when Bates stirs up a storm over this, because he will."

Meriwether's jaw muscles twitched as he ground his teeth in disgust. "Mind you both, this is fur company business, so Secretary Bates will *only* find out about it once Señor Lisa leaks the plan to him prior to it becoming public knowledge. And we all know that *will* be what happens."

I was seeing up close the deep-seeded rivalries betwixt these men of the fur trade, embedded within both the political and commercial arenas. And this Spaniard—Manuel Lisa... I really didn't know what to make of him. Was it true? Had he betrayed Pryor's party to the Arikara to save his own skin?

For a moment, I imagined Sheheke and Yellow Corn sitting on the back of a keelboat, peacefully traveling up the Missouri, little Lodge toddling in front of his mother, giggling and pointing at logs adrift in the muddy water, all of them unwary that just around the next bend a war-band of Arikara had been promised trinkets and Sheheke's life in exchange for allowing Manuel Lisa to continue on his way, untouched.

"When will you approach Jefferson to request funding?" I asked.

Will looked toward Meriwether, who said, "The request must come from my office, and I'll need to tap Jefferson before his term ends since we don't know who will be president yet. Elections won't end until December 7th, and with winter setting in, the post will face delays. We'll need to move on this now."

Will's next words were spoken low and somber. "And this time we must succeed because our honor and that of the United States is at risk."

※※※

Winter was upon us, and days were short, darkness descending by late afternoon. As I entered my final weeks of pregnancy, I struggled more with dispiriting depression and homesickness, invariably seeking pastimes to keep my mind occupied, for I'd heard how harsh winter could be in St. Louis. Sometimes Will caught me crying and missing family. Whenever he found me like that, I immediately forced myself to dry my tears and get busy around the house—anything to keep his concern at bay. Hopefully, the arrival of the baby would give me new focus.

And *dreams*!

I had dreadful nightmares concerning home, including a repetitious one of Mama dying, which made me crave letters from family even more. Since arriving in June, letters had trickled in from Virginia once or twice a month, and I'd write back the same week. However, I remained mindful of how winter would slow communication.

Still, I remained fortunate in getting several letters by month's end. Harri wrote how Georgie had taken a fall while out riding. Dr. John had examined him, of course, but found nothing damaged except youthful pride. Yet for some reason it upset me so that Will had Chloe give me a sleeping draught. Lastly, my sweet horse, Cassie—Will's gift to me—contracted the colic one morning and was dead by sunset. That was a dismal day. I'd only ridden her a few times before discovering my pregnancy and had looked forward to resuming horsemanship after having my baby.

Then as 1808 approached its end, change was in the air.

Will and Meriwether both cast their ballots for president, regretting the end of Jefferson's terms. After all, he was the idealistic philosopher president who had charted their paths as heroic explorers and honored them with positions of responsibility. Everyone waited breathlessly to find out who would win. Would it be the Republican candidate, James Madison or Charles Cotesworth Pinckney, the Federalist South Carolinian?

"Once winter ends," Meriwether announced one night after dinner while we sat next to the fire, "I'm going back east to Philadelphia to work on the journals. I need to touch base with my contacts there." That being said, he took a swig of brandy.

Will and I exchanged glances. By the look on my husband's face, it was the first he'd heard of this; they'd both assured colleagues that they needed to tend to things here in St. Louis for the first half of next year.

"That would be time well spent," Will said. "Unless you resume work on them soon, people will lose interest, as we've discussed before. Let me know how I might be of help," he added hopefully. "I could continue copying my originals into nice, neat journals for you."

By his tone, I sensed that assisting Meriwether with such was something of which Will longed to be a part.

Meriwether took another sip of brandy. "You've been kind to offer many times, and I know you've harbored concerns over my lack of progress. Good God, but it's inordinately difficult fulfilling my role as both governor of Louisiana Territory *and* striving to be an author at the same time."

I stirred honey through my hot tea. "Personally, I have no doubt that once published, those books will be a triumph. How could they not be when they tell the tale of such intrepid and adventuresome gentlemen as yourselves?"

They both chuckled at me, Will stretching his legs out. "Sounds like we both have hopeful plans for the New Year, then."

I was busy sipping from my cup, but my eyes flitted his direction, and I wondered what he meant. Swallowing, I cocked one brow. "Hopeful plans? What do you mean?"

He gave that sideways grin to Lewis, who shook his head. "Oh, just *tell* her, man! Don't be so miserly with exciting news."

I stared at Will, mouth hanging, piqued with interest.

"We may have yet *another* home this coming year. Not one let out to us, but our *own*."

"*What?* You've bought a house?" I swiftly set the tea aside, my face sporting an enraptured smile. "What's it like?"

"Quite nice, actually."

"I want to *see* it!"

"Of course you do. But my offer must be accepted first."

"Even a heron must patiently await its fish, Julia," Meriwether said with a wink.

I couldn't help but be a little hurt that Meriwether had already known about this. "Just when did you plan on telling *me*?"

Will shrugged sheepishly. "If the offer is accepted, it was supposed to be a Christmas gift. So Merry Christmas, angel. I hope."

I warmed. How could anyone be miffed about such?

Chapter XIV

St. Louis
December 1808–January 1809

Will's original intent had been to surprise me out of love, so when his offer for the house was accepted, we both rejoiced.

The home's previous owners were long gone, and the place had been abandoned for some time. It needed a deep cleaning—the hardwoods requiring wax and polish, the outbuildings needing light repairs, and the chimney's mortar demanding replacement. But the rooms were spacious and open, with more windows than any house in St. Louis—except for the Chouteau mansion, of course. And the yard was enormous. Will worried that the barn was too small, but we didn't own much stock right now anyway.

"In a few years, I intend to build an extension to the back of the house to display Indian artifacts."

"That sounds fascinating," I said, "but why specifically Indian items?"

"Because I fear someday the native culture of our country will either be gone or so displaced that nobody in the future will know what it was originally like. Somebody needs to preserve remnants of it."

It was a commendable idea, and I urged him to pursue it, but such things were for the future. We wouldn't be moving in for months. The baby was arriving soon, and our current residence was contracted through the end of summer.

Before becoming busy with motherhood, I began an inventory

of items on hand since arriving in St. Louis. Since Mama always kept her inventories detailed in a notebook, I wanted one of Will's red Moroccan journals that he used for copying his Corps of Discovery notes. He was in town with Meriwether and York was in Louisville, leaving Scott to manage Will's office keys, so I borrowed them to search for an unused journal.

Precisely arrayed on one section of his bookshelf were the red leather Moroccans, so I reached up, pulling one down. Opening the volume, I found it already full of entries. The page to which I'd turned was logged back to late November 1804—four years ago, when the Corps wintered at Fort Mandan. I smiled, realizing that it was written precisely when Will was first becoming acquainted with Sheheke. It said:

> *Last night late, we were awoke by the Sergeant of the Guard to See a Nothern light, which was light, (but) not read, and appeared to Darken and Some times nearly obscured and open, many times appeared in light Streeks, and at other times a great Space light & containing floating collomns which appeared to approach each other & retreat leaveing the lighter space at no time of the Same appearance . . .*

My fingers caressed the page, full of Will's imaginative spellings and bizarre capitalizations in the midst of sentences, particularly on words beginning with *S*. Granted, I was far from perfect as a writer, but Will's entire family poked fun at his penmanship, and the longer we lived as man and wife, the more I noticed it too. I'd never chide him for it like the rest of his kin, for I knew he had to be humbled by it—perhaps even ashamed. Especially in the light of learned men such as Jefferson, whom he so revered. William Clark was a man so loyal to family that he spent an hour or more nightly writing letters to brothers, nephews, sisters... He was remarkably steadfast to those he loved.

I pulled down several more journals, only to find them also complete with expedition material. Then, at long last, I discovered an empty one with crisp blank pages and claimed it.

Mama always said that "organization only begins with chaos," and such was true about inventories. Whenever one began, it created utter disorder. Nevertheless, Chloe and I proceeded, first with my shifts, undergarments, and corsets spread out across the room. I made notes in the journal of what I'd keep, and Rachel set those items aside.

We were moving on to my gowns when our work came to an abrupt standstill at the sound of cart wheels and hooves out front. Curious, I peered out the window, perplexed at what I saw.

Despite it being December with freezing temperatures, a lone black woman was bound by her hands and forced to walk barefoot. Thank the good Lord there was no snow on the ground. She staggered behind a rickety old wagon full of furniture and goods, completely at the mercy of the wagon's speed.

Chloe joined me at the window, gasping. "That's Nancy." She wagged her head. "Lord have mercy."

I nodded, thinking back and remembering Nancy—Juba's sister and half sister to York.

We both hurried downstairs, Chloe reaching the door before me in my pregnant state. She swung it wide-open just as the driver of the wagon sauntered up the path, holding a rope with Nancy in tow. His gravelly voice cut through the still, frigid air. "Just returning the general's slave-woman. Tell him she ain't worth piss in a pot."

Appalled at his choice of words, I recalled his name—Hinkle. A casual contact of Will's to whom I'd never been introduced. Now, I knew I'd not missed a thing by never knowing him. Will had said he was the son of a printer at the recently inaugurated St. Louis newspaper, and he'd been most gracious to him, even loaning him money to get himself started.

Hinkle untied Nancy's fetters, and she entered the house, dazed, shoulders slumped, staring at the floor. I was still on the staircase, studying her in shock. Emaciated, she was dressed in mere rags, likely the same clothes she'd worn to St. Louis upon first arriving from

Louisville back in June. Ill-fitting on her now malnourished limbs, they hung flaccid. One side of the dress was so threadbare I could see the curve of her breast beneath it. It was a wonder she was still able to stand, as cold as her feet had to be.

I hefted myself the rest of the way downstairs, one hand on the side of my enormous abdomen, glaring at Hinkle the whole time. "Have you paid your fee to General Clark?" I hated asking, but Will would be expecting it.

"You deaf or something, Missus?" he rumbled. "I said she ain't worth nothing, so don't go expecting to get nothing."

"What of her clothing? *Look* at her!" I cried. "She's starving and hasn't any shoes or decent woolens to keep warm. Providing her a new set of clothes was part of the contracted agreement, and you *know* it."

Hinkle waved me off, turning his back on me to hustle to his wagon. He sprang up onto the driver's seat to join a dark-clad, pale woman I assumed to be his wife. Two boys sat on the bench behind, surrounded by crates and a clothing trunk. He jawed harshly at the pair of skin-and-bone mules pulling the rig, and I watched as they left, grinding away and kicking up a chuff of dust.

"He doesn't even feed his team, so why should I expect he'd care for a woman in his service?" I muttered, seething.

Behind me, Nancy coughed, and I whirled about, far more concerned about her needs than chasing after that coldhearted bastard.

"Chloe, go upstairs to the pile we've started for charity. Find something warm that might fit her. Come, come." I gestured to Nancy. The mute fear on her face horrified me the most. Before being hired out, wasn't she the cheeky one, arguing with me to remain with us as a cook instead of Chloe? Dear God, what had Hinkle done to her?

"Nancy?" I repeated, softly so as not to add to her distress.

No answer. She stood as though rooted, shaking and staring down at her rough and cracked bare feet.

Chloe hesitated on the stairs, "Nancy, this be Chloe. You remember me, don't you? I'll be back in just a minute, but you go on with Missus Julia. She gonna help you."

I reached for a quilt folded neatly on the back of our settee in the drawing room, draping it gently over Nancy's shoulders. She shrank away at first, then pulled it tight about her bony form and even covered her head with it.

I tried to reassure her. "Follow me and we'll clean you right up and get you some warm clothes."

Oh, but Hinkle had lit a fuse of fury in my spirit, and I was *raging*. If I had no say whether or not we kept slaves in our household, I'd be *damned* before I'd have them without warm, suitable attire!

In minutes, Chloe hurried out to where Nancy and I were in the kitchen. She helped Nancy undress while I stoked the fire to warm the place and heat some water.

Sponging off was how most everybody bathed in colder times of the year. But when I finally went to apply a warm, moist rag to Nancy's face, she wrenched away, crying out, "Don't hurt me none! I ain't done nothing except work hard."

I froze, the cloth dripping water down my wrist. Chloe wordlessly took the rag from me, tending to Nancy herself.

I stepped back. Dear God, she was afraid of me because I was white.

Nancy just stood there, weeping silently, as I watched Chloe bathe her, removing her tattered clothes, speaking to her softly. I padded around behind her, and that's when I saw fresh lash marks on her back, raw and barely even scabbed over. In front, dark bruises colored her breasts.

Hinkle had used and abused her—there was no other answer for it. I stepped outside of the kitchen, tears wetting my cheeks, leaning back against the clapboard wall, sobbing for Nancy and for the fact that I could no longer withhold my biggest secret from Will.

Tonight, he'd find out *exactly* what I thought of slavery.

◈

I sat at my dressing table; agitated, mind whirling. There was nothing to do but confront my husband with the truth. I didn't want to be a tigress in my approach, but I was so angry it was difficult to rein in my emotions.

As always, Chloe came in to add logs to the fire and brush my hair. A real closeness between us was blossoming, a relationship of ease in her company that I'd never had with Megg back home. Yet as much as I wished her to remain with me for morale's sake, I had to do this alone.

"Chloe, if you don't mind, I need to speak to my husband privately."

"Yes, ma'am."

Shortly afterward, I heard Will's footsteps on the stairs.

God, give me strength...

He came into our room, shutting the door behind him like always, yawning and beginning to undress. Presently, he walked over behind me and leaned over, kissing my neck. He must have felt me stiffen, for he paused, asking in a low voice, "Is something wrong? You're not ill, are you?"

His hands moved to my shoulders, softly kneading.

I sighed. "That Mr. Hinkle sent Nancy back to us today. He didn't replace any of her clothes, and there were signs—*obvious* signs—that he'd *used* her." So far, I'd controlled my voice well, just above a whisper.

Will stopped rubbing my shoulders and turned toward the bed, pulling the quilt down and fluffing up his pillow. "Did he leave payment?"

I twisted around and stood up in disbelief. "Did you not hear me? I said he'd *used* her! Who cares if he paid? He should be *hanged* for treating her so! Handling a woman that way—*it's nothing more than rape!*"

I wasn't minding my volume now.

Will sighed, heading back over to console me. "Not all the world's ways are pleasant, angel," he breathed, outstretching his arms to enfold me.

I took a step back. "No. They're *not*." I held my hand up, stopping his approach. "I need to have my say about this." Here it came—all of my pent-up frustration on the subject. "*Slavery* is not pleasant," I hissed, and here came hot tears, searing my eyes again. I swallowed and paused, wiping my eyes with one hand and commanding my emotions to cease, to take control of myself. "I won't see *any* human being living under our roof treated in such a fashion."

His eyebrows raised, and he stared at me with a stunned expression. "My, but you're worked up—"

"Oh yes, I am. For this is something I'll stay worked up about. Will, despite my upbringing and being a Virginian, I *despise* slavery and everything about it. Now, I know you're like my papa in your beliefs, and you accept that way of thinking, but I—I *don't. I can't.*"

He was still calm, but his eyes were wide. "Does your papa know of these . . . these beliefs of yours?"

I shrugged. "Why does that matter?"

"It matters if they were *concealed* from me, and here I am now—your *husband*."

Anger or resentment was what I'd expected, so I was surprised to see hurt registering on his face instead.

Fair enough. "Mama knows. Papa?" I shook my head. "I don't know. But for not telling you before we wed—I'm dreadfully sorry. It was foolish of me, and I beg your forgiveness. I wanted to, I *planned* to, but there was just no easy way of bringing it up, and I . . . I was afraid."

"*Foolish* of you? I think so!" His voice rose too, but he corrected himself and lowered his volume so that his ardor came forth as a tremulous hiss. "In *this* household, you will manage *my* people as I see fit. Is that clear?"

I shook my head mournfully. "No. No, it's not. When I manage this household, I will treat your people like human beings, for that's what they are. I'll treat them with kindness and compassion because most of them have never experienced such."

Will was speechless. He took a step back, reached up, scratched his head, then murmured, "Damn. I sure hope this is merely your present condition."

That angered me. "It's got *nothing* to do with the baby or being near my time. It has everything to do with my *beliefs*, and I will never change them just because of your disagreement."

My voice had risen again, cresting like a vast wave, and though it was unintentional, it burst out as a victorious cry of avowal, and nothing less. "I don't expect you to join me in this regard, but its's something you'll need to accept, for there's no sense in hiding it anymore. It abides in my heart—it's part of me!"

He stood there for several seconds before speaking, and when he did, it was hushed. "My word, Julia. This has lanced me through to my very soul. It's true there will always be things upon which we'll disagree. But *this*—this is something you should have told me long ago. Before we ever wed."

Heart pumping, I asked the question I feared, "Would you have married me then? Would I still be Julia Hancock *Clark*? I'll tell you something, Will. I will always love you, but I am my own person, as are you. And I have my own mind on this matter."

He turned from me, crossing the room in measured steps. He still had on his boots, but next he snatched his tricorn—ever his favorite hat—smashing it onto his head. "Well, I find your 'own mind' to be distressing. However, it's something I must now live with, isn't it?" He punctuated his next point by jabs of his fingers. "But so help me, I'll expect you to keep it to yourself—within the four walls of this room, mind you. I won't have *any* of our people thinking they can gain sympathy with you. They're different than we are."

"And that's where you're wrong! They're the *same* as us. *Exactly* the same in God's eyes."

He shook his head and lifted himself to full height. "You just remember this, my girl. *None* of this conversation leaves this room, and I'll expect you to treat them as slaves because that's what they are."

As he spun away and out of the room, he thought he'd had the last word. My teeth were clenched so hard that my jaws ached. His footsteps stomped downstairs and out the door, most probably to go commiserate with Meriwether or ride over to Christy's Tavern for ale. His response didn't surprise me, and if anything, I felt an unbelievable relief.

It was out at last.

But that last demand he made? That I treat them like slaves? Could I comply with *that*?

My heart already knew the answer.

⁂

I praised God that, despite the truth being out, it became clear that my relationship with Will was miraculously intact. The very next morning, the ice broke and the breach began to heal.

York had just helped with Will's morning shave and had stepped out of the room when Will said, "Julia, I ask your forgiveness. After re-enacting our argument from last evening, I realize how indelicate I was in both my inaction and what I said. Thank you for tending to Nancy and her needs. As for your beliefs, we shall have to agree to disagree. However, I do see how our love has triumphed over our personal opinions, and for that, I am thankful."

Lord be praised.

He continued to respond lovingly, bringing me tea in the evenings by the fire or propping up my feet on a stool with an extra pillow. In bed, he'd lay his big hands upon my belly, eager to feel his child stir. We had stopped conjugal relations due to my condition, but ever since I'd told him the truth, I'd been anxious over losing our closeness and intimacy. What a relief that his desire was intact, for I wanted that part of our marriage to resume after the birth. The one thing I didn't think I could bear was losing *him*.

Even more promising, Chloe informed me how she'd overheard Will assuring Nancy that provided she always worked hard, she'd have a safe haven in his home for the rest of her life.

I was learning, discovering that marriage was just like seasons in a year.

Springtime was open and ripe, like flowers and all budding things, bursting with growth. Then came heated summer, passionate, sensual—demanding release. Next was autumn, when lovers harvested desire so abundantly they sometimes discarded the very fruit for which they'd originally longed—treating it as overripe, spoiled.

Then winter.

Coldhearted, argumentative winter, when it was easier to hide within one's self for warmth and protection instead of taking risks and walking out into a blinding storm.

Then it all began anew, spring embracing forgiveness, openness… and on and on it would go, cyclical… infinite.

I was thankful for this renewed "spring," but my last month of pregnancy was awful.

At least once daily, I had to change undergarments, for the baby used my bladder as a footstool, and with my stomach so distended, I could no longer lean over. God bless her, Chloe was ever near to help with my stockings and shoes, which were uncomfortably tight due to my swelling feet. In the mirror, I looked heftier than Jonah's fish, and even my loosest house-dresses were snug.

She kept saying, "You ain't got much longer, Missus."

Perhaps not, yet each day dragged into the next. Evening meals in particular made my stomach burn, so as much as I wanted to eat, I did so modestly. And sleep? That was near impossible, for I'd have to relieve myself at all hours.

Until the baby came, I wouldn't be going out anymore, so having Meriwether continue joining us for both breakfast and dinner was a pleasant distraction. On the morning of our first snow, I saw both men out the door following breakfast, nodding toward the scene outside. "It looks like December now. I only wish I could go walking in it."

Will leaned in and kissed me lightly. "Very soon you'll be so busy with our boy that you'll be too tired for walks."

"Still think it's a boy, eh?" Meriwether smirked.

"He'll love it just as much if it's a girl," I quipped.

"I've decided Colonel Hancock was correct and it's going to be a boy," Will declared. "I can feel it." Addressing me, he added, "Now, you take care of yourself. That cough hasn't improved."

"I caught it from you."

"My fault, is it? Well, we can't have it getting worse. You've had pneumonia once. Let's not go through that again."

Meriwether offered, "I could ask Dr. Saugrain to stop by."

I shook my head. "Please, neither of you worry about me. It's really nothing, and with winter stretching before us, I'll be sicker waiting for letters from home than I am with this cough."

"William told me he'll be curing you of that in the New Year," Meriwether whispered with a wink.

"Well, by God, man!" Will glared at his friend with real irritation. "You can ruin surprises better than anyone I've ever known!"

My face must have lit like a fire. "William Clark, could this mean a visit to Virginia? If so, we'll have *plenty* to discuss after you finish work today. I think my parents deserve to see their grandchild after all, don't you?"

"Indeed, they do. But it won't happen until the latter part of the year. We'll have plenty of time to plan. Oh—and one other thing. Major Christy's niece is visiting, and he mentioned to me that she intends to call upon you later this morning."

❦

Major and Mrs. Christy lived across from us along the river. They were wonderful neighbors and also the owners of Christy's Tavern.

Martha Christy was a quiet, private sort, but she made me a lovely satin pillow for the baby's cradle. Even more thoughtful was her assumption that her visiting niece would suit me as a friend. Once we were acquainted, Polly came over daily by midmorning, full of sunny smiles and long, thick golden blond hair cascading over her shoulders. Dimples punctuated a nearly permanent smile that made her hazel-gray eyes twinkle. She was a few years younger than me, but I was dumbfounded that this tender-aged girl knew more about what was to happen in childbirth than I did since her mother had allowed her to assist at family births.

A week before Christmas, she came for her midmorning visit. I was so weary and sore that she soaked and massaged my feet, helped me into my nightgown and robe, then settled me on the settee downstairs, adding a log to the fire before covering me with a quilt and slipping out the door.

I must have slept a good two hours when I heard someone lightly knock.

"Will?" I murmured.

"No, it's Meriwether," he responded, apologetically peering in at me from the half-opened door.

"What time is it?" Blinking, I pulled myself up to a sitting position.

"Half-past the noon hour. I'm sorry to have awakened you."

"No apology needed. Please come in."

He chose a wingback chair across from me that I'd fallen in love with in Louisville on the day we'd gone furniture shopping. "Not long ago, William mentioned that after leaving Jonathan's family last June, you missed a play you'd wished to see."

"Mmm. *The Taming of the Shrew*. It was advertised while we were visiting. If only it had played while we were there. You of all people know how much I love Shakespeare."

"A disappointment indeed—one I'd like to remedy."

"How's that?" Intrigued, I sat up straighter.

"I've prepared a little Shakespearean monologue for you. Consider it an early Christmas gift for a young lady who has everything—except tickets to a drama in Louisville, that is."

I grinned broadly at his thoughtful surprise. Two words would *never* be associated with Meriwether Lewis: those being inconsiderate and uncreative.

"Tragedy or comedy?" I queried.

"I won't spoil the fun. You have to figure out which play it's from and what character I am. Ready?"

"Yes, please!"

Meriwether showed me his back briefly, assuming character. When he turned about, he stood straighter and was no longer looking at me, but out toward an imaginary audience.

*"I shall have glory by this losing day
More than Octavius and Mark Antony*

By this vile conquest shall attain unto."

I couldn't help but interrupt. "One of the Roman plays, then—*Antony and Cleopatra*?"

Meriwether shook his head, diving back into character.

*"So fare you well at once; for Brutus's tongue
Hath almost ended his life's history—"*

"*Julius Caesar!* I remember this part. You're Brutus."

Meriwether grinned, nodding and slipping back into the soliloquy.

*"Night hangs upon mine eyes; my bones would rest,
That have but labored to attain this hour."*

Since I knew it, I jumped in to help, playing the minor roles. *"Fly, my lord, fly!"*

"Hence!" He gestured as if sending the man ahead. *"I will follow."*

I shook my head in rapt amazement.

*"I prithee, Strato, stay thou by thy lord:
Thou art a fellow of a good respect;
Thy life hath had some smatch of honour in it:
Hold, then, my sword, and turn away thy face,
While I do run upon it. Wilt thou, Strato?"*

Without hesitation, I took on Strato so he could finish. *"Give me your hand first. Fare you well, my lord."*

Meriwether grasped my hand with his left. *"Farewell, good Strato,"* he breathed.

He made a jerking movement, as though a real blade was piercing him. Slowly, like a tree falling after being cut, he collapsed sideways, not moving a muscle.

I sat breathless, deeply moved that he'd memorized and performed it especially for me. Once the pause of respectful silence had passed, I applauded. "Get up now. I don't wish you dead any more than Strato wished it upon Brutus."

He grinned from ear to ear as he rose in one fluid motion, brushing off his trousers and sweeping my hand into his before giving it a light kiss. "Merry Christmas, Mrs. Clark. I pray this gift was adequate."

I smiled at him. What a kindhearted person was Meriwether Lewis. I had to admit that we had such similarities it was a wonder that he and I hadn't wound up together. But Meriwether held no attraction to me the way Will did. William Clark was all muscle, brawn, and rugged strength. Meriwether was more refined. Perhaps it was true that opposites did attract.

"It was a most appropriate gift," I praised. "And what talent you possess, Governor."

This Christmas wouldn't be like any other I'd ever had. Because of my advanced pregnancy, we'd remain here at the house. But the New Year was knocking and would be so full of blessings—a new home of our own, a child to raise in love, and returning home to Santillane.

Chapter XV

St. Louis
January–March 1809

"Nothing wrong with this babe. Everything's gonna be fine. Don't you go a-worrying none."

These were the confident words of Midwife Mabel.

She came highly recommended by Mrs. Christy and Madame Chouteau, and now she came to see me daily, prodding my bloated belly and placing her ear upon it, listening.

"Start walking around your house. Is good for you to walk near your time." The old woman tapped her ear, gazing at me steadily. "You listen to Midwife Mabel, *oui*?"

Will spoke to Mr. and Mrs. Christy about Polly overnighting at our house until the birth, and everyone agreed it was a fine idea, especially if my pains began at night. During the day while Will worked, Polly and I strolled through the house. Arm in arm, I'd plod along next to her, up and down the stairs, even down into the cellar, back and forth through our dining room and into the drawing room. Then we'd start over again, all the while telling each other family stories and sharing trivial St. Louis news.

The only thing missing was Mama.

If only she were here to guide me through this ordeal that seemed so mountainous before me. Caroline had arranged to be at Santillane near Mama for Henrietta's birth so she could help her through it. Yet leaving had been my choice and now I lived with it, simply too far from family regardless of how much I craved their presence.

"Fidgety" was the only word with which I could describe myself. Will was solicitous and thoughtful, coming upstairs to our room every morning with a tray of hot tea, cream, and slices of Chloe's homemade bread and jam. On one of those occasions, I finally expressed a recurring thought that had plagued me more and more of late.

"Please, sit with me a moment. There's something I need to speak with you about."

He pulled up my dressing chair so as not to disturb my breakfast on the tray before me.

"At the birth, I want Chloe with me. She's promised to help Mabel if there's a need."

"I'm not sure that's appropriate," he said in a low voice, shaking his head. "None of my people should witness your birthing. It's a private affair."

"Chloe *will* be there, Will. She knows childbirth, and even Midwife Mabel suggested she come in case there's a need. And most importantly, she will be there because I *want* her there. If something happens and things go awry, you'd want me as calm and contented during my last moments as possible, wouldn't you? And if I died, she'd be the one to care for the baby."

"I'd have Polly—"

"Not all the way to Virginia you wouldn't. Because there's no way you could care for and raise a child on your own here without me. If something happens to me, take the baby to Fincastle. Mama and Papa would be more than pleased to raise our child."

Will's prejudice dissolved into empathy. "Oh, Julia, that's a possibility I won't even think on," he whispered under his breath." He sat down on the bed and pulled me to him, holding me tight. Too bad this attempt at comfort and intimacy was awkward due to my engorged stomach, for I'd learned in our abstinence how much I enjoyed relations with my husband. I craved his caresses, his kisses, his long, hard body against mine…

"If you must have Chloe there to comfort you, then so be it, though it's not my preference."

Regardless of how he felt, his words were music to my ears, for everyone heard enough stories about childbirth to know it was the hardest thing women faced and, like so many things in our lives, something else we couldn't control.

By January 10th, I had never been more ready to have my baby, and I complained so to Polly. "I can't tolerate another day inside these four walls. Please let's walk outside for fresh air."

"We really shouldn't," Polly said. "There's deep snow everywhere. What if you slipped and fell?"

"We'll lock arms. You won't let me fall."

"Not if *I* fall!" she laughed, flinging up her arms helplessly. "We'd both go down."

"*Please* just this once. Let's go outside and walk several laps around the house to keep me sane. I'll wrap up in so many layers of warm clothes that I'd be safe jumping from our second-story window."

Polly smiled wryly. "General Clark won't much like it if he hears about this."

"He's in town at a meeting today with Governor Lewis. We'll be back inside by the time he gets home."

Polly helped me into an old pair of Will's high boots. They were way too big, of course, but I was determined. I even wound up having to wear one of his old greatcoats since none of mine would make it around my waist.

As soon as we took our first step outside, frozen air shocked my senses, and I gasped at the frigid intake into my lungs. I started coughing—a leftover remnant from my bout with pneumonia that showed itself whenever I went out into the cold.

Like today.

"Will you be well enough?" asked Polly.

I nodded, forcing my fit to end and swallowing.

Arm in arm, we took tiny steps, tittering like little girls. The sky above was gray as slate, and it began snowing again. We stuck our tongues out, catching flakes, playful and making faces the whole time. Each inhale was icy, fresh, pure, and looking heavenward, I felt tiny stings of snowflakes dust my bare skin. Each step took effort, for Polly was right: drifts were knee-deep, and by the time we'd completed one lap around our house, both of us were breathing hard, half from the exertion and the other half from our mirth.

"One more lap," I urged.

"If you say so."

"I can't remember when I've felt so alive. It's a wonderland out here."

Stopping, I looked about, releasing one of Polly's hands to rotate around slowly, taking in my surroundings. She still placed her hands protectively atop my shoulders, following me and taking no chance that I'd lose my balance or slip onto the frozen ground.

I blinked in astonishment, realizing that what had first looked like a wide-open field was really the mighty Mississippi, completely frozen over, enormous chunks of jagged ice frozen topsy-turvy as the river stubbornly continued its flow underneath.

We completed the lap, but the river fascinated me, so I suggested, "Let's go across to your aunt and uncle's to look at the river frozen over. I've never seen such."

"Very well, but afterward we'll take you back inside and warm you up. It's snowing harder now, and look—the wind is picking up."

She was right, but we linked arms anyway, trudging across the road until we were in the Christys' yard, adjacent to the riverbank.

That's when it hit—a blinding gale of white that nearly blew us off of our feet. I tightened my hold on Polly as she cried out, "Where is your house? I can't see it anymore!"

I turned and saw nothing—nothing but white—but I felt something, for at that moment something hot and wet coursed down between my legs, causing me to tense. I'd made sure to empty my bladder before venturing out, so it wasn't that, but when a gripping pain seized my lower back, I knew.

Polly grabbed my hands. "Julia! Is it starting?"

I nodded, speechless. A moan escaped through my gritted teeth, accompanied by the usual cold-weather vapor of breath.

"We can't go back to your house when we can't even see it," Polly cried over the wind, her voice still almost lost against another furious gust of white blowing into us.

This was brutal. It had barely been snowing when we'd chanced going outside. And now it was nothing less than a full-on blizzard.

Another spasm.

This one felt as though some evil demon was twisting bones in my spine, and my midsection tightened like the thin skin on a soldier's drumhead. "We'll need to go inside your aunt's house," I cried above the wind.

She nodded. "Look, at least we have the fence. Use it to follow around to the front gate."

One step, two, three—don't think about the pain. Just move.

Polly was in front, moving forward hand over hand and plowing me a path, gripping the fence and making it to the front gate first. Turning to me, she shouted, "Stay here. Don't be afraid. I'm just running ahead to get help. I'll be right back."

I obeyed. Aside from the fence, which I felt through my hands, I couldn't see anything—not even the Christys' house, the walls of which were only feet away. It was unnerving seeing Polly disappear into a gale of white. The blowing snow was surreal.

And the *pain*...

It was the reason I'd stopped to begin with, but now I simply couldn't move at all. My skirts were too heavy in the gathering drifts to drag any farther, and the wind . . .

Out of nowhere appeared a bronze-skinned Spaniard I'd seen around the Christys' before, a hired hand built like a bull.

I blurted out, "I don't think I can walk."

He said nothing, just lifted me up in his arms, as Will had done before. Dear God above, but I wished it was Will now.

It didn't take much to start the pain again as another paroxysm passed through my lower half. I bore it silently, biting my lip. It was slow going, and I heard my rescuer breathing hard as he followed the fence line until we came to the front gate.

Polly was waiting at the entry above us, holding the door open. "Careful, Misael. Don't slip."

He made slow, careful progress up the several stairs. Then we were inside, and I could feel warmth surround me.

"We'll need her up in the guest room, Mizzy."

That was Mrs. Christy, and I heard her footsteps as sure-footed Misael carried me safely all the way up the flight of stairs.

"I've already pulled down the covers. What silly girls you are—out in such weather. Julia, my dear, you'll be more comfortable soon."

I sat on the edge of a soft bed with Mrs. Christy kneeling before me, one hand gentle on my knee. "Polly will bring up hot tea to calm you. The storm is raging for now, so it'll be a spell before we can send for the midwife, but Polly and I will be here for you until then."

I couldn't even respond because my back arched out of its own volition, and I squealed in more pain. It was dizzying, unbelievable anguish without any escape. Between breaths, I panted. "If it's safe enough, could you send for Chloe? Please?"

"It's already been done." Bless her! It was Polly herself answering as she brought in the tea. "Aunt Martha, should I start a fire?"

"Yes. I'll help her undress."

I heard Polly shuffling about near the fireplace, and by some miracle, my pains stopped. I was terribly embarrassed to have caused Mrs. Christy such inconvenience. Look at what my ridiculous notion to breathe fresh air had caused. It looked as though I'd be having my child right here at our neighbor's.

Tender and calm, Mrs. Christy was just like Mama would have been, helping me shed my layers, so perhaps it had all worked out for the best. I was in the company of women, at least. Once the fire crackled and I felt its warmth, Mrs. Christy took my hand. "Dear girl, drink the herb tea. I know it's the last thing you're wanting now, but it will help you relax."

Polly plopped down on the bed next to me, taking my hand. She was so serene.

"Next time your pains come, I've heard it helps to breath as much as you can," she said. "Great *gasps* of air. I've heard midwives say that breathing deep keeps you strong, so try to do that."

When Chloe arrived, she hurried straight to my side with words of encouragement, taking up both of my hands. "Sweet Missus Julia, now everything's gonna be just fine. You ain't gotta worry 'cause everybody in this room loves you and is gonna take mighty good care of you. You hear?"

I squeezed her hands tight. By now, the room had warmed and I found myself sweating.

Then the pains reawakened.

It took hours, but by evening the blizzard had let up enough for Midwife Mabel to arrive. Old Mabel panted hard from the stairs, porting a bulky chair with a slanted back.

Chloe drifted down her way as she examined between my legs, and Polly replaced her at my side, wiping my perspiring head with a cool cloth. Mabel spoke in a low voice. "Mistress, I's gonna help you sit up, for we need you up and a-moving about."

Moving?

Obediently, I sat up, and Polly helped guide me to my feet. All of my toes found the cool floorboards, which actually felt rather pleasant since my back was damp with perspiration.

Another lightning bolt shot through my back, shocking me and radiating toward the front. "I think I need to push," I whimpered, panting.

"Not yet," Mabel answered. "You'll be pushing a-plenty soon enough. You just take nice, deep breaths and walk. It will help. Trust me, girl."

Two more interminable hours passed into night's darkness while I paced back and forth over the Christys' creaky floor. I counted and memorized every line in the oaken hardwoods and could have drawn them from memory. Occasionally, I'd have to pause between steps, snatched in mid-stride by another stab of agony. Oh, how I wanted to push, but each time I asked, Mabel shook her graying head. "Not yet."

Finally, she asked me to come and sit on the edge of the bed again. I reclined backward while she peered between my legs, and I was oh *so* mindful that modesty had no place in childbirth.

"Well, mistress," Mabel announced, "you'll finally get to start pushing. But wait until we get you to the birthing chair."

Before moving me again, Chloe removed my linen shift, and now I was completely naked. With Polly supporting me on one side and Chloe on the other, they eased me down onto the wooden chair, Polly doing me the kindness of plumping a pillow under my shoulders to keep me as comfortable as possible. And there, utterly bare and exposed to this small audience of women, I prayed to God to deliver me—and the baby.

Another three hours passed, and somewhere in that span of time, Mrs. Christy entered with more tea. "General Clark is here and waiting downstairs for the news."

I was soaked. They had placed the birthing chair right in front of the crackling fire, for it was easier for them to see. My hair was wet and matted, plastered all over my face as perspiration dripped into my eyes, making them burn.

I pushed, I grunted, I cried out, I gasped...

Mabel's face reared itself before mine, her countenance stern and staid, her homely features unyielding and unbending. "You're very near your time, and you may feel like you need to take a shit. If you feel that, push even harder. *Comprenez?*"

What could I do but nod? Focused on my breathing, I sputtered something unintelligible, and now I knew why Mrs. Christy had brought in more tea. I drank it to the dregs, thirsty as though I'd wandered through a desert. When Polly offered me ice-cold cider, I drank it down too, gulping like a thirst-deprived animal.

"Good for you," she said. "I'll bring some more."

With each pressing convulsion of agony, I bore down, teeth bared, gripping each side of the birthing chair, and striving with all of my pulsing lifeblood. Each and every pain was stronger than the last. How that could be, I couldn't fathom. They'd been intense since the beginning.

Then at last, I had an odd feeling of something sliding.

"*Poussez!*" Mabel shouted.

"You's almost there, Missus!" Chloe cried.

For a moment, I stopped, simply panting like a dog, sweat dripping down my nose. Polly rushed in with the promised cider, and I drank, only able to nod my thanks.

Another piercing, white-hot pain, so deep and excruciating I screamed like a banshee, mystified that I could emit such a sound. Again, there was a shifting, some movement.

"Harder! We see the head—*push*!"

Was I pushing harder? I couldn't tell anymore. Stars danced in my vision as I sucked air. My flesh tingled, and my hands clawed the sides of that chair until my fingernails gored the wood, adding new grooves to those already carved by women before me.

Again and again, I strained, heaving my strength downward, feeling as though my groin would be torn asunder. Now—*please*!

"Yes, yes! Oh, sweet Lord Jesus, *yes*!" Chloe shouted in victory.

Next came a high-pitched, piercing cry of a newborn, and it was over. I'd done it.

"What—wha—?"

"You got a *son*, Missus Julia. And he's one *handsome* boy," Chloe crowed triumphantly.

It was still some time before things settled. There was more discomfort as I delivered the afterbirth. Following that, Chloe and Mabel were busy down between my legs, wiping, soaking, toweling me off. "We's cleaning you and cleaning the babe," Midwife said. "For a girl so young and it your first time, you done *très bien*. Maiden births can be trying, but not yours." She even flashed me a snaggle-toothed smile as she finished whatever she was doing. Chloe lifted a bundle, wrapped in clean, fresh linen, her grin irrepressible as a warm summer's day.

"Here he is."

All of the nightmarish suffering and toil was behind me when I first held my son. I laughed and cried, Polly kissing my face in happiness, Chloe wiping tears from her own eyes. She said it best, she did. "He be perfect, Missus Julia. Just perfect."

And he was.

Will named him Meriwether Lewis Clark.

After all those two had endured together, how could I argue? Really, it was perfectly natural for Meriwether to share in our joy of parenting and family, for *he* was family.

Several days after the birth, I managed to make it back to our house, where Meriwether came to visit, hauling in a splendid maple rocking chair. "It's for my namesake, and I want to see Papa William in it before I leave, rocking his boy to sleep."

"Give me my Man-boy," Will laughed, taking the child from me and sitting down in the rocker, moving it smoothly back and forth, Little Lewis perched on his shoulder.

Meriwether sat down on the wingback next to the settee where I rested in front of the fire, watching the show. How full was my heart. Being a mother was so eye-opening. Now, I understood the sentiments of other women, for I couldn't take my eyes off of my son. As he lay on Will's protective shoulder, my own eyes were fastened there. Little Lewis and Will—my whole life rocking in that single chair.

"Perhaps he'll travel all the way to the Pacific, like his Papa," Meriwether suggested, rubbing his forehead.

"Let's hope that if he does, the trail is much improved," Will said. "Especially over the mountains."

I chimed in, "He might be a soldier. Both of you were."

"Or a marksman as accurate as George Drouillard," Will said, nodding.

Drouillard had been the Corps's sharpshooter, though plenty of the men were excellent shots. Will was a known crack shot ever since his army days, and he and Meriwether originally became friends when they served together during their early years as marksmen. I'd heard that even York had become highly regarded at shooting while on the journey. York—who had still had not returned home, much to Will's vexation.

"I swear, Bates will be the death of me," Meriwether vented out of nowhere.

There had been subtle changes to his constitution this winter, ever since he'd performed for me before Christmas. He was paler, and something about him just wasn't right, although I was at a loss as to exactly what.

Both Will and I stared at him, waiting for him to continue.

"He questions everything I do. If I call for a meeting to openly discuss something, he sends some excuse about why he can't attend. On the few occasions that he does meet with me, he's contrary, opposing any suggestion or directive I make."

Will nodded. "You must learn to work around him and never discount anything he says. He's clever and will use anything and everything against you."

Meriwether sighed. "There will be no way on earth for me to quit St. Louis this year to work on the journals, as I'd hoped. Thanks to Bates and his cronies, I'm too overtaxed to think about anything except my affairs here."

"Then do as you must," I said sympathetically. "I hope you know that Will and I are always here for you."

"Julia's right. I'm available for advice if it's needed. Don't let that indelicate louse have the upper hand."

Meriwether managed a nod, but that was all.

We sat in silence, just watching the fire, the men nursing their ale, before my new motherly instinct awakened. It always happened once I started relaxing or engaging in an activity I chose. "He needs his first bath."

"I'll go get Chloe," Will offered, getting up and handing Meriwether his namesake, which made me smile.

"He's so tiny," the governor murmured in wonder.

"You'll think that until you hear him cry," I warned. "I swear he could shatter glass."

"Do you smell something?" Meriwether looked grim.

"Mmm—that would be a full clout. My apologies that he's being so indiscreet on your first visit."

Will re-entered the room, followed by Chloe, who carried a basin of warm water.

"Yes. It's definitely bath time," I grinned. "Our darling boy has managed to embarrass his mother on his namesake's first visit."

"Oh, let me see him." Chloe gave a throaty laugh, lifting him from Meriwether.

Once she cleaned Little Lewis up, she helped me rise and Meriwether said farewell.

"The rocking chair is perfect," Will praised. "Thank you so much."

"It should see plenty of use," I added.

As soon as Meriwether left, Will brought in a small flask of peppermint oil. Sprinkling the water with the refreshing scent, he took his wriggling, naked son from Chloe and placed him in the bath, carefully sponging him with a clean cloth, holding his head above water, and paying special attention to cleansing his backside. Little Lewis loved the attention, gurgling the whole time. "You'll not be an explorer *or* soldier when you're grown," he teased, recanting his original hopes. "You'll be a *fish*!"

I couldn't stop smiling, so overwhelmed was I with pride. Finally, my dripping infant was passed over to me for his first whiskey rub, a cleansing tradition passed down by both our families. Mama had written to me advising it, saying it helped keep fevers away.

"That smells perfectly delicious!" Will exclaimed as I finished toweling Little Lewis and began massaging him gently with fingers wet with whiskey. "I might get you to give me a whiskey rub," he went on, giving me a flirtatious wink. "I'd be irresistible too."

"Everyone in St. Louis would take one whiff of you and think you were a lush, General," I answered back.

There wasn't a thing I'd change about those initial days of bliss. Polly's continued visits, Chloe's attention and love, Will's support, Meriwether's gift. How thankful I was that I had a healthy baby with whom to snuggle during that first St. Louis winter, amid thigh-deep snows and howling winds.

"Chloe, do you mind putting him to bed?" I asked.

"You knows I's privileged to do so," she replied, instantly at my side and taking Little Lewis into her arms.

As she climbed the stairs, cooing to the baby, I whispered, "What a godsend is Chloe, Will. I don't know what I'd do without her."

He just grinned, taking me by the waist and turning me toward him. "This is what I can't do without."

Mabel had warned me not to resume relations until well over a month had passed. "I wish we didn't have to wait," I whispered.

"It will be worth the wait," he murmured, nuzzling and kissing my neck. "It'll be our wedding night all over again."

Chapter XVI

St. Louis
February-March 1809

A post rider knocked on our door.

Will was upstairs, having just returned to the house from his office. I called to him from the foot of the stairs. "You have a letter from Louisville. From Jonathan."

We both lived for news from loved ones, and Will was down the stairs in no time. He slid his letter opener under the wax seal, and I could tell immediately that something was very wrong. "My brother George Rogers has suffered an accident. Somehow, while unconscious, he fell into a roaring fire. His right leg is so severely scorched it's uncertain if he'll survive without amputation."

He paused, both of us staring at one another with the same thought. This letter had been written several weeks ago. What had happened since?

He looked back down, reading on. "George is with my sister Lucy for now. She told Jonathan he had a stroke, but personally I think there's more to it. So does Jonathan."

"Let me guess. Too much whiskey?"

Will nodded. "Exactly my fear. Lucy has ever been one to protect the rest of us from God's truth." Eyes closing in sorrow, he shook his head. "I hope he'll recover. He's so broken financially due to the government's refusal to compensate him for his good works. I tell you, sometimes such slights to a man's honor can become physically dangerous."

"Should you go to him?"

He shook his head. "I regret I'm not closer—in fact, it breaks my heart—but I've duties here, and I—*we'll* be taking a long leave later in the year when we return to Virginia. If he still lives by then, I'll be sure to see him on our travels."

I slipped my arms about him. "Don't overburden yourself with worry. We'll just have to pray and give our hope to God that he'll reach full health again."

He reciprocated the embrace, and suddenly we were kissing. I felt his hunger for me, and in my mind I knew it had been long enough. No more denying him or myself.

I yielded to his yearning and felt his lips brush my neck, rediscovering my mouth. Hungry for lovemaking myself, I whimpered a soft cry of desire, for wasn't this the intended way of marriage? Scripture even said a man must cling to his wife…

That night we made love, and oh, Will was so passionate. I opened myself like never before, feeling a pulsing, vibrant pleasure in our joining. It made me full again. Once more, we were man and wife in the physical sense, bringing me peace.

Yet peace never lasted.

Will was on edge about his brother, and it manifested itself in harshness to his people. While I scrubbed my face over a basin several days later, Scott was finishing Will's morning shave. A farrier was coming to re-shoe the mule team and horses, and he was anxious to get moving.

"Damn it all, Scott!" Will barked when the slave applied a cold, moist rag to his face. "It's February. A *warm* compress would be appreciated for once."

"I's sorry, sir," Scott said. "I didn't know that's the way you wanted things."

"If only York would get his ass home. Aggravating inconvenience is what he's become. I'll be giving him what-for when he sets foot here again." He looked about. "Now, where are my boots?"

After that exchange, I piped right up. "Probably downstairs, where you took them off last night. Right next to the door."

He muttered, "If only these ne'er-do-well people of ours would just do their jobs."

Scott stood shaking his head. "I's truly sorry, sir. Not meaning to be shirking nothing, sir."

"Don't mind him, Scott. He's overwrought. None of this is your fault."

Will said nothing but shot me a dark glance before leaving.

I was due at the Christys'. After spending the entire winter with her aunt and uncle, Polly was heading home. Mrs. Christy was holding a special ladies' tea for her. After several hours of delightful female company and showing off Little Lewis, I walked back across the street, only to find Chloe waiting for me at the front gate. By the drawn, set look on her face, I knew something serious had happened.

"It's that woman Venus, who's lazy and surly sometimes. General Clark told her to help Scott unload hay bales out in the barn after the farrier left. Now, it ain't the sort of work she be used to, so she told him off, like 'no, I ain't doing that,' so he grabbed her, hauled her to the back of that barn, and whupped her about fifty times with a riding crop."

My heart sank. *Fifty lashes?* "Where was Juba? He usually spends all day in the barn to help with work like that."

Chloe made an odd growling sound in her throat. "Nobody seen nothing of him today, so Scott done took care of them bales hisself, then brought Venus out to the kitchen, and I done tended her. She be lying next to the fire. I figure she'll be all right there for now."

I couldn't even find words, so horrified was I that Will had done such a thing—to a *woman*, no less. Chloe went with me out to the kitchen, where I examined Venus's back. I was relieved somewhat, for though Venus was bruised and had welts, none of the lash-marks had drawn blood. Though it didn't make the act any less heinous, Will must have beaten her through her wool dress, otherwise the damage would have been far worse. Still, I applied more of the salve Chloe made for minor kitchen burns and scratches.

"You'll be sore a while, Venus," I said. "You stay in here by the fire for the rest of today." I looked over at Chloe. "Where's General Clark?"

"Major Christy done come by while you was over at his house. He told the general he was needed in town for something."

After leaving Venus on some blankets in front of the kitchen fireplace, I put Little Lewis to bed and waited for Will. When he came home, he tramped in, snarling like a bear. Chloe hopped up from the stool in the drawing room where she'd been mending a shirt, grabbed Rachel's hand, and disappeared.

I stayed where I was, next to the drawing room hearth. "Will? You've just frightened Chloe and Rachel. And earlier today, you beat Venus? How *could* you? If these people must serve your every whim, they won't be pleased to do it when treated so."

He sighed heavily before speaking. "Julia," he rumbled, low and threatening, "your opinion of slavery belongs solely to you, so don't you dare tell me how to treat my people—especially when they're not worth a stale biscuit. You haven't heard the latest."

Lord in heaven, what now? Obviously, I'd chosen poor timing for a scolding. I fell silent, wary of upsetting him more.

"*Damn* that black bastard! He's disgraced me and become the most dishonest villain in the territory."

"Who are you talking about?" I asked, remaining calm.

"York's half brother *Juba*, that's who."

Juba? This was a shock since, after returning my stolen honey, he'd been helpful and hardworking—especially out in the barn with Scott.

Until this morning . . .

"He's shamed me before all of St. Louis," Will ranted, jerking off his topcoat and jamming it onto the wall peg. "He and some other slave from another household broke into a locked desk at Christy's Tavern and stole a good deal of money."

My jaw sagged. "Were they caught?"

"Oh yes—while running from the scene. Both were whipped well. One of Christy's employees saw to that. I had Juba follow me home, then when I happened to look back, he'd gone. I figure he's making a run for it."

"I can't believe this," I muttered under my breath.

Will finished stuffing gloves into his greatcoat's pockets, then turned around. "Well, Christy is an honest man and his money was gone, a desk broken into, and Juba was one of two thieves." He paused, his tongue pushing against the inside of his cheek, creating a bulge. Then he added, "After dinner, I'm riding back into town to visit Joseph Charless. I'll have him do a write-up in tomorrow's newspaper about an escaped slave. Honestly, I hardly feel like staking a reward on Juba's miserable head, but hopefully I'll be able redeem that loss if we catch him. I'll sell him in Louisville when we head east this fall. Slaves fetch better prices there."

No...

This. After trusting Juba and thinking he'd turned himself around . . . I felt sick at heart—for if caught and questioned by Will, the boy might just tell him that I'd let him off easy after the honey incident.

Once Will had gone to see Charless, I went back out to the kitchen, where Chloe was washing dishes. Pulling up a stool, I snatched a clean rag out of a drawer to rub more sulfur salve into Venus's back. She was sitting up now, broodingly silent during my ministrations.

"Chloe, what do you know about Juba's whereabouts? We both know he was missing earlier."

Chloe stepped away from the clean dishes air-drying in a rack on the counter. Reaching up, she hung the towel on a wall hook to dry, then turned toward me. "I know he's still an angry young man, and angry young men get stupid in their heads sometimes."

"So you know what happened in town?" I looked her square in the eye.

"Yes, ma'am," she said, low and mournful. "I knows."

"Why didn't you tell me?"

Venus harrumphed next to me. "Cause you's *white*! That's why!"

"Mind your mouth!" Chloe snapped back at her. "If you'd had a brain in your head, you wouldn't be in here with your back all swollen up like an overripe tomato." Then she looked back at me, her voice returning to utter calm. "It has nothing to do with black or white, Missus. Has to do with timing. I didn't know about Juba till right when I started serving dinner, after Scott done moved all that hay."

"Well, at this point I really don't care how you found out, but you need to tell me what you know."

"Yes, Missus. Juba and that boy of Major Penrose been planning to run all winter long. They's been a-waiting for just the right time. See, it's just that boy of Penrose's ain't trusty more than a cracked mug o' whiskey. That one's bad news, and he done befriended Juba."

Interesting. Another slave dragging Juba back down to his errant ways. I set aside the sulfur-smeared rag, wearily rubbing my eyes with one hand. "Chloe, next time you hear something like this about someone in our household, you need to come straight to me." I glanced askance at Venus. "Contrary to what some folk think, I can't help at all if I don't know what's happening."

"But, Missus, ain't nothing you could've done," Chloe expounded in frustration. "I just figured it was best nobody said nothing. Sometimes what people don't know don't hurt them, except Juba—'cause he's just plain stupid."

Venus snorted. "You done said I was stupid."

"Uh-huh." Chloe nodded, glowering down at her. "You wanna be trusted and live to see your grandchildren have babies, you best stop your whining and skulking and do whatever the general says, cause if you get trusted in a little, maybe you'll get trusted in a lot someday."

Defeated, I left them arguing, walking back outside toward the house. Why was it that when I tried my hardest to do good for Will's people, it just didn't seem there was anything lasting I could achieve? Or it was too late. Like tonight.

It was sheer frustration.

Little Lewis was crying when I stepped back inside the house, so I bustled up the stairs to him. After changing his clout and giving him my breast for a bit, I saw him back to sleep before retiring myself.

What a day. I crawled into bed, pulling the quilt high against the chill air, and flopped back.

Someone knocked at the door.

"Missus Julia! Missus—"

Chloe. What now?

"Missus, can I come in?"

"Of course."

Chloe opened and shut the door behind her, agitated. If ever I could have imagined a black woman gone pale, I saw it in the flesh now.

Her voice was low and trembling. "Scott's asking you come out to our cabin. Right *now*, Missus."

Down the stairs I followed, then out the back door again, past the kitchen to the tiny cabin where she, Scott, and Rachel lived.

Scott was waiting at the door, and as relaxed and easygoing as he usually was, his tight lips and palpable tension betrayed apprehension. "I needs you to come in here with us," he breathed. He glanced around cautiously, verifying nobody else was near, then he slipped the door open, motioning us in.

It was dark as ink inside, there being only one tiny window covered in worn greased paper, so I couldn't see a thing at first.

Slowly, my eyes adjusted. "Where's Rachel?"

"With Venus in the kitchen," Chloe said, shutting the door firmly behind her and remaining there.

It was *cold* in their tiny space. Why didn't they have a fire going?

Scott pushed in front of me. "It's safe," he said in a low voice. "You come on outta there now."

A peculiar scraping sound emanated from inside the fireplace flue, and there was an abrupt thud as a human form dropped from the narrow chimney space into the hearth. Slowly pulling himself up, the figure whacked his head on the brickwork and groaned.

"*Juba?*" I gasped.

He was shaking, staring at the floor.

Scott prompted him to speak. "Now, you stiffen up and tell the Missus exactly what you done told me. No lying or blaming. You tell the truth, boy."

Still trembling, Juba shook his head slowly. "I didn't steal no money, Missus Julia. I swears I didn't."

My eyes were adjusted to the dark now, so I ordered him, "Turn around."

As he did so, I saw blood smears through his shabby homespun. Though the sight made me want to weep, I breathed deep, trying to quell my emotion. "You'd best tell me God's truth from the beginning."

"Me and my friend Kitch, from Major Penrose's, we done decided to run. He says he has a free-born cousin in Pennsylvania who would let us live with him, and we could find work there."

I rolled my eyes. "*Pennsylvania?* Does Kitch even know how far away that is?"

"No, ma'am. But he done told me we was too poor to get there. He said we's gonna go in to Mr. Christy's but didn't tell me why. Now, everybody knows Mr. Christy's a kind man, and I just figured Kitch was gonna beg for a jug of ale or loose coins. Sometimes Mr. Christy gives something to us folks when he be feeling charitable and all."

"So you just followed Kitch into the tavern in total ignorance, and he did the stealing? Is that your story?"

"Yes, ma'am. I waited just inside and seen Kitch sneak into Mr. Christy's office, and I says, 'Kitch—what's you doing there?' He didn't say nothing, just took a hammer outta his pocket and crashed into Mr. Christy's desk. Somehow he knowed exactly where to look. He snatched that money, grabbed my arm, and we done run, fast as lightning. Then one of Mr. Christy's workers—a Mr. Geoffrey—he come running after us, shouting for help. Several other men from town joined in, and we was caught."

"And they whipped you?"

"Mr. Geoffrey did. But he showed me some mercy, Missus. I

only got fifteen stripes. Kitch? He got thirty since he was holding the cash."

"Where is Kitch now?"

"Sent back to his master, I guess. By then, General Clark done showed up and ordered me to follow him home, but I was scared of what he'd do and run here because I knew Scott would help me."

"I just hope he be telling the truth, Missus," Scott said.

I agreed with that much, for the entire story seemed far-fetched. Could Juba have really been that naïve? I debated with myself what to do. Will had threatened to sell him in Louisville, and I wasn't convinced I could change his mind, even over the course of six or seven months. Once he decided on something, there was usually no talking him out of such. Juba was bleeding, though I couldn't tell how bad fifteen lashes had left him.

"Missus, I's afraid the general might kill me or sell me somewhere bad," pleaded the youth. "I knows I stole your honey that time, but I ain't *never* stole nothing else. And I swears, I didn't know Kitch was gonna steal, or I'd have stopped him or left or something. I just wanted to run. Freedom is all I ever wanted."

I stared upward, sighing. Freedom was what they all deserved. Here would be my greatest test of faith, carrying out what was on my heart. I knew if I didn't do it, I'd live the rest of my life regretting it. But if Will found me out . . .

Dear God in heaven, please never let that happen.

I took Juba's hand, spitting my words out before I could swallow them. "Juba, do you still want to run? *Can* you run with your stripes so fresh? You won't make it to Pennsylvania, but you could head south, downriver, where nobody knows what happened. When you think it's safe, you could hire yourself out cheap to somebody headed to the Cumberland. From there, you might be able to make your way to Ohio, where slavery is against the law. You have to decide if you want this, for unless you turn yourself in to the general, this is really the only choice I can offer—a turned head and blind eye. You'll have a rough road ahead, but it might also mean you could eventually be free. You willing to take that chance?"

For a very long moment, there was no sound except for a rat scratching someplace in the walls. Then Juba nodded slow and sure. "Yes, ma'am. I knows it's gonna be hard, but I want to run where nobody gonna find me no more. And I ain't gonna run with Kitch neither."

"Then you have to go tonight, and you won't be able to tell Nancy or anybody else good-bye because nobody knows where you are. We have to keep it that way."

Juba nodded, face grave.

"Now, I'll give you what money I have in my purse. It'll be my gift to you, but neither of you"—I glanced at Scott and then back at Chloe—"*neither* of you must *ever* breathe a word of this to the general. Understood?"

"Yes, ma'am." They spoke in unison, their eyes wide and apprehensive.

"Juba," I whispered. "I'll be praying to the good Lord that you'll make it to safety. *Somewhere.*"

Chloe followed me back into the house, and I instructed her what needed doing. "When you go back out, stop by the kitchen and get that salve you made that we've used on Venus." Once upstairs, I counted out four dollars from my purse. Tears stung my eyes. I'd hoped to give him five or more, but this was all I had. Oh, how slim was the chance he'd even make it three miles before being caught, much less all the way to wherever he'd wind up. And in *February*, of all times.

"Tell Scott to go to the barn and find him one of our old quilts in the loft. He'll need something to keep him warm."

I searched through my dresser drawer, finding a small pink satin bag in which someone had given me a decorative comb. Into it, I placed the money and a pair of pearl earrings I didn't need. "Take this with you and be sure you cover his stripes with that ointment before he leaves."

Chloe nodded and disappeared.

My lips moved subconsciously in prayer as I prepared for bed, for now I could only give his life to God, knowing that at least I'd done something.

And here again was another secret kept from Will. But I was learning hard that some secrets could keep a conscience clear.

❧❧❧

I would not be dancing at this ball.

Oh, the music was lively, but the dances were all French or Creole, unfamiliar to me.

The boathouse in which this public ball was being held was next to the river, and March's frigid winds whipped against the rickety structure, assuring it remained terribly cold. No braziers for warmth, just lanterns placed near the dancing space. Attendees lurked in shadows against walls, and I joined them. No punch or cider—nothing even *resembling* a fun-filled ball back home in Virginia. Occasionally, I'd see a trader or boatman reach into a pocket to withdraw a Pitkin flask, guzzling its unknown contents. Gin? Whiskey? Rum?

Liquor was abundant in St. Louis.

It had to be the most disappointing social event I'd ever attended, and I was grateful I'd dressed in warm woolen tweeds, for I could actually see my own breath. Not that any of this was anybody's fault but my own. Will had warned me before coming, and my insistence to attend had been all my own doing.

"Seriously, Julia," he'd counseled. "You shouldn't bother. You'll be disappointed, for St. Louis public balls aren't genteel Virginia affairs. Most of the 'guests' are fur-trader types or scandalous women. Besides, Lewis and I have organized a meeting there regarding fur company interests. He's finally written the formal proposal for Sheheke's return, and I'm afraid I won't be able to dance or entertain you much. Why not just stay here at home and enjoy Little Lewis by the fire?"

Too late now.

Winter had been too long, and by the end of my pregnancy I'd had little social life. As much as I relished being a mother, I missed Polly and the easy friendship we'd had.

I spied movement out of the corner of my eye. Mademoiselle Escoffier, the brothel owner whom Madame Chouteau had pointed out to me last summer, was shaking hands with a sailor, undoubtedly a client. Escoffier looked elegant—hardly what I'd *ever* imagined such a woman to look like. Out of the corner pranced another brightly painted and youthful lady—younger than Escoffier, snatching the sailor's arm and smiling more than willingly. The two sashayed past me, slipping outside, heading only God knew where to have their tryst.

I tried to focus on the dance taking place. An out-of-tune clarinet squeaked, and I laughed to myself. How could any of those poor musicians keep an instrument on pitch in this frigid air? This ball was every single reason why Papa had hesitated in awarding Will my hand. But here I was—*more* than just surviving.

"Why, Mrs. Clark," a male voice inquired, "what are you doing here all by your lonesome?"

I'd been so busy witnessing the prostitute pimped that I hadn't seen the tall, lean form approaching to my right.

Frederick Bates. Could the evening get any more dismal?

"My husband is tending to business and should return soon." Was that enough to brush him off?

"You'd better hope he does. This time of evening is when drunken brawls tend to break out at these sorts of gatherings." He sniggered, crossing his arms and leaning back against the wall beside me.

I didn't reply, irritated and tacit.

After an entire dance was nearly done, he spoke up again. "May I ask you something?"

"Ask away."

"It's come to my attention that you and General Clark have been catering to Chief Shehekes every need. I'd like to know why. Is not the government's treatment of these people more than satisfactory? We've spent a small fortune on them."

I turned to stare at him. "Certainly, the barest of essentials don't cost 'a small fortune,' Secretary Bates. Moldy confines and dank, dark barracks aren't what any person might consider *satisfactory*, much less a family used to fresh air and open plains."

"Very well. Then I gather you and the general have been providing them feather beds, fine china, and linen napkins?"

"Why is this your business?"

Bates snorted. "No need for unpleasantry. It's just that I've found there's a fine line separating personal and government business, especially when it concerns your husband and the governor."

"And you consider *yourself* the judge that determines which is which? I've never heard anything so punitive. If anything, the people responsible for *leaving* Sheheke and his family in such egregious conditions at Cantonment Belle Fontaine in the first place should be blamed for infringing on their human dignity." I paused as a gall of anger rose in my throat. "Really, I don't owe you any sort of explanation; however, should it *deter* you from pestering the governor or my husband, I'll state that assisting the family was all *my* idea. Not theirs."

I began to walk away, but he stepped away from the wall and physically blocked me, his next words spoken in a low, menacing tone. "Well, I'd stop those visits if I were you."

"You're *threatening* me?"

The disturbing note Scott found in our door last fall came to mind. Since then, I'd received nothing more, but there were times at night, lying in the dark, when the thought of it kept me from sleep. Perhaps I'd just discovered its origins. In his bigotry and dislike of the natives, Bates was certainly a likely suspect.

I was still considering a response when he repeated his warning in a chilling tone. "Stop helping them. They're nothing but beasts and savages."

"That's your perception, sir. *Not* mine."

"I've insight into their barbarism."

I would have asked what he meant, but a huge crash resulted in some women's screams and the music coming to a sudden halt. A cluster of boatmen were knotted within a scuffle and had smashed right into the performing instrumentalists, who were scattering and shouting their outrage.

"Told you it was about time for a drunken brawl," Bates exclaimed, laughing at the violence.

Dancers were bolting, and I saw Will striding over from where he'd been in deep discussions with his business partners. I glanced around, expecting to say something more to Bates, but he was gone.

"Let's get home, angel," Will said, wrapping his arm protectively about me. "This is no place for my love."

In bed that night, my mind clung to the certainty that I'd found out who had either written that note or had someone else do it for him.

Frederick Bates.

What was it about that man? Was he so full of prejudice that he was blind to humanity?

"I spoke with Bates tonight," I whispered into the darkness.

Will was nearly asleep. "Mmm... my condolences."

I rolled over to face him. "Why does he despise Indians so much?"

With a sigh and stretch, Will also turned over, gazing at me with tired eyes. "I'm not entirely sure, but he's told me before that he thinks I'm too soft on them. Truth is I simply understand them better than he does."

"How so?"

"Jefferson's intent was for a gradual assimilation of indigenous peoples into the United States, but I'm telling you, it's not assimilation they want. *Land* is everything to Indians, and how can I blame them for that? To them, the earth is a living thing—something to which they belong. And I don't disagree. It's where they hunt, where they fish..."

"But there must be some reason Bates hates them so."

"When I first arrived as Superintendent of Indian Affairs, somebody told me that Bates lost a dear friend up in Michigan Territory due to an Indian attack. Supposedly, the fellow was scalped and had his limbs severed with a tomahawk. A pretty grisly way to go, and all due to some land dispute. I don't know if the tale is true or not."

I had a feeling it was.

Land.

Will placed great importance on it. All of us whites did, but then, it was our culture. How could an entire people be expected to change theirs? And how could the Indians possibly compete with the opening of the West? Eastern natives had already been pushed farther and farther westward. How long would it be before it affected tribes on the plains?

Tribes like Sheheke's people: the Mandans.

Chapter XVII

St. Louis
March-May 1809

Will bought me a new horse.

Older than Cassie had been, she was still responsive: a cream-colored mare with a blue eye that I named Sage. On a mid-March morning when the snows were mostly melted, I dressed warmly, seeing that Little Lewis was fed and safely placed into Chloe's care. Then I cantered out for a visit with Sheheke and Yellow Corn, bearing news from Will.

On the outskirts of the encampment, settlers in the village nearby were sowing their fields. I smiled and waved at them, knowing I needed to engage in similar work soon. But like many hardworking farm-folk, they barely responded aside from stares.

Dismounting, I tethered my mare at a post shared by militiamen's horses, then made my way toward the earth lodge. It was little Lodge who greeted me, smiling and missing a tooth, his hair tied back out of his face.

"Lodge!"

"Where baby?"

"I rode over myself today, so I had to leave him home this time." I usually only brought Little Lewis along when Will was with me.

"Inside, come!" he invited.

I followed as he flipped up the lodge flap and allowed me to enter first. Yellow Corn's dark eyes lit with pleasure when she saw me.

"Hąpe shí're," I greeted in traditional Mandan, beginning the routine we'd adapted over past visits.

Yellow Corn replied in English, "Hall-o, Julia."

"Where is the chief?"

She spoke some rapid Mandan to Lodge, who disappeared back outside. "Lodge find him. He with militiamen, teaching them talk with hands."

Nodding, I removed the shoulder pack strapped across my person, rummaging until laying hands on a package and presenting the gift with a smile. "I've brought you sugar to sweeten your cornbread."

She accepted, sweeping her hands toward the skins and cushions on the floor in invitation. "Sit."

As I settled myself, the flap of the lodge opened again, revealing both Sheheke and Lodge.

"When it's you, I hurry fast." Sheheke nodded, grinning. "Where is General Red Hair?"

"Omaha men are visiting St. Louis to speak with him. They are meeting today, so he suggested I ride out on my own."

"I see you have new horse. Is good horse."

"Yes, thank you, Sheheke."

Yellow Corn rattled off more Mandan, and Sheheke held up his hand to silence her. Then he said, "Two days past, Ramses Phipps came here. He tell us to stop stealing their dogs."

My memory of Ramses Phipps was vague, though I recalled he had issue with Sheheke about a chicken last year. "Why would he accuse you of such?"

"He says men in settlement are missing dogs. He thinks all Indians eat dog."

Shocked and appalled at the treatment these people had received so far from their home, I sighed, staring into the fire.

Sheheke said, "You no worry. Yellow Corn wanted me to tell you. But we have militiamen. Good men guard us." Changing topics, he asked, "Now, you have news for Sheheke?"

"Oh, Sheheke, I do."

He studied me hopefully, sitting down to listen. "I hope the news makes me smile again."

"It will. General Clark wanted me to tell you that you'll be going home this spring. Plans are in progress."

Yellow Corn understood enough to give a whoop, clapping her hands and bouncing with joy. "Home! To Mitutanka!"

Her delight brought a smile to my face.

"When in spring?" asked Sheheke. "After sunflowers are planted or when corn is seeded?"

Their understanding of time was so different, making it difficult for me to explain. "I wish I could tell you exactly, but I can't. There are still details needing to be determined, like the mustering of enough militia and acquisition of supplies. And you'll have more men with rifles to protect you. The general wants you to arrive home safe this time."

"How many?"

"I've heard well over one hundred."

The chief fell silent, then said quietly, "Pryor said four hundred were needed to face Arikara."

"True. I've heard that too. But there is another plan. Arikara enemies will be invited along the way to join the party upriver through dangerous territory. If it works, you'd have a multitude of native people *and* white men working together to see you home."

"General Red Hair will lead?"

I shook my head. "I'm sorry, but no. It will be Jean-Pierre Chouteau."

"Aha." Sheheke nodded approval. "He is a good man. This is all good. Thank you for the message."

I nodded. "It brings me joy to see you content." And it truly did.

Sheheke prodded the fire, and Lodge plopped down next to his mother, shaking a buffalo-bladder rattle and grinning playfully with his sparse teeth. Yellow Corn spoke some solemn-sounding words to Sheheke, and he nodded in obvious agreement, not taking his eyes off of me.

Clearing his throat, he said, "I learn much from these years on this journey to see the Great White Father, but my greatest lesson is that the season of my people is changing. It is a storm I cannot stop. None of the Hidatsa, Lakota, Arikara, or Omaha can stop it. This storm is a blizzard of white men that will change these lands forever."

I glanced at Yellow Corn, dismayed to see her cheeks wet with tears.

"Jefferson, your Great White Father, spoke peace," Sheheke continued, "but he also spoke power. My own eyes saw the white man's cities, armies, and people who number like kernels of corn at harvest. Jefferson's words invited peace—*or* it will be war. Americans have more guns, more people, more warriors. I saw this. I know this to be true."

My pulse pounded, for Sheheke saw what Will saw—what I saw now too. The west's gateway had been flung open, and nothing would ever be the same. How long the process of transition and change would take, none of us knew, not Sheheke and certainly not me. Would it be peaceful or forceful, with lives lost? Would it come in my lifetime? In Will's? Would there be enough room for white settlers and Indians to share?

Yellow Corn had risen and gone to a satchel, rummaging. She pulled out a long calumet—the traditional sacred pipe smoked by the Plains peoples, solemnly presenting it to her husband. Sheheke removed dried plant matter from a pouch at his waist, tamping it down into the clay pipestem. It made me smile, thinking of Papa or Meriwether doing the same thing.

He raised the pipe, a long eagle feather dangling from the stem and strings of buffalo-horn beads and a bushy coyote tail embellishing its length. In a high, mournful voice, he began crooning, chanting.

I bowed my head. There was no telling what his song was about, other than the sound of it was moving, reverent, timeless—a sort of blessing.

When it ended, I looked up, and Sheheke slowly brought the pipe back down. Yellow Corn brought over a braid of smoldering sweetgrass to light it. When I could smell its earthy scent at last,

Sheheke placed it to his lips, inhaling deeply and pausing before releasing a lengthy exhale.

He spoke, "Lone Man—a great spirit—did not bring us the pipe. No, our people and those of other tribes say that a woman brought us the first pipe and taught us to use it. It was sacred and good. Since then, we share pipes with those we wish to trust and call our own."

He extended the pipe to me with both hands, and tentatively I accepted, bringing it to my mouth. I inhaled a little—not much. I didn't want to dishonor myself or Sheheke by coughing, thereby not meeting his expectations.

Acrid, bitter—a gag started at the base of my windpipe, but I held my breath and sat motionless until the sensation eased, blowing the smoke out in a swift puff. Forcing myself to swallow hard, I took several rapid breaths, preventing myself from hacking, swallowing several more times, my eyes watering.

I gave the pipe back. He took another draw, waiting again and then sighing the smoke back out with relaxed ease, handing it over to me again. This went on a while until finally, after eight or nine exchanges, Sheheke handed the calumet back to Yellow Corn. He stood, motioning me to rise too, and as I did our hands joined above the small fire that continually burned inside the lodge.

I wasn't at all sure where this was leading.

"We have not traveled too far a distance together, yet we have come many miles, we four," Sheheke said, nodding at his family. "Today, you brought news making my heart glad. Today, you have become my daughter. From now on, I will call you Óti shí Míȟe—Kind Lodge Woman, for you have come bringing goodness through your gifts and your time. You have helped us make a home where we were not welcome."

On the other side of the lodge, Yellow Corn began singing in the same high-pitched, wailing sort of vocalese with which they made music.

It was the most moving experience I'd ever had in my life.

While riding home, I cried off and on. I was so filled with wonder and pride. What would Mama and Papa think? Their youngest daughter from Santillane being adopted by Sheheke—Chief of the Mandans.

I rode into the stable, and Scott scurried out of the house to tend Sage. He'd scarcely gotten to the barn when I lifted my leg from the sidesaddle's heads. I went to hop down but instead fell—the entire saddle flopping off unceremoniously onto the ground along with me. Sage snorted, sidestepping and tossing her head.

Scott cried out, offering me his hand to help me up. "Oh, Missus Julia! What happened?"

Perplexed, I looked about me where I'd landed on the barn floor, eyeing the saddle. Scott was already bending over, and he lifted the girth—or what remained of it.

"Look here, Missus," he said. "This here girth done been sliced, probably with a knife."

Cold fear tingled on my scalp as I stared at the cleanly severed strap of strong leather, which had been like new. Scott was right. It was intentional. Another threat? An actual attempt to physically harm me?

Bates? Who else would do this? My mind raced...

"Somebody wanted you to fall and get hurt," Scott affirmed, head wagging. "We best tell the general."

"*No!*" I got up, brushing off my skirts. "No, we mustn't." I wasn't sure I was making sense here, but I didn't want Will to know. In no way did I want to jeopardize any opportunity I had left to spend with Sheheke and Yellow Corn, since they'd be leaving soon.

"Scott," I breathed, "say *nothing* to him. Swear to me. I don't want him to find out."

"Now, Missus, you ain't gonna go out riding alone again?"

I shook my head. I'd have to show some sense. "No, I won't. Next time, you'll drive me. So are we in agreement? You won't tell?"

Scott worked his tongue around his cheeks the way he often did when faced with a difficult task. "I ain't so sure you's making a good choice here," he said. "But I won't tell nobody."

As I made my way back to the house, I willed my limbs to stop shaking and step inside as though all was well.

Yet another secret.

※

Now, I lived encumbered with the outlandish knowledge that someone wanted to harm me, so Scott always accompanied me whenever I went out. The only real place I felt "safe" was at home. I discovered a resiliency I never imagined I possessed, training myself to push the anxiety of it to the back of my mind, instead anticipating the joyous prospect of visiting home—even when it meant keeping one skittish eye open and glancing back over my shoulder with caution.

Mama, Papa, and the rest of the family would finally get to see Little Lewis, and letters from Fincastle brought even more bliss, for between Caroline and Mary, I was now an aunt several times over, and Harriet was due to give birth sometime in September. I'd get to see her new baby.

Every day, I allowed myself time to daydream about Santillane. Eyes closed, I'd envision the old log courthouse, the steep hill full of trees leading up to Fincastle's collection of clapboard and log buildings, and the peace of Johnny's gravesite, right beside our beloved Presbyterian church. In my mind was the scent of lilacs after late spring sunsets, whip-poor-wills calling at night, and the taste of sweet purple clover on my tongue, coupled with the dense, acrid smell of meat in the smokehouse—last winter's hams.

And of course, there was the grand Catawba tree, my beloved respite from life's quandaries.

Home.

It meant greeting friends outside of church on Sunday—something I missed a great deal, for aside from Catholic priests who still struggled to maintain a log parish, there was no connection to Protestant denominations whatsoever in St. Louis. After attending one mass, I was disheartened. Presbyterian as I was, I couldn't understand the Latin, and people were kneeling, rising, crossing themselves, and kneeling again. Thus, I spent time early in the mornings feeding Little Lewis and reading a Bible given to me by Pastor and Margaret Logan for our wedding.

I had always felt closest to God outside amid smells of the earth. I sensed His presence most when surrounded by breezes, plants, and rustling branches. It delighted me. Chloe, Nancy, Venus, and little Rachel would sing while watching with pride as our lettuce, beets, asparagus, and kale popped up near the flowers we'd planted. Peonies in particular were a favorite of mine, their deep pinks and stand-out petals lifting high and proud toward the sun.

On a balmy afternoon in May, Little Lewis napped in his cradle as we worked the garden, Rachel beside him, giving him gentle nudges to keep him rocking. Sweet, sweet Rachel—what a good-natured child—her hair ever tightly plaited.

"Keeps it off her face," Chloe always said.

As lively a thing as Rachel was, she was still naïve as to what her life would be—that of a slave. I was determined to soften that blow as much as I could. Struck with creativity at Christmas, I gifted her with a rag doll whose face and hands I'd stained with coffee, turning it to Rachel's own skin tone. Delighted with the gift, she carried "Suzy," as she called it, everywhere. How blessed she was to still be child enough not to have prejudice marring her mind.

I loved her just like Little Lewis.

A cool breeze tugged at my bonnet, and I sat back a moment, squinting up at the blue sky and inhaling, savoring the day. It felt good to have dirt on my garden gloves and feel sunshine on my face.

Chloe began another song, and hearing her, joined by the others, I figured I was attending church in God's ultimate cathedral—His creation. Deep and resonant, Chloe would lift up a song like a tithe, so full of faith, music about Jesus, deep rivers, chariots, and arks. Then little Rachel chorused in, her instrument high, clear, and flute-like, a contrast to her mother's mellow contralto.

We'd become so close, Chloe and I.

She was entirely different from other slaves I'd tried to befriend, even back home at Santillane. Megg had always been pressured by Papa's expectations and demands and ever mindful of Mama's supervising eye. At Santillane, there was always that stiff formality of "they are them and we are us." However, here in St. Louis, Chloe, Scott, and Rachel lived and worked alongside me like family. My hope was to eventually see the others experiencing that feeling, those who still had reservations of being too close to the "Missus."

In the midst of our gardening, a sudden commotion arose from the other side of the house. Chloe stopped singing to listen too, but it was difficult to gauge whether something good or bad was happening. But then I heard Will shouting, so I pulled off my gloves and stood up.

"Chloe, come with me. The rest of you, stay here and keep up the good work. Rachel, watch over Little Lewis for me," I ordered.

I tossed my spade into soft-turned earth and, lifting my skirts, walked briskly around the house, Chloe at my elbow.

There—with his wrists bound to a stout tree branch and his shirt stripped to his waist, was someone I'd not seen in months.

York.

He must have arrived on one of the later boats from Cahokia since he hadn't been here this morning.

Right then, it was as though I'd traveled back in time years ago to when old Sticks Howard whipped poor Ares and Virgil senseless. That dreadful day when I'd felt so helpless to do anything for them. The very day I'd first met Will.

And now Will's back was to me as he wielded a wicked-looking bullwhip. Before I could protest, he swung his arm back in a wide arc, the lash flying back straight toward me. I'd never moved so quickly in my life. Reflexes heightened, my hand shot out, snatching the end of the leather lash in midair. Of course, I couldn't hold it; it whizzed through my palm, stinging my flesh, but sent enough of a sensation to the other end to cause him to whirl around.

My, but he was surprised to see his wife. My hand was still smarting and blood was rising up, but I didn't care.

Chloe moaned behind me, "Sweet Jesus, help us…"

Will froze, a look of shock on his face. "*Julia?* What are you—"

"*Don't hurt him!*" I bounded forward several steps.

He was breathing hard, hand tight on the whip, shaking with pent-up rage. His voice went soft and slow when he spoke. "I'll damned *well* do to my property whatever I need to because he's due a lesson."

I doubt my mind had ever worked as nimbly, for suddenly I had a lesson for *him*. The very words he'd spoken in response to the people of Fincastle shot through my head like a rifle's lead ball. "'To respect the rights of humanity . . . will be the leading principle of my life,'" I recited boldly. "That's what you said to folks in Fincastle? *Isn't it?*"

He stood there, mouth agape and red-faced, sweat beading his forehead and soaking through his linen shirt. Did I catch a fleeting look of shame in his eyes?

Undeterred, I continued. "You *said* those words, William Clark, so don't be a hypocrite. Leave him be and respect *his* right to humanity!"

Will's chest heaved. Slowly, he lowered the whip and took a step toward me.

I shuffled backward. "No—*no*! Don't you touch me."

"He was *months* late returning, Julia—you know that. I have to discipline him. There's nothing else for it; can't you see? My word must not be ignored. I won't stand for it among my soldiers, and I sure as hell won't stand for it with my people!"

I faced him, trembling but holding my ground, begging him, "Leave him be. Please! Put the whip down..." My inconvenient pneumonia cough tickled and I tried to suppress it by clearing my throat. It liked to raise its annoying head if I was out of breath.

Peripherally, I saw Scott striding over from where he'd been, way down in the cellar, organizing and packing tools for our relocation. And from around the house, here came Nancy and Venus, far too curious to remain in the garden as I'd asked.

"You go back into the house now," Will whispered softly to me. "I've business here to tend to, and it's best for you not to be here while I see to it. Go on now. Go back inside."

I stood there dumbly, head shaking and tears stinging my eyes.

This time, I couldn't find any elaborate words, simply entreating, "No . . . *no* . . ."

He nodded at Chloe. "You get your mistress inside, you hear?"

Chloe took my arm, urging me toward the house. Part of me wanted to shake her off, but Will was bent on this course, and as single-minded as he could be...

I kept mouthing that one word, sobbing, shaking my head, "No."

Once more I turned back. "Don't do it, Will. *Don't do this!*"

Chloe steered me to the porch, Will tapping the whip handle on his hand as the spectating slaves all stood by in horrified silence.

"We gots to go inside," Chloe intoned gently, her hold on my elbow firm.

She guided me through the door and into the drawing room, both of us sinking onto the settee, and she held me, humming in my ear, cradling me in her arms and rocking me gently back and forth. Resonant and soul-melting, her music was sweet as ever, but no melody could completely mute the crack of that bullwhip outside.

⁂

It was dusk, and I'd already put Little Lewis to bed. Chloe met me downstairs with a basket of clean rags and whiskey.

"Thank you," I acknowledged, feeling numb. "We can't let infection set in."

Will didn't return to the house after the whipping. I imagined he'd gone to town. He wasn't the drinking sort, but when stressed, he didn't mind downing a few mugs of ale, and I doubted he was eager to confront me.

Oh, eventually that time would come, but I dreaded it.

Chloe returned from the kitchen with the whiskey flask, and I asked, "How will I ever be a wife again, Chloe? How?"

"Mmm... You will. 'Cause you has to, and you's a good woman. That's how."

She sat down on the other end of the settee from me, waiting a spell before speaking. "You know, men ain't nothing but watermelons, and girls is always hungry for melon, but when you pick one out, how you gonna tell if the melon's sweet or too seedy? You can tamp it on the outside and listen for a holler sound. You can look for black buttons on each end and squiggles on the rind, but when it all comes down to it, until that watermelon is done sampled, you ain't knowing *what* you got."

My emotional exhaustion lapsed into sudden laughter at her ridiculous analogy and the seriousness in which she'd shared it. Yet it held truth.

She reached out to me, taking my hand. "Look what you done did to yourself taking a stand for York out there."

I studied my hand, now bearing a bloody slice on the palm where I'd snatched at the whip.

"We gonna fix you up first," she said, reaching for the whiskey and one of the clean linens.

I sat motionless, allowing her to clean and bind my hand. Strange, but I felt nothing until the whiskey drizzled into the wound, and even then the burning couldn't possibly be as painful as what poor York had endured.

"You think Juba got away, Chloe?"

"Ain't no way of knowing."

"I hope he's safe. I hope he found a boat and stowed away. I hope he's in Ohio."

"Mmm. Juba be York's brother, so he'll take care of hisself unless somebody nabs him and turns him over."

"I've been praying nobody does."

Together, we carried the bandages, whiskey decanter, and a full-to-the-brim basin of cool, clean water toward the barn. Sweat trickled down my back and dampened the linen chemise under my workdress. The air was still and humid, even for May.

A bolt secured the barn from the outside, and Chloe hauled it open. There was a grating sound, and evening's soft light streamed from slight gaps between the clapboard, miniscule particles of dust floating before me while my eyes adjusted to the splotchy light.

York was facedown on his stomach atop some hay inside the

nearest horse stall. Flies buzzed around his back. Hearing us, he pushed up with his arms, turning his head to see who had come, his eyes hard, jaw set. When he saw me, he turned away, flopping back down with a grunt.

I set down the basin, and Chloe lowered the basket, both of us crouching beside him. "I'm going to clean your wounds," I said. "I'll be gentle."

He said nothing, but I could hear his teeth grind.

Maybe he didn't understand, but I cared about his plight and wanted him to know this mercy was coming from *me*—a Clark—not Chloe or anyone else. I didn't hesitate, but reached into the basket for a clean linen towel to dip into the basin. Lightly, I blotted, removing dried blood and dirt. Several times, I folded the soiled cloth, not wanting grime returning into the wound. York's back was a crisscrossed thoroughfare of cut flesh, and it was measured work. My hackles rose in virulent resentment at what my husband had wrought. Some of the stripes had severed deep and would probably drain for days.

"I'm going to apply whiskey now. We can't have it fester."

No response. York stared straight ahead, face buried within his crossed arms—not unlike the way Will often lounged about.

"It's going to burn," I warned.

Nothing.

Chloe handed me the bottle, and there was a little pop as I removed the cork. With a steady tilt, I eased the liquor out. York's night-black flesh quivered as it made contact, his only manifestation of pain.

"I've been told that as children you and General Clark were close as brothers."

Not a sound.

"There's not much I can do to bring peace between you, but if there are ways I can make the lives of his people more tolerable, I shall ever strive to do so."

"No white lady gonna make no difference for me," he finally muttered, his voice like gravel.

"Think as you will, but this white lady won't let your wounds go intended."

He didn't reply to that.

Perhaps I was finally beginning to understand York. The man had so much anger and antipathy inside. I thought aloud, "You know, you're the only black man to have ever gone all the way to the Pacific."

That triggered a reaction.

"And you know what I got for that? While all them white men on the expedition was getting their share of money and lots of land to go with it—them *wise* white men in Washington City done gave me nothing but an extra bagful of army rations. That's what I got. After all my hard, sweating work, just like the rest of them. That's all, and Master Clark—he didn't say nothing 'bout old York."

The injustice made me stiffen, and I felt heat rise to my face. As I applied Chloe's sulfur poultice, I agreed with him. "Reasons for your bitterness are clear, but cling to the fact that you're ahead of your time in firsts for your people, York. Always remember that. I've seen in the general's own journal how you and Sakakawea were allowed to vote for a preferred campsite when you reached the Pacific. Think about that. This was a military expedition, and no black man or woman of any race has ever cast a vote in this country, so your vote was a landmark of achievement in itself. Don't let anger harden your heart. Think of your achievement."

After a pause, York asked, "You think I'll ever get to see my woman again?"

"I don't know. But if there is a next time, you'd best come home when you're expected."

He grunted. "I should have done run—made my break, just like Juba." His hands tightened into fists.

Chloe had been silent until then. She snapped, "Then you's more a fool than I thought. Running might well get you killed. Juba might not have no younguns, but what would your woman and children think if you run and got shot or hung? Hmm? Lot of good you'd do them then."

"She's right," I agreed. "It would be a very dangerous move, especially following all of this. Now, I'm truly sorry for the way things are, but remember something. I'm the general's wife and I'm your *ally*. I'll interject on your behalf when I can, but you have to do your part too. By making General Clark angry, you're merely rubbing salt into burning wounds."

York said no more, no thanks for my care—nothing. But the important thing had been done. I'd planted a few more seeds to make a difference. And isn't that what Reverend Mitchell had encouraged? To do whatever I could?

"Chloe and I will be back tomorrow to tend to you again."

Finished, we left strips of whiskey-moistened cloth on his wounds along with the remainder of the whiskey for him to drink to dull the pain.

Late spring's longer shadows seeped through the barn slats as sunset approached. They set a picket-like pattern amid the hay and sawdust motes, which stirred with our movement again as we left. Chloe secured the bolt from the outside, imprisoning York within, but I reminded myself that our intent was different from Will's. Right now, it was to save York from himself.

We walked side by side toward the main house, Chloe striking up a haunting song, and I realized it was the melody she'd hummed to me during York's whipping. Now I heard the words for the first time:

I held my brother with a trembling hand, I would not let him go
I held my sister with a trembling hand, I would not let her go
   Wrestle on, Jacob,
   Jacob, day is a-breaking
   Wrestle on, Jacob
   Oh, I will not let you go.

How was it that in one afternoon my marriage had been reduced to nothing but an awkward burden of avoidance?

Will came home late the night of the whipping. He found me in the drawing room before the fire. Little Lewis was teething and as irritable as his father.

Will turned his back to me, removing his boots. "We need to talk."

"If I speak my mind right now, you'll be sure to take offense," I said evenly.

"York was in the wrong. He's my property, and I handled it. That's the end of the matter."

I buried my face in Little Lewis's softness, not wanting an argument when the baby was just going to sleep.

"Come on up to bed now," Will said.

"If I come up tonight, it won't be our bed I sleep in," I whispered.

Will paused, then stiffly headed upstairs, his footfalls slow and heavy all the way to our room.

In the days that followed, I took to sleeping in the empty upstairs guest room by myself rather than joining Will in ours. Thinking too much about what I'd say made me overemotional, and he remained defiant, so I discovered that neither of us was ready to talk about what had happened.

Not yet.

At mealtimes, I was pleasant but aloof. Meriwether, who always dined with us, had to be well aware that something major had happened betwixt Will and me and steered clear of any thorny conversation. Table topics were mostly between the two men and I kept my peace, excusing myself early to help Chloe clear the table.

A few weeks after York's whipping, Lewis made an announcement at breakfast. "My physician, Dr. Saugrain, is administering smallpox vaccinations. He's been involved in some of the scientific studies in the inoculation's preparation, and I strongly urge you to have my dear namesake treated—and be treated yourselves."

Dr. Saugrain was well respected in the territory. He preferred administering herbal medicines whenever possible, but was also an intelligent adherent of scientific study, and the smallpox vaccine was saving lives. I'd heard of it, but wanted more information.

"What does it entail?" I asked.

Meriwether explained, "Just a minor pricking or cutting of the skin on one's arm or hand. Then the vaccine is administered to the wound. It's over quickly, so the pain is minimal, but there is a reaction period in several days' time. However, it's nothing compared to suffering from the disease. Truly, I urge you both to act while Saugrain has it available."

I'd been sipping tea, and my hand was resting beside my cup. Unexpectedly, Will reached over and covered it with his. Though I started to pull away, he took hold, firm but gentle.

"Neither of us want the Man-child hurting. However, if he were to contract the real virus, it would be far worse—probably fatal at his young age. Smallpox runs rampant at times."

He continued holding my hand. I stared down at the contact, trying to concentrate on the important discussion at hand, but I had been unprepared for Will's touch.

Meriwether cleared his throat. "From what I've read, the vaccine is derived from a cow disease appropriately called cowpox, which is no threat to humans. I think it's remarkable that it protects against smallpox."

"I'm going to have it," Will announced. "And I want Little Lewis to have it too."

He was looking directly at me, his fingers rubbing my hand. "If all three of us have it, Julia, it could preserve our lives."

That wasn't all he wanted. He was using this moment to woo me back, but this decision was important—anything having to do with the life and health of our son was significant, and as a new mother, I was becoming more conscious of that fact daily.

"What do you say, angel?" Will coaxed, using his favorite nickname for me.

Meriwether added, "If it gives you more comfort to know this, more and more people back east are receiving the vaccination. I've heard of no ill reports, and as governor, I've done my share of reading on it."

Everyone knew of a family member, relative, or friend who had succumbed from the disease, for smallpox was a lethal killer. Of course I wanted my son safe. "Then I give my blessing. Little Lewis shall have the medicine, as shall I."

"Good, *good*!" Will crowed like a cock, releasing my hand and clapping enthusiastically. "Now, we'll never have to worry about our boy ever getting smallpox."

"But there are others I love and care for who also need it," I said. "Could we request Dr. Saugrain to visit Sheheke's camp so they could receive it too?"

A slight pause, then, "That's an excellent idea," Will concurred.

"And all your people should get it too."

"That's not necessary." He shook his head.

For a split second, Meriwether's eyes met mine and he smiled knowingly. "Actually, Clark, it would be more than wise if you wish to preserve them. Jefferson has record of his own slaves' vaccinations. He saw to it that they received them, and none became ill."

Will paused, this time longer—looking directly at me. "Very well, then. *All* of my people shall be vaccinated, as shall Sheheke and family—if they wish it so."

I nodded my assent, thinking, *Thank you, Meriwether.*

Chapter XVIII

St. Louis
May 1809

Dr. Saugrain rode out to Sheheke's encampment with Scott and me on a brilliant May day. His final patient rounds in St. Louis ended late, however, so by the time we arrived, late afternoon shadows stretched clear across the path, covering us with shade.

Usually, Lodge was always the first to scamper out and greet us, but today it was Yellow Corn who met us at the hitching post. Her mouth was set in a grim line.

"Lodge hurt," she cried out. "Settler boys hit him with stones and chase him home. Lodge run fast, get here safe. Sheheke take gun outside and shake at them, then they run off."

Dr. Saugrain and I exchanged fearful glances. How thankful I was that he'd come, today of all days. Inside the lodge, Sheheke was sitting with his son, the boy stretched out and fighting back tears with balled fists. His face was badly bruised, with several serious cuts demanding stitches.

Next to the boy's cot of soft bear furs, Sheheke's rifle rested against a lodgepole.

After the doctor administered willow tea to Lodge, helping him relax, Yellow Corn stationed herself next to her son to calm him while Dr. Saugrain began stitching.

I stood amazed.

The child uttered not a sound—even when Dr. Saugrain explained that he'd also need to make a tiny cut in Lodge's arm for the smallpox vaccine.

"Lodge, what a brave boy you are," I whispered in awe as Dr. Saugrain applied vaccine into the incision with a tiny spatula.

"Every hour or so, I suggest more willow tea," Saugrain instructed. "His face will be sore with more bruising tomorrow, and the tea should relax him some. There are still chunks of ice floating downstream in the river. I suggest riding over and getting some before nightfall. Ice compresses will lessen any swelling."

Sheheke and Yellow Corn also accepted the offer of the powerful medicine. Smallpox had already proven fatal to the Mandans when thousands died back in the 1780s due to an epidemic raging northward from the southern plains.

Saugrain addressed all three patients to the care of their inoculations.

"Remove your bandages tomorrow. Within a few days or a week, you'll all form pustules. Leave them be, and they'll form itchy scabs, but try not to scratch. Eventually they'll fall off, leaving only tiny scars."

Sheheke spoke solemnly in awe of Saugrain's work. "This good medicine. None of us get sick now."

"At least not from smallpox," Dr. Saugrain agreed with a smile.

I followed the doctor out of the lodge as he departed to ride home. "Thank you so much. Who knew Lodge would have that scrap with boys in the settlement? Your timing today was perfect."

"*Avec plaisir,* Madame Clark. It is disheartening to see how cruel children can be." He glanced at the western sun. "It is getting late. Should you not begin the ride back too? I could accompany you and your driver back to town."

"Thank you, but I have a few more things to discuss with the family."

"Very well. *Au revoir* until my next visit to your home."

That would likely be soon, as Meriwether had been showing more signs of illness lately.

Back in the lodge, Yellow Corn had made her son as comfortable as possible, and the willow tea had relaxed him into sleep. The rest of us, including Scott, gathered around the fire for a brief chat.

Sheheke asked his usual question. "Is there news of when we go upriver?"

I had to be honest. "Nothing more yet. I'm sure that when the time is near, the general will come to inform you."

Sheheke sighed. "You are always welcome here, Kind Lodge Woman, but I miss seeing him and speaking my heart to him."

"I'm sorry. He's been very busy—partly in preparation for your return trip." I left it at that, having no desire to bring up the fact that Will and I were estranged, that being the main reason he hadn't accompanied me in visits Scott and I had made these past few weeks.

"I must speak to General Red Hair soon," Sheheke persisted. "Yellow Corn feels shamed to be in place where we are not welcome."

What could I possibly say? I glanced in her direction. She sat staring down at the fire, her eyes troubled.

I nodded. I couldn't imagine her dilemma with a lonely child and nobody with whom to spend her own days except her husband and boy. They were so isolated here. Strange, but before coming to St. Louis, I imagined I'd be the same way, but my days had been busy and full, even without Will in my bed.

Yellow Corn spoke again to her husband, rather sharply, and he nodded, offering translation. "She says she's glad to go when the time comes. White men here are not friendly. I go to settlers after Lodge was hurt. I told them it was wrong that my son was beaten, but that man Phipps has a poisoned tongue. He was there and spoke for other settlers, saying we are bad people, stealing their land, hunting and planting on it." Sheheke became impassioned, raising both hands to make his next point. "How can I steal land when it is not theirs?" Then he raised his fist, declaring, "It belongs to all men."

As Scott and I prepared to leave the lodge, Yellow Corn followed.

I wrapped one arm about her shoulder. "I'm so thankful he's safe. If he needs anything . . ."

My sentence didn't need to be finished. Her nodding told me she really would seek help were it necessary. I would have to tell Will about this. There was no excuse for Lodge to be bullied and bloodied by other children, chasing him like a pack of feral dogs.

Yellow Corn said, "I want Mitutanka, Julia."

"I know."

"Soon, Julia."

I nodded. All I could offer was a hopeful smile and brief embrace. It was getting dark, and Scott and I needed to get back before anyone got worried.

❧❧❧

I glanced westward. Already, the sun was setting. We'd stayed too long.

Scott helped me up onto the buckboard. Usually, the creaking wagon and its churning wheels set me at peace. Not this evening, as the day's last throes descended into still and quiet, Scott and I were both uneasy.

Two previous threats along with Frederick Bates's words at the ball haunted my mind like ghosts. What a pity to be so anxious, for warm nights on the prairie were wondrous. Toads squeaked from hidden places in the brush, and the melancholy, low coos of prairie chickens rose in a nocturnal chorus, somber and mild—blissful music all its own, whose adagios would have lulled me to sleep at any other time. All was quiet, and aside from sounds of the grasslands surrounding us, we heard only the tread of the mules' hooves on solid earth.

Two miles or so into our return, we entered a wooded stretch, the prairie melodies dissipating. Somewhere nearby, a lone owl hooted his presence when Scott abruptly halted the team.

"What is it?" I whispered, my heart accelerating.

"Them mules hear something," Scott breathed, his voice barely audible.

Sure enough—their ears stood tall and at attention. Rupert, the big male, pawed at the ground, snorting and tossing his head.

"Rupert ain't one to get all nervous-like," Scott said.

Ahead of us, the tall shadow of a man materialized from the

trees, as though out of nowhere. On foot, he paced toward us leisurely with a long, purposeful gait. Miniscule hairs on the back of my neck rose, and my hands went clammy. Now at the front of the wagon, he stopped.

Scott hailed him, "Evening, sir. Do stand aside, if you will, so's we can pass."

"I ain't moving a muscle until Mrs. Clark there gets off that wagon and comes over here, nice and quiet-like."

He knew me, and it nagged at me how I'd heard that voice before.

"Who are you?" I demanded.

"Well now," the stranger drawled, his hat pulled down low in the darkness, making any identification impossible. "We met once. My poor brother lost his home because of your husband siding with them Kickapoos."

Phipps! It was that man Phipps. Hadn't Sheheke just told us how he'd been inciting trouble? Had I been wrong about Bates? Or was Phipps working with him?

He stepped toward us, hat still low over his brow, shading his eyes. "So I figure since General Clark took something of my brother's, I'll take something of his."

I hissed, "*You* left that note in my door?" A tingling fear swept over me. I gripped both sides of the wagon seat tight.

Scott reasoned right along with me, "Then you's also the one that cut Missus Julia's saddle strap."

"Aw, now. That's one dirty accusation a-coming from a lowborn niggah."

"You're making a mistake not visiting General Clark and discussing this grievance man to man."

"Already tried that, remember? You was right there, in Sheheke's lodge last fall, when I retold the tale. See, your husband pretty much destroyed my family. After Odysseus was forced off his land, he didn't have nothing to eat—or nowhere to go. By the time he walked all the way to Cape Girardeau to try and find work? Well, he done collapsed with the pneumonia. Least that's the story folks from them parts told my mama. He died homeless. Alone, without no family with him to soothe his soul." Then his final words coursed out in a venomous hiss, "All because your bastard of a husband took some militia and forced him off his land."

Attempting a calm that I wasn't feeling at all, I kept my own voice low, trying not to escalate the situation. "Mr. Phipps, General Clark explained that it *wasn't* your brother's land to begin with. It was Indian land on which he chose to squat. I'm terribly sorry he ended as he did, but he made the wrong choice. Now be reasonable and kindly move aside so we can pass, and I'll tell the general to see you at his earliest convenience."

"Oh, he'll see me, sure as shooting. And he'll see my folk at the settlement too. I done worked them up to a damned frenzy, and they're ready to take him on, make no mistake about that. They'll be a-looking for him when he comes a-looking for *you*."

He was still directly in front of the mules, and before I could blink, he rushed at Scott, reaching up and snagging his arm, hauling him off the wagon roughly. Scott landed on his side with a heavy thump but managed to scramble up. Rupert and Nell danced a few nervous steps forward, so I reached down and snatched the reins, pulling them to a standstill. It would be too easy to panic. I needed to stay calm and think.

By then, Phipps—a huge brute of a man—had hauled Scott over to the side of the road and was pounding him with his fists.

"He gots a knife, Missus!" Scott screamed, helpless and unarmed.

Rifle . . . beneath the seat . . .

Will always made sure that loaded, half-cocked gun was there before using the buckboard, but had he remembered to put it there this time when I'd announced we were riding out?

Frantically, my hand reached beneath the seat, trailing, groping—dear God, let it be there—let it—*yes*! Thanking the Lord, I lugged it out clumsily, settling back on the bench and aiming while holding steady and fully cocking it. It clicked, and I shouted, "Stop, or I'll fire!"

The two men were still struggling, Scott managing to force the knife out of Phipps's hand. I heard it drop softly to the ground, but then I saw Scott's head snap back as Phipps bashed a fist against his temple.

One last warning: "I said *stop!*"

Phipps's hand let fly again, smashing into Scott's face a third time.

Kli-FOOF!

Flames blazed from the rifle's pan on my right side, but there was no report.

No—a flash in the pan? It didn't fire? Was this really happening?

Phipps stood up and turned around to me slowly, laughing between heavy breaths. "Well, ain't that shitty luck? Looks like it's just you and me now. I'll have to hand it to the general. He's got decent taste in women. And I've always liked 'em frisky. I'll secret you away someplace *real* special, and maybe he'll learn next time that us farmers deserve the land we pick."

Everything was happening so fast. I feared he'd killed Scott because my eyes caught the brief flash of the knife in the dark. It was back in Phipps's hand. He had retrieved it.

Now he was coming for me.

One advantage was left to me. I was still atop the wagon holding the rifle.

Closer, just come a little closer.

I waited until the timing was right, then I smashed that rifle butt into his head as hard as I could, hearing his nose crunch and having the satisfaction of seeing both his hands reflex toward the pain—the knife dropping again—*dropping*—

I jumped, landing painfully on one ankle, off-balance. In a blink, I scrambled down for the knife, two rough hands snatching me by the armpits and ramming me against the wagon so hard my breath was gone. Then Phipps's forehead thudded into mine, his sour breath filling my gasps as I tried to recover. A steady trickle of blood was dripping down the front of his face where the rifle butt had struck.

"Naw—you ain't gonna get away now," he exhaled, his unclean smell invading my person. Arms moving upward, he pinned me firmly against the buckboard, and I felt his crotch grind into mine, a lustful smile curling onto his mouth.

Rupert began to bray, lifting and twisting his head around, and then there was the strangest sound—a *whoosh* followed by a thud, seemingly out of nowhere. It was only a split second since I'd glanced away, hearing the soft, odd noise, but when my eyes refocused on Phipps again, he had frozen, his mouth drooping open and his eyes listless. He exhaled with a long wheeze, his weight folding over me, both arms falling limp. I felt spatters of hot blood shower my face.

How—what had just happened?

In a voice more welcome than an angel, Sheheke called, "You hurt?"

My head shook as I watched Phipps ever so slowly crumple away from me, down to the ground. As he dropped to one side, I saw the single arrow protruding from his back.

My adoptive father had just saved my life.

Quivering, trembling, feeling sick, I stared down.

Motionless, but was he really dead?

Sheheke swiftly came to my side, pulling forth a soft shred of doeskin. Gently, he wiped my face and began to sing softly…

"Hi-yi-yi, Hi-yi-yi, Hi-yi-yi, Hey-yah…"

When he removed the cloth, I saw the blood he'd wiped away. Phipps's final breath had sprayed me crimson. Horror gripped me, but I came back to myself when a moan faintly joined Sheheke's song from across the road.

"Scott?"

I ran to him, sinking to his side in three strides. "Scott, it's Missus Julia. We'll get you home. You rest easy now. Stay still."

Oh, he was still indeed, slipping back into unconsciousness again.

Oh God, don't let Scott die!

I lowered my head to his chest, satisfied and relieved only when I heard his steady heartbeat. For a moment, I just sat there, listening to Sheheke's song.

"Hi-yi-yi, Hi-yi-yi, Hi-yi-yi, Hey-hey…"

I looked over my shoulder at the chief. He had started moving rhythmically and slowly around Phipps's body, as though apologizing to it in song.

Scott moaned again.

I turned back to Sheheke. "I'll help you load Phipps into the wagon," I called, hating to interrupt his spiritual rite but also troubled by Scott's suffering. "Between us, we should manage, but we need to get Scott home."

Before lifting the body, Sheheke braced himself with one foot atop Phipps's buttocks and jerked his arrow out clean. Then together we heaved, Sheheke taking Phipps's arms and I his legs. Carefully, the chief climbed up onto the buckboard, and I labored with all my might, both of us grunting and breathing hard, as I gave Phipps's hip a final shove—both arms above my head. The body thudded into the back of the buckboard.

Wordlessly, Sheheke climbed down and we proceeded over to Scott, who was now struggling to sit up.

"The more you help us, the more you make a Mandan smile," Sheheke told him.

Each of us supported Scott on one side, guiding his foot to the high step of the wagon without falling. Nor did he even complain about having to bed down beside a corpse to get home.

While Sheheke tied his horse to the back of the wagon, I climbed back up. The chief sprang up to the driver's seat next to me, and I shook my head in wonder. "Sheheke, I owe you my life. It's a miracle you came when you did. How—how did you know we needed help?"

He picked up the reins. "Lone Man told me. He's a good spirit."

I blinked in puzzlement, marveling. Had some goodly native spirit really visited him? It was uncanny, and I had no more words.

Sheheke glanced back at Phipps, musing with a shrug, "At least Ramses Phipps won't tell me not to steal dogs no more."

❧

"I was coming to search for you!" Will cried, bounding out of the house to us, followed by Chloe, who carried Little Lewis.

Though I saw them, I had withdrawn into myself. My mind kept repeating the sickening feel of Phipps's blood splattering my face, his weight upon me, and his vile lust. The night's terror was fresh within me.

Will reached the wagon and climbed up, taking me into his arms with relief that I was safe. But I was as unresponsive as Suzy—Rachel's doll. Arms limp at my sides, I turned my face away from him.

Following that was a flurry of activity, and though I was aware of everything, I sat dazed and silent, overhearing that the night hadn't ended; there was unfinished business. Will was now in charge, and in my sorry state I vaguely heard him tell someone that he'd need my presence to prove I'd been attacked. I braced myself, for now he'd discover that I'd kept certain facts from him. The note Scott found in the door, the sliced girth…

As if things between us weren't already tangled enough.

Several of his male enslaved, including York and Ben, carried Scott around to the kitchen, where Chloe could tend him. He'd be staying here. Little Rachel appeared, taking charge of Little Lewis, every bit as capable as her mother.

Ben brought out some old quilts from the barn, wrapping Phipps's body up in the back of the buckboard while Will sent York over to the Chouteau mansion with some important message, of which I knew nothing. I just sat atop the buckboard in my bloodstained clothes, and the only thing Will allowed before our hastily planned return trip to the settlement was for me to drink some tea and wash my soiled hands in a basin of water brought to me for that purpose. For that, I was most grateful.

When we departed, Will rejoined me in the wagon, placing his hand atop mine. "I'll need to ask you questions tonight, angel. I know you've been through an awful ordeal, but for us to come out of this unscathed, I must know everything. St. Louis has but a measly four-man police force who know little of native affairs. I want this handled as quietly as possible."

I looked down at his hand covering mine and felt my heart stir at its warmth.

Not long thereafter, I was bouncing along in the buckboard again, this time next to my husband. He slapped the reins hard atop Nell's and Rupert's rumps, both mules winded and trotting as fast as they could. Ramses Phipps's corpse, now wrapped in musty quilts, bumped and rolled about in the back of the buckboard whenever the wheels hit a rough spot. Sheheke trotted alongside us on his horse.

Will explained to him what the present mission would be—to see that his family was transferred safely into Jean-Pierre Chouteau's hands to begin their journey upriver the very next morning.

And indeed, Will had been gravely concerned over my absence; his solicitude had been evident in his urgent greeting, to which I'd felt numb. I had also anticipated him to be angry that I'd withheld danger from him. Beneath all of his immediate responsibilities, he probably was, but for now his real feelings were buried beneath duty.

Within the woods, not far from where the night's drama had played out, he pulled the mules up. Will clasped hands with Sheheke once more, thanking him for rescuing me. "Alert the militiamen at your camp of my imminent arrival. I'll need them, as we need this to look as official as possible. I don't want you blamed for murder."

Fear nagged at me, for I'd been considering that ever since the attack. A voice in my head kept telling me that few men sitting in judgment would take kindly to the murder of a settler by a native chief—regardless of his reason or affiliation with Will and Meriwether. The settlers would see Sheheke dead once they learned he'd killed Phipps. They'd show him no mercy at all. And what of Lodge and Yellow Corn? The very thought of them in harm's way made me tremble.

Will was quiet for a moment after Sheheke spurred his horse to leave, then he said, "Now tell me everything. When did you first receive a threat?"

It was time to be open and honest. "Late last fall—October, November?" Oh, how hard it was to think clearly.

Will reached over, taking my hands into his. "That was the only written message you received?"

I nodded, still unable to meet his eyes. "Yes." Earlier, while at the house, I'd confessed where I'd hidden it behind a loose brick out in the kitchen. Now it was tucked inside Will's coat pocket.

"And the next incident?"

"On the only day I rode out alone to see the family by myself, someone sliced through my girth. I assume Phipps cut it, but we'll never know for sure. Scott and I challenged him about both the note and the saddle girth, but he didn't confess."

"Did he mention anyone else's involvement?"

I thought hard about that, closing my eyes and swallowing another terrifying flashback—reimagining Phipps's hands on my shoulders, unyielding, his blood spraying my face.

Forcing myself to respond, I said, "Well, folk in Phipps's settlement have been downright hostile to Sheheke and his family. Phipps was goading them on with lies or misinformation about the Indians and their intentions to plant corn, remain where they are, provide food for themselves—"

"How did the settlers manifest Phipps's insurgency?"

"Just last night, Lodge was struck repeatedly by rocks and eggs when he tried to innocently visit the settlement, curious and lonely. And when Sheheke confronted the settlers about his son, Phipps was stirring them up against him. Lodge's injuries may have come by bullying children, but their parents did nothing to stop it."

And those same settlers would be out for blood against Sheheke and his family once the truth about Phipps's death became known.

I paused, pondering if I should bring up my first suspect. Dear Lord, after all that had transpired, I owed it to Will to be an open book. "Part of me wonders if Bates was complicit—perhaps as the initial instigator. Have you ever seen Phipps in his company?"

"Never. And after meeting Phipps in Sheheke's lodge with his stark reminder that I'd 'wronged' his brother over that illegal land claim? No. I would've remembered that." He glanced at me before adding, "I agree Bates is one unpleasant bastard, and after Odysseus

Phipps's land dispute, he told everyone I favored Indians too much, but I can't imagine he'd go out of his way to harm you. Lewis? Maybe, but not you. Now if I had *proof*—"

I shook my head. "You won't find any. At the boathouse ball, he told me to stop giving goods to Sheheke and his family and was so intimidating I gave him a piece of my mind." At that point, I felt the first tears from the ordeal tracking their way down one side of my face.

"Damn it all!" Will swore, his ire seeping out at last. "Julia, do you think I'm so callous a man not to be disturbed at these threats against you? You should have told me about all this at the beginning!"

I sniffled, looking away to stifle a sob, and it softened his frustration, so that he eased his tone. "You're right," he admitted. "There's no solid evidence that Bates hired Phipps to harm or kidnap you. His comments could have been pure coincidence."

Will clucked to the mules, resuming our ride toward the Indian encampment. "With Phipps dead, I'll need to speak to the farm-folk where he lived and return his body. We can't have a death without any explanation. Regardless of who's at fault, he's still dead. If there is conflict between the settlers and Sheheke's family, they'll likely lay blame on me too. I fear that if we approach this the wrong way, it could mean more violence."

His words prompted another thought, which came out more emotional than I'd expected it would. "And they're expecting you, Will," I warned fearfully. "Phipps told me that. His attempt to kidnap me was in part to lure you to the settlement."

He reached down with his right hand and gripped mine firmly, driving the rest of the way with his left.

Upon arriving at Sheheke's camp, Will rousted five sentries from the militia to accompany us. Once they'd armed themselves with rifles, lead, and powder, Will briefed them as to the situation and his intentions. Before departing, he posted the remaining three militiamen in close proximity to Sheheke's lodge to protect the family. The other five soldiers rode in the back of our wagon along with Phipps's corpse, and we arrived at the settlement right before dawn.

Will stopped just within sight of the buildings.

"What is it?" I managed, exhausted and apprehensive after what last night had wrought and what might still transpire.

"I don't see any stock," he murmured, brows furrowed. "Horses, cattle, sheep—they've corralled them someplace out of danger or free-ranged them. It's too quiet."

He was right. In the darkness preceding daybreak, I heard dogs barking from within houses, yet nothing else stirred. "Remember, they're waiting on you. Be careful."

Will gave me a curt nod, then turned to the militiamen. "Gentlemen," he began in a soft voice, "I suspect they already know we're coming or are at least expecting something. I need two volunteers to make an initial approach with me." He looked at the nearest man to him. "Get up here behind the driver's seat. If things get bad, take this wagon and get the hell out of here. Report straight to Governor Lewis. You other two, cock your rifles and follow me." Then he looked my way. "You stay right here, understand? Get into the back of the wagon and stay down—out of range."

With my heart thudding in its cage, I obeyed, but only after turning toward Will a final time. "Be careful—*please*!"

He said nothing more, just hopped down, striding away, back straight and fearless like the explorer and soldier he was, the two sentries flanking him, rifles at the ready.

There was no gunfire, so I kept my head high enough to watch for movement within the settlement's picket-fenced space separating abodes and barns from fields beyond. Then I saw movement. As Will and the two militiamen proceeded on, steadily sweeping their rifles one way and another, more shadowy figures crept out from corners and crevices between outbuildings, from behind trees and unhitched wagons.

Did Will and his men see them? My vantage point in the wagon was higher than theirs. With the settlers appearing and sneaking about in the predawn light, it was apparent that Will and his two men were hopelessly outnumbered.

No longer could I stand it. I sprang up, leaping down from the wagon, not even considering the risk. The militiaman at the front of the wagon hissed at me as I ran toward my husband, "Ma'am! Come back here!"

I didn't. Because if Will was destined to die here, then I'd die too. For all I'd kept from him and *still* kept from him. For the love still fighting within me that wanted to forgive and forget—

The two militiamen whirled around at the sound of my footsteps. Will's head snapped back at me. "*Damn it*, Julia! You disobeyed me!"

"Well, if they have a modicum of decency," I panted, coming up next to him, "then they'll be less likely to harm you if a woman is present. Isn't that what Sakakawea did for you and Meriwether among the Indians?"

He stared at me with both anger and respect, brow cocking and eyes narrowing.

"Who's that there?" shouted one of the settlers—a man acting as their spokesman, rifle poised, ready to shoot.

"Hold your fire," Will called back. "It's General William Clark, Superintendent of Indian Affairs, and I come peacefully."

The name William Clark was household jargon, and several more of the armed settlers continued forward, curious, rifles at the ready.

"Get off our land, Indian-lover!" another shouted. "We knew you'd be a-showing up."

The first speaker said, "General, we's a peaceful folk, but them Indians yonder settled here without asking."

Will shook his head. "You're misinformed. They didn't have to ask. That land isn't being farmed by any of you. That's exactly the reason Jean-Pierre Chouteau advised them to *temporarily* camp there."

"One of our men—Phipps—says you's always protecting Indians! You listen to 'em, invite 'em into town, treat 'em like kings." That was Spokesman again, his rifle aimed directly at Will. "When's somebody gonna speak up for *us* instead of giving ear to a bunch of savages?"

"And where *is* Phipps?" someone else called. "He should've been back afore now."

Will ignored the question. "Lower your gun," he ordered Spokesman. "We're just having a conversation."

Slowly, hesitatingly, Spokesman relaxed his rifle's muzzle, propping the butt onto the ground beside him. With a motion of his free hand, he signaled the other men to lower their weapons as well.

Will nodded, grateful. "Thanks for the courtesy. Now, it's true that I host Indian delegations. It's part of the way we're able to live in peace with them. Our way of life is coming directly into conflict with theirs. They know it as much as any of us. Entertaining them amiably is the best method I know of to promote understanding between our peoples."

One of the farmers yelled, "Them Indians over there in that lodge could rob us blind or kill us in our sleep. Damned chief's family has no business here. *None!* And them Kickapoos who was on Odysseus Phipps's land had no business there neither."

"You're wrong," Will explained patiently. "First off, that lodge you speak of holds but three souls: Chief Sheheke of the Mandans, who is a personal friend of the president, his wife, and his young son—who was physically harmed by some of your own children. How can they possibly be a threat to any of you? Secondly, Odysseus Phipps *illegally* settled on Kickapoo lands."

Spokesman pointed out, "Phipps says that chief could call for more of his braves to come and massacre us in our beds."

"He lied. Sheheke's people are clear up along the northern Missouri. He's a kind, honest man and should have been treated with neighborly welcome instead of distrust."

"Where is Phipps?" another man brought up. "He should be here."

There was a brief moment of silence before Will made the admission, "I know his exact whereabouts. But first, I'll ask each of you here to lay down your rifle so we can continue talking like gentlemen."

Spokesman shook his head. "Sorry, General. We ain't playing

that game. If you know where Phipps is, out with it." He lifted the muzzle of his gun again, pointing it at Will, and the others followed suit.

I barely dared to breathe when something odd caught my attention. Dawn was just breaking; the sun was cresting on the horizon. I was afraid last night's horrors had thrown me into madness, for in the blinding morning rays I saw a woman limping forward on a cane. She was perfectly aligned with the sunrays, burning my weary eyes, making me squint in disbelief.

Real or apparition? A spirit, like Sheheke's Lone Man?

I decided not to wait and find out. Heart sprinting and with my impulsive Hancock nature, I stepped forward before Will or my own common sense could stop me. "Ramses Phipps is dead," I declared loudly. "But before any of you start shooting, you need to believe my husband, for he's telling the truth. It was *Phipps* who was spreading lies and mistruths all over your settlement."

"Julia," Will hissed.

But my words threw them, many of the men lowering their sights and staring at me. I had momentum, so I kept going. "Ramses Phipps tried to kidnap me last night on the road to town. He beat my driver, stabbing at him with a knife. And look at my clothes," I challenged, gesturing toward myself. "I had peacefully visited our three Indian friends, as we have for months, but Phipps assaulted me with ungentlemanly intent. When his knife fell to the ground and he leaned over to retrieve it, I snatched a rifle from beneath the wagon bench and shot him in the back."

In a low voice, Will growled, "Go back to the wagon, Julia. Now."

"Wait."

Every head turned, including mine.

The voice had come from the apparition, now fully visible, limping unsteadily out of the rising sun's blaze so that we all finally saw her. Older, crippled, she was a middle-aged woman whose weather-worn skin and clothing spoke of a rough life and impoverished conditions. Her rheumy eyes took in my blood-spattered bodice.

Nodding, she turned to the menfolk. "Ramses left yesterday afternoon, never coming back. Ain't seen him all night."

"Your name, madam?" Will inquired gently.

"I's Regina Phipps."

Will nodded, glancing at me and decisively running on with my lie. "You have my sympathy, ma'am. I regret things came to this, but what you see evidenced here by my wife's attire are the results of self-defense. However, we are honorable people and have brought your son home to you. We'll hand him over, asking only one thing"—his voice rose toward the gunmen who still threatened—"that you folk allow us to resume our own lives, free of accusation. My wife merely protected herself and her driver."

A silence as loud as winter's gales ensued; my wrists aching from clasping my hands so hard, while my pulse drummed in my ears.

Regina Phipps turned toward the men, speaking loud and clear. "Everybody here knows my son had a mouth on him. He could stir up trouble outta nothing, and I knew he had it in for Indians. He was always thinking they'd try to plant on our fields and hunt near our homes because of my other son's history. Ramses didn't trust 'em, and I a-feared he'd try to do something stupid, but a mama's love never made no child the wiser. For all of the interfering, lying words, and accusations he used to turn you men against the general here, I ask forgiveness, for I's a peaceable woman. I just regret burying a second son today. Both my Odysseus and Ramses have destroyed themselves."

Spokesman replied to her, "You might be willing to let the general off easy, but we menfolk wanna know what deal we get by letting this woman go when she killed one of our own. What'll we get, General?"

"I'll tell you what you'll get," Will called out—and far from pleasantly, ready as he was be done with the whole business. "Tomorrow morning, Chief Sheheke and his family are leaving you, never to return. You'll have no reason to rise up each day with hatred or prejudice, and your anger toward these people who have never harmed you in any way can die, just as Phipps did."

With that, he whirled about, snatching my arm and guiding me toward the wagon, ordering the militiamen still perched in it to bring Phipps's body to his mother. Then, lowering his voice in my ear, he ordered firmly. "Get up there."

Little did I like his timbre, but indeed a disobedient wife like me probably deserved such in his eyes.

❧❦❧

This particular stretch of the Mississippi was so broad it even dwarfed Jean-Pierre Chouteau's sturdy keelboat. Yet my friends' journey home would begin on this very vessel, and God willing, this time they'd make it the entire way. Handpicked marksmen from area forts would escort them both on shore and in canoes until the second boat with more men and supplies was ready to depart and could catch up.

"You I will miss," Yellow Corn whispered to me, her hands lifting a necklace of shiny black jet and rawhide from her neck. "This comes from a place of sunsets," she said. "It is my gift to you."

"But I've nothing for you," I replied regretfully.

Just as she had when we first became friends, she took my hand, placing it over her heart, and I took hers. Once it was in place above my left breast, she whispered, "You give heart. Greatest gift of all."

We embraced, rocking back and forth, both of us knowing how unlikely it was that we'd ever behold each other again in this lifetime. Perhaps we would in another. We could pray for such.

Sheheke and Lodge came over.

"Thank you, Miss Julia," Lodge said in perfect English.

I knelt so we were eye to eye. "I'll miss you, Lodge. Now show me your arm." The bandage had just been removed, per Dr. Saugrain's instructions. "No picking at it, promise? Remember, the doctor placed great medicine here to keep you safe from smallpox."

The boy smiled, nodding.

I stood, and Chief Sheheke of the Mandans took me protectively in his arms. "Kind Lodge Woman. Daughter, you are forever painted upon my spirit. Be at peace."

With my fingers, I brushed away my tearful emotion, managing a nod and watching the family board the boat, joining Chouteau. Boatmen began hauling the craft's lines up against the current while others poled, commencing their labor upstream. Their journey would be long and arduous.

"Safe travels!" called Will, lifting one hand.

Sheheke did likewise. We stood watching until their party disappeared around a bend in the river, winding slowly north and west.

Back on the buckboard, Will clucked to Rupert and Nell, who began plodding their weary way toward St. Louis. I stretched, rubbing my temples, anxious to crawl into bed and try to begin healing from the previous night.

Will broke the silence, "My, but I married a tenacious and impetuous girl, just as her father warned. And a clever one too—accepting blame for Phipps's death to protect Sheheke as you did."

"Living on the frontier forces one to be bold," I replied, realizing what a cool head I'd kept when it had been necessary and how adeptly I'd lied, ensuring the chief's safety. My, how I'd changed since coming to St. Louis.

"Julia," Will pleaded gently, "swear that you'll never again hide things from me that could prove dangerous. This business could have been far worse, and you know it."

That was reasonable, so I nodded. "I promise."

"If anything had happened to you, I don't know what I would have done. Losing Scott is one thing, for he's just a slave, but the thought of losing you—"

My breath's swift intake at his return to prejudice was audible, and he glanced at me. He'd left me with no words, just more sorrow to accompany my heavy soul.

You're so wrong, I thought. *Life is precious. It doesn't matter how it's packaged or from where it comes.* I shook my head sadly. Moments ago, we had been close—so *very* close. I thought perhaps today would end with things changing, that I could forgive or that he would ask forgiveness for treating York and the others so.

To be fair, I'd earned his criticism for being hardheaded back at the settlement. But he had to voice his hard-nosed, slave-owner sentiments.

"Julia?" he queried, sensing my wall of defense returning and probably not even conscious of what had offended me.

"What a shame you haven't considered valuing the lives of enslaved black people as you do native Indians," I remarked, my eyes straight ahead as his bored into me.

We rode on—me wishing his heart would change or that mine could soften. The rest of the way home was silent and troubling, interposed only by the clopping hooves of two exhausted mules.

Chapter XVIII

St. Louis
June 1809

I plumped up my pillow, setting aside the copy of *Gulliver's Travels* that Mama and Papa had sent me for Christmas. Our hall clock chimed eleven, so I extinguished the oil lamp next to the bed and settled in for the night.

Since the day of York's whipping, I'd slept in the smaller upstairs guest room. Will and I remained cordial but not intimate, and I could tell he regretted that. So did I, for that matter. Lying alone in the cool room with a fire down to embers, not feeling him next to me...

Here came the tears. It was the same every night.

I missed him—how we made love, his touch, his caresses. *Desperately*, I missed him, but I also possessed a stubborn resolve. My heart had not yet forgiven him, and I didn't know when it would.

However, tonight Will wasn't even at home. He was attending a fur company meeting, and it was late, and since his wife was not sharing his bed, it had likely turned into a tavern party.

For a long while, I lay awake. Since the Ramses Phipps attack, I often had trouble getting to sleep. Having Little Lewis next to me in his cradle helped. I'd rock him until finally dozing off, and sometimes, if slumber deserted me completely, I'd steal out to the kitchen and make bread dough. Better to do something useful, in my estimation.

Sometime after midnight, there came a loud pounding on the

front door, startling me awake. Sleep still had me blinking as I sat up before scrambling about in the dark for my moccasins, pulling them over my heels and sliding out of bed. Still fussing with my robe, I shuffled to the stairwell. Chloe was already at the door, lantern in hand.

Something was wrong.

Will came in huffing and grunting, supporting Meriwether as best he could, his friend leaning haphazardly against him. Meriwether's face shone pale like the moon.

Instantly, I thought of his visit to Santillane. "I'll turn down the guest bed. Chloe, fetch some cold water and clean rags."

I hastened in front of Will as he half dragged Meriwether through the dark drawing room. In the guest room, I jerked the counterpane and linens down from the top of the bed, snatching a candle from the mantel, then darting back to the drawing room fireplace to coax the coals into providing light.

By the time I returned, Will had propped a wilting Meriwether on the edge of the bed, and I settled the wavering candle upon the side table's pricket. Turning to Meriwether, I reached over, feeling his clammy forehead.

"Too much to drink," Will confessed with slurred speech, wiping his own face of sweat. "Both of us, actually."

"Well, he's not just drunk. He's hot as an iron."

Godsend Chloe bustled back with a basin of water. I snatched the rag from her apron pocket and immersed it, wringing the cold, wet cloth and placing it on Meriwether's head.

He moaned.

"Go on to bed," I said to Will.

He looked at me with pleading eyes, but if he thought this moment was the time for romancing, he was dead wrong. I worked at loosening Meriwether's shirt, making sure his head was elevated, and when I turned back toward Will, he was gone.

Chloe and I stayed awake the rest of the night, tending to both Meriwether and Little Lewis, who woke up crying and hungry. Whoever had come up with the adage that a woman's work never ended, had to have been female herself.

Meriwether suffered that night. At one point, his fever raged so high he began shuddering.

"Shaking in a fever means they's hot like hell inside," Chloe said, head shaking. "Let's put some of them cold, wet rags under his armpits."

It was sound advice, for the care proved beneficial. Before dawn, his temperature abated, thank the good Lord.

"Governor Lewis has the summer fever," Chloe sighed. "I's seen this here sickness many times in Kaintuck."

I muttered a prayer to myself that it wasn't contagious. Like any mother, I wasn't as much concerned for myself, but for my son.

Morning's soft light ignited a warm peace, and Meriwether slept, although I expected he'd have a miserable headache once he awakened. Will did, and he looked haggard at breakfast, limiting himself to dry toast and dark coffee Chloe made right before I sent her off to sleep.

"Serves you right," I quipped, sipping my hot tea.

He cast an irritated glance my direction but admitted, "Probably so. Still, Lewis had good news for our company last night. The War Department has budgeted us with seven thousand dollars to pay for Sheheke's return trip. *Excellent* news considering he's already been sent back. That was *my* reason for drinking. Lewis's reason was Frederick Bates. He's giving him more grief." He raised one hand, rubbing the space between his eyes.

"Seven thousand?" I echoed. "Is that enough to cover everything?"

He gave a short shrug. "It's not as much as I'd hoped, but we'll make it work." A slurp of coffee and a crunch as he bit into his toast.

"Will, Chloe and I were up all night nursing Meriwether out of a severe fever. He may have been drinking, but he's quite ill. Might we send for Dr. Saugrain? I think he should be examined."

After another swig of coffee, Will frowned, nodding. "Definitely. I'll send Scott over to see if he'll stop by sometime today. Why don't we have Lewis remain here, where our people"—he paused, correcting himself— "*my* people and you might care for him."

Indeed, it was a logical plan.

To my relief, Dr. Saugrain arrived later in the morning with his precise, short stride that always conveyed efficiency. Hair in a traditional queue, physician's bag in hand, he was courteous and professional as always, shutting the door of Meriwether's guest room during his initial examination.

After a quarter hour or so, he came out, speaking with me privately. "*Le gouverneur* is still quite ill, madame. Since he is in your care, he has asked me to discuss his condition with you, provided it remain confidential."

"Of course." Men like Bates would thrill at using a severe illness to exploit Meriwether's weakness.

"He has the ague—a common but serious illness here in Louisiane. It commonly has three stages which I have noted: chills with severe shaking, a burning fever accompanied by nausea, pain, delirium, or other symptoms, and lastly, sweats which typically lead to a period of remission."

"How long does all that usually last?"

"It varies," he replied, lifting one hand in a helpless gesture. "However, *le gouverneur*—I have noted his episodes to be increasing, and he is aware of that."

"He told me about this last summer. What treatment can you offer?"

"Ague is not curable, but there is a therapy of sorts. I prescribe a tree bark found in l'Amérique du Sud, called quinaquina. Since his symptoms have stabilized, I have merely given him a purgative of Glauber's salt. Have a bedpan readily available."

"I'll see to that."

By default, we had two other houseguests besides Meriwether. His servant, John Pernier, mostly stayed in Lewis's room, tending to him, which pleased me. He was a quiet sort and obviously knew a great deal about Dr. Saugrain's remedies.

The second guest was Seaman, Meriwether's enormous black

dog. I had always liked the furry beast, and since Will and I were sleeping apart, he slept with me at night. It put me at ease, for with Seaman present I finally found it easier to drift off to sleep.

The miserable ghost of Ramses Phipps was kept at bay.

※

Will knew *exactly* how to tempt me and win.

"There's to be a public ball at the Chouteaus', and my heart's desire is that my wife would attend it at my side," Will said. "During my bachelor days, I stayed as an overnight guest at the mansion, and they live in utter elegance."

There was no way I'd miss an opportunity to visit the grandiose Chouteau mansion.

I wore a gown that was untouched since Mama had packed it inside my trousseau. A wedding gift from the Earlys, it consisted of cascades of emerald silk with delicate, hand-wrought ivory lace on the neckline. A thick, ivory-colored satin ribbon made a neat bow in the back. It was exquisite, as was the Chouteau mansion.

I'd seen it from the outside, of course, the grand house supposedly rivaling Mt. Vernon. Since the only other public ball I'd attended in St. Louis had been in a boathouse, I anticipated this one to be far removed from drunken sailors, trappers, and loose women, who had all been present there. I wasn't disappointed, for I'd never attended such a glamorous event, and how ironic that of all places—not Paris, New York, or Washington City—it was happening *here* in little old St. Louis.

"That gown is perfect with your blue eyes," Will whispered in my ear as I descended the carriage. He kissed my hand, and my, but my husband did look dashing, as did Governor Lewis, quitting the carriage behind me. Will was bedecked in full military finery, sword at his side. And as territorial governor, Meriwether wore a fashionable tailcoat and stylish, striped cravat from neck to chin. He may have been ailing from the ague, but the man knew how to dress.

As we entered, a slave with a booming, resonant voice announced our names, his powerful instrument echoing throughout the ballroom and over the music in three different languages—French first, then English, and lastly Spanish. Will led me toward the receiving line, where we were met by Monsieur Auguste Chouteau.

"*Cher* Guillaume!" Chouteau exclaimed. "I see you have brought along *votre fleur de la Virginie.*"

Will responded formally, clicking his heels together in a curt but military greeting. "Indeed. Julia, once again, I present Auguste Chouteau."

"Monsieur," I smiled politely, extending my hand, Chouteau immediately sweeping it up and kissing it with gallantry. At previous meetings, I had thought him reserved, but tonight he seemed more relaxed and inclined to be talkative. Perhaps his star burned brighter in his brother's absence since Jean-Pierre was away, leading the Missouri Fur Company's men northward to return Sheheke.

"Madame, my hope is that you will save me at least one dance this evening."

"I'd be honored, monsieur."

"*Ma mere* told me that you favor literature," Auguste remarked casually, changing the subject and winking at Will.

"Why, yes. I'm afraid there aren't enough books for me in all of St. Louis."

"*Ce n'est pas vrai!*" he declared. "Jean-Pierre and I have a taste for literature *aussi*, so we have developed our own *bibliothèque privée*. We have volumes in multiple languages—French, English, Latin, Spanish, and one or two in Greek."

"Really? Might I borrow a book or two?"

"*Bien sûr,* madame! Shall I send you my newest volume of Voltaire? For it is an extraordinary English translation."

"Yes, please. Have you any Rousseau? I've never read his work but would be fascinated to do so."

Will gave one of his irresistible smiles and remarked to Chouteau, "You do realize that now the dam has broken, you'll be fated to loan her every book in this house."

Chouteau laughed heartily, replying, "If I must, I'll do it *avec plaisir.*"

I extended my own appreciation in French. *"Merci bien. Vous êtes très gentil."* Chouteau was gracious at my attempt, bowing respectfully.

Next in the receiving line was Madame Chouteau, matriarch and keeper of bees. She had been talking in rapid French Creole with Auguste's wife, but when she saw me, she gave me her full attention, tilting her head just enough to inspect me with her steely, gray-blue eyes. Her austere head-to-toe dark attire was the same, hair bound beneath another of her bland-looking wool turbans that common Creole women wore about town.

I gave her a respectful curtsy, as I always did when greeting the Mother of St. Louis. "Madame, I'm most pleased to see you. Our household so appreciates the monthly supply of honey you send."

"Ah! It is always a joy to give to you and le Général, and how lovely you look *ce soir, ma chérie.*"

After exchanging warm acknowledgments to one another and moving on to where others were socializing, I felt her approving gaze follow me.

An impressively adept ensemble of string musicians that the Chouteaus had hired all the way from New Orleans alternated between minuets in the familiar Viennese style to energetic jigs, along with some more traditional French Creole dances. Once we'd found a table, Auguste Chouteau strode over, asking for his promised dance. In turn, Will danced with his quiet, sweet-natured wife, Thérèse. What a pleasant surprise when a reel began—something with which I was familiar. I'd probably been dancing reels in Virginia since I was two years old.

As at any Virginia ball, there was much clapping, hooting, and merry-making, and I have to say that Auguste was a spritely dancer. Here, in this setting, I felt welcome and was having the first real fun I'd enjoyed in too long a time. Smiles surrounded me, and at one point, as we swept across the floor, the inertia of our movement made me laugh in glee.

After my turns with Auguste, the musicians played a minuet, which I danced with Meriwether, and I noted how hot he felt to the touch. After that came several waltzes—still considered a rather scandalous dance in some people's opinions. There was only one man I dared dance them with, and as soon as the first bars began, he was bowing before me.

"I've never been as natural a dancer as you, my love," Will said, his voice just loud enough to hear above the strings.

"Actually, I've always considered you a fine dancer."

He grinned broadly. "Well, it is a waltz after all. I only have to count to three in my head."

How could I not smile, for Will wasn't predisposed to loving dance. His participation at this moment had more to do with me, I was certain. Lately, he had been trying his best to win me back. For a time, we were silent, and as much as I longed to resume our intimacy, my stubborn heart remained unyielding and hard.

"When will you forgive me?" he whispered low, his gleaming blue eyes boring into mine. "It pains me to think we've wasted a good month of loving in our separation."

"Part of me…" My voice trailed off.

"Part of you what?"

"Wants to feel you next to me at night. But I'm not ready. I beg you—let it be for now."

His face fell. Was I being cruel? Oh no. He had been *more* than cruel, I reminded myself.

Once the waltz ended, he bowed. "You grieve me, wife. You hurt my heart." He left me, trailing off toward the refreshment tables.

Unlike the public dance at the boathouse, here there was fine china, crystal, fresh strawberries with cream, and punch, most likely mixed with rum.

Meriwether motioned me over to our table where he sat with a handsome, dark-eyed Spaniard. "Julia, I want you to meet Señor Manuel Lisa."

Ah. The power wielder in the fur trade who helped doom the first party trying to return Sheheke. To me, he was ruthless, opportunistic, and self-serving.

"A pleasure, señor." Usually, lies tasted bitter upon my tongue, but not this time. Not over this man, who betrayed so many to the Arikara.

"Señora Clark." His lilting Spanish accent blended with a husky voice that certainly most women found beguiling. "The pleasure is all mine. What a shame that my wife is not here to meet you."

"I'll look forward to making her acquaintance another time."

"I hear you're journeying east."

"Yes," I confirmed. The mere thought of Santillane and my family cajoled my artificial smile into a genuine one. "My parents have yet to meet their grandson."

Meriwether seized the opportunity. "And you *know* for whom he was named!"

"Ha, Lewis!" Señor laughed heartily. "Who in Louisiana Territory does *not* know that, eh?"

Señor Lisa excused himself, moving on to another group of rougher-looking men—probably fur traders in their Sunday bests, though their ragged beards and greasy, unkempt hair always gave them away. This was still a public ball, and though it was held at an extravagant location, anyone could attend.

Meriwether leaned in toward me. "Lisa is a bigamist. Bigamy thrives out here. His legal wife, Molly, lives here in St. Louis, leading a lonely life in his many absences. While among the Omaha, he married a chief's daughter—a girl by the name of Mitane. It suits him to keep these two lives: one for St. Louis society's sake and the other helping to promote trade business with the natives."

"Scandalous," I muttered, unsurprised. "And men do this all the time?"

He nodded. "Men in St. Louis often lead two lives—one in the west and one in genteel culture." Then Meriwether snatched my hand, leaning in confidentially, the heat from his fever branding my flesh. "But you should know something, Julia Clark. When it comes to women, you've *nothing* to worry about. You two may have your differences, but William Clark's word means loyalty, and that's the end of it."

Undoubtedly, Will had informed him of our current problems,

so I smiled and gave him a courteous nod but removed my hand from his. Close as a brother he was, but I didn't have any intention of allowing him to influence whatever happened between Will and me.

On the dance floor, lively quadrilles had begun and couples were forming groups of eight. I was satisfied just to watch since this was a dance with which I wasn't as familiar. Will returned with glasses of champagne for us all, then made a second trip to bring us a plateful of sugared nuts mixed with the delicious-looking sliced strawberries. Just as he sat down, the Chouteau slave raised his robust voice, announcing another guest.

"Secretary Frederick Bates!"

Meriwether was seated right next to me, and I saw his posture stiffen. It was my turn to place my hand atop his, whispering, "I know there's plenty of history between you two, but don't let it ruin tonight. Enjoy yourself."

"History?" he harrumphed. "That man despises the very mention of my name."

I squeezed his hand, hoping beyond hope that he'd relax, for tonight he looked so pale. His ague was returning.

Bates descended the stairs into the ballroom, avoiding the Chouteaus' reception line and veering toward the table next to us, where some of his friends were sitting. He had a way of smirking arrogantly, his smile full of sarcasm. Energetic male voices welcomed him, while next to me Meriwether remained stiff as a board.

Will leaned in, giving his friend a nod and whispering encouragement. "Do what you must, Governor. Go right over and greet them all *pleasantly*. Prove who is the real gentleman at this party."

I shot a desperate look at Will, for he wasn't aware of Meriwether's present physical condition, and if these phases led to impaired judgment and erratic behavior, now would be the *wrong* time to send him over to Bates.

"If you'll both excuse me, then," Meriwether managed, courteously nodding to us. He swiveled his chair around to where Bates was sitting right behind us. In a sociable way, he reached out, placing one hand upon his rival's shoulder, uttering a stiff but affable greeting.

Instead of being cordial, however, Bates arose so quickly that his chair toppled backward, thudding to the floor. "I daresay, it's the insolvent *wreck* himself!" His words were followed by raucous laughter clear around the table.

"*Damn* that man," Will seethed under his breath. "He can never leave anything at peace and *looks* for excuses to cause trouble."

Loudly, Bates addressed the other men around him. "You must all pardon me, but I have no interest in rubbing shoulders with useless debtors." He turned on his heel, pacing swiftly toward the front of the ballroom.

Meriwether snapped, veritably roaring, "Bates, you will *not* show your back to me!"

In one fluid motion, Will and I also stood up. Still nearest to Meriwether, I snatched at his hand, but I was too late to hold him back, for he shook me off to stalk after his prey.

Everyone in the ballroom sensed a disturbance, and the music ceased, all activity coming to a standstill. Those who'd been dancing froze, breathlessly staring at Meriwether, who shouted, flinging his arm downward to demand Bates to halt. "You heard me! If you're a gentleman, *stop and face me!*"

Bates did stop but turned slowly, leisurely, a smirk budding like a wicked little flower upon his lips. In measured steps, he approached Meriwether, encircling him, hissing, "Do you even know what a joke of a governor you are? Improperly funding an expedition for that money-sucking Mandan, then cloaking your commercial fur trading beneath the guise of official business? Do you?" he raged. "You're an *embarrassment!*"

Will and I had hurried up behind Meriwether to try to dissuade further argument, and I prayed no one else had heard their exchange. However, nobody could have prepared me for what Meriwether did next. Fevered as he was, it was as though a lion possessed him. "Sir!" he bellowed. "I demand the satisfaction of a challenge. Bloody Island will suffice, so choose your second. I myself already have one!" Clumsily, he snatched Will's arm.

A duel? Dear God—no!

All around us, I heard mutterings and gasps.

Will, still in Meriwether's claw-like grip, whispered, "Come with me, friend. We'll discuss this privately."

By some miracle, Meriwether turned and followed Will away from Bates toward the back of the ballroom, where French doors beckoned.

Unsure what to do with myself under the gaze of hundreds of eyes, I followed on their heels, red-faced at being the subject of so many. What a relief when the musicians resumed their playing, attempting to restore normalcy.

Through the French doors we went, merry strains of another folk dance fading as Will shut the doors firmly behind us. I glanced about. It was a spacious alcove with a high ceiling and cushioned benches. Chouteau family portraits gazed down upon us like jurors, their somber eyes seeming to cast judgment.

Meriwether's voice stormed like thunder, resonating through the capacious recess. "How *dare* he insult me in public!"

Will kept his voice soft and steady. "Lewis, *you* are governor of this territory, and *you're* the one who must compose yourself. You just challenged the man to a duel in front of everyone. What if he accepts?"

Meriwether had taken to pacing from one end of the alcove to the other, his face pale and wax-like. I stood like a statue in front of the French doors, furtively glancing back every few seconds, praying nobody had followed us.

"Damned War Department's refusing to authorize payments owed to both me and *you!*" he fumed. "And I'm talking reimbursements for returning Sheheke to the Mandans. There's an accountant in Eustis's War Department—name of Simmons," he blathered, still pacing from one end of the alcove to the other. "That man is harder-assed than Eustis and had Jefferson and now Madison wrapped around his finger in complete trust."

"Meriwether," I heard myself say gently, "you must calm yourself."

"*Calm* myself?" roared the lion. "How am I supposed to remain composed when both Simmons and Bates are dedicated to my demise? Why, even the *post* is against me! Some of my own mail and Simmons's has been delayed or perhaps lost. My God, but there may be debt I'm still unaware of—stuffed in some saddlebag somewhere in Indiana—*vanished*. Oh, the question of what Simmons and Eustis will next refuse to reimburse me for is eating me alive. Go ahead—call me paranoid, but what if Bates, Simmons, or both of them are purposefully delaying my mail to hasten my ruin?"

"Don't be ridiculous," Will scoffed.

"Well, just remember," Meriwether warned, "as more of my bills are turned in for review and declined outright, it will have its effect on you too. We both may be bankrupt before it all ends. I tell you, the out-of-pocket costs, the debt I'm faced with—"

"Lewis!" Will barked sharply. "Get hold of yourself, man! You're overcome. We'll sort this out—but *elsewhere*," he insisted, trying to prevent his friend's emotions from escalating any further.

"Oh, I assure you Simmons has already 'sorted' it for me," Lewis retorted. "He *and* Bates. Hear me out here. What you don't know is that despite Jefferson's blank letter of credit for our expedition, Simmons accuses me of owing the government almost *ten thousand dollars*, and I recently learned that he included that amount in a published Treasury report, currently in the hands of the War Department. Simmons is a man who's been in communication with *Bates*. Now tell me the two of them don't intend to destroy me, bring me down."

"Oh no—that can't be," I breathed.

Will stepped forward, trying to reassure him. "Then, my friend, it's up to both of us to clear your name, and we will do that. *Together*."

Meriwether was still traipsing back and forth, ranting. "Then there are tracts of land I snapped up after first assuming my position here as governor. I would've paid them off in installments, but then came the Simmons debts, which turned out to be far more than I'd expected, so now I'm negligent there too."

Will suddenly looked concerned, his brows closing together into a frown. "Wait—are there fur company debts involved here too? If so, how much are we talking about?"

"Old skinflint Simmons doesn't want to reimburse Chouteau for the four-hundred something he spent for Indian trinkets, which you and I both know are essential. God, if he's loath to repay the leader of the expedition—a man taking militia straight into proven danger—it concerns me that other amounts for which I've requested settlement will also be declined."

As I listened, one thing was loud and clear in all of this: Louisiana Territory was both far removed and misunderstood compared to the rest of the United States. Here, we dealt with an entirely different culture and set of necessities compared to the east.

Will intercepted Meriwether's pacing, managing to place an arm around his friend's shoulders to offer comfort. "Let's keep this business between just us," he told him, his voice steady and firm. His eyes glanced over, locking on to mine.

Meriwether shook his head, his face a montage of apprehension and stress; tears even sparkled in his eyes, and I feared he'd fall apart completely, here and now. "It's too late," he whispered, voice cracking. "You heard Bates out there. He'll shout my shortcomings to the world and continue writing to his allies in Washington about what a mess I am as governor. And there's only one way to stop that from happening."

"Please—not *that*—not a duel!" I pleaded, shaking my head.

Fist clenched and raised, Meriwether's voice ground out, "I *require* the satisfaction of meeting him. It's Bloody Island tomorrow at dawn."

Bloody Island—the well-known, low island in the Mississippi where St. Louis men shot one another in the name of honor.

"No," Will said flatly, his voice stern and echoing through the open space. "I'll have no part in it."

Snarling through his teeth, Meriwether lunged at Will, grabbing him by the collar, yelling into his face, "*Go get Bates!* You're my second. Go *now*, Clark!"

Will neatly twisted free of him, taking a step back and standing firm. "I will not."

"*Go tell him!* We'll meet at dawn!" Unhinged, he was, voice livid and raging. "You go, or I shall, for you know that right now my reputation's already tarnished. It matters *not* what sort of spectacle I stage."

Despite my issues with Will, what a boon it was that married people were sometimes able to communicate in a mere glance, without words. Once I'd caught Will's eye, I was hoping to convey my deeper intent. "This is so important to Meriwether's honor, so perhaps it's best that you go find Bates. Just go *look* for him…"

Will's eyes lit up with understanding as Meriwether resumed pacing, at times muttering to himself. Now, I'd have to trust in the deep friendship he and I had built.

"Dear Meriwether," I cooed, stepping toward him. On his turnabout, he saw me in his path and hesitated, at first raising his fist, as though he didn't know me.

"Julia—" Will gasped.

Scarcely daring to breathe, I reached out, taking Meriwether's stiffened, clenched hand into my own. Hard as it was, I held it, gently rubbing, soothing. "You're like a beloved brother, and it breaks my heart seeing you like this. *Please…* put all anger aside so we can go home?"

Meriwether met my eyes, his face pallid and rampant with fever, his fist relaxing in my hand.

Peripherally, I saw Will glancing down the hallway adjoining the alcove. He'd been a guest here. He knew where the exits were. We needed to get Meriwether out of here—quietly and quickly.

"Will, I think we're going outside," I said. "I know I need some air, so Meriwether will see to it that I get some."

Meriwether's hand strayed from mine to his head. "Oh God—the pain is back. Yes, cooler air would help."

Will moved swiftly, his long stride leading straight toward the back of the house. There he paused, and I saw him beckon, opening a door for us and stepping away.

Voice held low, I spoke in a soothing manner. "As soon as we get you home, I'll send for Dr. Saugrain."

"He's away, tending patients in St. Charles."

"Then Chloe and I will nurse you back to health. We did it once. We'll do it again. Come, it's pleasantly cool out."

It took me nearly a quarter of an hour to get him clear around the Chouteau mansion, for he balked occasionally, his head paining him and his mind so badly affected. Will trailed close behind, no doubt worried something might happen to me.

We finally located our carriage in the long string of conveyances lining up all the way to the main road. The hired driver sprang into action at our approach, helping Will pull Meriwether inside. By now, he hardly knew us, shaking and talking gibberish, even laughing at who knew what. I feared that the Governor of Louisiana Territory had gone quite mad.

"I need to go back in and speak to Bates. We don't want this ending in a duel."

"I'll stay with him. He's relaxed more now."

"Julia—"

"*Go*, Will."

His eyes were full of concern and worry. "What if he harms you, not realizing—"

"*Go*. The driver is here. I'll be fine."

He wasn't gone long past the tenth hour of the evening, but it still seemed an eternity. Meanwhile, Meriwether lost consciousness, sagging against me—his body heat like an iron brand.

I feared for his life.

Finally, footsteps, then the sound of the carriage door reopening. Will jumped into the seat in front of me, rapping on the exterior to signal the driver.

"He's unconscious," I whispered, gazing down at Meriwether's head, now resting on my lap. "Did you find Bates?"

"Yes, and I managed to speak with him. When I told him that I couldn't bear to see two friends waste their lives firing upon one another, he scolded me for calling him 'friend.' Said he's unable to separate my opinions from those of Lewis since he and I have 'trod the ups and downs of life.' He thinks my words to him were solely for Lewis's convenience, but no matter. At least we've avoided a duel."

"Such a relief," I whispered. "But what a hard-hearted person that man is."

Will leaned back, puffing his cheeks out in a sigh. Seeing Lewis finally at peace, he said, "You never cease to amaze me, Julia. Lewis responded to you like a kitten to cream."

After that, we bumped along in silence during the short ride home. My fervent prayer was that Meriwether's troubled mind would be put at ease.

Chapter XIX

St. Louis
June–September 1809

It was agreed that Meriwether remain with us indefinitely so we could assist with his care. Thus, Dr. Saugrain became a familiar face.

"Summers are exhausting for me," he confided. "There are numerous cases of the ague to treat."

With my own eyes, I observed the destructive nature of the disease ravaging Meriwether. His fever would rage and break, rage and break, like a storm on wildly thrashing seas.

"*Notre gouverneur* is acute now," Dr. Saugrain confirmed, though it was already obvious to me. Meriwether's body was tiring, and something deep within him seemed broken too. Vanished was the confidence of a well-respected man whom people had loved and esteemed. More and more, he retreated into himself. His appetite faded, along with his judgment. Meriwether's quiet, efficient servant, John Pernier, held a vital role. He saw that the governor presented bathed, shaved, and dressed daily since, in the throes of his illness, he often had difficulty with even those ordinary tasks.

Dr. Saugrain trained me to administer Meriwether's medicines, and Will always accompanied his friend to his office in town whenever he felt up to working. There, the two men worked side by side at separate desks. When work was too demanding, Will took over many governmental duties, especially since he was better at ignoring Bates's taunts and obstacles.

As late June's warmth brought the songs of meadowlarks, afternoon storms, and bumblebees droning above clumps of clover, Chloe and I sat on my bed in my guest room, working on our 1809 household inventory, organizing items to remain in St. Louis versus what we'd take east with us at summer's end. Rachel sat next to Seaman on the floor, stroking the dog's thick fur, and Little Lewis babbled happily on the rug nearby. We boxed and crated possessions to be moved into the new house, setting aside smaller pieces of furniture we could go ahead and send over.

Will came home early and found us working. "I brought Lewis home. He's in bed," he said. "I think his fever is back."

I looked up from writing. "I hate to hear that."

"Where did you get that?" He was pointing toward my lap, in which rested the red Moroccan journal I'd inventoried in for the past year. "Did you—did you *take* that from my office?"

Ever responsive to the edge in his voice, Chloe scooped up Little Lewis, and shooed both Rachel and the dog out of the room, leaving the two of us alone.

"I've had this journal for my inventory for a solid year, and you've not missed it," I countered.

"Very well," he answered squarely. "But those journals are meant for my use in rewriting the original Corps of Discovery field notes, and they're not cheap."

Bristling, I stood up. "Expensive like the midwife, are they?"

Will gave a heavy sigh. "There seems to be nothing we can do to please one another since—"

"Since you whipped York senseless? Ever since he came back late because all he wants is to be with his family?"

"By God, Julia," he growled under his breath. "We must have it out about this—now." He strode to the door, shutting it. "What happened that day..." His face was red with frustration, and I could see he was baffled at how best to express himself. "I'm responsible for soldiers, as you well know. Even on the voyage west, Lewis and I had to discipline men—sometimes by whipping. It's as common in the military as it is for slave masters, but if you think I *enjoy* it or take some perverse pleasure from it, you're dead wrong. If that's what you think, then you've gravely misjudged me. Remember, I allowed York to visit his wife, per *your* suggestion. It was his responsibility to return in a reasonable amount of time, but instead he was gone for months. Therefore, I will not explain myself any further. I needn't because my people are my property and that's the end of it. Now, I'm grateful for your meticulous care of York's wounds, and I'm sure he is too." After pausing, he added, "So I ask for your forgiveness if I frightened you that day. I was very angry."

What an understatement.

"You should know that I'm seriously thinking of selling York. I hate to do it, but I'm weary of his sullen behavior. There are boatmen who pay good money for slaves, from here all the way to the Ohio."

No. Oh no. "I've a much better idea that will also serve to make money for you, if that's your intent. Send him to Jonathan in Louisville. Have him hire York out for you. Will, you'd be rid of the problem, and he'd be nearer his family. It would solve everything."

"I needn't bother Jonathan with any more of this—"

"He doesn't mind, and you know it."

He paused, and I sensed him yielding. "Actually, it would make sense."

I sat there in utter relief, not knowing what more to say, my eyes watering with conflicted tears. Inside, my heart twisted and burned, for despite our differences, I *loved* Will. But *why*? *Why* did I love him after what he'd done to Venus, to York, what he would have done to Juba had he caught him—*why*?

"Can we not enjoy our life together again?" he entreated.

He wanted me so much.

"I *love* you, Julia." That intoned as a gentle whisper. "I vowed that to you and you alone, and that will never change. You made the same vow to me, so let's put this behind us and begin again."

He knelt before me, brushing some stray hairs back behind my ear. Then, leaning forward, he kissed me, his tongue seeking mine. There was an urgency between us both that took me by surprise. This had to be what poets called passion, what I loved to read about and imagine in all of my womanly fantasies.

His hands were running firmly up and down my back, even reaching beneath me, squeezing my buttocks, drawing me toward him. He was so hungry, and my own body was responding like a morning glory opening at sunrise.

But then came the anguishing memory of York tied to the tree, and my tenacious heart was simply not ready to forgive or accept compromise—despite my commitment to him. Why I couldn't let it go after several months had passed, I wasn't sure, but I just couldn't.

My hands left his auburn hair and turned to fists upon his chest, pushing him away before we became too entangled. He released me with a groan of vexation, and I reached back, grabbed the red Moroccan journal off the bed, sprang up and rushed out of the room, tears in my eyes and a terrible void in my heart.

※

Work.

In a thriving household with a growing babe crawling everywhere, I seldom sat down.

When the year's first vegetables demanded picking, I joined Chloe, Rachel, Scott, Nancy, and Venus in harvesting behind the house. We'd eat well this summer and into the fall. In fact, I believed our yield would be so abundant that we'd be able to carry a whole crate of fresh-picked as far as Louisville for Jonathan and Sarah.

Toward midday, Chloe and I were working side by side in the garden when I heard the front door open and shut. Curious as to who was home early, I went back into the house.

Through the kitchen, around the corner, I nearly ran headlong into Meriwether, who startled me by snatching both of my arms for support. Liquor lay heavy on his breath, and I staggered back under his weight, smacking into the wall. Why, if Will came through the front door, I feared that what he'd see might be misinterpreted.

"I just wro-wrote Eustis," Meriwether stuttered, his grip like a vice. "I'm in debt now for four thousand dollars—fo-four thousand more…" his voice trailing off.

He was hurting me, his grip tight as a vise. "Please!" I hissed.

"Let go!" He was unyielding despite my struggle, clutching at me fast, his head drooping in shame against my shoulder.

"Cr-creditors are after me," he continued, his speech slurred, muffled against the fabric of my work-dress. "Four came to-to the office today. Word's out. I'm ruined."

"Let me go," I repeated through clenched teeth. "Let me go, and we'll talk." Keeping calm was a struggle.

He swayed a moment, and I thought he'd topple. Oh, it was true. His ague was back again; the fever had nearly set me afire and his clothes were damp, stale with sweat. Drunk and ill at the same time—the sorriest of states. I tried to focus on his mumbled words as they dribbled out.

"All over town, it's rumored I won't be reappointed as governor. Bates—Bates," he snorted. "Probably to blame…" Off-balance, he wheeled away from me, back into the drawing room, careening into the stone fireplace.

"Be careful!"

He slumped against the stone hearth, still standing, but barely. I nearly shouted for Scott, but I hated anyone else to see the territorial governor like this.

"Let's get you to your room." I grasped his arm, hauling him up, trying to lead him, but he sagged against me again. Thankfully, his room was on the first floor, only a few more steps away, but he stubbornly pulled me in the opposite direction as though lost.

Back to the drawing room.

Crates, baskets, and satchels were stacked all over the place in preparation for relocating to the new house, and at present the drawing room was our catch-all for anything to be moved. Lewis was a pacer when agitated, and he began, narrowly missing piles of goods.

There had to be a way to settle him. I'd done it at the ball, so couldn't I do it again? I wiped my soiled hands on my apron and simply stood by, praying for an idea to strike.

Back and forth, back and forth, from wall to wall he strode, scarcely missing boxes full of Little Lewis's clothing and toys and some of my odds and ends. Presently, he seemed to remember someone else was in the room and directed his thoughts toward me.

"I'm forever shamed, you hear? Damn that man Bates to hell!"

Oh no. Here came the fierce lion. I needed an idea *fast*. "Oh, Meriwether," I breathed, "calm yourself—"

"It was Bates who let the word out—*Bates*." Unexpectedly, he dropped to his knees facing me, panting and lifting his hands toward heaven. "Have I not been an honorable man? *Have I not?*"

"Shh, you're overcome." In two strides, I reached him in the center of the room, heart hammering. Sinking down with him, I took his hands in mine, compassion demanding it.

His frenzied eyes sparked brightly with malaise, a clumsy grin forming, followed with joyful laughter. "Letitia! I knew you'd finally come to your senses. You're here just in time—you'll restore me!"

Good God—he thought I was Letitia?

Before I could panic, he pulled me forward, pressing his lips to mine. On my knees as I was, my balance failed, and I slumped sideways. Lips still on mine, he rolled with me, hot and fevered in the summer heat.

I scrambled with my legs, finally finding purchase when my foot landed against the wall. Pushing with all my might, I extricated myself from beneath him, scooting frantically in the opposite direction until I ran into a crate.

Meriwether pulled himself up to a seated position, and we both stayed where we were, breathless, rooted, until he spoke again. "Oh, darling girl, forgive me. Those several years with the Corps of Discovery were my glory days. I was at my best; in better health and respected by the president, by my men, the American people... And *now*? I haven't even time and energy enough to edit the Corps journals. I'm too ill. How can you possibly love me like this, Letitia? How?"

Oh God, he was delirious. Just when I thought he'd relax and we'd turned the corner...

"And my *debt!*" he cried out, panting and pallid. "You won't marry me because of that, will you?" Eyes bulging, he stared at me, frantic.

An idea began budding in my mind so I opted for a different tack. It was something to which Lewis could relate, something we had in common, the two of us. Voice soft and meek, I said, *"Misery acquaints a man with strange bedfellows."*

In an instant, Meriwether's pupils jerked, refocusing on my face, rekindling, and I witnessed his rigidity dissolve. "*The Tempest*, ohh—Act II, yes?"

"Yes!" Another—*think of another!* Desperate, my mind scrambled. *"We know what we are, but know not what we may be."*

A pause, then Meriwether rubbed his face, comprehension dawning. *"Hamlet,"* he murmured.

I swallowed hard, inhaling in relief. Meriwether—*my* Meriwether—was returning, be it ever so slowly. I eased myself up from the floor, remaining before the fireplace.

Head back down, eyes widening, his next words were a mere expulsion of air. *"Julia?* I didn't know you—Julia?"

"Yes." I nodded frantically. "It's me." Tears of relief dripped down my face.

His eyes flitted about nervously. "What have I done?"

"We won't speak of it. All will be well, but you have the ague again." There couldn't have been a more opportune time to remind him that justice would prevail on his behalf and that, eventually, his name would be cleared. But to persuade him, I needed words of exoneration, words he'd accept as eloquent, full of truth, and meant specifically for him. And here they came, tumbling forth as though they'd resided inside me forever and a day, awaiting their moment: *"I am a man more sinned against than sinning."*

He stared at me, incredulous. "Shakespeare wrote that?"

"He did. In *King Lear*. I swear, there could never be more suitable words for you, Meriwether Lewis."

Mouth open and sagging, he wiped sweat from his face with both hands.

"Come. You need rest," I counseled. "Chloe will bring dinner in to you tonight."

I stepped to him, steadying him gently but firmly. He was so weak now that the worst had passed. Together, we shuffled through the short hall into his room.

He sank onto the edge of his bed, still somewhat adrift in his mind.

"Rest now," I whispered as he eased back. I caught his feet, removing his shoes one by one. "Things will look brighter once you've slept."

Only once his breathing became calm and even did I chance to slip out, closing the door behind me and sinking down against it in relief.

Again. I'd done it. I'd calmed Meriwether, hopefully saving him from himself. What worried me was what might happen if he found himself as ill as he was today—but also alone.

❦

"Go to Washington City," Will urged Meriwether that night. "Face your demons down. There, and only there, you can meet with Madison and Eustis personally to clear your name once and for all."

Will's advice was sound, and Meriwether tabled the deeds of his lands in the territory for surety against his debts. It was likely that Will and I would face some losses too. Ironically, both men opted to sacrifice the very acreage granted to them for their success in the Corps of Discovery. Meriwether hoped to sell it down in New Orleans, for Will urged him to take a boat south, then catch a ship for the American east coast. This route would make the journey less taxing on him physically. And perhaps the sea air would strengthen his constitution.

I sat in front of the fire, rocking Little Lewis. Will leaned in from where he sat on the settee, his voice low. "Earlier today, I found a letter in Lewis's office from Simmons. Madison himself gave Simmons permission to reject any other payments above the initial cost of returning Sheheke."

I gazed at him uneasily but said nothing. Will shook his head despondently, leaning back on the settee and running his hands through his hair. "Thank you for caring for him today," he murmured. "I stepped out of his office to settle a dispute with some Osage warriors. When I went back in, he was gone."

"Will he even be able to reach New Orleans?"

"I have the same concern, but John Pernier will be with him. That's some support, I suppose."

Though the thought made me wince, we considered Meriwether family, so I asked, "Should we postpone our journey to Virginia? Should you go with him yourself?"

Will paused. "No. He's a man and will want to stand on his own two feet."

"I remember when Meriwether visited Santillane before we wed," I reminisced. "Even back then, he was feeling poorly with a fever. Drinking too."

"Just like today," Will sighed.

Not exactly, I thought. Back then, he didn't try to assault me, thinking I was someone else.

"Do you know what he told me tonight?" Will mused. "He said that after New Orleans and Washington, he intends to visit Philadelphia after all, to continue work on the journals."

I stared at him, mouth agape. "Really? He's done nothing on them, Will. I wouldn't hang your hat on his word with his health so compromised."

"Now, now. Don't be so pessimistic."

"Pessimistic? I'm not. I'm *realistic*." Frustration overtook me. "Regardless of his ailments, he's had a year and a half or more to do something with them."

He nodded. He of all people knew I was speaking the truth.

I placed Little Lewis on my other shoulder—finally, he was asleep. "I'm just fearful that your journals will never come to light when they're the ones that should've come out first—not Robert Frazer's or Patrick Gass's—*yours*. Those documents contain our country's greatest adventure. They're a treasure. They simply *must* be published."

Both of us sat staring into the fire a while, listening to its hissing and popping. Will said, "If he truly does mean to work on them, then I'm going to see to it that he takes every copied version I've got—even my elk-skin journal—*everything*."

"Do that," I agreed. And I thought how refreshing it was having such a meaningful and agreeable conversation together. "Those journals of yours are different than those of the other men from the Corps. You and Meriwether were the *captains*, and your version contains science and an official record of events. Not only do they belong to the United States military, they belong to *all* Americans."

"You know," he sighed, "Lewis was completely different out west. Of course, it was a terribly difficult and physically taxing mission. When stressed, he could be snappy and terse, but we all were sometimes. His military background guided him the entire way to the coast—that same military background which Bates detests, by the way. But there was a side to Lewis that none of us on the journey possessed: that of a scientist. It was extraordinary, the knowledge he had and how he'd log flora and fauna along the way."

"When will he leave?"

"Very soon. God above, but I can only hope that time away itself will be restorative for him. In the past, travel has always been a balm for both our souls—but now? The way things are . . ."

Slowly, I arose from the rocking chair Meriwether had given us right after we'd become parents. Leaving Will with his distressing thoughts, I eased my way upstairs and into my room, placing Little Lewis gently in his crib. For a while, I knelt down, moving the tiny bed back and forth, assuring his slumber. It was a hot night, and my eyes sought the moon's benevolent, comforting face, shining through the sieve of white linen curtains and speckling the floor with luminescence. After leaning down to kiss my son's rosy cheeks, I stretched and climbed into bed, trying to still the disquiet my heart secreted for Meriwether, along with the usual unrest over Ramses Phipps.

Soft footfalls made me glance up from bed, half expecting it to be Will.

I couldn't help but smile. It was Seaman, cautiously entering with a slight tail-wag and gingerly sniffing at Little Lewis's crib. He approached my bedside, flopping down next to me on the rug. I reached down, relieved to have his company again. What comfort a dog could be.

Hand lost in thick black fur, I closed my eyes, finally confident that rest would come.

❦

September brought a chill to the air, forecasting autumn's resolve. Close, humid air from summer was chased away by breezes stirring branches that rustled with the promise of burnished color.

Was it fresh, cooling air coupled with the promise of seeing loved ones that lightened my steps? Maybe it was both, for I felt renewed at the thought of imminent travel.

On the day of Meriwether's parting, Will and I accompanied him to the docks to wish him a safe passage. Seaman shuffled along with us on a lead, for Lewis had entrusted him into our care.

"We'll be following you eastward in no time," Will promised.

"In my absence, do what you must to see to anything of mine," Meriwether instructed.

"And have no fear concerning Seaman," I assured, my hand upon the big dog's head. "He'll be traveling to Virginia with us."

Meriwether smiled, kneeling down for a canine farewell. "We already know he's a fine traveler, so he shouldn't be any trouble. Thank you for taking him in, as I can't quite imagine him joining me when meeting with President Madison."

We all shared laughter, imagining that. Then Meriwether turned sober, taking a step forward, embracing Will. "You're a steadfast friend, William Clark. There is no man on earth with whom I would rather have traveled to the Pacific."

Then it was my turn, and I embraced him, this man who had become another brother. Oh, how thin he was, his shoulders bony and frail. "Take your medicines, and should you be stronger, consider coming overland next spring through Fincastle. Mama and Papa would love to host you again."

"Julia's right," Will seconded. "You could travel back to St. Louis in our company. That would please us all."

"We'll see how things fare," Meriwether said. "For now, I shan't make promises."

Will clapped him on the back once more before he and John Pernier boarded a boat bound for New Orleans. Pernier ported the hefty wooden case I recognized, containing medicines and concoctions prescribed by Dr. Saugrain, delivered only days before. Among other healing remedies, fifteen pounds of the Peruvian bark were inside, the quinaquina Lewis required to combat his fevers.

As the boatman poled off the shore toward deeper water, Will and I stood watching until the craft gradually disappeared from view.

※※※

With Meriwether's departure, our own was only weeks away. Never had I been as eager to embrace family, friends, and everything familiar. There would be the Clarks in Louisville and my own parents and siblings in Fincastle. My imagination was bursting, daydreams staging the moments when I'd be surrounded by loved ones cooing over Little Lewis.

Chloe and Rachel accompanied me over to our new place, located at the southeast corner of Main and Vine. They hadn't yet seen it, and today Will, Scott, and a few militiamen were hauling our packed crates and baskets over. It would be up to me to direct them where everything needed to go. Chloe and I arrived early so I could give her a tour.

"Have *mercy!*" Chloe declared. "This kitchen's huge!"

"Big like a castle be, Mama," Rachel imagined.

Indeed, it was all red masonry with a magnificent stone fireplace in the central wall.

"Just think of the space we gonna have for cooking."

"And I still need to show you that family recipe of ours for vinegar pudding."

Rachel ran ahead, back into the main house, twirling childishly across the wide-open dining room, creating her own dance.

"Now, don't you be scuffing them floors none, girl," her mother warned.

I showed Chloe the five large bedchambers. "Well, Missus Julia, either you's gonna have plenty of guests or the Lord's gonna heal whatever's wrong between you and the general so's you'll have more children."

Did she notice how I inhaled sharply at her words? They hit their mark upon my heart, for when Will had first spoken of buying this house, all had been well between us. I answered her tactfully and honestly. "Hopefully, this place will lure family and friends from both Virginia and Kentucky to visit. And the general often has out-of-town business guests who have lately been forced to billet elsewhere, hiring out rooms for let in peoples' homes or businesses."

After our smaller pieces of furniture and the many packed crates arrived, I realized how much work I'd have upon returning from our journey east just unpacking. However, 1810 felt a million years distant, and I wouldn't trouble myself looking ahead to returning to St. Louis when we were just now preparing to head east.

The next few days saw further preparations for our leave-taking. Will had tasked York to build a wooden frame around our buckboard wagon, topping it with heavy canvas treated in linseed oil to resist rain. Fitted with upholstery-covered cushions stuffed with straw and ground cornhusks, the benches would pass as padded seats, their backs built of sturdy, sanded rails.

I passed by York outside the barn while he was putting finishing touches on the canvas top to prevent any of us inside from getting too wet. "It's fine work you're doing there," I called, pausing for a moment to look at his handiwork.

York glanced up, staring at me with his vacuous, sad eyes that were always so troubled and full of sorrow. Sometimes it was hard looking at him because it stirred my soul so. I resumed walking on back toward the house.

"Missus."

I stopped in my tracks. Never once had he addressed me. Slowly, I turned around, facing him.

"I ain't got no fancy words, but thank you for all you done."

Why had he chosen that moment? That day? It didn't matter. It lit my heart like a bonfire.

Only days later, with York's job on our buckboard complete, Will sent him on to Louisville as we'd previously discussed. He had arranged for Jonathan to hire him out, and though he could easily be passed off to someone cruel, like his sister Nancy had been, I reminded myself that at least he'd be near his family.

As for Scott, Chloe, and Rachel, I insisted that they come with us and that Chloe and Rachel ride in the covered part of the wagon with me.

"They can either ride on the very back where the extra mules are ponied or they'll walk, as is their place," Will argued.

I'd thought this through and suppressed a smile as I gave my planned excuse. "I'll need help with Little Lewis should I require a nap or respite, so Chloe must be near, and we can't expect a child as young as Rachel to be outside in the wilderness without her mother."

Will swallowed that whole and didn't make any more fuss. Chloe was my cherished friend, and I didn't want her and Rachel open to the elements, especially with autumn upon us.

Will charted us an overland course. I hadn't even given thought to the fact that the Ohio wouldn't be navigable upriver this time of year, as summer's heat had dried up the river. Indeed, I'd be seeing much more of these United States.

Chapter XX

Eastward Bound
September–October 1809

Our journey began by flatboat, crossing the Mississippi from St. Louis to docks near Cahokia. From there, we'd head toward Louisville, where we'd enjoy sweet respite with Jonathan, Sarah, and family.

Built for carrying people and freight, flatboats offered reliable transport down the Ohio in spring and summer and back and forth on the Mississippi and downriver from St. Louis to New Orleans. Still, I always eyed them with a certain trepidation, making sure I was safe in the central part of the boat since they had no guardrails.

Halfway across the river, a cold crosswind blew up, so Chloe and I stayed inside the wagon, wrapped up tight together in a blanket while the men readied the mules and horses for debarking. Once off the boats, they'd be hitched to the wagons again.

As we approached Illinois, people gathered on the port side, their weight causing the craft to scour the river bottom along shoals near the docks. Chloe and I laughed, feeling the slight bumps accompanied by a scraping sound emanating from the shallow bottom.

Suddenly, a male voice from the top of the small shelter bellowed, "Slave overboard!"

Next came Scott's voice, shouting to Chloe, "Mama, you got Rachel?"

Chloe's mouth dropped as she tossed aside our blanket and

leaped from the buckboard. "No!" she cried, her voice wavering. "I figured she was with you . . ."

I jumped down from the wagon too. Even more passengers had gathered portside, eager to get off, with yet more folk queued up on the Illinois dock, standing at the edge of the waterfront, some of them pointing down into the water.

Dread gripped me.

The same crewman who had first sounded the alarm shouted again, "Who's missing a slave girl?"

Scott and Chloe were fighting their way through the crowd, not making much headway. Most of the flatboat passengers saw that they were slaves and pushed them back, ignoring their distress.

Chloe shrieked, out of her mind with terror, "Where is she? Rachel, *where you at?*"

To my horror, I saw Will near the edge of the boat, lifting his arm in the midst of all the people, calling, "She's mine, sir." Gradually, the crowd parted, allowing him through.

Scott and Chloe were still caught up behind crowds of passengers, who were only now surging forward toward the gangplank. Bless Chloe, she was panicked, screaming and keening. "Master Clark, is it Rachel? Please, Lord Jesus, *don't* let it be Rachel!" She glanced back, searching for me, eyes brimming with tears. "Our girl don't swim none, Missus Julia…"

Little Lewis was alone in the wagon, but he'd been asleep, so I sprang forward to comfort my friend. A fear I'd never known gripped my heart with steely fingers, making my breath shallow: a mother's distress at the thought of losing a child, especially in such a chilling and unforeseen manner. My heart beat in rhythm with Chloe's—both of us mothers and facing a terror for which no parent was ever prepared.

Scott was finally at the edge of the flatboat with Will, and the sound that emanated from his throat was something from a nightmare. A moan, long and loud, pierced like that of a banshee over the confusion, carrying over people talking, stepping off the boat, greeting loved ones, calling for their bags, going about their business…

How was it that life was carrying on in such normalcy when a little child was lost?

As tall as he was, I saw Will's red head bobbing through the crowd toward us. Oh God—he was carrying her—*Rachel!* Drenched and dripping from her watery fate, she was limp as the cotton rag doll I remember Harriet losing as a child, left outside during a summer storm and hanging over the wrought-iron rail on our back stairwell, soaked and drooping.

She was also still as stone, blood dripping from her head, staining Will's cotton shirt. I willed her to lift her head and say something—*anything*. Still holding Chloe, I shielded her as long as I could, but when she finally saw her daughter, her scream clawed its way up my spine. She ran to Will, and I stood helpless, my emotion spilling its way down my face.

Chloe snatched Rachel from Will, lowering her to the deck and holding the girl's bloody head in her hands, swaying from side to side.

Will crossed over to where I stood. "She must have gotten too near the edge. My best guess is that she lost her balance when we hit ground back there."

"She couldn't swim," I murmured. "Will—is she—"

My answer came when arms encircled me, and it wasn't the one I wanted. "I need to know. Did she drown?"

His arms gripped me tighter as he spoke softly in my ear. "The boat was docking and crushed her head when she was flailing about. Let's pray she went quickly."

Oh, Sweet Lord…

"Nooo—" Chloe was on her knees, rocking Rachel's lifeless form in her arms, her protest a guttural screech at the top of her lungs. Scott stood sobbing behind her, wiping both eyes with his worn, patched shirtsleeves and shaking his head in disbelief.

At the sound of their grief, other travelers crossing the gangplank to Illinois stared back at our group, heading on their way and leaving us in our shock.

Will released me, turning and walking slowly toward the wagon.

"Where are you going?" I cried, balling my fists. My tone turned accusatory and bitter. "How can you just leave us to hitch the mules when *this* has just happened?"

He stopped in his tracks and turned about to face me, patiently and quietly answering, "Julia, I'm going to the wagon to find something to wrap her in."

※※※

Will wrapped her himself in a shroud of the same stiff oiled canvas that sheltered us in the buckboard. Inside, hidden away with Rachel's body, was the brown-faced doll I'd given her at Christmas. Will had placed it there. Chloe and Scott were both too occupied in their grief to notice—but I did.

Due to the accident, we stopped well before dusk at an ordinary. Sheltered in the Illinois woods, Will voiced his intent to me as we took our overnight bags up to our room. "We'll have to bury her in the forest near here. Scott will help me dig the grave if you'll tend to Chloe."

"I'm going to spend part of the night with them in the barn. I don't want them alone in their grief."

Will hesitated a second, then said, "They might want to be alone. It's really not…" He simply stopped mid-phrase, shrugging and turning away.

"Not what?"

"Never mind. I won't start any sort of argument while there's so much sorrow. Do as you will."

Will paid the innkeeper to keep dinner warm for us until we returned, and Scott unloaded Rachel, carrying her behind Will, Chloe, and me into the woods behind the ordinary. Following a small trail past a dilapidated shed, we continued onto a game-trail that wove its way into the dense forest for at least a mile. Presently, the trees opened into a small glade. Will stopped and turned to Scott and Chloe.

"We can keep going or use this site."

"This'll do, General," Scott panted, gently setting Rachel down.

Chloe knelt down, peeling apart the canvas nearest Rachel's face. "I just gots to see her one more time."

I sat with her, and there were no words, just Chloe rocking Rachel back and forth, humming softly through her tears. Beyond us, a stone's toss away, the two men were wordless. Only sounds of their spades chinking into the earth accompanied a mother's final lullaby.

Too soon did Scott come over. Blubbering tears and apologies for no reason other than to pity his beloved, he peeled Rachel's little body away from Chloe. She followed the two men to the gaping grave, falling to her knees again in a shattered lament as Scott and Will used hemp cords to carefully lower the child down.

There, in an unmarked grave, we left precious Rachel. My innards churned and felt rancid as butter left untended. As miserable as I felt, I couldn't even fathom what Chloe and Scott were experiencing.

As I'd intended, I spent part of the night inside the innkeeper's barn, where they huddled together. My heart was broken for them, and I wept as they wept. Yet I discovered that Will had been right. In no way did I feel unwelcome, but they needed to sort out their hearts on their own.

When I left the barn, it was a crisp, early autumn night with clear, starry skies and a chill breeze. Relieved to have brought my shawl, I sat down just outside the ordinary entrance on a rickety chair, gazing up at the heavens.

Why, God? Why did you take the very best, the smallest, the most precious from us?

My brother Johnny... lost. Now Rachel.

Oh, Rachel...

Though I knew we were supposed to see through a glass darkly, in this I was uselessly blind. If this was faith, then it was a desolate journey indeed.

My mind kept re-enacting those horrific moments on the flatboat, and even though I thought I'd cried every drop of fluid from my body, more tears came. However, this time I wept because I'd seen something different in my husband today—how he'd cradled

Rachel with a quiet but solemn sorrow. And he'd placed the doll I'd given to her in the canvas, letting her hold it in her arms for eternity.

Sometime well after midnight, I crept back to the room where Will and Little Lewis slept together in the ordinary's largest bed. Not wishing to wake either of them, I took an extra quilt and wrapped up with it and a pillow on the old rug next to them on the floor.

For a long while, I stared up at the ceiling, lost in the lowest emotional wasteland in which I'd ever journeyed. Now, I had but a taste of the desolation and grief Mama had suffered when Johnny had died. Eyes burning, tasting the salt of my own tears, the only thing giving me any peace whatsoever was when Little Lewis awakened, crying—wanting sustenance.

Never had I been so pleased and thankful to hear my own child's cries.

※

After sixteen days of travel, we reached Louisville.

Jonathan and Sarah gave us the expected joyful greeting with all of the excitement, though I was numb to it. I let Sarah sweep Little Lewis from my arms, crowing with praise for him. But the joyous triumph I'd imagined of showing off my son had been sucked from me by the cruel, greedy Mississippi.

"Such a healthy, robust child, Julia," she appraised my boy adoringly. Then she paused. "But are you well? You're mighty quiet-like—and pale too."

"Chloe. She lost her little daughter when we crossed the Mississippi to Cahokia. Rachel's head was crushed against the docks, and I'm still grieving—I still keep *seeing* it and reliving the shock in my mind. I'm sorry. It's just that the pain is still too fresh. Chloe and I are very close, and neither of us can sleep."

Sarah patted Little Lewis's back. "Oh, how dreadful. I see Rachel was loved dearly. I always thought she was a lovely little girl."

I nodded impassively; the sorrow returned, descending like a dark fog sucking joy out of family reunions and first glimpses of new babies.

"I'll make you a sleeping draught and one for Chloe too." Sarah promised. In her loving effort to put a positive face on tragedy, she cast a glance down at Little Lewis as she held him, smiling. "Just remember the blessing you still have. Look at him, Nanny," she cooed to her daughter. "Isn't he fine? He even has William's red hair."

"I prayed for you last winter, Aunt Julia," Nanny said sweetly, dimples ornamenting her smile. "I hated that you had to bear him all alone without a woman from the family to help."

Oh, I hadn't been without family. My sister Chloe had been there.

I was beyond words. It was simply impossible to feel happy. Not now. The foremost wound was losing Rachel, but another thing burdened me too.

Excluding that first night, Will and I had shared a bed at every inn, ordinary, friend's cabin, and tavern we'd stopped at along the way. Weighed down with grief, I found myself sleeping as close to the edge of the bed as I could, despite wrestling with feelings of arousal and desiring to turn to Will for comfort.

My heart said, *"Damn your pride! Be a wife again,"* only to be answered by my stubborn, obstinate will, which did nothing. My fickle, *fickle* self took no action, fearful of awakening what I expected would be earth-shaking craving or baiting Will into another quarrel that neither of us needed after such horrific loss.

Yet during each of those nights abed with me, he never pursued lovemaking. Caring and polite during our travel, Will respected my grief, being a gentleman in every way.

He was also more than supportive of devastated Scott and Chloe, not even ordering them to their usual tasks, but harnessing the mules himself at dawn to allow Scott extra rest and private grief. He even made sure they had a hearty breakfast each morning on the trail, as did we.

Buried within all of these layers of conflict, I was also constantly mindful of Little Lewis's well-being and the fact that I still had a child while Chloe did not.

On our first full day in the Louisville area, Will, Jonathan, Sarah, and I all rode into town in the buckboard to purchase supplies for the rest of our journey. After Jonathan and Sarah took off to buy flour and cornmeal, Will turned to me, smiling hesitantly.

"At the risk of causing you more pain, I have something I want to give you." He reached into his fringed buckskin jacket and pulled out a tiny black braided lock of hair. "This was Rachel's," he explained. "Before we buried her, I cut some off and braided it."

I stared at his offering, stunned.

"I have an idea." He paused, brows knitted and staring down at the plait in his hand. "There's a jeweler here in Louisville. I'd like to take you there so you can pick something out for Chloe. A locket, perhaps? Might that be appropriate?"

All I could do was nod and remember to inhale.

❦

On our second day at Trough Spring, Will and Jonathan left at the crack of dawn to visit their convalescing brother. Chloe and Scott showed up on the front porch after they'd ridden off, when smells of pork-back and corn cakes heralded the household's stirrings. Ever loyal, the two had chosen to set aside grief and were prepared for whatever work needed doing.

Finished with breakfast, I politely excused myself, meeting them outside. "Scott, do you mind me borrowing Chloe for a walk?"

Really, we'd spent little time together. Ever since that night in the barn on the day Rachel had died, I'd tried my best to allow them privacy to grieve.

Scott nodded assent and I clasped Chloe's arm in mine, and for a time we said nothing, relishing the hush of morning's tranquility. I remembered back to when we'd first arrived in St. Louis. When I'd asked Chloe to tell me something about herself, she'd said that her father had been an African prince prior to being enslaved.

It struck me how that made her royalty. Her blood was bluer than mine would ever be, and yet she'd never held court, learned to read, or lorded over anyone in her life. Here was a woman who still managed to live with dignity and grace, carrying out any request Will or I had, often before it was even asked of her.

Finally, I stopped in front of a big haystack next to Jonathan's barn—ironically, the very first place I'd ever set eyes on Scott and Chloe. "I have something for you." I slipped a hand into the embroidered tie-on pocket inside my petticoat. There, I felt for the gift I'd selected, then presented it. "This journey has been anything but pleasant so far, so this is for you."

Chloe pinched the delicate chain between her thumb and forefinger, lifting it in awe.

"See the latch?"

She nodded, pushing at the minute button so that the locket's face sprang open slightly. When she saw what was inside, her face screwed into another moment of tearful sorrow, and I drew her close.

"Now, you have something tangible to remember her by, so you can keep her next to your heart forever."

Her head was shaking in disbelief.

"There's something more I want to tell you about this," I added. "This gift wasn't my idea. General Clark clipped Rachel's hair for you. It was *his* idea to do such. And he's the one who drove me to the jeweler to get this for you. *He* did, Chloe."

She wiped her eyes. "Have mercy. Well, the Lord does work in the strangest of ways. Oh, Missus Julia. Ain't no person, black or white, ever given me something so grand as this..." Her voice trailed off, lost amid tears, and I wordlessly took the locket, fastening it around her neck.

Once done, she reached out, taking both of my hands. For the first time in over two weeks, I saw a slight, unforced smile play on her full lips. She lowered her voice to a whisper. "Now, just you listen to Chloe. Remember—you gots to live in the same house as the general and sleep in the same bed."

I laughed lightly at that, and she went on.

"Life be too short not to share the time the Lord done blessed you with. No man be perfect, Missus. *No* man. Not my Scott, and not your general. They's human flesh and bone, and we womenfolk is made to love them even when they's acting like fools. I's a-hoping I'm giving you a priceless gift here, just like you done gave me."

I squeezed her hand, for she knew I had some serious mending to do. With Chloe and me, there were times when words were unnecessary, but these had been. They were the final prompting my obdurate heart needed.

※※※

When Will and Jonathan returned from their two-day trip to visit the convalescing George Rogers Clark, I hurried out to the barn.

I could see by the look on his face how genuinely surprised Will was to see me coming out to welcome them. "Jonathan, I have much to speak to Will about," I said. "If you don't mind, we'll be in presently for dinner."

"Well, then. I'll see you two inside, I reckon." Jonathan gave his brother a wink, and I could just imagine how Will had probably spoken to him of our discord.

Once we were alone, I said, "Will, if Rachel's passing has taught me anything, it's how fragile life is. I don't want to waste any more of my life without you."

"Could this be you forgiving me at last?"

I walked right up to him and reached up to his face, brushing one finger over some wind-wrought lines on his forehead. He closed his eyes, sighing, his relief palpable.

"Yes. That's what it is," my lips breathed in his ear.

"Ah. Then it was worth the wait."

Edging closer, I smiled, lacing both arms around his neck, slowly kissing him full on the mouth. He remained frozen at first—still astonished—but in mere seconds his hands had found my waist, and he returned my kiss. It was a gentle moment that seemed to span eons. Just Will and me, lost in forgiveness and reunion.

At last.

He broke away first, quipping, "There's not much privacy up in Jonathan's guest loft, is there?" No need to answer. With a sweeping gesture, he lifted me, carrying me to the back of the barn. He removed his buckskin coat, draping it across a large pile of hay.

It would do. I had a feeling that this would not take long.

"The door?" I prompted. Grinning, he strode back over near where his horse still stood tethered, closing the barn doors for more privacy.

I arranged myself as comfortably as possible, hoisting my skirts enticingly, and then he was back, covering me with himself, his body warming mine. My hands wandered seductively to his lower waist, popping open the buttons on the fall-flap of his breeches, making him moan into my mouth with want. He fumbled about, trying to negotiate the lacings on the back of my travel dress. My turn to offer up an amused smile. I arched my back and pressed into him, allowing his eager fingers guidance to what he sought, and soon I lay back in nothing but my loose chemise, my legs wrapped tight around his waist.

Oh, I'd almost forgotten how it felt!

Lips on my neck, he shifted up a bit, and I gasped in delight, opening myself as wide as I could, never wanting him as much as I did right then. We'd made love many, many times in the short time we'd been wed, but tonight was the most passionate, crazed frenzy of intimacy we'd ever enjoyed—an evening I'd keep hidden to revisit again and again as a vivid memory.

Here we were—two very imperfect and different people. One sometimes harsh of heart and the other too full of secrets, pride, and too fearful of disclosing full truths. Yet when we were paired, I couldn't help myself but to cry out at just how perfect it felt.

And no—it took no time at all.

Chapter XXI

Eastward Bound-Fincastle
October-November 1809

Travel by a mule-driven buckboard with a baby was slow going. Ten to fifteen miles a day was usually the best we could expect, depending on road conditions, which deteriorated the farther we went into the more rugged country leading to Appalachia.

Shelbyville, Kentucky, brought us to Shannon's Tavern, lodging with which Will was familiar, promising a good meal and decent beds free of vermin. Little Lewis was teething, and Mrs. Shannon offered him a clean rag dipped in a mixture of whiskey and honey, settling his temperament nicely. Come breakfast the next morning, I applied her treatment again, for it soothed him well. While I tended the baby, Will decided to walk into town to find a newspaper. "I haven't read a single word since leaving Jonathan's," he mused, striding out of the tavern.

Little Lewis slept in Mrs. Shannon's arms while I helped Chloe and Scott load our overnight bags onto the buckboard, which was hitched and ready. Will returned from the small nearby village of Shelbyville, grinning in victory and brandishing a freshly printed paper.

"It's still early, angel," he said, giving me a quick kiss and joining me inside. "And it's cold. Let's enjoy coffee and biscuits before we leave while I read the news."

Kind Mrs. Shannon, humming folk melodies to Little Lewis next to the fire, nodded to an empty table, where Will and I sat down. Mr. Shannon brought us our steaming beverages and hot biscuits with jam. Will wasted no time diving into his newspaper, hungry for whatever was going on in the world.

"Whatever did you do at Fort Clatsop?" I teased. "You couldn't get local news when you were out there." Playfully, I nudged his leg with my toe under the table.

He grunted, giving me that sideways grin of his, eyes poring over the front page. Then his expression changed from lighthearted flirtation to horror.

"Dear God, *no!*" He stood up so quickly his wooden chair screeched on the hardwoods, waking Little Lewis to yowling and drawing eyes from other tavern guests in the seating area.

William Clark always tended to be on the calm, collected side, ever conscious of his station and professional responsibilities. I'd never seen him react like this—especially among other people.

"Sweet, you awakened our boy," I whispered, stunned. "What's wrong?" I recognized the same emotions that Chloe, Scott, and I had had when Rachel died—unexpected, overpowering *grief*.

"No. *Nooo!*" he cried out, slapping the paper down and backing away from the table.

A few other lodgers were coming downstairs into the social area of the tavern, and seeing them, Will came to himself enough to turn on his heel and rush outside. All of us were left staring after him. His cast-off news article lying squarely on the table before me. Looking down, I gasped.

> *It is with extreme regret we have to record the melancholy death of his excellency Meriwether Lewis, Governor of Upper Louisiana, on his way to the City of Washington. The following particulars are given us by a gentleman who traveled with him from the Chickasaw Bluffs.*
>
> *The governor had been in a bad state of health but, having recovered in some degree, set out from the Chickasaw Bluffs, and in traveling from that to the Chickasaw nation, our informant says, he discovered*

> *that the governor appeared at times deranged, and on their arrival in that nation, having lost two horses, the governor proceeded on, and the gentleman detained with a view of finding the horses. The governor went on to a Mr. Grinder's on the road, found no person at home but a woman: she observed something wild in his appearance, became frightened, and left the house to sleep in another near it, and the two servants that were with him went to sleep in the stable. About three o'clock, the woman says she heard the report of two pistols in the room where he lay and immediately awakened the servants, who rushed into the house, but too late! He had shot himself in the head and just below the breast and was in the act of cutting himself with a razor. The only words he uttered was, "It is done, my good servant give me some water," and expired a few moments after.*
>
> *He was decently interred as the place would admit.*

Slowly, unbelieving of the news, I lifted the paper and reread it in a haze of stupefaction, stunned and unsurprised all at once.

Hadn't he been ill? Was he not drinking at times—unstable and out of his mind at others? Didn't the thought of him traveling cause me to fear for his madness and wonder if he was fit enough for such? But now—seeing it in print? It was too sudden and oh *so final*.

After the egregious loss of Rachel, another death of a loved one was simply too much to bear. I cast the paper down and hurried outside.

Hoarfrost—cold and stark as my spirit felt—coated the ground and roofs of the tavern and outbuildings. Though I hadn't even a shawl, I hurried to my husband, ignoring the cold.

He stood against the buckboard, utterly broken, his face tilted against the wagon's rough wooden sideboards, attempting privacy while he sobbed so hard that his shoulders heaved. I embraced him from behind, my head against his back. Really, there was nothing more I could do than that.

"Will—oh, *Will*..."

What could I say? There were no words, only my presence to grieve with him, for it was my loss too. Kind Meriwether, the best of men, unmarried, so lonely, and terribly ill. Like a brother to us both, Will's stalwart companion, his closest friend. In my heart of hearts, hadn't I even felt a stab of envy for what the two men shared? Their history of exploration, camaraderie, and discovery was a relationship I would never fully understand, one demanding enormous sacrifices of risk-taking, unknown dangers, and unexplored territories.

No. Only Lewis and Clark ever shared that.

Out of the side of my eye, I saw Scott and Chloe. They stood together, having just retreated from loading the buckboard and seeing Will explode outside in a tempest of emotion. Outside of the Shannons' barn, they stood watching, their faces troubled, never having seen their general so devastated. Still oblivious to the source of his agony, they knew only too well what true loss was like. They understood. They'd endured their own nightmarish anguish on this journey.

Finally, I was able to turn Will around and take him into my arms, whispering, "You were the richest of men to have known him so closely, and a true friend in every way."

It took him time to find his voice. "Not, not at the end, Julia. Not if he died the way they said he did. And is it even true?" his voice escalated. "How can it be? This is unreal."

"Shh," I whispered, fearing that nothing so macabre would have been published in such detail had it not been factual. "His own mind was so heavy that it took him, along with whatever illness he suffered. That's what it was, for we know he wasn't always himself, was he?"

God above, but *I* knew it.

Will nodded slowly, reality still sinking in. "You're right... the weight of his own mind. It became too much. Oh, I cannot fathom a future in St. Louis without him at my side. We've worked together so closely..."

Shaken I was, but in gathering my own thoughts, they were speeding forward to a new impasse in particular, along with all of its uncertainty. Lewis had taken all of the Corps of Discovery journals with him—his and Will's—since he'd sworn to finally work on them in earnest.

If the paper had printed the truth, and Lewis was really dead, then where were those documents now? Had some tavern-owner disposed of them, not realizing their value or what they were? Or had they been discarded by some unknowing, illiterate fool with no respect for a dead man's property?

"The journals," I gasped in a hoarse, fearful voice.

Eyes swollen and with a face as red as his hair, Will raised his head, his eyes meeting mine with a spark of panic. "What's become of them?"

Firmly, I took his face in my hands, nodding. "You must find them, Will. You *must*!"

❧❦❧

Where *were* they?

And where was this obscure place the newspaper described where Lewis had died, owned by a Mr. Grinder? I kept asking myself, was it the ague that had caused his mind to snap or the deep dishonor he'd felt due to his public humiliation?

And was I wrong to consider Frederick Bates partially responsible for Lewis's death?

As we conversed with travelers at inns, trying to learn more, another troubling facet to the disturbing scenario was that there were now rumors of murder. At first, I was alarmed. After all, I'd experienced personally the lawless nature of men in St. Louis and the spite that rivals harbored for both Meriwether and my husband. As governor of such a lucrative territory, bitterness between men could often turn bloody, as evidenced by the challenge he'd made to Bates at the ball.

However, Will didn't accept any murder theory. He was convinced that Meriwether's demise was his overwrought mind and male honor trumping his will to live. Still, gossipmongers cast shadowy doubts on what had happened at the place now known as Grinder's Stand, some folk almost seeming to favor murder over a desperate act of suicide.

No.

In the end, it was the ague that killed Meriwether.

His all-consuming fevers led to pain and insanity, driving him to the brink, ending in irreversible tragedy. I would accept the truth, but the rest of posterity would ever argue his fate, and I was afraid he wouldn't be remembered for what he did, but instead for the controversial manner in how he died.

While people around us disputed his end, we proceeded on.

The temperate weather we'd enjoyed since leaving St. Louis ended abruptly after the news of Lewis's death. One day, it poured without ceasing; on another, sleet mixed with rain. Chloe, Little Lewis, and I remained under the protection of the buckboard cover, huddling under blankets for warmth. With weeks of travel still ahead, the weather was worrisome.

The buckboard's bench-like seats on which we spent our days were far from comfortable despite York's upholstery and stuffing. Bruises formed under my thighs from being bounced about so often whenever Scott was forced to drive through potholes due to the trail's narrow width. It got to the point where he'd shout, "Hold on, ladies! This one be *deep*!"

We jarred in and out of depressions and over rocks that he couldn't gauge, but even more frightening was when the wagon slid on slick red clay as though it were ice. I'd never been on an ocean voyage, but I wondered if this was what it would be like on a ship in a storm.

"This here mud's slicker than grease on a melon!" Scott shouted in complaint at one point, maneuvering the mules as best he could.

Somewhere approaching the Virginia border, Chloe nudged me. "Missus, look here." She peeled back Little Lewis's linen baby cap that I'd spent months embroidering.

"What *is* that?" I exhaled, so unwilling to have any more ill fortune along our way. My nails dug into the bench of the buckboard as it pitched again. We were due for another round of jostling.

Chloe pursed her lips, frowning. "Some kinda pox, I reckon."

I gave her a look of panic. She knew children so much better than I and was my rock when it came to advice or explanations about Little Lewis's needs. I grazed my forefinger lightly over the round, raised bump on his forehead just beneath his baby cap. It had a disquieting red hue to it. I took him from her and felt him.

Warm. Too warm.

Dear Lord above, please, please *don't let him get sick out here.*

"Where would he have contracted a pox?" I wondered aloud.

"We's been all around folk. Just two days back, them children on the trail was passing him around, taking turns loving on him. And there was all sorts of folk a-staying at the places where you been sleeping. Ain't no surprise that he done caught something 'cause he's little and that's what they's good at when they be babies."

What a blessing that Meriwether and Will had persuaded me to consent to the smallpox vaccination. At least that could be ruled out. But by the next day, more small red lumps had formed on his torso, accompanied by a pronounced fever that kept Will and me up for most of the night as Little Lewis wailed his distress.

We discussed staying put and waiting out his illness, but in the end we decided to continue. Each mile traveled meant we were one mile closer to Fincastle and home than we'd been the day before. On this journey that had been such a terror in so many ways, Santillane became the proverbial carrot dangling in front of the mule.

Chloe concocted an ointment from chicken fat and boiled willow leaves. "I used it once on Rachel when she had the itchy rash."

God bless her, it helped.

"It's so unfair," I reasoned aloud while bouncing along in the wagon. "How could a loving God have allowed Rachel to die like she did? I can't comprehend it. Such a darling child snatched away."

Chloe pursed her lips, thinking before she answered. "He allowed it 'cause this here earth is the devil's battleground. See, earth ain't part of His Kingdom. If it was, white folk and black folk and Indian folk—they would be living happy-like, side by side, and there'd be no such thing as slavery. So I believe my Rachel's in a better place. And in the meantime, we just have to carry on and make this here battlefield as good a place we can."

I clasped her hand, feeling the dry callouses of the work-worn. "I wish I could free you, Chloe," I said, shaking my head. "If I could, I would."

"You don't need to worry yourself about that, Missus Julia. Besides, if I was free, where would I go? I's not altogether godly, but I don't never see a black or white child. They's all the same in His sight, and they's all the same in mine too. Let's just live in this moment and see if Little Lewis be feeling better by tomorrow."

Chloe's heart of hearts astounded me. Such simple faith, so unadulterated and pure with an innate comprehension of right versus wrong. Here she was—consumed with concern about my son, with her own loss still so all-pervading.

Bless her. *Never* was there a better woman than Chloe.

❧❧❧

Listlessness, crying, hot to the touch, and no interest in eating.

Little Lewis gave me every reason to worry over his pox, but we kept going toward Fincastle. Chloe made more of her liniment, settling him and even doctoring Will, who developed a sore shoulder. Exposed to the elements as we were daily, winter's teeth snapped at us with bone-stiffening cold.

At a fork in the road, we lunched with a man from Tennessee who had been raised near Grinder's Stand, where Meriwether died.

"Honestly, General," he said to Will as I listened, "the place ain't much of a going concern. Just a little cabin. Ain't much there. It's a place for tired folk to sleep and then move on."

Will garnered information, asking questions; trying to glean more facts about what had happened. But he hadn't spoken of Meriwether once since learning of his death, which troubled me. He'd bottled up his emotions regarding the loss.

Stiff, sore, and sick of another minute inside the wagon, I chose to walk outside beside Will for the afternoon. He dismounted, leading his horse so we could talk. Seaman trotted at our side. Poor dog, whose master was lost. At least he had us, and I suppose in a way he was Meriwether's gift to me. Never a burden, he was friendly with children and gentle with Little Lewis.

"You know," Will confided, "there was a time on our return trip when Lewis headed up to explore Blackfeet territory and I took men south along the Yellowstone. When we rejoined, Lewis was in a desperate state. Pierre Cruzatte, who was a talented fiddler, traveled with his company. Something was wrong with Cruzatte's eyes; his vision was skewed—couldn't hunt—I tell you, the man couldn't shoot the broad side of a barn!" He chuckled at the memory. "Anyway, for some reason I'll never understand, Lewis gave him a gun."

"You mentioned Blackfeet territory," I said, encouraging him to talk. "Was that when Meriwether had to kill an Indian warrior or two?"

"Yes. Rascals tried to steal their horses and were ready to kill anyone in their way. Lewis acted in self-defense. Anyway, they were only a day or two away from meeting back up with my party, and Lewis decided to try and hunt something to supplement dinner. Half-blind Cruzatte still had that damned rifle, and when he happened upon Lewis lying on his stomach in the grass, he mistook him for an elk and shot him right in the ass!"

"No!" I burst out laughing; I'd never heard this story.

"That he did. When I arrived, poor Lewis was still prostrate on his stomach with a bloody backside and had to stay in that position all the way to Fort Mandan."

"What a blessing it didn't turn septic."

He nodded. "Yes, he was fortunate. But you know, it was after that injury when his fevers worsened." Shrugging, he added, "Maybe being shot weakened him in some way."

"This past year was such a nightmare for him."

After a lull in conversation, Will confessed, "I worry those journals are lost. To think I even sent the elk-skin account with him—my *favorite*—one that I stitched together along the trail four years ago."

"My fervent prayer is that someone trustworthy has them and is keeping them safe." Another thought had rooted itself in my head, and I needed to voice it, for somebody had to give Will encouragement to take on the task since he was ill-prepared for such.

While pondering the best way to bring it up, Will spoke again. "Once we get to Fincastle, I need to travel on to Washington City. I need to see to the fate of all Lewis's personal belongings. And since he can't speak for himself anymore, I also want to meet with President Madison on his behalf to clear his name."

"Oh yes, and it *must* be you. Little Lewis and I will be fine at Santillane."

We walked on. Sparrows were arguing in thickets next to the path, causing Seaman to pause every few steps, cocking his head and barking. My heart was full to bursting with what needed saying, so I stopped walking and just blurted it out. "Will, *you* need to publish those journals yourself."

He glanced back, scoffing. "Not a chance." Then he stopped, looking away, emotion forcing him to swallow hard.

My poor husband. He probably felt it unmanly to find release in tears, but his eyes were brimming. Abruptly, he changed his tone, gruffly shouting at Scott, "Give those mules some what-for on these steeper grades. We can't afford that wagon getting stuck or falling backward."

Scott cracked the whip, and the mules lunged forward. I watched, clenching my jaw, for Chloe and Little Lewis had to have felt that arrhythmic heave.

Will caught my attention again by grasping my hand and protectively guiding me up a steep embankment. Alongside us, the buckboard rumbled by, Seaman following in his unending dogtrot.

Once the wagon passed, I tugged on Will's hand, stopping to face him, repeating myself. "Finish the journals. You *must*. Do it for Lewis."

"I haven't the education for such," he argued, shaking his head in frustration. "True, I enjoy writing letters to family and friends, but

I'm no editor. My spelling is awful, and so is my punctuation. It's a joke among us all—you know that!"

I smiled, taking up his hand and kissing it. It really was a source of humor in the Clark family and had been between Will, Meriwether, and me in St. Louis. Afraid to rub salt into what could be a sensitive wound, I never teased him about it, like some of the others. Indeed, it was I who was really literary-knowledgeable, but I'd never done any real writing or editing, for that matter. I'd just always fancied I could do such.

"I'll help and support you every step of the way," I offered.

His next words were surprisingly bitter. "Publication *should* have come already—from Lewis—before Pat Gass ever published his account and before Lewis made allowances to anyone else."

Scott cracked the whip again at the base of another precipitous rise. This time, Will urged me to scramble up ahead of the buckboard, keeping it behind us in case of a mishap. I lifted my skirts, scrambling up with Seaman and waiting for Will at the top.

Once together again, I challenged, "Find an editor to help you."

"Good God, Julia!" he groused. "I don't know the first thing about finding someone like that."

"I'll ask Papa, and you'll ask around when you go to Washington City. Papa still has connections, and you have them in Washington too." And this time, he didn't shoot down the notion, so I felt I'd planted one more seed, challenging, "Who else would Lewis have preferred to take over his work? Answer me that."

His eyes met mine, and he swiped away another tear of emotion. We both knew the answer.

"Pursue this, Will," I insisted. "Lewis is gone, so make it your mission. Finish what he never started. *You* be the one to complete Jefferson's hope for the journals and that will be your lasting legacy to the whole nation, by leaving record of what you saw before any of it is tamed and gone."

"Judith Julia Hancock Clark!"

That voice!

Seaman was barking, indicating a stranger—

I sprang up, clutching Little Lewis in a cotton sling Chloe had made me so my hands could be free. Steadying myself against the rocking wagon, I stepped forward, peering outside.

Papa!

We were in Virginia, and it had been long since I'd heard his thunderous bellow that used to make me shrink in fear whenever he was angry or cause me to melt against him when it rumbled like a lion purring. Flurries of happiness stirred my heart, for this meant home wasn't far away.

I glanced back at Chloe. "Do you mind taking him?"

Wordlessly, she extended her arms for Little Lewis. The buckboard ground to a halt, and I leaped down onto cold-packed red clay, surrounded by the rugged, rocky hillsides of the Blue Ridge Mountains.

"Papa! Oh, *Papa!*"

He had already dismounted and swept me into his arms. What a relief to see that he hadn't changed in the year and a half since I'd left. No—if anything, he seemed more robust, his cheeks rosy from the cold. Nor was I anxious about how to think of him anymore. He was my *papa*. That was all that mattered.

"I've missed you, girl."

"Colonel Hancock, sir!" called Will, trotting up on his horse and hopping down beside me.

"Oh, William," Papa groaned. "My heart grieves at the news."

Will nodded. "I mourn him daily."

"I hope the rest of your journey hasn't been a struggle."

Sighing, Will answered, "Colonel, it's been a right trial, I'm afraid. Right now, we've a sick child, and along the way we've met up with plenty of potholes and rocky terrain. Much harder travel with this wagon than solo by horse. Then, ten days ago, our sway strap snapped and the whole bed listed. Julia and the baby were both inside. Thank God they weren't hurt."

Papa whistled, eyeing the back right wagon wheel and leaving me to stroll over for a closer look. "Strake needs replacing; be best to just get a whole new wheel. Let's hope it makes it to Fincastle."

Right then, Little Lewis began crying.

"Is that your boy demanding to see his grandpapa?"

I gave a slight smile. "Oh, Papa. His fevers are lessening, but travel has been hard on him." I returned to the wagon, calling for Chloe, who brought Little Lewis out, placing him back into my arms.

Papa was guffawing, "Hard on him? This one better learn to travel, with a Papa like *his*!"

"Look here," I fretted, presenting the baby to his grandfather. None of this journey had been how I'd first dreamed. "See his blisters? They're *everywhere*—even inside his mouth. He's been crying day and night."

Papa took Little Lewis in the crook of his arm, his other hand flipping back the baby quilt covering his face from the cold. With a nod of recognition, he said, "I'm no physician, but all of you young ones had chicken pox. That's what it looks to be." Then, bouncing Little Lewis a bit to try and settle his crying, he added, "Oh, William, he looks just like you with the red hair and blue eyes."

"How far are we from Fincastle?" I asked. "Might Dr. John look him over?"

"I know he'd be happy to do so, but Fincastle is still days away. I knew you'd be along this road, so I've been staying at Fotheringay and riding out each morning to intercept you. It's less than three hours' ride from here."

Fotheringay was Papa's project of sorts. He'd started its construction around the same time as Santillane, intending that someday he and Mama would spend their final years there. I'd only been there once or twice, much earlier in my life, so I barely remembered it.

As we approached, I saw the house's thick walls rise dramatically, the residence set upon its hill like a crown on a queen's head. With squared chimneys at either end, the red-brick exterior stood out in magnificent contrast against the gray November sky.

Inside, our rooms awaited, each fireplace lit, and Hector, Papa's slave-butler, was ready to serve us hot cider and sweet biscuits. Sitting around the table together, we shared more details about our travels.

"All of this hardship has made you tired and sick at heart," Papa declared as Hector replaced the cider with glasses of port. "But soon you'll return to Santillane, and all will turn about. There will be no more tears of grief, fear, or trials, for the love of family will prevail, and we've prepared the warmest of welcomes back home."

Chapter XXII

Fincastle, Virginia
November-March 1809-1810

First came the familiar contours of hills, the smell of smoking meat permeating the air as strung hams hung curing, excess smoke filling the hollows. Then the road improved with our approach to Fincastle, a road much-used in comparison to the rough-hewn trail we'd taken most of the way.

Next were the voices of people working outdoors, spiting the cold. Snug cabins stood close—most I recognized; the chimneys emitted gray plumes as we passed. Just as it began to snow, I felt the mules turn up the hill leading to Santillane. As we crested, the house was in sight, and tears of relief blurred my vision.

"This is it, Chloe," I murmured, reaching down to clasp her hand in mine. "This is home—Santillane."

I held Little Lewis closer. He coughed, and I pressed my cheek to his, feeling a rough scab against my skin.

Soon, precious one. Soon your Uncle John will tend your illness.

Everything accelerated. Mama was fussing at Georgie as they hurried down the steps to greet us. Papa's people ran around the house in excitement while Seaman barked at so many new unfamiliar sights and sounds. The buckboard finally halted and I climbed out, Little Lewis in my arms.

"Mama!"

"Oh, Julia—let me see him!"

"He's sick, Mama. Papa thinks it's chicken pox."

My eyes found Georgie, who was barely recognizable as a younger brother. He'd sprouted since I'd seen him last. Gangly and slender, he bore that youthful promise of filling out into manhood. My, what a fetching gentleman he'd be, with Mama's pronounced cheekbones and Papa's height.

Mama held me tight, covering me with kisses, Little Lewis cradled between us. Then I handed him over.

"Oh, sweet one," she cooed. "Yes, it looks like chicken pox."

"Please, let's send for John!"

"Yes. Georgie," she called, "tell Cap to saddle up Major for you and ride up to John and Harriet's. Tell them we have a baby here needing healing."

"Sure, Mama."

"And ask them to dinner. We've much to celebrate!"

Scott was already unloading our bags, assisted by two more faces I knew, though they were young men now. Ares and Virgil both nodded courteously in my direction with welcoming smiles.

"Thank you so much," I called to them.

Soon I was in my old room, standing in front of the window, gazing outside. Beneath me, carved on the windowsill, was the inscription I'd made. I ran my fingertips over it. Why did it feel as though I'd done that in another lifetime?

JL+MC

How drastically I had changed since inscribing those initials into the wood. Here I was, both a wife and mother with a husband who was an important man—an authoritative gentleman much in demand.

JL & MC

Finally tearing my eyes from the initials, I looked around my old room. No longer was I an inexperienced girl who had charmed America's beloved explorer. Now, I was a woman in my own right, with my own opinions and beliefs. I had even persuaded my husband to pursue the task his colleague hadn't completed. All of the editing and completion of the Corps of Discovery's journals now rested upon Will's shoulders—provided they were located.

Travel weary, Will came in behind me, collapsing on the bed. "Your papa just gave me a letter that arrived several days ago. It's full of excellent news. Chouteau and the fur company were successful. Sheheke is back with his people."

Hearing that made me feel exultant and relieved. "What wonderful news greeting us on our first day home at Santillane."

"Yes. And I intend to celebrate with a good nap. There's enough time before dinner, and if the whole family's coming, I'd like to be awake for it."

"Sleep and rest well, then," I said, leaning across the bed to kiss him.

Will turned over, eyes closed in the pursuit of rest. I closed my own eyes momentarily. My fancy traversed over the Blue Ridge, west to the high plains. Somewhere, next to the Missouri's ever-flowing confluence, stood a woman holding a little boy's hand.

Yellow Corn, I see you...

I soared about her, smiling, and seeing her raise her right hand, placing it to her left breast, lightly tapping. My own hand lifted, tapping gently too.

We're both home, friend.

❧❦❧

I made my way downstairs, gazing at framed silhouettes on the wall of me and my siblings as children. Funny, but I'd always taken them for granted. No longer.

Mama declared as I entered the drawing room, "You've made us awful proud, turning into such a mature wife and mother." She was sitting before a roaring fire in a rocker, easing it back and forth as she grandmothered Little Lewis.

"I hope so," I replied, joining them and relaxing next to Papa on the settee's softness—a far cry from the bumpy buckboard bench.

"You know," Mama whispered, lifting Little Lewis to her shoulder, "I think his fever may have broken. His visit with Grandmama and Grandpapa is proving to be a healing balm."

I beamed, so grateful to be warming myself at Santillane's hearth again. "Then I'm so thankful. He's been a poorly little mite."

"How do you find the Clarks?" Papa ventured, teeth on his pipe-stem.

"Such loving people. Sarah Hite and I write often, and we've grown close. I call her 'my Kentucky Mama,' though nobody can compare with my *Virginia* Mama."

"No, ma'am," Mama clucked, patting Little Lewis's back. He had fallen asleep, and I had to admit his color looked healthier.

"Papa, due to Lewis's death, Will is going to press forward with work on the Corps of Discovery journals."

"I was wondering what had happened to that project. People keep asking."

"They're not even edited."

"What?" he muttered, pipe still in his mouth, sucking. "I thought Lewis had contracted with a publisher and all those scientific types."

I nodded. "But he did nothing more on them. As soon as we moved to St. Louis, his health declined and he had all sorts of other problems with staff, money—everything falling apart. Anyway, Will now needs an editor."

"In my opinion, his wife could do the job," Mama stated smugly under her breath.

Papa harrumphed, removing his pipe. "Now, don't you start getting ridiculous, Peggy. You know it won't do having a woman mixed up in a man's learned work."

I ignored their banter. "Will plans to leave for Washington City in the next day or two. He intends to meet with President Madison, and hopefully they'll be able to locate all of Lewis's personal items, for the journals were among them. We've heard nothing about their whereabouts—or even John Pernier, Lewis's servant."

"Have mercy," Mama fretted. "Where on earth would we be if someone tossed those accounts as rubbish?"

"Exactly," I nodded, "and Will has lost sleep over that possibility for days. We're trying to remain hopeful, praying they'll be found. Papa, can you think of anyone capable of editing?"

Papa's head shook slowly as he took a long toke on his pipe. "Well, there's myself and Breckinridge, who are more than literate, but that's far from being qualified as an editor of literary works. There's nobody I know of here in Fincastle. Surely, Jefferson would have a name or two in mind; he's such a learned man. Persuade Will to task him with the matter."

Oh, that I would. I would indeed.

❧❀❧

Dr. John smiled while examining Little Lewis.

"Oh yes, it's chicken pox, and I see he's had it a while. He's starting to turn about. Look at these scabs on his face." He rubbed at one gently; one edge lifted up as though ready to fall off. "See, they're drying. I'm a bit concerned that he's coughing so much, but he's been traveling out in the cold for weeks. I've some peppermint balm for you to rub on his chest, so we'll try that and keep rocking him near a warm fire."

"Thank you so much, John." God had heard my prayers and was healing my boy, who had never been surrounded by more love.

With joy, Harriet and I resumed our kindred spirit as though we'd never left each other. Both of us were now mothers, and we sat up together until well after midnight, swapping stories and talking about our lives as married women. Her firstborn, Willie, was presently the youngest of the grandchildren, and Harri was loaded with baby questions for me.

Oh, and we reminisced about old times as girls.

"I'll never forget the day you first met William," she laughed. "You were always up for mischief. Remember that stubborn old horse? Does Uncle Hancock still have him?"

"Old King George, you mean? I have no idea. If he's still alive, he's probably out to pasture, as is the *real* king! Have you heard? It's rumored all the way in St. Louis that he's gone mad. Another reason to be free of England."

Griff and my sister Mary visited often in the days following our arrival, and it pleased me to see Papa more friendly with Griff, who was a hardworking man doing his best for Mary. I watched with satisfaction while the two men sat together, discussing the newest marketable goods on order. Mary had a winsome little son named after Papa, so how could he not love them dearly?

Caroline was expecting another child any day and was too near her time for travel all the way from Wythe County. I was disappointed not to see her, but her health and that of her child came before anything.

Our first few days at Santillane were sweetened with family and plentiful dinners. Since St. Louis still lacked a Protestant church, Pastor Logan offered to baptize Little Lewis, and Will stayed long enough to see his son sprinkled.

"We hope you'll be back for Christmas," Mama said to Will when he was ready to leave.

"I fear my business may consume me for several months," he answered. "However, Julia and I will write, and I trust she'll keep me abreast of all the social celebrations you're enjoying."

Everyone gathered on the front steps of Santillane to see Will off. He and I stood beside Papa's dogcart, which Will was driving to Washington City. A smaller rig, it still offered adequate storage in its undercarriage, for our buckboard was at the wheelwright and looked to be there for a while.

I linked my arm through Will's, raising my voice to address the entire family. "The torch has passed to my husband," I announced. "It may take time, but he'll see that the publication of the Lewis and Clark journals become reality."

December 29, 1809

My dearest Angel,
   Forgive me for not writing sooner. I have not stopped since leaving Santilane.
   My first visit was with Lewis's mother.

Understandably, She is Shattered about her Son's untimly death. I have ashured her that in St. Louis we provided him the best care we could find and I offered her Simpathy.

In Charlottesville, I was hosted by Jefferson at Montichello. I only wish you had been there. Like you, his daughter Martha is well-read, and surely a feeling of mutchual friendship would have Sprung from Such an introduction. In the foyer there, Jefferson displays the Skins, Indian blanckets, and artifacts that Lewis and I Sent to him. Seeing that with my own eyes did my heart much good.

Next, I traveled to Washington City and met with President Madison. He offered me the office of Louisiana Territory's governorship. I thanked him for his generosity but declined for now. I did stress 'for now'—as that will leave things open-ended as to persuing the governorship at a more oppertune time.

Madison Shared Something in confidence—a letter from Lewis Sent during his final journey. I found it trubling. Lewis's Script was erratic all the way thru, with entire phrases and words Scratched out. I know how my friend used to write and how his penmanship was impressive and masterfly Scribed. Therefore, I cannot fathom that he would have Sent Such a document to the President unless his mind was Seriously compromised.

Next, I Share good news. The journals are Safely in my hands. A Major James Neely, who was with Lewis toward the end, returned his papers and posessions to Washington. They were waiting for me there.

Presently, I am in Philadelphia, for Jefferson persuaded me to meet with the men with whom Lewis had formerly contracted. One of them—Dr. Barton—recommended the Services of a certain Nicholas Biddle. He is Said to be extremly intelligent, inquisitive, and Should be my first choice for editing the work. Unfortunately, we have missed

Seeing one another here, so I have left an inquiry, hoping he'll respond Soon via your address at Fincastle. Do expect his post.

I have also heard from C. & A. Conrad and Company, who had originally contracted with Lewis and prepared the prospectus. It relieves me that they are willing to work with me, in light of Lewis's passing, and we have agreed in writing to move forward.

I miss you desperately and hope this finds you and the family well. Please give the Man-boy a hug and kiss from his Papa.

I am ever your faithful husband,
William Clark

Will returned in late February. I stood on the porch with Little Lewis and Seaman, who wagged his tail uncontrollably, accompanying Papa down the stairs to greet him.

"Welcome back, William—and Happy New Year!"

Will laughed, "Colonel, the year's not so new anymore. It'll soon be March."

"Ah, but it's still young, and Peggy and I don't want you and Julia rushing off too soon," Papa explained. "You barely took off your boots before heading to Washington back in December." Papa clapped him on the back as he hopped down from the dogcart. Scott climbed down too, assisting Cap with crates and baggage.

Will fondly placed his arm around my father's shoulders, guiding him up the stairs to greet me with a kiss. "How's my Man-boy?"

I handed him over, "He'll be walking before you know it."

"Haha!" Papa slapped his knee in amusement. "Why just last week, Megg caught him crawling out the back door. He's already taking after you—exploring the wilderness!"

Will grinned at the jest and turned to me. "Anything from Biddle yet?"

"Nothing."

He frowned and twisted his lips, thinking. "Then I shall write him again. Let's hope persistence pays."

"It will. It already has, for you've possession of the journals, God be praised."

Persistence was something my husband possessed in immense quantities, and over the next several weeks, whenever hoofbeats drummed up the road to Santillane, Will habitually quit whatever he was doing, eagerly hoping the post was bringing word from Biddle. When a letter finally did arrive, he rushed breathlessly into the library, where I sat reading, Biddle's letter in hand.

"Read it aloud!" I begged.

He scanned it briefly, beginning someplace in the middle:

> "...it will be out of my power to undertake what you had the politeness to offer, and the only object of the present is to renew my regret at being obliged to decline complying with your wishes. My occupations necessarily confine me to Philadelphia, and I have neither health nor leisure to do sufficient justice to the fruits of your enterprise and ingenuity."

"Damn!" Will sighed, flopping down in the wingback and drumming his fingers on its arm. "I have no idea where to go from here."

"Don't give up," I entreated. "Write to Jefferson. He'll know of someone else, or perhaps he'll do it."

"And I'll write Dr. Barton again. He's good friends with all the educated types in Philadelphia. You're right. Somebody out there is *meant* to be our editor."

Oh, my heart soared that he'd become so zealous in this project.

⁓⁓⁓

Papa took Will hunting.

Harriet, Dr. John, Mary, and Griff were all coming for dinner, so we'd have a houseful. Mama was hoping for fresh venison.

Will rose for the hunt before I awakened. We'd made love again the night before, and I was sated and lazy. At this rate, I figured

I'd be pregnant again before leaving for St. Louis, the same way it happened after we wed. It was nigh time for me to give him another child. Little Lewis was just over a year old, pulling himself up and wobbling before losing all sense of balance and plopping back down onto his haunches. The time was ripe for him to have a sibling.

After brushing my hair into place, I pulled on a frock. Half the day was gone when the clock struck eleven, so I had tea downstairs and slipped out the back door, intending to walk into town to visit Mary and Griff's mercantile. I'd not been there since before I'd married.

As much as I loved being here, whenever I gazed westward, my heart was conflicted. Despite St. Louis being such a rough, ofttimes uncouth place, I still ached for the western horizon—I guessed I always would. Still, the thought of leaving Santillane grieved me. Yes, I was prone to homesickness, but I also knew my destiny.

Will.

I'd wanted something more than being a planter's wife, hadn't I? God had granted me that. My place was at my husband's side, and without Lewis with him in St. Louis anymore, he'd need me more than ever—having to deal with the likes of Frederick Bates and his bevy of troublesome friends.

These thoughts jumbled through my head as I jaunted along, shaded by my bonnet in the brilliant sunshine. When I heard thudding hooves along the road, I stepped safely to one side. It was a post rider, and when he saw me, he reined in.

"I'm looking for Santillane."

"I've just come from there. It's my parents' home."

"It's not for them, but for Brigadier General William Clark."

"He's my husband. I'll deliver it."

"Then I thank you, madam."

He reached into his saddlebag and pulled out a letter. It didn't look like anything official, but when he handed it down, I gasped at the return address.

Nicholas Biddle?

Why would he write again, unless to suggest someone else as an editor? If so, then that would help us.

As the rider cantered off, I stayed where I was, under dogwood trees that flirted with their half-open blossoms. With my finger, I flicked open the wax seal, unfolding the page and reading down a-ways to the heart of the message:

> *"I will therefore very readily agree to do all that is in my power for the advancement of the work; and I think I can promise with some confidence that it shall be ready as soon as the publisher is prepared to print it. Having made up my mind today, I am desirous that no delay should occur on my part, as therefore you expressed a wish that I should see you, I am arranging my business so as to leave on Wednesday next..."*

Sweet Lord, what news!

Overcome with excitement, I hoisted my skirts, bolting back home, Biddle's letter flapping in the breeze. Ascending the hill, I saw Cap wiping down two horses I recognized as Will's and Papa's. Beyond that, male laughter echoed off of brickwork between the kitchen and smokehouse.

Cap called out a greeting. "Afternoon, Missus Clark."

Panting, I managed, "My husband—"

"Just outside the smokehouse, ma'am. They's dressing a doe they brought home."

I snatched my skirts up again, hurrying around the side of the house, breathlessly calling out, "Will, you'll never guess!"

"Angel, look what your father and I brought home for our dining pleasure tonight. How does roasted venison sound—with gravy, of course."

"Will, *look*!" His hands were all bloody from skinning the deer, so I just blurted it out. "This is from Biddle. He's changed his mind and is already on his way here!"

He looked astonished. "*Truly?* That's what it says?"

"Look for yourself." Still breathing hard and grinning like a fool, I held the letter up for him to read.

He read, shaking his head in wonder and smiling from ear to ear, his bright blue eyes twinkling like sapphires in joy. "Well, I'll be damned. Colonel, it looks like we'll be imposing on you for a bit longer."

"Papa clapped him on the back, laughing, "Good!"

"You know, the editing process will take weeks," Will said, wiping his red-stained hands on a rag Papa tossed him. "Biddle will need lodging, so we'd best think on this."

"Don't be ridiculous," Papa insisted. "We've plenty of room, my good man. He'll be made most welcome."

Chapter XXIII

Fincastle, Virginia
March-April 1810

Never had Will worked with such fervor, trying to finish his journal copies, transferring "original scribbles," as he called them, to neater work within his favored red Moroccan journals he held so dear—ones he'd once reprimanded me for using. I special-ordered more of them at Griff and Mary's mercantile, requesting them posthaste.

One thing that amazed me was how most of the account was *Will's* material.

"Lewis didn't write as much because he was busy doing research, collecting samples, taking distance measurements, and the like. He left it to me to record thoughts along the way." Laughing at himself, he added, "What he got were copious details written with incorrectly spelled words and poorly executed phrases."

Will's stress and anticipation of the editing process caused him to be short-tempered at times, and the frustration he faced in trying to complete his own copies for Biddle's perusal resulted in the first harsh words I'd ever heard him utter about Meriwether.

"Damn it all! Lewis did absolutely *nothing* on this since '06. By God, but I wish he'd spent less time in taverns, frittering over Frederick Bates, and more time using some self-discipline while he still had his mind. This part could already have been done."

Anxiety did his constitution no good either, and following another hunt with Papa and the nonstop task of copying documents,

Will complained of persistent pain in his shoulder again. John examined him, gently extending Will's bare arms around to determine the affected area.

"Ah—yes. There's a tenseness there," John said. "However, I don't think it's serious. By middle age, many people begin feeling aches and pains."

Will gave him a wry look. "Must I be reminded?"

Come August, he'd be forty years old. Strange, but to me he no longer seemed like an older man. Affable, handsome, energetic, loving father, astute decision-maker, capable lover... Why, few younger men possessed William Clark's physique or stamina.

Certainly, Nicholas Biddle did not.

When he arrived, he was *far* younger than I'd expected. Most probably, he hadn't but five or six years on my own age. Short and slightly built with a boyish face, he wore thick, circular spectacles, presenting himself neatly dressed and amiable with a very proper manner. However, he shared the same sort of fastidious work ethic as Will, so they got on extremely well together. His interests were of the scholarly nature, not the outdoors type, as were my husband's.

On the day he arrived, Biddle presented a lengthy list of questions. "These," he explained, "are meant to draw out more information from General Clark's memory to embellish what has already been written."

This was my first opportunity to become involved, posing each question to Will while Biddle recorded his answers.

> *~What sorts of native hairstyles did you see, and did they vary much between men and women?*
> *~Do native women get venereal disease as frequently as their men?*
> *~Which tribes pierced the noses, and were there spiritual reasons for it?*
> *~Could oysters be found along the Pacific coast?*

I was stunned at how much I *didn't* know about the expedition. No topic was left out, be it sexual or cultural, and by the time Will managed to answer every question Biddle asked, we'd been at it for nearly a week already. In fact, answers to Biddle's additional questions alone filled up an entire Moroccan notebook.

Once the actual editing commenced, I couldn't help myself, so fascinated was I with the work. "Mr. Biddle," I risked, "might I try transposing this phrase of concern into more sensible prose?"

Spectacles perched low on his nose, he looked at me in surprise. "Why, of course."

Will cocked a stern eyebrow at me, but I ignored him, and the rephrasing didn't take long. "Will this do?" I handed Biddle the scrap of paper with the corrected phrase, smugly gazing at Will.

"My, that's much improved. Thank you. Could you work on some other sentences I've noted?"

Delighted to have assisted, my foot was clearly in the doorway now. Only one day later, Biddle presented me with another set of marked items to rewrite. "I've two paragraphs here. Several of the sentences don't seem to flow. Could you possibly—"

"Yes!" He never needed to ask twice. I dashed back into Papa's drawing room, fumbling about in his desk until I found several sheets of blank paper on which to write. Diligently, I rewrote each one into a more sensible phrase, presenting the new versions to Biddle, who grinned.

"Excellent work! Should I require more assistance, are you willing? It will speed up our work."

Was I *willing*? I was stunned, *overjoyed* in getting to share in some way the gifts I'd always felt were inside me, lying dormant, waiting to awaken and be useful. I'd felt this way since first developing a love of reading.

From then on, Biddle often turned over paragraphs to me to rephrase or shorten.

"Mr. Biddle, may I suggest that some of the work's spelling be revised?"

That's where Biddle stopped me. "I would prefer the captains' own personal style and spellings be respected in that regard."

I'd have to be satisfied with table scraps, but still, it was marvelous to work with the two men. Biddle and Will often asked me to read portions of the work aloud, listening to how things were worded. Privately, I thought how overjoyed Meriwether would have been that I—Judith Julia Hancock Clark—had contributed in *some* way to aiding in the work's publication.

⚜

To have gained both Biddle's and Will's trust in the editing process moved me to express my gratitude. I did it over a dinner, when both my parents, Harri, and Dr. John were present.

"Mr. Biddle," I began, "allow me to express my deep appreciation for the privilege of reading over and providing you with edited fragments. It's given me the greatest joy imaginable."

"Why, of course, Mrs. Clark," Biddle replied. "In turn, I must compliment your husband and father on what a charming, kind, gentle, and educated young lady they have in their lives. You are indeed the perfect wife for such a gallant and adventuresome explorer."

Seldom needing an excuse for such, Papa cleared his throat and took the opportunity to lift his mug of ale. "I propose a toast to my stalwart daughter Judith, who, two years ago, left as a blushing bride, expectant of my grandson. She faced the formidable Louisiana frontier, and since her return last November, I have become reintroduced to a mature young woman with thoughts and opinions of her own. Shall I credit my son-in-law with that?"

"William deserves nothing of the sort!" Mama scolded, causing Will to freeze as he lifted his glass. "George Hancock, you give credit where it's due and allow a simple fact to sink in. Julia is a Hancock and a woman who has done us proud. Yes, she has her own opinions and thoughts, and I shall grant nobody but *her* credit for that!"

I raised my own mug of ale. "Huzzah to that, Mama."

Everyone at the table lifted mugs and wineglasses toward one another with resounding clinks, small ale overflowing onto the seasoned wood of our old dining table.

⚜

While sheltered in the library during a rainstorm, Biddle said, "I still need more of your memories, General. Think for a moment—what is something specific you regret not writing more about?"

After a few moments, Will ventured, "There was a dancing rite among the Mandans that was unique."

"Tell me," Biddle said, dipping his quill into the ink and readying himself.

"They called it the Buffalo Dance because they believed the ceremony would call the buffalo toward their villages, and they allowed all of us to watch it."

Biddle jotted some notes, then waited for more.

Will hesitated.

"Well?" Biddle asked. "Is there more? Did they paint themselves or wear something bizarre?"

Will snickered. "You might say that. Each dancer was a virile young man who would offer up his naked wife to their elders so that the old ones' strength and past hunting prowess would be transferred from one man to the other through the women."

Biddle's mouth drooped, and his face registered moral outrage. "*God in heaven!* You're repeating this in the presence of Mrs. Clark?"

His shock made me giggle. "Mr. Biddle, I'm sitting here rather impressed that the Mandans consider women capable of such a biological feat. Please, you mustn't worry about me hearing such. Remember that General Clark and I have a child between us, so I'm obviously familiar with *how* that child was conceived. I'm more curious to know whether any of the expedition's men became involved?" I cocked an anticipatory eyebrow at Will.

He laughed aloud in his hearty, uninhibited way, nodding. "Yes, they did, but be assured that both Lewis and I abstained."

Biddle's jaw still hung slack. "I cannot include this in the manuscript," he breathed, removing his spectacles and dabbing his flushed face with a handkerchief.

Well, he asked...

"Why not include it?" Will argued. "It's a traditional ceremony among an indigenous people. They even had a name in their language for the ceremony of which it was part—the Okipa, they called it. And it worked! Within days, the buffalo appeared, providing their winter stores."

Biddle pursed his lips but finally set the handkerchief aside and replaced his spectacles as he began writing.

"What do you think made certain Indian groups more welcoming than others?" he queried afterward.

"That's an interesting question," pondered Will.

I voiced, "Those awful Sioux were so hostile to you."

"Why?" Biddle asked.

"You and Lewis used to talk about that incident a lot," I added.

"Yes, and we decided that the tribes on either of the foothills surrounding the Shining Mountains, as they called them, were far friendlier. Lewis concluded that they hadn't had previous contact or had only *limited* contact with white men, and I agreed."

"Didn't you tell me once that the Clatsops on the Pacific coast were unfriendly?" I asked.

"Not *all* of them, but they'd been exposed to the vices of our darker sides, like Indians on our present frontier in St. Louis. Before the last century ended, an American captain, Robert Gray, navigated up the Columbia a short distance. And he wasn't alone—other merchant vessels seeking furs visited the Pacific coast before us. They traded with the Indians and gave them spirits before we ever arrived. It's sad, really, how we've sullied them so."

※※※

Papa's hemp crop was coming in, promising hot, humid weather on the way. It also meant my time at Santillane was ending.

Will was becoming more and more anxious to leave for St. Louis.

I've been told how all good things must eventually end, but I hated seeing time peter out when it meant leaving. My parents were glorying in my little boy as they came to know him, and days alongside Will and Mr. Biddle were merry and brought me great contentment.

How miraculous that Biddle had changed his mind, traveling to

Fincastle to work with Will on the project. In fact, not since Lewis died had my husband been so fixated upon anything as he was with the work accomplished with Biddle each day. And Biddle knew exactly how to entice more memories and information out of Will that he typically kept to himself—like the Mandan Buffalo Dance we joked about.

"We should consider hiring someone with cartography skills to draw up a map for the publication," Biddle suggested, poised and ready for the day's session.

"Oh, Will, you should draft a map," I exclaimed.

"I've not touched cartography since the expedition," he reminded me.

Sometimes he frustrated me; such constant humility in the face of opportunity.

Listening to our exchange, Biddle said, "Actually, I think Mrs. Clark is right. I've seen your sketches in your field notes." Both of his eyebrows lifted above his spectacles, his enthusiasm accelerating. "Yes! If you did it yourself, it would add ownership and a personal touch to the work."

"But those field sketches you're talking about are crude—drawn in a hurry while sitting inside a tent or next to a river."

I reached out, grasping Will's hand. "Do this. It's one of your many gifts."

"I insist," Biddle persisted. "It would be most appropriate if you were the one to do it. In fact, it would be a *selling* point. Could you do a sample draft before I leave, just to give me an idea of what it could look like? That way we can discuss it and you can take your time working on the final copy once you're back in St. Louis. And don't feel rushed because it'll be a good year or so before I'm finished editing everything."

"If only distance wasn't an issue," Will said regretfully. "I'd help you in any way I could if we were closer."

"Indeed," Biddle agreed. "I've an enormous task ahead, and once I'm home, I'll be wishing I had an assistant."

A thought struck me, and I turned to Will. "What about George

Shannon? You mentioned he'd been pursuing more scholarly paths. I'll bet it would be an encouragement, focusing on something as worthwhile as this."

Addressing Biddle, Will explained, "Georgie Shannon was the youngest member of the expedition. I sent him upriver on a mission to return Chief Sheheke of the Mandans a few years back when his party was attacked by the Arikara. He was badly injured and lost a leg as a result. Julia's right. He'd be a perfect assistant. He's been studying in Lexington, Kentucky, and is intelligent, with a keen memory of everything that happened on the journey. I'm sure he'd jump at the chance to help."

"Then I'll look forward to hearing from him," Biddle said appreciatively. "And think of what it will mean to readers that one of the captains crafted a map for the journals himself."

"Daa-daaa—" The sound of my son's gurgling voice brought me upright.

We all froze. Little Lewis was toddling over to a chair where Will had set his favorite field journal, the one he'd made of elk-skin, sewn by his own hand and covered with hides from an elk the Corps had hunted for food.

He'd just taken his very first steps!

Little Lewis picked up the book and teetered back over to Will, offering it up to him. Will took the journal, then lifted his son up into his lap. "Ah, well. I guess you're right, Biddle. It looks as though the entire family wants me to finish this project, and I'll throw in a map or two for you too."

❧

Nicholas Biddle departed in mid-April, taking with him a significant portion of Will's life, namely a stack of red Moroccan journals, full of paraphrased and corrected writings, documents for Dr. Barton to review, a few pocket field journals from the expedition, and a large map of the United States that Will gifted him, encompassing the Mississippi all the way to the Pacific. Indeed, Biddle's baggage was far heavier upon leaving than when he'd first arrived.

Once he was gone, days were lazier and quieter without the constant rehashing of the Corps's journey. Mama, Papa, Will, and I all spent one peaceful afternoon in the drawing room. Little Lewis napped in Mama's arms, Will and Papa shared a relatively new edition of the *Virginia Argus* of Richmond while I read a copy of *Evelina* that Mama had purchased for me.

"A book written by a woman," she informed me. "It might spur you on to writing, sometime."

When a post rider clattered up the drive, everyone jumped to attention.

Megg entered the room, presenting Will with a letter from Louisville. After reading it, he grumbled something incoherent and got up, stalking out of the room and heading upstairs. I exchanged a quizzical look with my parents, excused myself, placed *Evelina* aside, and ascended the stairs. The door to our room was now shut, so I opened it slightly, peering in before entering. Will was standing in front of the window, his back to me, staring outside.

"Will? Has something happened?" I treaded carefully, detecting frustration. It was often said that redheaded people possessed tempers. Fortunately, Will's didn't rise up often, but when it did…

"My nephew Johnny O'Fallon wrote that York was hired out to a man by the name of Young in the Louisville area."

"Isn't that what you wanted?"

"Yes." He turned around, staring downward.

"Then why are you bothered?"

He shrugged. "Johnny-O says he's happy there, working hard, thriving. York actually told him that even though he wishes things were better between he and I, he's never been more content than now because he's closer to his wife."

I smiled to myself. "Then that alone should give you great satisfaction. You've succeeded in giving York some happiness. Why, I think this instance shows how erring ways can be altered through kindness instead of severity."

He shook his head. "Well, by the end of the year, York's contract will have ended. I think I'll have him—"

"Don't say it, Will!" I snapped. My hackles bristled, but I tried tempering my voice. Mama and Papa were right downstairs. "Don't you think he learned a lesson when you shredded his back? If you're not wiser with your people, then someday slavery's horrendous stain may serve to blacken your name and sour your reputation. In the future, I believe slaves will be free men and women and that some people will look back at those who owned them with disdain. Even *I* feel guilty for 'owning' Chloe and Scott—and all of them—though you already know my sentiments."

"*Enough*, Julia," he emphasized, holding up a staying hand to prevent my saying more. "You're right about one thing: I'm *well* aware of your 'sentiments' on this subject. No matter, I've decided—"

"You've decided to bring him back to St. Louis again? Where he'll be miserable?"

"Please stop," Will said, his voice soft, his hands reaching out, imploring.

Did I give a damn?

"No, William Clark. On this, I'll speak my mind, no matter what you say. York followed you clear to the Pacific, and what did he ever gain from it? From *loyalty*? You and every other man in the Corps received the accolades of men and women with whom you've come into contact. York received *nothing*, Will. Nothing but continued misery, being forced into leaving Louisville time and again, when that's where his heart is—"

"Julia—"

"I'm not finished!" My voice had risen, and no doubt my parents heard us downstairs. "It's high time York finds happiness. Let him *stay* in Louisville. It's within your power, but you're too damned stubborn to do it!"

"Finished now?"

"Yes, and I hope your heart is open to what I've said because it's time you allowed him to make of his life what he will!"

Having said my piece, I knew he was furious with me, so I spun on my heel, rushing out of the room and down the stairs, nearly colliding with Chloe, who was carrying up an armload of clean linens. Still, I didn't stop, but ran straight out the back door, fleeing past the smokehouse and down the hill into the field leading to the mighty Catawba tree.

Once there, I stopped, sobbing. Down I sank onto that great, sweeping branch, spring's breezes cool against my wet face. The tree's heart-shaped leaves still hadn't appeared, and the branches looked skeletal, dead.

Like my marriage now?

In that episode upstairs, had I once and for all ruined the relationship I had with my husband? It was so exasperating, for my inward truth was that, far beyond our differences, I *believed* William Clark was still worth fighting for, and so was our marriage. But would *he* believe that anymore?

For a bit, I just sat on Papa's branch. Strange, but whenever I spent time by myself at the foot of the Catawba tree, feeling nature's own breath dry my tears, comfort always came.

Somehow.

That old Catawba tree was home.

My shelter.

A refuge.

I tilted my head back, gazing up into its gnarled branches. What a magnificent creation it was. No wonder Papa's horses, cattle, and yes, his people came here frequently on summer days to abide in its shade—relaxing in its cool security. I lowered my head, gazing westward, the sun shimmering on the horizon, kissing distant treetops with its golden rays.

"Julia?"

I stood up at the voice, turning about.

Will was descending the hill toward me. Rooted, I stayed where I was, breathing hard with emotion and biting my lip as he made his way over. Papa's sweeping branch hung between us like a barrier.

"Julia," he breathed my name again, looking at me and shaking his head. "You didn't let me speak."

His voice was patient and gentle, not angry or scolding, the way

I imagined it would be. He moved closer, stepping over the branch so that we were together again—nothing between us.

"I need to say something," he began, taking my hands into his. "First off, I love you. I love the woman you are, even as an outspoken advocate for something I cannot yet fully embrace. However, I respect you and see very well how all my people adore you. *That* I understand. I even see them willing to go an extra mile for you that they're not willing to travel for me. It's because of your kindness. *Kind Lodge Woman*," he sighed. "Sheheke knew your heart better than I. Maybe someday I'll come to see things differently, but in the meantime, you'll need to show me how to be kinder.

"When my parents first introduced me to York, we were children. They encouraged our friendship—for us to play together, to become close. I've never been separated from him for long periods. He's always just been there, and frankly . . . I miss him when he's not, for I'm a selfish creature of habit, and he knows how I prefer things." He paused, searching for the right words. "However, I've decided that I need to sever the cord and let him stay in Louisville. I need to back away since our bond is so broken. He has too much anger pent up to remain at my side. And me? Well, I did the real damage to cause it, didn't I? For now, it's best we maintain distance." He shrugged, genuine sorrow on his face.

"Oh, Will," I breathed, stunned and momentarily closing my eyes. "You're doing the right thing."

"Yes. I believe I am."

"Do you think you two might ever be able to heal what is so wrecked?"

He shook his head. "I doubt it. So much bad has passed between us that mending what I thought was once there is impossible."

My breath caught in my throat. "Oh, I overreacted badly, didn't I? I thought—I thought you were going to insist on punishing him further or forcing him to return to St. Louis."

He chuckled low in his throat. "My impetuous angel, jumping to conclusions."

"I was. I'm so sorry. Forgive me?"

He leaned in, hands soft on my shoulders, and kissed my head. "I already have. Now, I have something I want to give you for when we return to St. Louis."

My concern about Will and York morphed into curiosity as he reached into his ample greatcoat pocket, drawing out a brand-new red Moroccan journal.

"Last year, I recall being frustrated and miffed with you for taking one of these from my office and using it for your household lists and such. It was wrong of me, for whatever is mine is also yours. So today, I'm giving this new journal to you—but it's not for household inventories."

My heart rushed ahead of his words with anticipation.

"I want you to *write*," he whispered, placing the journal into my hands. "You've always had a gift and love for words, and Lewis saw it well before I did. You've an impressive education, so write what you want. Create something and make it heartfelt. Make it *yours*."

Had my happiness at that moment been a fire, then that old Catawba tree would have gone up in smoke.

"You know," Will pondered, offering me his arm as we sauntered back up the hill toward Santillane. "It's occurred to me that when Lewis and I returned from our adventure, your adventure was just beginning. Perhaps that's what you should write about."

I snuggled into his side, closer. He was right. Everybody knew about Lewis and Clark, but my adventures were yet untold.

Author's Notes

I was finishing the Antonius Trilogy when COVID-19 rolled its ugly head around the corner. Since there would be no travel, no opportunity to visit museums or meet with historians for an extended time, I realized I'd need to select a new project much closer to home. It needed to be something I'd be able to research in my armchair and love just as much as my previous projects. Lewis and Clark had always fascinated me, so when I discovered that Julia Hancock had been born and raised in my own Botetourt County here in Virginia, I knew I'd found my next book.

Like so many women of her day, Julia was a silent voice next to the influential personality that was her famous explorer-husband. We have but one portrait giving us her likeness, a stunning set of jewelry (necklace and earrings of gold and carnelian), the baby cap made for Little Lewis, some handwritten items, including a letter written to her brother George Jr. in 1814, along with a red Moroccan journal containing household inventories. From the tidbits that William wrote about her to his brother Jonathan, we know she did suffer from a certain amount of homesickness and tended to catch colds easily. The inventories, needlework, and even a recipe for "Vinegar Pudding" all suggest that she was hands-on among "Will's people" once she moved to St. Louis.

Sadly, Julia Hancock Clark died in 1820 at the age of 28 at her father's Fotheringay estate in what is now Elliston, Virginia. She is buried there in a mausoleum built by her father for himself and immediate family members. Ironically, her father, George Hancock, followed her in death only several weeks after her own passing.

It's not 100 percent certain what caused Julia's death, but the best guess is breast cancer, despite her young age. In a September 16, 1814 letter to Biddle, Clark used a somber tone, sharing very personal details about Julia's problems with her breast. He stated, "I am apprehensive it will terminate in a Cancer."

In her final days, Julia rallied, and Clark was persuaded to return to St. Louis to resume his duties as governor while she remained with her parents, convalescing. However, shortly after arriving home, he received word that Julia had died. Clark had a glass pocket locket made containing Julia's hair on one side and his daughter's on the other. Little Mary Margaret Clark followed her mother in death after a fever in October 1821. She was only seven years old. This two-sided piece is housed in the Missouri Historical Society Library and Research Center in St. Louis. I imagine William Clark pocketed this keepsake to remember his wife and little girl, keeping them somehow close in the only way he could.

We don't know whether Julia was as gifted in the literary arts as I portrayed her. However, she certainly appreciated Shakespeare and was passionate about the arts. Therefore, it's not completely out of the question. It is true that she bemoaned not getting to attend a play in Louisville, which Jonathan Clark and family saw. It was Shakespeare's *Taming of the Shrew*, so I ran with the Shakespeare theme, concocting the scenes between Julia and Lewis. And he really *did* give her a complete Shakespeare collection to celebrate her wedding, which worked beautifully in my story. I chose Brutus's tragic scene out of *Julius Caesar* as a poignant foreshadowing of Lewis's own demise that wasn't far off by that time. This particular monologue of Brutus's comes in the final Act V, Scene V.

The 1814 letter Julia wrote to her brother George is written in a graceful script and is *much* easier reading than documents written by either Lewis or Clark, a testimony to her penmanship, intelligence, and education.

Julia and William Clark were married as the story detailed, on Tuesday, January 5, 1808 at Santillane. And yes, Thomas Jefferson really *did* send her a gift of jewelry. She bore five children to William Clark, the first being Meriwether Lewis's namesake, Meriwether Lewis Clark. Next came William Preston Clark, Mary Margaret Clark, George Rogers Hancock Clark, and John Julius Clark.

There is absolutely no evidence of any mistreatment or cruelty toward enslaved individuals by Julia Hancock Clark. Therefore, I depicted her as loving, gracious, and humane toward enslaved people.

William Clark was very much a man of his day. Most Virginian planter families were slave owners, and the Clark family was no different from anyone else in that regard. The Hancock family also owned slaves, per my depiction.

Clark stated in a March 1, 1809 letter to Jonathan that he'd "trounced" all of his slaves except Sillo, Ben, and Sip (Sep). The incidents depicting York's vicious whipping and Venus's severe punishment are both mentioned in Clark's letters as well. There really were some severe disciplinary actions administered to some of Clark's enslaved people, and from the wording of his letters, it's likely that he executed their punishment himself.

That being said, William Clark acted most admirably on other occasions. Beginning in 1810, probably not long after returning from his trip to Virginia, he began to oversee and provide an education for Sakakawea's son, Baptiste (Pomp), and daughter, Lizette. Julia would certainly have connected with Sakakawea in some way and had to have met her. Clark also eventually freed some of his enslaved people, including York.

In his comprehensive biography, *Wilderness Journey*, William E. Foley wrote, "It is not difficult to identify William Clark's shortcomings, but his modern critics would do well to remember that he lived in a time and place far removed from their own. Even though the core issues he struggled to address may not be so very different, the setting was." (pg. 268, *Wilderness Journey*)

I paraphrased the speeches by both Major Patrick Lockhart and William Clark which were delivered in Fincastle on January 8, 1807 in honor of the Corps of Discovery's homecoming. Copies of these original speeches are found in Gene Crotty's book, *The Visits of Lewis & Clark to Fincastle, Virginia* (Published by The History Museum

& Historical Society of Western Virginia, 2003) and *Lewis & Clark: The Fincastle Connection* by Dorothy Simmons Kessler (Published by Historic Fincastle, Inc., 1995). The original manuscript of Clark's *Response to the People of Fincastle* resides in the Missouri Historical Society Library and Research Center in St. Louis.

Webster's Dictionary wasn't published until 1828, so in early America there weren't established spellings for vocabulary like there are today. Clark's spelling was all over the place, and to a certain extent, Lewis's was as well. Be forewarned: if you decide to read the *Journals of Lewis & Clark*, get used to some pretty creative spellings and overly florid prose, which (as letters from the period prove) was the style of the day.

If the old Fincastle legend is true, that William Clark met Julia and Harriet out riding on a stubborn horse, then he met *both* of his wives on the same day—*and on the same horse!*

Yes, Clark married Harriet Kennerly Radford in 1821 after Julia died. Harriet's husband, Dr. John Radford, died tragically in a wild boar attack while hunting. Suddenly widowed with children needing a father, Clark's proposal in 1821 was instantly accepted. Together, they had three children: Jefferson Kearny Clark, Edmund Clark, and Harriet Clark, who died as a child.

Meriwether Lewis wound up with all the makings of a tragic hero. He was Thomas Jefferson's top choice to lead the Corps of Discovery. At that time, his health was sound, and decisions he made during the expedition years (1803-06) were overall intelligent and wise. His foresight in selecting a second officer to replace him in case he became debilitated is to be commended, for he and William Clark were indeed the "dream team."

Things began to look different upon their return.

Both Lewis and Clark suffered from the "ague," the common term for malaria. After reading about the manifestations of this disease, I was *astonished* at how differently it can affect people. Thomas C. Danisi wrote an impressively researched work called *Uncovering the Truth About Meriwether Lewis* (Prometheus Books, 2012). It includes a lot of detailed medical research showing how malaria is capable of breaking down one's physical and mental state. Danisi also presented some powerful documentation showing Bates's and Simmons's behavior that destroyed Lewis's good name.

On May 13, 1809, Lewis requested government reimbursement for Indian gifts for the Missouri Fur Company's mission to return Sheheke. A two-volume compilation of well-organized letters collected by Donald Jackson (*Letters of the Lewis & Clark Expedition*) shows that Lewis did not actually receive a denial for this request until late July or August of the same year, right before leaving St. Louis. Thus, I did take one month's liberty by allowing Lewis to have already received this news thirty days earlier in June at the Chouteaus' ball.

By this time, Lewis's physical and mental condition were rapidly deteriorating, with frequent relapses from his disease. Sadly, he wasn't too good with finances, and there were apparently discrepancies in his accounts. Lewis "kept" the pay of John Colter, a Corps of Discovery veteran who had not yet returned from out west. Colter's earnings from his Corps of Discovery years totaled $559—back then, a hefty sum! Colter had a tough time acquiring his pay once he returned from exploring what is now Yellowstone National Park. His only option was ugly—suing the deceased Lewis's estate. Whether Lewis intentionally kept the money or simply lost track of it and forgot about it is unknown. Due to the nature of his illness, I tend to assume it was the latter.

Three years after Lewis's death, the Secretary of War declared that the department had been *erroneous* by not reimbursing him. The Lewis estate was awarded an adjusted amount of $636.

Heartbreaking—and *far* too little, too late.

In Search of York by the late Robert Batts was one of the most valued books I read while researching this novel. Though York remained fairly content hired out to a Mr. Young in 1810, by 1811 he was hired out to a Mr. Mitchell, known for being hard on slaves. Also around this time, York received more bad news. Whoever had owned his "wife" relocated to the lower Mississippi valley, known in York's day as the Natchez, taking both the woman and York's children.

York never saw his family again.

In more research after Mr. Batts's death, it was discovered that William Clark finally freed York around 1815. Clark set him up with a drayage business: a wagon, horses, and some cash. However, York had no idea how to be a manager, so it never took off. Most historians believe he contracted cholera and died, never returning to St. Louis again.

When I needed an additional plot thread in the St. Louis section, I kept coming back to Chief Sheheke-Shote. One hears so much about the Cheyenne, Lakota, and Shoshone Nations as well as Sakakawea's involvement in the Lewis and Clark expedition. But the Mandans? Not so much. The more I researched, the more I was persuaded to include a portion of Sheheke's story in my book.

It isn't known for certain where Pierre Chouteau housed Sheheke and his family after they left the moldy confines of Cantonment Belle Fontaine. Therefore, I snatched that gray area and encamped him just outside of St. Louis, adding a plausible but fictitious plot including Julia's involvement with his family. Ramses Phipps was also a figment of my imagination and Odysseus Phipps, his fictitious brother, was based upon a real person, though I never found the squatter's real name. Therefore, while Julia undoubtedly came into contact with dangerous men, and her husband had many enemies, her face-off with Phipps is purely fiction.

Sheheke survived the first scourge of smallpox in the 1780s, for he was apparently away from his village at the time. That first epidemic reduced the Mandans to just a few thousand. However, an epidemic affecting *all* of the Great Plains in 1836-37 nearly annihilated them. Sheheke-Shote didn't live to see his people's demise, for he died in the autumn of 1812, fighting the Hidatsa.

Santillane still stands and remains privately owned. There really is an old Catawba (Catalpa) tree on its property, down the hill from the house. I've been privileged to visit Julia's home numerous times and consider it an honor to have walked through the same kitchen, halls, library, and drawing room as she and William once did.

Santillane was badly damaged by fire in 1811. Nobody seems

to know much about the extent of the damage other than the fire somehow began on the roof. My best guess is that a fireplace flue or debris from the chimney may have ignited. In discussing this with several Fincastle historians, I have concluded that the conflagration consumed most of the original house since at that point George Hancock promptly moved his family to Fotheringay. The months Julia spent at Santillane after her return in 1809-10 in this story would have been the final time she ever really got to return "home" to Fincastle.

The Botetourt County Historical Museum has the original bell from the old log courthouse that once rang during New Years' celebrations, and young John Hancock's grave can still be seen in an outside corner next to the Fincastle Presbyterian Church.

Around the turn of the 20th century, Reuben Gold Thwaites prepared to launch his new edition of the Lewis and Clark Journals. In doing so, he offered this golden truth: "The story of the records of the transcontinental exploration of Meriwether Lewis and William Clark (1803-1806) is almost as romantic as that of the great discovery itself." (*A History of the Lewis & Clark Journals*, Paul Russell Cutright, 1976.)

In his book, Cutright notes that since the Corps of Discovery was a military expedition, the journals should have been turned over to the US government. However, at the time Jefferson was relying on Lewis to publish them, and they needed to be reprinted neatly in more legible fashion before any real editing could begin. Thus, the original field journals remained in the explorers' possession.

The young amputee George Shannon was sent to Biddle as an assistant, as Clark and Julia discussed in my story. But there were many delays in the publishing. Conrad & Co., the original publisher, went bankrupt, so Biddle contracted with Bradford & Inskeep to finish the job.

However, when Biddle began a political career, he turned over the final edits to a man named Paul Allen, who wound up taking credit for *all* of the editing. Biddle never received any recognition, so I'm pleased to say that he was honored posthumously since the very first publication has become known as the "Biddle Edition." It was entitled: *The History of the Expedition Under the Commands of Captains Lewis and Clark*.

In 1814, William Clark received a letter from Biddle informing him that the journals were finally completed. However, Clark didn't get to hold a copy of the work until mid-September in 1814—and it was a *borrowed* copy. Due to the poor economy brought on by the War of 1812, Bradford & Inskeep also went bankrupt, so incredibly a letter from Clark to Jefferson in October 1816, stated that he *still didn't have his own copy*! Nor did Clark ever receive any royalties for fulfilling the promise he kept in Lewis's memory.

In the end, Biddle chose not to accept *any* payment from Clark for his expertise. His exact words to the explorer were, "I am content that my trouble in the business should be recompensed *only* by the pleasure which attended it, and also by the satisfaction of making your acquaintance, which I shall always value." Indeed, he did always value it. He and the Clarks remained close friends.

No, the Lewis & Clark Journals are not easy reading, but Elliott Coues, who published the second edition after Biddle, eloquently summed them up in 1893: "The story of this adventure stands easily first and alone. This is our national epic of exploration, conceived by Thomas Jefferson, wrought out by Lewis and Clark, and given to the world by Nicholas Biddle."

And perhaps by Julia to some extent? Hey, I can hope!

To avoid as much confusion as possible, I changed a few duplicated names. The Hancocks' enslaved woman known in my story as "Megg" was actually "Pegg." Since Julia's mother was typically known as "Peggy" Hancock, I thought it best to change it. Since the Christys' niece went by Polly, I changed Manuel Lisa's wife's name from Polly to Molly. Also, the tavern owners in Shelbyville, Kentucky, by the name of Shannon were (to my knowledge) of no known relation to George Shannon from the Corps of Discovery.

Foley states that in childhood, William Clark's nickname was "Billy." I chose to let Julia choose her own name for him since Billy Preston, Julia's brother-in-law, is mentioned occasionally in the story.

And I think it would be natural for a married couple to have nicknames for one another.

In writing historical fiction, there are always embellishments and things that need to be changed due to plot structure. There are several changes that historians familiar with this history will immediately note. First of all, Clark's niece Ann Anderson actually joined Julia and William on their first trip to St. Louis. She stayed with them until October or so of 1808 before demanding to return home. I wound up removing her completely from my plot since she'd be leaving the action so early.

Juba was supposedly York's half brother and really was accused of stealing money from a St. Louis business. He was whipped and may have eventually escaped, but at a later date. Lastly, Rachel's death actually occurred on the way back from Virginia to St. Louis along the Ohio River, and not on the way across the Mississippi, as depicted. This was a pacing necessity that I took the liberty to change.

I must also note that any italicized excerpts from the *Journals of Lewis & Clark* were from the Bernard DeVoto edition.

Now comes the special moment in my copious notes when I'm able to thank many incredibly talented people involved in this book. My husband, Carlton, puts up with my obsessive writing habit. He is the prince of patience and *so* generous, driving me across Lolo Pass and helping me locate Lewis & Clark's latrine sites at Traveler's Rest. I hope we have many more research adventures ahead!

Then there's Jennifer Quinlan—Jenny Q—whose editorial eye is my *lifesaver*. She also has patience of gold with this goofy woman who's still figuring out how to write. Your talents are extraordinary and I simply couldn't do without you, Jenny.

Three creative women deserve special thanks for their artistic/graphic gifts. Cathie, Dee-Dee, and Roseanna—the lovely touches you put on the cover and interior content of this novel were simply outstanding.

Next, a special shout-out goes to both Molly Kodner (archivist) and Hattie Felton (senior curator) at the Missouri Historical Society Research Center. These ladies gave me a once-in-a-lifetime experience, as I privately toured items from the Clark family collection and actually *handled* Lewis & Clark documents—some containing Julia's inventories firsthand. Yes, I actually *held* the skewed letter that Lewis wrote to James Madison and Clark's *Response to the People of Fincastle*!

Shannon Kelly of Lewis & Clark's Fort Mandan Historic Site in North Dakota was an absolute *treasure*! From reading my work to catching inaccuracies, sharing her ideas, and making suggestions, as well as tolerating my phone calls. This lady is the *final word* on discussions about Frederick Bates—a million thank-yous!

To add realistic native touches to my work, I turned to Bheri R. Hallam of the TAT Culture and Language Department. I owe her a special thank-you, for Bheri is a Nuu'etaa (Mandan) Language Apprentice of the Mandan Nation and was kind enough to translate both Yellow Corn and Kind Lodge Woman into the original Mandan language. The phonetic pronunciations are as follows:

*Yellow Corn (Sweet Corn) - Sííka' (one word, pronounced "see-kah," but it stops short at the end, like the H gets cut off)

*Kind Lodge Woman (Good Home Woman) - Óti shí Mííhe (pronounced "oh-tea she mee-hey")

Dr. James J. Holmberg, curator of the Filson Historical Society Research Center, has made a life study on the correspondence of William Clark, and believe me, I benefited from it. I was delighted to have him be the first to share Julia's recipe for vinegar pudding with me, and I'm humbled by his knowledge and willingness to share—even on weekends.

Mr. Stephen Blake, who harbors an intense love for Clark Family-associated history and Fincastle history, recommended extremely helpful resources which enhanced my work. And he's an amusing dinner guest when visiting Botetourt County too!

I'd like to extend sincere appreciation to the Botetourt County Historical Museum, the Historical Society in Fincastle, Virginia, and the Fincastle County Courthouse for private tours, access to courthouse records, and sharing their love of Julia Hancock with me as I first began this novel's research.

So many people have influenced this book. I fear I'll forget someone, but here goes... To my team of beta/advance readers, Elizabeth St. John (oh, the insights this woman has!), Amy Maroney, Pam Lecky, Dr. Wendy Dunn, Shannon Kelly, Tonya Mitchell, and Sharon Doane, I cannot thank you enough. And to the gang at the Coffee Pot Book Club, you all are my *TRIBE,* and I could not do any of this without your cheers of encouragement.

Last, but *not* least, I extend deepest appreciation to John, Angela, Harper, and Barrett for welcoming me and letting me investigate their world. Angela, I will *forever* be indebted to you for introducing me to the "Catawba tree."

FOR MORE INFORMATION ON THIS STORY...

Betts, Robert B., *In Search of York*, University Press of Colorado, 1985.

Cutright, Paul Russell, *A History of the Lewis and Clark Journals*, University of Oklahoma Press, Norman, Oklahoma, 1976.

Danisi, Thomas C., *Uncovering the Truth About Meriwether Lewis*, Prometheus Books, Amherst, New York, 2012.

Fenn, Elizabeth A., *Encounters At the Heart of the World: A History of the Mandan People*, Hill & Wang: A division of Farrar, Straus and Giroux, New York, 2014.

Foley, William E., *Wilderness Journey: The Life of William Clark*, University of Missouri Press, 2004.

Holmberg, James J. (editor), *Dear Brother: Letters of William Clark to Jonathon Clark*, Yale University Press, New Haven & London, 2002.

Jackson, Donald Dean (editor), *Letters of the Lewis & Clark Expedition with Related Documents*, (Volumes I & II), University of Illinois Press, Urbana and Chicago, 1978.

Morris, Larry E., *The Fate of the Corps*, R.R. Donnelly & Sons, 2004.

Potter, Tracy, *Sheheke: Mandan Indian Diplomat*, Farcountry Press and Fort Mandan Press, Helena, Montana/Washburn, North Dakota, 2003.

Robinson, Michael C., *History of Navigation in the Ohio River Basin (pamphlet)*, National Waterways Study 13 U.S. Army Engineer

Water Resources Support Center/Institute for Water Resources, January, 1983.

Ronda, James P., *Jefferson's West: A Journey with Lewis and Clark*, The Thomas Jefferson Foundation, Inc., 2000.

Stoner, Robert Douthat, *A Seed-Bed of the Republic: Early Botetourt*, Kingsport Press (Kingsport, Tennessee), 1962.

van Ravenswaay, Charles, *Saint Louis: An Informal History of the City and its People, 1764-1865*, Missouri Historical Society Press, 1991.

A Special Message from Brook Allen

Dear Readers,

Thank you for reading this book. My sincere hope is that you develop a hunger for history, for that's the magic of historical fiction—to read an entertaining story and then be compelled to learn more about the facts behind it.

If you enjoyed West of Santillane, *kindly consider writing a review on Amazon, so that others will be able to benefit from this book. Julia was a fascinating woman. Help me share her with the world.*

Read on, everybody!

Sincerely,
Brook Allen

Printed in the USA
CPSIA information can be obtained
at www.ICGtesting.com
JSHW080021270324
59981JS00004B/9